THE VALLEY OF SHADOWS

Also by Mark Terry

DEREK STILLWATER SERIES
The Fallen
The Devil's Pitchfork
The Serpent's Kiss

STAND-ALONE NOVELS
Hot Money
Edge
Dirty Deeds
Monster Seeker
Battle for Atlantis
Catfish Guru

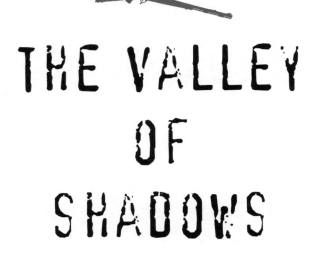

THE VALLEY OF SHADOWS

A Novel

Mark Terry

Oceanview Publishing

LONGBOAT KEY, FLORIDA

ISBN: 978-1-933515-94-6

Published in the United States of America by Oceanview Publishing,
Longboat Key, Florida
www.oceanviewpub.com

10 9 8 7 6 5 4 3 2 1

PRINTED IN THE UNITED STATES OF AMERICA

IN MEMORY OF MY PARENTS

Leona Terry, April 2, 1927–August 25, 2010

Robert Terry, September 7, 1926–October 12, 2002

THE VALLEY OF SHADOWS

PROLOGUE

ISLAMABAD, PAKISTAN
OCTOBER 20

The new guy said, "Do you trust any of these people?"

Agent Dale Hutchins stood in front of his locker, adjusted his flak jacket, and took a moment to consider the question. He had worked here for five years, at first directly with Pakistan's National Police Bureau and now in the FBI's own headquarters.

"Some of them," he finally said. Hutchins checked his SIG-Sauer P220 for the fifth time, and slipped it into his tactical holster.

The new guy, Jason Barnes, said, "You want to give me a hint? Who can I trust at my back, man?"

Hutchins didn't like chatter before an op. He knew Barnes was running his mouth because he was nervous. It wasn't a bad question, though. He darted his gaze over to Sam Sherwood, sitting in front of his locker in his black tac gear, leaning forward, elbows on his knees like he was praying. Maybe he was.

Finally Hutchins said, "I trust our people here, and I trust one guy with the Pakistanis. His name's Firdos Khan Moin." A grin crossed his tanned face. "We call him Frito."

Barnes laughed a little too hard. "Yeah? He lets you call him Frito?"

Hutchins shrugged. "We've been through some hairy shit. I trust him at my back." *More than I trust you, newbie.*

Sherwood stood up, his praying done. He started to pull together his gear. "Okay, ladies, time to get it together. Let's focus."

Hutchins knew the boss was right and nodded at Barnes. "You can trust me. Stick with me."

•　　•　　•

Kalakar watched the final suicide bomber through the video camera. His five jihadists were almost finished making their videotapes. The Afghani, Sardur Mazari, sat on an old brown sofa next to the Pakistani, Abdul Fareed.

Mazari talked into the camera: "I think it is imperative for the jihad that I act. I can no longer stay on the sidelines and watch while my brothers and sisters in Afghanistan, Iraq, and the Land of Two Holy Sites are violated by the infidels. We take the jihad directly to the land of the infidels, to the crusaders. I will bring the wrath of Allah's righteous anger down on the Americans for the deaths of my brothers and sisters who have gone before me. It is a glorious day for the jihad, and I will be rewarded by Allah, praise his name. I am content and at peace."

The Pakistani, Abdul Fareed, smiled and nodded along. His own videotape had shared the same sentiments. All of Kalakar's jihadists had plagiarized from each other, coached along by his suggestions.

Kalakar clicked off the video camera and checked his watch. His people, his jihadists, were ready. His cell phone chimed and he glanced at the screen. It was a text message. A single word: now.

Kalakar's heart thudded in his chest. Now? It was too early. Anger burst like a flame in the pit of his stomach, searing into his chest.

Now?

He stared at the cell phone, the signal disconnected. Now.

"I'm going out," he said. He hesitated, mind racing to catch up with this unexpected change in plans. "I have preparations to make."

Fareed jumped up and embraced Kalakar, face aglow with emotion. Kalakar knew the crusaders called it the Suicide's Grin. He preferred to think of it as the reflection of Allah's joy. "May Allah be with you."

"With you also, my brother. Also with you."

Kalakar nearly choked at the betrayal. Kalakar hugged all his jihadists. *"As-sallamu aleykum."*

"We aleykum-us-sallam."

Peace be unto you.

And to you be peace.

He slipped from the apartment, keeping to the shadows.

Hutchins's FBI team hooked up with the Pakistani National Police team in the F-10 district, just off Sumbal Road. The Pakistani team was made up of five men, led by Frito.

"It is a three-story apartment building," Frito was saying, laying out a map. "Entrances in the front and in the rear. The apartment is on the main floor."

The U.S. team leader, Sherwood, asked, "Where's your observation team?"

Frito, who looked very thin and short next to the bearlike Sherwood, pointed to another apartment building on the map across the street from their target. "They have had it under surveillance for six days. They believe that all of the cell is currently present."

Hutchins said, "They *believe* they're all present or they *know* they're all present?"

Frowning, Frito said, "It was difficult to get placement for both entrances, although anybody leaving by the rear needs to pass by our observation post if they're getting to the street. At the corners, see?" He pointed to the map again.

"So how many?" Sherwood asked.

"Six."

The new guy, Barnes, asked, "Armed?"

"Most assuredly."

Hutchins said, "That's a given. The problem is whether or not they have bomb-making materials."

Sherwood said, "Or bombs all ready to go." He frowned at the map. "Main floor. One door? They have a patio? If we go in through the door, are they going to jump out the windows?"

"I suggest we put a man on each window," Frito said.

Sherwood nodded. To Barnes he said, "But be careful about bombs."

Kalakar slipped out of the building, sweat beading up on his neck and trickling down his back. At the rear entrance of the flat was a small parking lot facing a tall wooden fence that bordered the back of a shopping center. He hurried toward the fence, pushed aside two loose boards, and squeezed through.

Within seconds he was in his Honda, driving away. Only when he was out of sector F-10 completely did he relax. Pulling the Honda into the parking lot of the Jinnah Supermarket, a bazaar of shops and stores crowded with people, he leaned forward and pressed his forehead to the steering wheel and prayed to Allah for strength.

It had been so close. Their mission had almost come to an end before it began. He thanked Allah and prayed for continued success. Finally, praying done, he reached into the glove box of the car and retrieved a small notepad. He wrote in Urdu:

Raid premature. Hot site not deleted. Proceeding as planned.

Folding the paper into a tight square, he pocketed it, climbed out of the Honda, and strolled into the crowd of shoppers. He walked for ten minutes, appearing to any observers to be a man out shopping. Kalakar stopped and bought a cup of tea. He paused to look at a store selling shirts and pants, pretending to shop. Finally, convinced he was not being followed, he sat down on a bench beneath a lime tree. There were half a dozen limes rotting on the ground, attracting fruit flies and bees. The air was strong with the smell.

Kalakar relaxed, watching. He bent down to pick up one of the limes. When he did, he reached down and slipped his message into a small, black plastic box attached beneath the bench seat. Picking up the lime, he made a face and tossed it away. Rising to his feet, Kalakar headed back to his car.

Hutchins raised his hand. He was lead on the dynamic entry. Three fingers up.

Barnes stood to the left of the door, a BlackHawk Thor's Hammer in both fists. The newbie got to bust the door down, but he'd be one of the last ones in. His lean, bony face had a look of excitement and anticipation on it that Hutchins wished would go away. The rest of the team was arrayed behind them on either side of the door.

Two.

Hutchins gripped his H&K MP-5 in his right hand, one finger of his left hand in the air. His heart raced. Adrenaline surged in his veins.

One. A fist.

Barnes swung the BlackHawk cudgel, striking the apartment door. It exploded inward.

Hutchins rushed into the room, followed by the rest of the team.

There were three men in the living room. A TV played Al-Jazeera. The jihadists shouted and leapt for guns stacked in one corner.

"Don't move! Don't move! FBI! Don't move!"

Frito, behind him, was shouting the same thing in Urdu, Hindi, and Arabic.

They didn't listen. Two of the men were reaching for their guns. The third was going for a backpack.

Hutchins focused on the backpack. "Don't—don't—"

He fired. The jihadist screamed, falling.

Gunfire rang through the apartment. Hutchins spun, trying to keep track of all the people. Where was Barnes?

Out of the corner of his eye he saw a fourth figure lunging for a laptop computer. "Don't move! Don't move! Freeze!"

Hutchins heard Barnes shout, "Down, down, down—" A rattle of gunfire followed. Men shouted in what seemed like half a dozen languages.

One of the jihadists got hold of a gun. It looked like an AK-47. Barnes shot him.

Hutchins took out the third jihadist.

Barnes said, "Hutchins, where's five and six? Where the hell is—"

Hutchins dropped into a crouch, scanning the room. Three were down. The flat was crowded with friendlies. Into his throat microphone, Hutchins said, "We've lost five and six. Where is five and—"

Sherwood, in his ear, said, "We've got five. There is no six. Site is secure. Repeat, site is secure."

Sudden silence enveloped the apartment. Most of the men relaxed, lowering their weapons. Hutchins felt as taut as a guitar string.

Barnes stepped back and wiped his forehead with his sleeve. He grinned and Hutchins knew the new guy was totally spiked on adrenaline. Barnes said, "That wasn't too bad."

Hutchins nodded. "Fairly clean." His jaw ached from clenching his teeth.

Barnes leaned down to pick up the laptop the jihadist had been trying to reach.

Hutchins bolted, hands outstretched. He screamed, "Don't touch that—"

The laptop exploded, tearing the new guy to shreds.

CHAPTER 1

Jeff Cohen, an FBI agent assigned to the Homeland Security Operations Center, jerked upright, staring at his computer screen. Fingers triggered over the keyboard. He called out, "We've got reports of an unidentified explosion at the Fort Totten Metro station."

Eric Mayer, with the CIA, two seats down from Cohen, called out, "Fort Totten explosion confirmed. It's a Green and Red Line—"

Jennie Mills, with the Department of Homeland Security, called out, "We've got a report of an explosion at the Metro Center station, that's where the Red, Blue and Yellow—"

Mayer called out, "Another report, Archives Navy Memorial station—"

The HSOC suddenly lit up with activity. A large plasma screen on the wall glowed to life, a map of the Washington, D.C. Metro System appearing. The sites of the bombings glowed red. Another plasma monitor flicked on showing details of emergency response as the HSOC made calls.

Mayer shouted, "Fire and D.C. transit police on scene. The entire Metro is shut down. I repeat, the Metro is shut down, they are evacuating the trains."

Cohen, voice strained, yelled, "Another bombing at Pentagon station—"

The atmosphere in the operations center felt explosive, as if the air was filled with kerosene fumes. The agents leaned into their computer monitors, faces intent, shoulders hunched.

Another agent, from the Office of National Intelligence, Joe Barry, said, "I've alerted all stations with multiple lines to look out for explosions. That means Pentagon, Gallery PI-Chinatown, Stadium—"

Cohen interrupted. "Agents have apprehended a possible suicide bomber at the Pentagon station. Yes, confirmed—"

Jennie Mills gasped. The buzz in the room intensified as everybody studied their computer monitors. She turned and said, "Dr. Stillwater—"

Derek Stillwater paced the long, narrow room like a caged lion. Scowling, he raised an eyebrow.

Mills's voice was hushed. "We've got a report of an explosion on Pennsylvania Avenue in front of the White House at the top of the Ellipse. Apparently a truck bomb—"

Cohen blurted, "Too far from the White House to—"

Mayer swore. "Radiation monitors going off! It's either a small nuke or a dirty bomb. We're contacting the White House, suggesting evac—"

The door opened and General James Johnston, secretary of the Department of Homeland Security, walked in. Derek nodded as Johnston approached.

Johnston looked up at the plasma monitors. "This your scenario?"

Derek nodded.

Johnston studied the monitor for a moment. "Multiple suicide attacks on the Metro as a diversion for a dirty bomb near the White House?"

"It worked."

"How was the response?"

Derek grinned. "Not bad. They never really got ahead of the situation, but they responded appropriately and alerted the stations and caught at least one of the bombers, but the White House attack slipped past them."

Johnston nodded and raised his voice to the room. "Attention everybody."

All eyes turned to Johnston, a gruff, stocky man in his sixties who never lost the military bearing of a career in the Army. "The drill is terminated as of now. We're going on full alert, Security Level Red. This is not a drill. I repeat, *this* is not a drill."

Johnston turned back to Derek. Derek thought his friend looked pale. "I need you over in the Hoover Building by four thirty. We've got actionable intelligence and we're forming STARTs. Take your Go Packs with you."

Derek swallowed and followed Johnston out of the operations center. "Where am I going?"

Johnston scowled. "They should decide that by the time you get there. We've got five targets: Washington, D.C., New York City, Dallas, Los Angeles, and Chicago."

Derek headed for his locker to retrieve his Go Packs. Johnston walked with him, seemingly lost in thought. Derek's head felt light. He took in a deep breath, let it out. Don't get freaked out, he thought. Not yet. Get information, then you can freak out.

"What's the threat?" Derek's specialty was biological and chemical terrorism.

Johnston looked ill. "Everything. The threat is everything. Bombs, biological, chemical. Everything. So watch yourself."

CHAPTER 2

FBI Agent Aaron Pilcher ran the briefing, a slim blond guy whose hair was doing the middle-aged fade. Derek had worked with him before, and although they weren't buddies, Derek knew Pilcher was a pro. He was an easy guy to underestimate if you based your opinion on his initial appearance. He looked like an accountant or a second-tier golf pro.

About thirty people were scattered throughout the auditorium. Derek recognized a couple of them as being fellow troubleshooters for the Department of Homeland Security like himself.

Pilcher stood before them and brought up a photograph of an apartment building on the plasma screen at the front of the room. "On October twentieth, a Bureau team in Islamabad, Pakistan, working a joint antiterror task force with the National Police, made a raid at this building. We had intel indicating there was a six-man al-Qaeda cell living there, making plans for some sort of attack on the U.S."

Pilcher clicked a button on his remote and another photo came up, this one of the interior of an apartment. It was severely damaged, the walls and furniture scorched, at least three people dead.

"The raid was essentially successful. Although it was believed there were six men present in the apartment, only five were found. Four were killed during the entry. One was wounded and taken into custody. Unfortunately, one of our agents picked up a laptop computer that was booby-trapped with a small packet of plastic explosives. It detonated, killing him and wounding another agent."

Pilcher paused, scanning the crowd. "There were a total of three laptop computers in the apartment. All three were booby-trapped. One was destroyed. One was damaged while being disarmed and only gave us partial evidence. The third laptop's trigger failed to go off, was disarmed effectively and transferred to bureau labs and the NSA. It took us nearly two weeks to decrypt and translate the contents of the computers."

Another click of the remote and photographs of two Toshiba laptops appeared. Another click and four faces appeared, three of them obviously dead.

"These are four of the cell. There was nothing recognizable of the fifth, who was shot in the face during entry."

Pilcher paced over to a lectern and took a sip of water. His gaze scanned the room, lingering on Derek. Their eyes met and Pilcher nodded briefly before continuing.

Pilcher clicked another button and a memo appeared on the screen with the words: TOP SECRET written across the top.

"Each of you will receive a packet detailing the information found on the laptop. This is the front page of the NSA, CIA, FBI, DHS, NCTC, and ODNI report." Pilcher took a deep breath.

"This al-Qaeda cell had plans to conduct an ambitious terrorist operation in the U.S. on November fourth, which I need not remind you is national election day. The files on the computer indicate they planned to conduct multiple attacks in five major cities using a variety of tactics—suicide bombs, dirty bombs, biological and/or chemical attacks."

A woman raised her hand. Derek's heart sank when he recognized her. Cassandra O'Reilly. She was an expert on nuclear weapons. They had worked together in Iraq as members of an UNSCOM inspection team. It had not gone well. She said, "Does this report indicate they have a small nuclear weapon in the U.S.?"

Pilcher shook his head. "It does not. However, the likelihood of a dirty bomb is very high." He raised his hands in a hold-off gesture as the room began to buzz with conversation. "Please, let me get through the briefing. I'm sure you'll all have questions." He gestured to another agent off to the side of the room who began walking among the group with file folders. Each person had to sign for them as they were distributed.

Pilcher continued. "John's handing out the dossiers now. These are top secret, people. Handle them appropriately."

Derek received his file and signed for it. He didn't bother opening it yet. He was waiting for the other shoe—or shoes—to drop.

Pilcher said, "The computer files do not indicate specifics about the attacks, although there is a vague indication it may be polling places, which does not narrow things down."

Someone called out, "What cities?"

Pilcher sighed and nodded. "Five cities were indicated. Washington, New York, Dallas, L.A., and Chicago."

More talking. Pilcher raised his hands again. "Nothing in the computer indicates which types of attacks are being planned for which cities. The Bureau, ODNI, and DHS have been alerted to this operation, from this point forward called Operation Daybreak. Local law enforcement has been placed on high alert, but no specifics have been given."

Derek leaned back and closed his eyes. He could feel a headache coming on. It was obvious to him what was coming next and if he just opened the folder he'd have more details. But he didn't want to get that far ahead. Instead he raised his hand.

Pilcher said, "Yes, Derek?"

"Why'd it take so long to get this out? It's been almost two weeks."

"It took a day or so to get the computers disarmed and transported to the U.S. Then it took time to get the computers decrypted and translated. The translations took some time. There were files in three different languages: Urdu, Arabic, and Farsi. Then it was analyzed and the various agencies had to settle on a coordinated plan."

Pilcher scanned the room. "Okay. Here's the plan, then. We have formed multiagency Special Terrorism Activity Response Teams from the bureau, Homeland Security, and the Office of the Director of National Intelligence. Each team will contain five members. Each member has a particular area of expertise relevant to terrorism activity. A member has been chosen to lead and coordinate that team's activities. Each team will go to these cities and consult and work with the various bureau and DHS offices in locating and stopping these attacks from happening."

A man with jet-black hair worn long for a federal agent raised his hand. "What about the sixth man?"

Pilcher nodded and brought up a slide on the screen. It showed the silhouette of a faceless individual. Below it was a single word: Kalakar.

"The sixth man was never described. He is believed to be the leader or recruiter of this particular cell. He is believed to be a Pakistani national. The only other thing we know about him is he goes by the name of Kalakar, which translates as the artist, or perhaps the craftsman. We don't think it's his real name and we have no idea why he has chosen the designation. Our people and the Pakistanis are trying to find out more. Although this has not been verified, they believe it's possible he is now in the U.S."

Derek raised a hand. "If the apartment was under surveillance, why aren't there any photographs of Kalakar?"

Frowning, Pilcher said with a shake of his head, "The Pakistani surveillance team took a lot of pictures and video, but either Kalakar isn't in them, or he's so obscured that they're useless."

"Don't you think that's a little odd?"

Hesitating, Pilcher finally said, "It concerns me, yes. Please, let's continue with our action plan."

Cassandra O'Reilly raised her hand again. "Are these attacks being supported in the U.S. by al-Qaeda sleepers? Do we know anything about al-Qaeda teams already in these five cities?"

Pilcher nodded. "Good question. Yes, the computer files indicate there were al-Qaeda sleepers, or perhaps sympathizers is a better word, here in the U.S. who would be handling at least some of the preparations and support for the attacks. The individual attacks, as best we can tell, were going to be coordinated by Kalakar, and each one led by the remaining five in the cell. Those five were going to be involved with as-yet-unidentified operatives in the five cities."

There were more questions, but Pilcher finally referred them all to the file they had received. "Good luck, people. And be safe."

Derek tore open his envelope and pulled the file out. The top sheet said:

START TEAM BLUE
OPERATION: DAYBREAK
LOS ANGELES, CALIFORNIA

Fredrick Givenchy (Captain, Navy, retired)
Office of the Director of National Intelligence
Counterterrorism

Cassandra O'Reilly, Ph.D.*
Office of the Director of National Intelligence
Nuclear/Radiological

Shelly Pimpuntikar, CPA, MBA
Federal Bureau of Investigation
Financial Intelligence

Derek Stillwater, Ph.D. (Colonel, Army, retired)
Department of Homeland Security
Biological and Chemical

Jonathan Welch
Federal Bureau of Investigation
Counterterrorism

*Designated Team Leader

He saw the asterisk and felt a sharp pain in his gut. Derek closed his eyes, and when he opened them again, the woman in question stood directly in front of him. Blonde hair to her shoulders, blue eyes the color of gun metal, and an expression somewhere between rage and disgust.

"For the record, Stillwater, I don't want you on my team. I don't want to have anything to do with you. If the clock wasn't ticking I'd protest, but we don't have time for that. So let's play nice."

He stood up and stuffed the sheet back in the folder. Scowling, he said, "It says you're with the ODNI. That true?"

O'Reilly nodded.

Derek nodded back. "For the record, O'Reilly, I don't want to be on your team, either." He walked out of the room.

CHAPTER 3

The chartered jet was well out of Washington, D.C. when Derek looked up from the file he was reading. It was a small Lear and with their gear and the five agents, not as spacious as one might have hoped. Despite the lack of room, they had split into two groups. Cassandra O'Reilly, Jon Welch, and Fred Givenchy clustered toward the pilot's cabin. He and Shelly Pimpuntikar sat toward the back.

Shelly Pimpuntikar met his gaze. Slim and petite in a crisp gray business suit, the FBI agent was of either Indian or Pakistani descent, Derek didn't know which. Voice soft, she said, "I don't think they like us."

He caught the same vibe. Flashing a smile, he said, "Well, I know why O'Reilly doesn't like me. Why doesn't she like you?"

Surprise spread across Shelly's face. "You don't know?"

"Uh, no."

"I am originally from Pakistan. I am a U.S. citizen, though." Her English had a slight accent, almost a lilt, that Derek found very pleasant.

"Ah," he said.

"And I am a Muslim."

"'Ah' again. Yes, well—" He wasn't sure what to say, actually. He settled for silence, which often worked well for him.

"Why doesn't O'Reilly like you?" she asked.

He took a deep breath. "We worked together in Iraq. We were weapons inspectors. We didn't get along very well." Not quite true. In fact, they had gotten along too well—and too often. Unfortunately, it was only later that she had told Derek she was married, a little factoid she had kept to herself during their time together. There were other issues, but that was one of the big ones.

Shelly Pimpuntikar's large brown eyes were penetrating. "There is, perhaps, more to this story than you suggest?"

Derek nodded. "Perhaps."

Shelly seemed to consider that. Derek glanced out the window. Cloud banks to the left. To the right he saw a large river, a wide meandering stretch of brown. He wondered if it was the Mississippi.

"And why," Shelly said, "do the others not like you?"

"You're rather forward, aren't you?"

Shelly blinked, expression hurt. "I'm sorry. I don't mean—"

"Let's just say that my reputation probably has preceded me. I'm not known for being a team player."

"You are a Homeland Security troubleshooter?"

He nodded.

"I didn't think they were meant to be team players."

Derek nodded again. "Then I'm very well suited for the job." He gestured to the file. "What do you think?"

"I think it is a very large, complicated, ambitious, and expensive operation this cell had planned. Very expensive."

Derek hadn't given a lot of thought to the expense of the operation as he read the file. Shelly's expertise was financial intelligence, called "finint" in intelligence jargon, so of course she had looked at the op from that point of view.

He was intrigued. "How much money?"

She frowned. "Five cities. It appears they are supporting a sleeper cell for logistics, perhaps aid and comfort, housing, transportation, documentation in each city, as well as operatives. I would say, conservatively, several hundred thousand dollars. Depending on how long the sleepers have been in the U.S., and what they are expected to do, it could run well over a million or two in U.S. dollars—for each city. In fact, I don't know how this operation could be done without spending more than ten million dollars, U.S. Six members in the cell, they're traveling to the states, and those figures don't bring into account the weaponry. I don't know much about biological or chemical weapons. Are they expensive?"

"Not particularly, but like most things, it depends. How big is the attack going to be? Sarin's not terribly complicated to produce and if all you plan to do is lob a gallon jug of it into a polling station, then it's not very expensive at all. The problem with biologicals, like anthrax, is getting and manipulating the actual cultures. But it's not expensive. On the other hand, if you're intending to rent several planes and dump several tons of it over a city, the expense goes way up."

Shelly nodded. "Although Agent Pilcher said there was no evidence of a nuclear device, I find the references to a nuclear/radiological explosion to be rather vague. The nuclear device bothers me."

"No shit."

She shook her head. "No, not like that. It bothers me from a financial point of view. How much would a suitcase nuke cost?"

From the other side of the plane Cassandra O'Reilly said, "Millions of dollars."

Derek looked up, startled that their voices had carried. O'Reilly said, "Let's assume for a moment that this cell somehow got hold of a single suitcase nuclear device. One report suggested that al-Qaeda bought twenty of these in nineteen ninety-eight for thirty million dollars."

Givenchy's Texas accent was thick. "It was bullshit then and bullshit now. That claim was that Osama bin Laden bought them from a former KGB agent. It makes no sense that he'd have that many and not use at least one of them."

"The point isn't their possible existence," O'Reilly snapped. "The point is a single one would cost about one and a half million dollars. At a minimum."

They all paused to consider that. Derek said, "If I had only one of these to use, I'd probably plan on blowing it up by the White House when the president was home."

O'Reilly said, "If I had five of them and they were functioning, I would try to blow them up simultaneously in five different cities."

Givenchy said, "We've got, what, four different time zones in five different cities. That's an interesting logistical problem if you're trying to make a big statement in each city."

Derek silently agreed. He was skeptical of the suitcase nuke concept. Too expense and too technical. But he found the psychology of this operation interesting. Election day and multiple attacks on polling stations. If it leaked, people would stay home and not vote, which would be a success for the terrorists.

But to really make the point, you would make it simultaneous, and that was a separate issue. Do it first thing in the morning so the polls shut down and the U.S. election was screwed up? Or do it at peak times? But there was a three-hour time difference between Washington, D.C. and Los Angeles. Peak times in D.C. might be first thing in the morning, but the L.A. polls wouldn't even have opened yet.

Shelly apparently was thinking along different lines. She said, "The one and a half million isn't a domestic transaction, correct?"

O'Reilly squinted. "Meaning someone in the U.S. paid for it *from* the U.S.?"

"Yes, that's what I mean."

"I wouldn't think so. There are probably only two countries sophisticated enough to produce suitcase nukes, or nuclear mines—in the U.S. they're called small atomic demolition munitions, or SADMs, and they were designed for use by Special Forces." She looked pointedly at Derek. "Are you familiar with them?"

He nodded. "Not my area of expertise, though. Are they all accounted for in the U.S.?"

O'Reilly nodded her head, although the set of her jaw suggested she wasn't 100 percent certain of that statement.

Shelly said, "So if we exclude the largest U.S. transaction—for the suitcase nuke—and I assume we have been trying for years to track the Russian nukes, then I will need to focus on finint related to the sleeper cells here in the U.S."

Jon Welch spoke up for the first time, pushing up his wire-rimmed glasses. Round-faced and balding, he looked like everybody's favorite uncle. "If OBL or AQ had a suitcase nuke, they would've used it a long time ago. I suggest we focus on the sixth man. The sixth man's the one who pulls the trigger. That's where I'm focusing my efforts."

Everybody nodded in agreement.

CHAPTER 4

ISLAMABAD, PAKISTAN

FBI Agent Dale Hutchins limped into the office at the FBI Headquarters in Zone 5 of Islamabad. It was early in the morning, he hadn't been able to sleep, so he had decided to come in. His left arm was still in a sling.

When the new guy, Jason Barnes, had picked up the booby-trapped computer, Hutchins had spun to his right, ducking his head, trying to throw himself behind a wall.

He hadn't been fast enough. Shards of plastic and metal had knifed into his left side. The wounds in his thigh, butt, ribs, and head had been relatively minor, although it hadn't been any fun getting over fifty stitches, ten of them in his ass. What had really screwed him up, though, was a chunk of metal about one inch long, that had torn a gouge along his left shoulder, ripping muscle, nerve, tendon, and bone as it went.

The Pakistani surgeon who repaired his shoulder informed him that with aggressive therapy he should have almost 100 percent use of his shoulder in time. Then he had told him that the metal shrapnel appeared to be the pin from one of the laptop's hinges. "You were quite lucky," the doctor told him. "Had it struck you in the back or the head, you would have been dead. It was like a bullet."

Jason Barnes had not been lucky.

Sam Sherwood, Barnes's group leader, already slouched over his desk in his glass-walled office. He looked up when Hutchins came in, wheeled his chair to the door, and said, "Welcome back."

Hutchins dropped gingerly into the chair behind his desk. His ass still hurt. "It's good to be back."

"How's Teh?"

Hutchin's wife, Tehreema, was Pakistani. She worked at the U.S. Embassy, which is where they had met. He smiled. "Good. Not completely happy with me these days."

Sherwood laughed. "I talked to her a couple times to check on you."

"I know. She told me."

"She said you were driving her crazy at home. I told her you weren't coming back until the time was right."

"That's now."

"I know. The files on the raid are on your desk. We also just got a summary of what was on the laptops we captured. Read it, we'll talk later. It's actionable."

Hutchins laid his hand on the folder. "Thanks. The sixth man?"

"Not much luck. Frito's coming in to talk about it in a couple hours."

Hutchins had talked to Frito Moin a couple times since the raid. The Pakistani had visited him in the hospital and expressed his apologies and sympathies about Barnes.

Sherwood said, "If you're up to it, I want you to work with Moin on finding out as much as you can about Kalakar. We've had a few other projects on the burners, so we turned that over to Moin and his people, but now that you're back, I want you on it. You're not going to be doing any raids until you're completely healed, anyway. We've got to track him down, particularly now that we found out what was on the computers."

Hutchins felt oddly disconnected from that information. He was angry about the sixth man, angry about Barnes. He wanted revenge, pure and simple. "I'll get on it."

"You sure you're up to this?"

Hutchins thought of Barnes, dying before his eyes, his face a blasted, bloody wreck of bone and burned flesh. He nodded. "Definitely."

CHAPTER 5

Derek Stillwater burst out of a nightmare gasping for breath. Sweat soaked his body. It took a moment before he was able to figure out where he was—on a small jet headed toward Los Angeles. Shelly Pimpuntikar had shaken him awake.

She said, "Sorry. We're coming into LAX in a few minutes."

Derek ran a hand over his fevered brow, trying to shake the images and emotions in his head. His heart raced in his chest, his stomach twisted and turned.

Images:

- sitting on the dive platform of his cabin cruiser off the coast of St. Bart's, serenading a tiger shark he had named Mistress Sonia with his guitar
- his brother David next to him, saying the Congo wasn't too bad if you didn't mind all the parasitic diseases, holding up a stump of a hand rotted from within
- a mushroom cloud just off the horizon

Derek lunged from his seat and flung open the bathroom door and vomited into the sink. Glancing apologetically back at the rest of the START team, he pulled the door shut. He ran the water in the sink, his stomach doing backflips. Splashing cold water on his face, he straightened up and cautiously studied his image in the mirror.

He shook his head, wiped his face, took in a deep breath, rinsed his mouth with water, took a drink, and pushed his way back out of the bathroom to strap into his seat across from Shelly. With some embarrassment, he noted that both Givenchy and Welch looked mildly amused. O'Reilly wore a familiar expression of disgust, and Shelly looked alarmed.

O'Reilly said, "Don't mind him, Shelly. He always does that."

Derek felt pressure in his ears as the plane began its descent. Glancing out the window he saw they were dropping down between the mountains, Los Angeles a scatter of lit jewels below them. He saw that Shelly was studying him.

"She's right," he said. "Don't worry about it."

She nodded. "Who's David?"

He gave a little start. "Excuse me?"

"You were kind of talking in your sleep. And you said something about somebody named David. You sounded worried about him."

"He's my brother."

"Are you close?"

He grunted. "Sort of. For two people who haven't seen each other in about five years. The joys of e-mail. He lives in the Congo. I'm in Baltimore, and I travel all the time."

"What's he doing in the Congo?"

"Doctors Without Borders. And his hands are fine."

A puzzled expression flashed across Shelly's face. "What?"

O'Reilly interrupted. "We'll see what needs to be done once we get to the Federal Building, but I want to make sure we can stay in contact with each other. I want everybody to exchange sat phone and cell phone numbers."

They all pulled their respective devices out and each of them read off their numbers and programmed them into their phones.

"Now, Shelly," O'Reilly asked, "What kind of field experience do you have?"

Shelly's mouth clamped into a hard, unforgiving line. "Field experience?"

Derek felt his heart sink.

O'Reilly rephrased, "You've had field training, correct?"

"Yes. I've been through the FBI's standard training course."

"You have a firearm?"

Shelly nodded, although Derek noted that she dropped her gaze when she did so.

He asked, "What kind of weapon?"

She looked at him. "It's the 10-mm standard—"

Derek, voice quiet, replied, "You have no field experience, do you?"

Her expression was determined. "I don't think that matters."

"It matters. How long have you been with the bureau?"

"Are you questioning my ability?"

"No. I'm questioning your field experience. How long?"

"If you must know, I completed my training three years ago."

Givenchy groaned. "Oh, dear God. And spent it behind a desk, I bet."

Derek met O'Reilly's gaze, eyebrows raised and said, "She can partner with me."

O'Reilly nodded. "That's a good idea. Don't get her killed."

"I'll try not to."

Shelly started to protest, but Derek said, "Trust me. If you go out of the Fed Building, you go with me. We can get lost in L.A. together."

Within minutes they landed at LAX, hauled their gear to a waiting Suburban, and were driven to the Federal Building in downtown L.A. on Wilshire. After passing through security, they were met by Simon Ferguson, the assistant special agent-in-charge, who led them into a conference room. Except for a large conference table and chairs, it was an empty room.

Ferguson hadn't grown up in L.A., that much was clear. His voice was Boston through and through, and his carrot-colored hair matched his name. "Feel free to spread out in here. We'll get you badges shortly. I can't tell you how screwed up this is turning out to be. We've got teams crawling all over the election precincts checking for bombs, but I gotta tell you, there's a hell of a lot of them and we're already spread pretty thin because we've got both Vice President Newman and Governor Stark flying into town several times over the next couple days for rallies and we're involved in the security for that, as well."

O'Reilly said what they were all thinking. "On Tuesday?"

"Sure. Both of them will be coming in Tuesday. Are you kidding? California's one of the undecided states this time around. And yes, I know what you're thinking. Don't think we haven't thought that, either. Security is ultra tight, and we're keeping their travel routes under wraps, as best we can."

Derek felt his pulse quicken, the familiar sensation of a ticking clock in his head, telling him they had to move, move, move. He pushed into the conference room, dropped his Go Packs on the table and withdrew a tablet computer. "Fine. Who's your bio and chemical person? Let's get going on this thing."

CHAPTER 6

Derek knocked on an office door on the seventeenth floor of the Federal Building. It was whipped open by an older woman who wore her silver hair in a long braid that trailed down her back. Tall enough to meet Derek's gaze straight on, she said, "Oh, good God, it's Derek Stillwater. Killed or tortured anybody today?"

Behind him Shelly gasped.

"Not yet, but I've still got a couple hours. How are you doing, Helen?" Derek walked into what was a relatively small, windowless office that had apparently been hit by some sort of new bomb that scattered paper instead of shrapnel.

To Derek, Special Agent Helen Birch looked like a lumberjack cook. Round face, barrel chest, square, broad hips. She was like a walking, talking piece of beef jerky.

"It's been a long time, Derek. Last I heard you were shacked up in the Gulf of Mexico with some Russian spy on that boat of yours."

"She's not a spy and it was mostly the Caribbean."

"What happened to her? You shoot her and dump the body overboard?"

"If you knew her, you'd realize if it had come to that I'd be the one feeding the sharks. She went home."

"Got tired of your bullshit, huh?"

Derek sighed, rolled his eyes, and shot the FBI agent an annoyed look, which she ignored. "You like giving me shit, don't you?"

"No, Derek, I *love* giving you shit." Helen reached out and gave him a quick hug, turning to look at Shelly. "Who's this?"

Derek made introductions. Helen said, "Oh, you probably want to talk to Gerald Miller. He's heading up the finint section."

"He's out of the office at the moment," Shelly said.

"Oh. Well, come on in and have a seat."

Derek stayed standing, staring at a large map of Los Angeles that took up most of one wall. It was a mass of colored thumbtacks and Magic Marker scrawls.

Shelly sat. "Do you know everybody in the business, Derek?"

Helen laughed. "Derek? He gets around. I think people know him more than he knows other people."

"He said his reputation preceded him."

"That's for damned sure," Helen said.

Derek shrugged. "Helen and I did some work together out here in L.A., when I was sort of attached to the bureau's HMRU. What're you working on here?" He gestured to the map.

Helen crossed her arms over her ample chest and frowned. "The red tacks are all the precincts in our jurisdiction."

The map looked like it had broken out with the measles. Derek said, "Jesus. What's the green?"

"Mosques. And the blue marker indicates high concentrations of Muslims."

Shelly said, "You don't believe this cell will strike at precincts in areas with mosques or high concentrations of Muslims, do you? You really need to get synagogues on your map."

Helen shook her head. "No. I'm just trying to get the lay of the land. I'm not sure we can—"

Derek said, "How about those self-storage places? Can we get those up on your map?"

Helen held up a sheaf of papers. "Here's my list. I was just about to start working on those."

Shelly said, "What are you looking for?"

Helen looked at Shelly through her bifocals. "You can set up a bio or chem lab almost anywhere, in the basement of a house or in an abandoned building, but self-storage places work well, too. And you decrease the risk of there being an accident and killing yourself and everybody around you. They've worked pretty well for meth labs."

Staring intently at Helen, Shelly queried, "Are you trying to find what site the sixth man is going to attack, or the support network, the sleeper cell? What are you focusing on?"

Helen and Derek turned to study the young woman. Derek said, "I don't think there's any way we can predict where they might attack, at least not where we stand now. I imagine O'Reilly and the nuke people will be focused on the Port of Los Angeles, storage areas, and trucking companies. With bio and chemical weapons, the ingredients and facilities are hard to track."

Shelly flipped open her laptop. "Okay. I've got the location of every ATM and every Western Union station in this area on my computer. If we correlate those with the storage places and Muslim areas, we will really narrow things down. Also—"

"Whoa," Derek said. "This really isn't my approach. How long is that going to take?"

Shelly continued. "I've also got the office locations of a number of *hawaladars* in the area, although many of them are probably underground now since nine eleven."

Helen said, "*Hawaladars*. Those are the informal money transfers?"

"Roughly, very roughly equivalent to the Western Union, but they operate back and forth between countries, especially Islamic countries, and there are no promissory notes. It's entirely on the honor system. I imagine Gerald Miller can expand on my list. This is really my area of expertise, *hawala* and *hawaladars* and terrorism, finint."

Helen rubbed her jaw. Slowly she said, "Derek, why don't you go do your thing? Agent Pimpuntikar and I will spend some time seeing if we can narrow down the likely location of our sleeper cell and get back with you."

"Sounds good."

Shelly seemed startled. "What are you going to do?"

Derek smiled. "Hit the bars. There's a couple old friends I need to track down if they're still alive and in business."

CHAPTER 7

Derek started with Little Pedro's Blue Bongo on First Street in downtown Los Angeles. The exterior was southwest faux adobe, tucked away between Little Tokyo and the Artists District. He parked his bureau car—what they insisted on calling a bucar—on the street, half hoping someone would steal the decade-old Ford. All the good bucars were taken, he had been told.

It was a Sunday night, so Little Pedro's was caught somewhere between dedicated partiers and dead-and-gone. He glanced around the place and took a seat at the bar. The barista approached, gray eyes flinty, suggesting a hardness that her mid-thirties wannabe actress face didn't. "What can I get you?"

"Corona."

She delivered a bottle with a lime slice in the neck. He paid and she started moving on, but he said, "You see Greg Popovitch around here tonight?"

Her expression hardened. "Who's asking?"

"A friend."

She shook her head. "Haven't seen him."

Derek took a drink of his beer, sampled some chips and salsa, and thought for a moment. Another bartender walked by. Derek waved at him. He was older, graying hair, eyes the color of peat.

"Seen Greg Popovitch around?"

This bartender shrugged. "He's not here much any more."

"If I want to find him, where would you suggest I go?"

"Try Little Tokyo. He's developed a taste for sushi."

Derek took another sip of his beer, tossed a couple bucks on the table, and headed out. He wasn't very far before he realized he was being paced by a broad-shouldered black guy in jeans and a black leather jacket.

Derek had noticed him at the far end of the bar, sipping something from a low ball glass.

Derek paused. "Can I help you?"

"I don't know. Can you?"

Derek's gaze flickered. "Why don't you just lay out your ticket, buddy, and save us both some time."

"All right. Just keep your hands where I can see them, seeing as how you're carrying."

"And why don't you move real slow, seeing as how *you're* carrying," Derek said.

The guy did as Derek suggested, reaching slowly into his jacket pocket and retrieving a badge holder, which he flashed. Derek rolled his eyes and held out his hand. "I'll want a little more time to see your ID."

The guy reluctantly dropped the badge into Derek's hand. It was an LAPD shield and identified the man as Detective Stephen Connelly. Derek handed it back. "All right, Detective. What can I do for you?"

"I overheard you asking about Greg Popovitch. I'm curious as to your interest."

Derek didn't blink. He said, "Patriot Act notwithstanding, what business is it of yours?"

A feminine voice behind them said, "Oh for God sakes, Derek, show him your ID."

Connelly and Derek turned to see Cassandra O'Reilly walking down the sidewalk toward them. Connelly asked, "Who are you?"

O'Reilly reached into her handbag, and Derek saw Connelly tense. "Easy," Derek murmured. "She's with the Office of the Director of National Intelligence."

She presented her creds to the cop. Derek took the opportunity to pass over his identification with the DHS. O'Reilly said, "I take it you know something about Greg Popovitch, Detective?"

"I know he's bad news and people who want to talk to him are usually worse news. What's this about?"

"National security," O'Reilly said. "Do you know where we can find him?"

"We?" Derek said.

She ignored him and waited for Connelly to provide an answer. The detective nodded. "If he's not here at Little Pedro's, you can usually find him at the Suehiro Café in Little Tokyo or sometimes Kwan's if he's in the mood for Korean barbeque."

"Thank you, Detective. We appreciate it."

"What's this about?"

"Business as usual," Derek said. "Stopping bad guys."

"I hear that. Anything more specific?"

"Not that I'm going to talk about with you," Derek said. "Why don't you go find some junkies to harass or something. We've got work to do."

"Jesus," O'Reilly muttered under her breath.

"Maybe I'll take you two over to the PAB to discuss what you're doing here."

"Give it your best shot," Derek snarled, stepping toward the cop. "But keep in mind that my first phone call will be to my immediate boss, who happens to be James Johnston, the secretary of Homeland Security."

The cop didn't budge. Connelly was taller and broader than Derek. Probably few people intimidated him. The cop started to place his hands on Derek's chest when O'Reilly shouldered Derek aside. "We don't have time for this shit. Detective, we're following actionable intelligence that there's going to be a terrorist attack in the city in less than forty-eight hours, and if you were in the office instead of a bar, you'd probably already have heard about it."

To Derek she said, "Grow up. Come on." She started off down First. Derek followed. Connelly said nothing and stayed where he was.

Little Tokyo was lit up like a carnival, all energy and brightness, but not crowded late on a Sunday evening. Once they were out of earshot of the L.A. detective, Derek asked, "Were you behind me or ahead of me?"

"Behind. I was heading into Little Pedro's when I saw you coming out. I didn't like that there was a guy behind you. Did you know you were being followed?"

"No."

She stopped, studying him. "That's not very operational of you. And why the hell didn't you just try to diffuse the situation? You always make things worse."

"It's a gift."

"I'm the team leader, Derek. It would be my pleasure to have your ass sent back to D.C."

"If that's how you feel about it, go right ahead."

Sighing, O'Reilly poked him in the chest with her index finger. "I am not impressed with your bullshit. I think you try remarkably hard to get thrown off teams. We don't have time for this, so I expect you to live up to this reputation of yours for cutting through BS and getting things done. Impress me."

"Okay." He turned and walked away. She tagged after him.

"Get your game on, Derek. This is serious."

"I'm aware of that. But at the moment we have nothing. I'm just looking for a thread to start pulling on. Were you looking for Popovitch?"

She nodded. "Great minds think alike. Where's Pimpuntikar?"

"Back with the feebs being a computer geek with Helen Birch."

"Let's go find Popovitch, then."

"All right. Suehiro Café or Kwan's barbeque?"

"Let's try the Japanese place first. If Popovitch is in one of his zen phases, he's more likely to go with Japanese."

"And if he's not, he's likely to shoot us the second we walk through the door."

O'Reilly said, "That's one of two reasons why I want you to start paying attention."

"Okay. What's the other?"

"I want you to go through the door first."

CHAPTER 8

Charlie Daniels thought the Dallas, Texas night was sultry. *Yeah*, he thought, *sultry*. I like that word. Hot and wet. Like that line from that movie, what was it, that's all right if you're with a woman—that movie with Robin Williams, the DJ in Vietnam, what's the name, *Good Morning, Vietnam*, that's what it was, yeah, funny movie.

Charlie pushed an old Schwinn alongside him, its three metal baskets jammed with all of his life's belongings—a sleeping bag, a blanket, a little pillow with Santa Claus embroidered on it in red, a photo album wrapped in a black garbage bag, another black garbage bag full of the beer and soda cans he had picked up so far today, two dozen newspapers he had collected from trash cans, and a half-box of stale Ritz Crackers.

He pushed across the Brookhaven College campus toward the Loos Field House on Valley View Lane. Charlie liked college kids because they were wasteful. They threw out the best stuff, especially food. Pizza slices, french fries, fruit that hadn't gone completely bad.

And one of Charlie's favorite places for Dumpster diving was behind the Loos Field House.

Sweat soaked Charlie's skin, not just because it was sultry, but because he wore almost all of his clothing—a pair of graying Army boots that were holding up well, a pair of dirty jeans that were rotting around him, three pairs of white tube socks, just a single pair of jockey shorts he had recently scavenged from a Dumpster, three T-shirts, a brown and red checkered flannel shirt, a Dallas Cowboys sweatshirt, and an Army jacket he'd also found in a Dumpster. Charlie started wearing all his clothes after he was robbed once while sleeping in an alley downtown and he'd been left with only the clothing on his back. From that time on he'd decided he was always going to wear all the clothes he owned so it never happened again.

Charlie pushed his bicycle toward the back of the Loos Field House, keeping an eye out for campus cops and students. He wasn't sure which were more dangerous; he'd had problems with both from time to time.

Nobody.

It was a hot night.

"Sultry," he said, his voice an unfamiliar croak.

Don't start talking to yourself out loud now, he chastised himself. *That's the beginning of the end. You know you're really going downhill then, gonna be one of them crazies, those schizos talkin' to God.*

Charlie leaned his bicycle against one of the Dumpsters and climbed up to lean in. It was a sticky stew redolent of rotting food and, thank the Lord, beer and wine and spirits. Charlie pushed the lid off and crawled in, peering through the gloom. A shaft of light from a nearby halogen pierced the interior of the Dumpster.

He picked up a plastic cup half-filled with stale beer and tore the top off and drained it, the beer dripping down his matted beard.

Up to his knees in trash, he wallowed through it, picking up a partial box of popcorn, half a hotdog, more stale beer, and a plastic container of nachos, the cheese sauce congealed and cold.

"Good eatin'," he mumbled, not correcting himself for speaking out loud. His gaze caught sight of what looked like a small garbage can about two-and-a-half-feet tall, made of gray-green metal, the top sealed.

"What's this?" He floundered over and tried to peel back the lid. It wouldn't open.

Charlie set down his treasures and applied both hands to the top of the metal can lid, finally getting purchase with his fingers. With a tearing sound the lid came up. Charlie peered myopically into the interior of the can, his disappointment mixed with a rare curiosity.

Clearly there was no food in the can, but maybe whatever it was he could scavenge and sell.

It looked like some sort of electronics—a circuit board, something from a cellular phone, all connected with wires to some packages wrapped in plastic. Maybe it was some junk the guys who ran the sound system and stuff in the field house had ditched.

Charlie reached in and tapped the circuit board. Years before, back before the booze sunk its claws in, Charlie had worked at a factory that built radio-controlled cars. The circuit board looked like something from one of those cars.

With a shrug, he grabbed hold and pulled.

The explosion was instantaneous.

CHAPTER 9

Derek and Cassandra O'Reilly finally found Greg Popovitch at Kwan's Korean BBQ, a green faux-pagoda building tucked between an Asian market and a noodle shop. After the woman at the desk told them Popovitch was in a private room, O'Reilly said to Derek, "Let me do the talking. You piss everybody off. You've really got to work on your interpersonal skills."

Derek raised an eyebrow, but didn't comment.

Running a hand through her blonde hair, O'Reilly headed for the back room. Derek followed.

He and O'Reilly had dealt with Popovitch in Iraq, back when the man was some sort of contract operator involved with the CIA. Derek had never been able to quite put a job description on Popovitch's résumé. "Intelligence asset" was probably one possibility, as were "smuggler," "snitch," "spy," "soldier of fortune," "mercenary," and "unreliable self-interested asshole." Since his return to the U.S., Popovitch kept his fingers dangling in a stream of information about all things illegal and illicit on the West Coast.

Popovitch was holding court in a private room with two steroid-juicers. Only a blind man could miss the handguns they carried under their warm-up jackets. Popovitch took one look at the two of them as they walked through the door, shook the dark hair he wore past his shoulders, and said, "Jeee-sus Christ! It's been a long time. C'mon in, have some barbeque. Want a beer?"

Derek pulled up a chair and took the bottle of Hite beer offered him. O'Reilly stayed standing. She said, "We're in kind of a hurry, Greg. We need some information."

Leaning back in his chair, Popovitch's black silk shirt stretched over his bulging belly. He laced his hands together behind his neck. "Sandy, how are you? How's that husband of yours?"

"We're divorced."

Popovitch grinned. "If you don't mind my saying so, I could have seen that coming from a thousand miles a way. Hell, I *did* see it coming from about ten thousand miles away. From Iraq, as a matter of fact. Who you working for these days, babe?"

"ODNI."

Derek saw something saurian move behind Popovitch's dark eyes. Derek turned his attention to Popovitch's buddies, one of whom was seated at the table eating. The other roamed the room, dark blank eyes taking in everything.

"Yeah? And Derek, I hear you're with Homeland."

Derek dipped his head in assent.

"So what can I do for you? And might I add that it's a bit unusual to find you two together—again." A leer edged his voice.

O'Reilly said, "There are two things specifically you might help us with and maybe some general things."

"I'm sure we can work out some sort of arrangement, assuming I can help."

Derek said, "Have you heard of an al-Qaeda op that goes by Kalakar?"

O'Reilly shot him a squint-eyed look.

Popovitch rocked in the chair. "Kalakar, Kalakar. Hmmm, nope. Sorry. Guess that one's a freebie. Besides, those al-Qaeda assholes keep to themselves pretty much. Nasty fucks, generally."

Still standing, O'Reilly leaned forward, fists resting on the table. "Any unusual shipments lately that you might have heard rumors about, Greg?"

Popovitch tipped forward on his chair and laughed. He picked up his own beer bottle and knocked back the remaining half and set it down with a clunk. "Can you be a bit more specific, babe? This is La-La Land. We get unusual shipments every day."

Popovitch's minions chuckled as if he'd told a really good joke.

O'Reilly's voice was so low Derek could barely hear her. She said, "We've got actionable intel that al-Qaeda intends to set off a major attack in the next two days. L.A. may be one of the sites. That unusual enough for you?"

Popovitch scratched at his jaw, an expression both contemplative and crafty on his broad face. "Info of that nature would carry a significant price tag."

Flipping open his sat phone, Derek asked, "You want cash or do you have an account somewhere?"

Hands splayed in an of-course gesture, Popovitch said, "Cash is always welcome, but I do have some offshore accounts that would work well for this piece of business." He reached into his pocket. Both Derek and O'Reilly tensed.

"Easy." Popovitch slowly retrieved a PDA from his pocket. "Easy." He tapped keys for a moment and passed the instrument over to Derek. It listed a Grand Cayman bank and an account number.

"How much?"

"Ten."

Derek shook his head. "Nice opener, but I'm not committing to that much until I know what it is."

Popovitch shrugged. "The problem with information—"

Both Derek and O'Reilly's phones rang almost simultaneously. Derek pointed to O'Reilly. "You take it." He let his own phone pick up. O'Reilly answered hers with a curt, "Yes," and walked away from them to stand by the door.

Popovitch continued. "As I was saying, the problem with information is you pretty much have to buy it without knowing its value. And it sounds as if you folks are in real need." He grinned his shiny white grin. Derek remembered an old biology instructor warning them not to anthropomorphize: "If an animal grins at you, it's not smiling. It's showing you its fangs. It's a sign of aggression."

Derek leaned forward. "Greg, for all we know you could be at ground zero for an attack. If this is good information, I can go to twelve. If it's crap, we'll go five. But I'm not paying you anything until—"

O'Reilly clicked off her phone, strode over to Greg Popovitch, caught up a fistful of his long hair and slammed his head down on the table. Her Beretta was in her left hand and she dug it into the underside of his jaw.

The big thug who'd been roaming the room rushed toward Derek, ham-sized fists swinging. Derek got his arms up and took the blows on his forearms, but toppled backward in the chair. He tried to roll with it, but still hit the floor hard enough to rattle his bones. The thug kicked out, catching Derek's thigh with his cowboy boot. Derek yelped, reached out, caught the toppled chair and arced it sideways into the bruiser's legs. With a shout the thug collapsed to the floor. Derek leapt up, gun out, and aimed at the other guy.

O'Reilly snarled, "Enough. Listen to me, Greg. A dirty bomb just went off in Dallas. They're still sorting out the radiation counts and they don't know if anybody's been killed yet. Whatever al-Qaeda's got going is starting, and if this is their opening salvo, things are going to turn to shit big-time. So don't fuck around with me, or I will kneecap you and we can have this same discussion in an emergency room."

"I don't know anything about attacks," Popovitch said in a muffled, strangled voice. "I know some people have been asking about suitcase nukes. Jesus, back off."

Derek thought: shit.

O'Reilly stepped away, gun aimed at Popovitch's head. Derek moved back so he could keep his gun trained on everybody. His leg hurt like a bastard, but at least he hadn't taken the kick to his bad knee.

Popovitch glared at O'Reilly for a moment, then grinned. "Didn't know you liked it rough, babe. Maybe you are my type after all."

Derek said, "Who's been asking about a nuke?"

Popovitch turned to look at Derek. "Good cop, bad cop?"

"She *will* shoot you if you drag this out too long, Greg."

Popovitch said, "About five, six weeks ago. A guy came around, asking for something special. Once we got past the foreplay, he asked me about suitcase nukes. How much and if I could get them."

"And your answer?" O'Reilly said.

The guy on the floor finally clambered to his feet. The look on his face as he glared at Derek said paybacks would be in order.

Popovitch shrugged. "I told him that if I could get such a device, it would go about three million, that I would have to get half up front. But I'd have to know more about who wanted them than just handing over money."

"A fine, upstanding citizen like you?" O'Reilly said.

Popovitch's hands twitched, as if he were imagining strangling her.

"Shocking as it might seem to you, I don't think having a nuke go off in the States would be to my or anybody else's best interest, money or not."

"What happened?"

"He went away and didn't come back."

"Do you think there's somebody else who could get suitcase nukes?" Derek asked. "Somebody in town?"

"Maybe, but I'll tell you what, they're pretty damned hard to come by."

"What was this guy's name?" O'Reilly asked. "What did he look like?"

"I was told his name was Abdul Mohammad. He was Pakistani."

"Goddammit, Greg," Derek said. "Abdul Mohammad is practically Muslim for John Smith. Who referred him to you?"

"None of your fucking business." Popovitch made a gesture with his left hand. The guy who had attacked Derek lunged at O'Reilly.

She spun and brought her elbow up into his face with a crunch. Spinning, she struck him in the neck with her other elbow. The guy went down hard and stayed down, blood pouring from his nose.

Derek moved in on the other guy, who had remained seated and silent, hands on the table. Derek kept his gun trained on him.

A knock at the door preceded a heavily accented voice. "Meester Popovitch? Ever . . . thing okay?"

"Yeah, it's just fine. Thanks," Popovitch called. He shook his head. "You're gonna get my ass kicked out of here and I like the food."

"What was his name?"

"None of your fucking business."

O'Reilly moved toward him. He scowled at her. "Don't bother, Sandy. I'm not telling you. Derek doesn't have enough money in his account to turn on this guy, and you don't have enough balls to make me."

She raised her gun, but Derek said, "Give us another name. Someone to talk to about al-Qaeda in L.A."

Popovitch smirked. "An imam. Ibrahim Sheik Muhammad. He's what you might call an al-Qaeda sympathizer."

"How do we find him?"

Popovitch frowned. The guy on the floor groaned. Popovitch said, "You don't need me for that. You need the goddamned Yellow Pages. He's in L.A., Masjid al-Falah. And you didn't get referred by me."

O'Reilly headed for the door. "Come on, Derek."

"I'll be along in a minute."

She glared at him. "I'm the—"

"Shut up. I'll be out in a few minutes."

Her gaze was flinty, and she pushed her way out the door. Derek shook his head after she was gone. "That information's worth ten. I've got a couple other questions, though."

Popovitch said, "You were always a straight guy, Stillwater. What're you doing teamed up with her?"

"I'm not. She was along for the ride. Tell me why you didn't sell this guy a suitcase nuke?"

Popovitch laughed. "Because I can't fucking get a suitcase nuke. If there are some out there, and I'm not completely sure there are, I don't have access to them. They're too hot for me. And despite what you and that bitch might think, I'm not crazy enough to want to try and get one into the States. That's the kind of animal that bites back."

"So what did you sell him?"

"Like I said, I didn't sell him anything."

Derek looked down at the guy on the floor, who was now sitting up, looking dazed. His face was a mask of blood. Derek said, "You know, I'm not sure I believe you about this. Tell me what you finally hooked this guy up with."

"Why?"

"How much?"

Popovitch splayed his hands. "I'm telling you the truth, Derek. I sent him on his way."

"How about medical supplies?"

"Ah," he said, leaning back again, patting his belly. "Onto your specialties. Sorry, not much going on around here in the biological and chemical front. Also, they don't need me for that. That's what the Internet's for. There might be some specialists in the area selling expertise, but that's just a rumor on my part. I'm not privy to it."

"Give me a name. Someone who might be able to connect me to someone with that expertise. Come on, Greg. You know everything that's going on from Mexico to Vancouver. Talk to me."

Popovitch seemed amused. "Sure. Robert Browne. He's a professor of sociology over at UCLA. Studies terrorism. Has a particular interest in biological and—"

"I've heard of him. Thanks." Browne was bullshit and Derek knew it. Browne was an academic with no particular real-world ties.

"You're welcome."

Derek flipped open his sat phone and made a call. "Francis? Derek. I heard about Dallas. Yeah, I need ten thousand operational capital transferred into this account." He read off the number and clicked off the phone.

"Take care of yourself, Greg. And if I were you, I'd get out of town for a couple days."

Popovitch leaned forward. "A word of advice?"

"Is it free?"

Popovitch grinned and again Derek thought of a baboon showing its teeth. "Yeah, it's free. If you ever come back here, don't come back with O'Reilly."

Derek nodded and walked out. He found Cassandra O'Reilly pacing back and forth in front of the restaurant. "What did you get in there?"

Derek kept on walking, heading back toward his car. She set off after him. "Derek, talk to me."

"Gee, Sandy, that was fun. I'm all for beating up people if it's necessary. But it wasn't necessary. You handled that all wrong. Greg's not a bad guy. And you'll never be able to utilize him as a source again. I was making sure that I can. You need to work on your interpersonal skills."

"You don't think Greg's a bad guy? He's a smuggler and an arms dealer and—"

Derek turned on her, snapping, "I don't trust him. He's greedy and unreliable and can be bought. But he's not who we're after."

"You're just pissed because that guy got the jump on you."

Derek stopped, feeling his blood pressure rise. "Sandy, I'm not your partner. I'm not your employee, and I'm not your friend. Go talk to the imam. I'm going to work my own angle."

He turned and started down the street. She called after him, "Ron and the kids live in Dallas, Derek."

He stopped. Ron was her ex-husband. Kids? She hadn't had any kids when they were in Iraq.

Derek turned to look at her. "Are they all right?"

"I don't know."

Derek nodded. "I hope they are. I really do. But that doesn't mean I want to be partners with you. Good luck with the imam. You might want to take a man with you and let him do the talking. Or a Muslim, like Shelly."

He headed for his car.

CHAPTER 10

Agent Dale Hutchins just finished reading through all the after-action reports when Firdos Moin walked into the office. The slender Pakistani smiled, though his eyes looked haunted. "Dale, you're looking much better than last time I saw you."

Dale reached out and shook Firdos's hand, gesturing for him to have a seat. "That's right. I'm much better looking now."

Firdos's smile widened. "Still not as good looking as me, but maybe the doctors can do something about that next time you visit. It is good to be back to work?"

Dale nodded. He gestured at the files scattered over his desktop. "I was just reading through the reports. How goes the hunt for Kalakar?"

Firdos's smile faltered. "A dead end, I'm afraid. I've also been distracted by a new case. I apologize, but you understand, I'm sure. I was hoping you might help me with another set of eyes."

"I'd like that."

"Another look at the apartment?"

Dale nodded. Face your fears, he thought. He really didn't want to go back to that apartment building. The associations with that place were only pain and death.

Firdos drove, his radio tuned to some local pop station that made Hutchins want to pull his own ears off. He kept his mouth shut, though. Firdos was unusually quiet. Something was on his mind, but Hutchins decided to wait and see if the Pakistani would share it with him.

When they arrived at the apartment, Firdos parked across the street and they walked over. The door had been fixed. Firdos unlocked it with a key he had on a separate ring and they entered.

A sensation like spiders slowly creeping up his back made Hutchins shiver. For a brief hallucinatory moment he smelled cordite and the distinctive, pungent stench of Semtex, then it was gone.

"Are you all right?" Firdos asked.

"Yeah, just had a moment there." He walked over and looked at the bare floor. Someone had torn up the carpeting and not replaced it. The walls were scorched. A sofa that had been both burned and ripped by shrapnel still stood against one wall. The apartment smelled of mildew and something darker and gamier that Dale thought might be the residue of death—blood and torn and burned tissue and bodily waste.

He wandered the empty apartment, trying to get a feel for things. Pausing, he said, "In the after-action reports your recon team insists there were six people."

Firdos seemed lost in thought. He looked up, startled. "Yes, six. I've looked at the photographs myself."

"Do they have anything better than what you shared with us? The sixth man, Kalakar, if that's who he is, is never clearly identified."

"No. He was very careful."

"But there were only five people in the apartment."

"Yes. Did you watch their suicide tapes?"

Dale shook his head. "No. Maybe later. Did Kalakar have one?"

Firdos shook his head. "No, but perhaps he was planning to. Or perhaps he was just the person sending them out to end their lives."

"You're still interrogating the survivors?"

"Survivor. Yes. That is how we know he was called Kalakar, although the survivor does not know why he was called Kalakar. It's not his name. It's a label, a nickname of some sort. It means artist or artisan, or, I think in English another word might be craftsman."

Hutchins thought: *He was here and then he wasn't. He must have split just before we arrived. Where did he go?*

He thought also of something the new guy, Jason Barnes, had said in the locker room before the op: do you trust any of these people?

"Did you go back and look at the surveillance tapes to see if Kalakar got out of here somehow and they just missed it?"

Firdos gazed out the window toward the surveillance post across the street, another apartment building, four-stories, made of pink-gray stone. He shuddered as if startled. "Sorry. What?"

"Did you go back and look at the surveillance tapes to see if Kalakar somehow got out and they missed it?"

"Yes. Nothing. We think he left out the back and jumped the fence. There is a shopping mall over there and he could have parked there."

"He had advance warning." It wasn't a question and Hutchins tried unsuccessfully to keep the anger out of his voice.

Firdos looked at him. "Come with me."

They left the apartment, Firdos locking the door after them. He led Hutchins toward the back entrance, into the apartment building's tiny parking lot. The back of the property was enclosed by a six-foot-tall unpainted wooden fence. It would have been difficult to climb, but not impossible.

"Did you guys examine the fence?"

Firdos shrugged. "It wasn't our top priority. The forensic team may have. I don't know."

Hutchins started at the far left corner and studied each board in each section of the fence. He had no idea what he was looking for.

The sequence of events didn't make complete sense to him. More than an hour before their dynamic entry, the surveillance team reported the complete terror cell was in the apartment. The surrounding apartments had been emptied earlier while the cell was gone. A loose tail had been placed on members of the team, who had been out eating lunch at a restaurant together. And yet no one had captured a clear image of Kalakar. Almost as if he knew he was under surveillance.

Hutchins's FBI group and the Pakistani National Police group had stormed the apartment.

In the interim, the leader of the cell had left, disappeared. And if the surveillance team reports were reliable—Hutchins didn't know if they were—then this guy hadn't just left, he'd left in a way that the surveillance team couldn't observe.

Two-thirds of the way along the fence, Dale said, "Hmmm." He carefully pulled aside two boards, looking at Firdos. "I think we know how he got out. He planned it. He knew there was an observation team out front. He probably kept a car over here in this mall parking lot."

A look of sadness crossed Firdos's face. "That may explain it, then."

Hutchins shot him a questioning look, eyebrows arched. "Explain what?"

"Two days after the operation, one of the surveillance team was murdered on his way home from work. He was found in his car on a side street, his throat cut."

Hutchins stared at Firdos. Slowly he said, "You think Kalakar was tipped off that we were coming and left just before we got here? That one of your team tipped him off."

"Perhaps."

Hutchins let that sink in. There were many, many questions he wanted to ask. Where to start? He asked, "If so, why didn't Kalakar get them all out?"

"That is a most excellent question, Dale. A most excellent question."

CHAPTER 11

Derek walked back to his bucar from Kwan's, lost in thought. He had been hit with a lot of things over the last few hours and his brain was buzzing. Not least of all was his concern over his own mental state. Upon walking through Helen Birch's office door, her first comment had been about him shacking up with a Russian spy on his boat in the Gulf of Mexico.

In fact, he had spent two months on *The Salacious Sally* touring the gulf and the Caribbean, contemplating whether he was going to retire from DHS and take on a quiet life as an academic or consultant. Only two of those weeks had been spent in the company of Irina Khournikova, and she finally got fed up with his brooding and returned to Moscow with a final, "I don't know where your head is at, Derek."

He decided to return to work in Washington, but something was missing and he didn't know what it was. And that guy at Kwan's should never have been able to get a jump on him like that. Had he lost his edge? Where was his fire?

The bucar awaited him and he popped his key into the lock and was ready to climb in when Steven Connelly, the LAPD detective, melted out of the shadows. "Have a word with you, Stillwater?"

Derek turned to stare at the detective. "About what?"

Connelly waved him to follow and set off down the street. After walking two blocks in silence, they came alongside a white van parked at the curb. As they approached, the door slid open and Connelly jumped inside, gesturing for Derek to follow. Hand on his gun, Derek climbed in. Two men lounged in the van, which was crammed with communication equipment.

"Have a seat."

Derek sat in the proffered chair and looked around. "You have Popovitch under surveillance?"

"Yeah. You and your partner walked right into a sting, which I suspect is blown now. Popovitch was waiting for a guy linked to the local Russians to show up and make the payment for a shipment of AKs. It might still go down, but I doubt it."

Derek rubbed his cheek. "Sorry, man. You heard about Dallas?"

Connelly nodded. "And we heard every word you and O'Reilly said. I'm not sure Popovitch is being straight with you."

"Not a surprise. What makes you think so?"

Connelly nodded at one of his partners, who pushed some keys on a keyboard and brought up a digital recording. The guy had a bushy Afro and wore heavy-framed glasses like he was refugee from the 1970s. He said, "This is from right after you walked out."

Popovitch: You got beat up by a girl, Jeb.

Jeb: Fuckin' bitch broke my dose.

Popovitch: Not the first time. Need to see a doc?

Jeb: Do.

Unknown: Might improve your looks.

Jeb: Fug you. Jus' sat there with your hands on your dick. Didn't even move.

Popovitch: Yeah, Larry. You didn't say a word the whole time.

(A rustling sound.)

Larry: Nobody broke my nose or hit me with a chair, either. You also didn't tell them everything.

Popovitch: O'Reilly's full of shit if she thinks she can intimidate me into giving her information.

Jeb: I'll kill that bitch I see her again.

Popovitch: Back off her. Back off both of them. They're both trouble. And don't think because you got a drop on Stillwater that he's a pussy.

Jeb: He suckered me with the chair.

Larry: He *reacted* with the chair. Pretty damned fast. He surprised the hell out of me. One second he's on the floor, the next second he's kicking your ass and back on his feet. He could have put a bullet in your head and mine before either of us got a gun out. I didn't think he and the bitch were in sync.

Popovitch: They weren't. They don't get along.

Larry: So I gathered. You want I contact Valentin, call this off?

Popovitch: Change location, I think. Just postpone it. Tell him this site's hot now. Give us a couple hours or he can pick something.

Larry: I don't trust him.

Jeb: Yeah, me neither.

Popovitch: Call him. Tell him—tell him I'll get back with him in an hour with a new location.

Larry: I understand why you didn't roll over on the bitch, but Stillwater seemed to be playing straight with you.

Popovitch: If you don't cross him. He can slash-'n'-burn with the best of 'em if you fuck with him. He just didn't ask the right questions.

Larry: Okay, I'm out of here. I'll call Valentin. Be back in five.

Afro clicked off the recording. Derek said, "Who's Valentin?"

"Mafiya," Connelly said. "Know what that is?"

"Russian mob. Selling AK-47s here in the U.S.?"

"Bringing them in; Popovitch is the wholesaler."

Derek nodded, thinking. "Which guy is yours?"

Connelly laughed. "We don't have anybody inside Popovitch's organization."

"Larry's not yours?"

Connelly's expression darkened. "What makes you say that?"

Derek shrugged. "So Kwan's is bugged. I need to talk to Popovitch about what he didn't tell us."

Connelly exchanged a look with the third man, a short, heavyset guy who looked like the Michelin Man. Michelin Man nodded. Connelly said, "We think we know what he held back. Abdul Mohammad."

Derek said, "The LAPD has a tap on a guy who is asked to acquire a suitcase nuke and you follow up. I can't tell you how encouraging that is."

Afro said, "We're not amateurs."

"You arrest this guy?"

"No."

"Jesus, don't tell me you lost him."

"Sort of," Michelin Man said. "He's at the morgue. Somebody slit his throat. And we don't think it was Popovitch or one of his crew who did it."

Derek leaned forward, blood starting to boil. "If you don't think it was Popovitch, who do you think it was?"

Connelly shrugged.

"Then who was Abdul Mohammad?"

"A guy who works as a courier for a law firm here in L.A.," Connelly said. "Jamieson, Perzada, Suliemann and Hill. They're entertainment industry attorneys. We can't figure out any connection with the firm, but we think the building he worked in was kind of interesting."

Derek splayed his hands in an out-with-it gesture.

Michelin Man said, "The law firm is in the Avco Center on Wilshire. It's about three blocks from the Federal Building. You probably drove right by it."

"Okay. So?"

Michelin Man said, "Maybe it's a coincidence, but the Pakistani Consulate is in the Avco Center."

Derek let that sink in, nodding. "All right. Popovitch still at Kwan's?"

Connelly shook his head. "Stillwater, you're done with Popovitch. Don't go screwing with us. We've had a lot of time in on this operation and we don't need some Homeland asshole screwing it up."

Derek ignored him and said to Afro. "He leave Kwan's yet?"

With a shrug, Afro tickled the keyboard and studied something on the screen. "Looks like he's on his way out now."

"What's he drive?"

"Stillwater—"

Afro said, "Black Mercedes SUV, tinted windows. Why?"

"For God sakes—"

Derek shoved open the door and jumped out. The Emerson knife he wore inside his pocket was in his hand. Bending down he slashed the front tire. The Emerson blade was made of carbonized steel, was razor sharp, and it cut through the tire as if through Swiss cheese. It flattened with a whoosh.

Derek took off at a dead run, the complaining shouts of the LAPD a distant echo behind him.

Jumping into the bucar, he raced toward Kwan's. He didn't get far before he saw a black Mercedes ML320 with tinted windows. There appeared to be three figures inside. Derek swerved the bucar into a skid, blocking the road.

Jeb, Larry, and Popovitch piled out, reaching for their guns. Derek was already out, Colt in his hand.

"Are you fucking crazy?! What's the matter with you?" Popovitch's face turned the color of a basketball.

Derek reached out, caught Popovitch by the hair and dragged him toward the bucar. "I've had a change of plans. I'm deputizing you to the Department of Homeland Security. Gentlemen," he said to Jeb and Larry, "you can go ahead and make your deal with Valentin, but I wouldn't recommend it. You're hot. I'd call it a night or turn over a new leaf and go straight, because there's some prison time in your future if you don't."

Dragging a protesting Popovitch over to the bucar, he opened the front door, shoved him in, and slammed it. Racing around he jumped in, waved to Larry and Jeb, and stomped his foot down on the gas pedal. He smiled at Popovitch who seemed stunned.

"You'll thank me later."

"What the fuck are you doing?"

"You know what a fish out of water needs to do?"

"I don't know what you're talking about. Let me out."

"He needs to find a local dog to direct him to the local watering holes. Sorry for mixing metaphors, but you're the local dog. Let's talk about Abdul Mohammad."

CHAPTER 12

Donna Price paced around her hotel room in the Sofitel Chicago Water Tower, alternating between watching CNN, clicking on her PDA, and glancing out her window at the lights of Chicago. Winter had come a little early to the Windy City, and a few flakes of snow were whipping around the high-rise. Her cell phone chirped. A peek at the screen only indicated a D.C. area code, not who the caller was.

"Donna Price here."

The voice on the phone sounded like it needed a good sanding. "Ms. Price, this is Homeland Secretary James Johnston. How are you this evening?"

She stopped pacing, eyes drifting to CNN. "Mr. Secretary—"

"I'm sure you're aware of the incident in Dallas. I'm contacting both of the candidates to update them on the situation and to let them know that I'm going to be discussing their security with Director Mallard shortly. That will be coordinated through their Secret Service details, but I want to make sure you know their safety is our greatest concern and we are evaluating it now."

"Thank you, sir."

"You're welcome. And of course we're aware the candidates will need a briefing so they can prepare their political positions."

Price wondered if there was a hint of sarcasm in the secretary's voice. Johnston was notorious for his lack of political sophistication. She ran a hand through her long blonde hair. "We appreciate that, sir."

"Now, Ms. Price, I didn't know if Governor Stark was in the middle of something right now or not, so I decided to contact you directly before talking to him. He's not at a rally or in a press conference, is he?"

She brought up her PDA again. "He's taking a short break, then we're going to have a strategy session. Then we've got a crew from ABC that's going to conduct an interview with him."

"A late night for presidential hopefuls," Johnston said. "Particularly this close to the election."

"Yes, sir. We work almost nonstop this late in the game."

"Ms. Price, in the next forty-eight hours or so, if I understand this correctly, you will make stops in New York City, Washington, D.C., Dallas, and Los Angeles. Is that correct?"

"Yes, of course. Tonight's the last rest before it's nonstop. It'll be constant travel from tomorrow morning until about midday on election day, then he'll head back home to Phoenix to vote and wait for the polls."

"Will you be returning to Chicago?"

"Yes, for a late rally tomorrow evening."

"Thank you, Ms. Price. That's very useful information. May I speak with the governor now?"

"Of course. I'll go get him."

Governor William Stark also had CNN tuned in, but he was on the phone talking to his wife, who was campaigning separately in their home state of Arizona. Just for a little while he was hanging loose, his jacket hung up, stripped down to a T-shirt. He was alone, not surrounded by aides, consultants, strategists, media, or security. It was a fifteen-minute window, and he wanted to talk to his wife in peace.

Stark's tall, lean frame was sprawled out on his suite's sofa, bare feet up on the armrest. His gray hair was short, and he ran a blunt-fingered hand through it as he talked. "Yeah, I feel like I've got tennis elbow. All those grip-and-grins. And my feet are killing me. How about you?"

"They keep harping on your lack of foreign policy experience, Bill. We've got to come up with something new here."

Stark nodded. "They always nag governors about that. I'll mention it to Donna, see if we can craft something fresh. I haven't had an update on Newman's day yet. Heard anything?"

"He's hitting the South. Florida, Georgia, Carolinas, Alabama. There was a sound bite on Fox about his experience fighting terrorism under President Langston, how he was the head of some task force or something."

"Yeah? Anybody ask him why he authorized letting the Fallen Angels loose in exchange for—"

"You know that's classified."

"Maybe it should be—"

A knock on the door interrupted and Stark frowned. "Hang on, hon." He called out, "Who is it?"

The door opened and Jeremy Murg, one of his Secret Service agents, stepped in. "It's Ms. Price, sir." Murg glanced at his watch. "I know you asked to be undisturbed for five more minutes, sir, but—"

Stark waved Price in. "Sorry, hon, I guess I have to get back to work. I love you. I'll call you first thing in the morning."

Stark clicked off and scowled at Price. "All I wanted was fifteen minutes, Donna. Just fifteen. What is it?"

Price held up her cell phone. "Secretary Johnston wants to fill you in personally."

Stark scowled. "Did you ask him if he called me first or Newman?"

Price sighed. "I would think Newman was higher on the list than you. Same party, plus he's vice president. Let's not get all paranoid this close to the election, Governor. You're ahead in the polls."

"Yeah, by three points. Let's see what Johnston has to say."

He took her phone. "Mr. Secretary, busy evening."

Johnston said, "Sorry to have to interrupt, Governor. I need to fill you in on Dallas."

CHAPTER 13

In the bucar, Derek held out his hand to Popovitch. "I'll take your piece, too."

Popovitch laughed. "Or what?"

Derek's Colt was in his lap. He picked it up and aimed it at Popovitch's knee. "It might be worthwhile to remember that I'm not as nice a person as Cassandra O'Reilly is."

Popovitch muttered, "But close," and slowly reached into his jacket and retrieved a .38 Smith & Wesson Model 36, holding it out to Derek. Derek took it, slipping it into his coat pocket.

"I didn't think anybody used revolvers any more. What's your backup piece?"

"Revolvers don't jam. And I don't know what you're—"

Derek backhanded Popovitch with the Colt. "Don't fuck with me, Greg."

Popovitch touched his lip with his fingers, which came away red with blood. "Jesus, Stillwater. What's your problem?"

"Backup. Hand it over. I'll frisk you later."

"Okay, okay." He bent over, pulled up his pant leg to reveal an ankle holster carrying a small semiautomatic. He handed it over. Derek glanced at it.

"Walther PPK? Figures."

"It's a good gun and no, I don't like my martinis shaken."

Derek smirked. "Okay, Greg. Where are we going?"

"How the fuck would I know? You're the kidnapper."

"So turn me into the Feds. We'll have a great discussion. Tell me about Abdul Mohammad."

"I told you back at Kwan's."

"Yeah, and you also mentioned he was a referral. I can't imagine that some guy walking through the door asking if you can sell him a suitcase nuke is going to get a free pass from you. For some reason I don't think you're as accessible as Wal-Mart."

"I'm not really in the mood to teach you the basics of how I run my business, Stillwater."

Derek glared at him. "I know where the LAPD is fixing a tire right now, and I can just drop you off with them. But the fact is, I need your help."

"Could've asked. Didn't have to fuckin' kidnap me."

Derek shot him a look. "Oh, really?"

Popovitch fell silent. They passed over the L.A. River, which at the moment was barely a trickle through its concrete crib.

Finally, Popovitch said, "Yeah, he came twice, as a matter of fact."

"Twice." Derek took a turn and they passed by the Cathedral of Our Lady of the Angels. It didn't look like a church. It was modern with no steeple, and could have been a museum or a large office building except for the cross on the glass box attached high on the front. Derek could just imagine his father complaining about it; and his mother responding that a church was the people, not the building.

He focused on driving. Derek didn't know where they were, exactly, but was trying to stay in the downtown L.A. area as much as possible.

"Go straight until you get to Alameda, then go right."

Derek nodded, not asking where Popovitch was directing him. For the moment, Greg seemed willing to cooperate. It was time to give him a little bit of slack and see where it led. He said, "Tell me about the first time."

Greg was quiet until Derek turned onto Alameda heading south. Although it was late on Sunday, heading quickly toward Monday, there were a fair amount of people driving around this section of town.

"I was at Bongos the first time," Popovitch said. "Don't go there too often any more. Too many cops. I like the food, though, and the chicks are pretty hot. Anyway, he comes to the bar and sits down and asks if I'm Greg Popovitch; he heard I was good at getting hard-to-find items."

Since Popovitch didn't give him directions, Derek stayed on Alameda.

"I told him I sometimes had luck finding things other people couldn't. Then I asked him how he heard of me. He gave me the name of somebody I work with on occasion and I told him to come back in a couple days after I checked him out. He told me his name and took off."

"The name of the person?"

Greg leaned back. "You know, Derek, although I appreciate the money the government gave me for my initial assistance, this information will cost you a lot—"

Derek fired his Colt. The bullet passed within inches of Popovitch's head, shattering the passenger window into a million little squares of glass. The sound of the gunshot was deafening in the confines of the car. Cool night air flowed in.

"Jesus Christ, Stillwater! Are you fuckin' crazy?" Popovitch brushed glass chips off his pants.

"Don't start thinking this is a negotiation, Greg. You're helping me out here or I'm dumping your body in a landfill. I tried doing this your way and O'Reilly's way. Now we're doing things my way. What's his name?"

"Shit."

"Name."

"This is a guy who will think nothing of shooting you just because he doesn't like the way you look."

"I'm a pretty good-looking guy. I'll take my chances. Name."

Popovitch sighed. "Ishaq Mohammed Mukhtar."

"Great. Another guy named Mohammed. Just what I need. Okay. Good. Let's go talk to him. Give me directions."

"Jesus Christ, Stillwater. Aren't you listening? Are you trying to get us both killed?"

Derek held up the Colt. "I'm trying to keep a lot of people from getting killed. You, on the other hand, are expendable."

"All right, all right. Get on the Ten and head west. It's coming up. We're going to Playa del Rey. Jesus, Stillwater. Mukhtar is not a guy to screw around with."

"I'll be very diplomatic." Derek glanced over at Popovitch and waggled his eyebrows. "Promise."

CHAPTER 14

Kalakar paced around the bedroom his hosts had provided. He had finished his prayers for the evening and was trying to set his mind for the Tahajjud prayers he would rise early in the morning to make. But he was jittery, so he paced.

The sound of hurried footsteps were followed by a tentative knock on the door. "Yes?"

The door crept open and his host, John Seddiqi, peered in. "Kalakar, I have—you need to see this, I think."

Kalakar followed John into the living room, where the TV was on. It showed a news broadcast from CNN. A reporter was talking about a bomb blast in Dallas.

> It has been confirmed that the bomb was a so-called dirty bomb. A dirty bomb is not a nuclear weapon, but a regular bomb using regular explosives—gunpowder or plastic explosives or dynamite—that also has radioactive isotopes present, so it spreads radiation. The immediate area around the blast, which took place at the Loos Field House outside Dallas, has been evacuated. The building was not in use at the time. It's not known at this time whether or not there were any casualties. We're going to go live to Dallas.

Kalakar clenched his fists. What had happened? It wasn't supposed to go off now. This was too early. He paced, running his hands through his dark hair. Turning to John, he asked, "What else have they said?"

John shrugged, his dark eyes worried. "Not much. It caused some damage to the building and people are panicking because of the radiation, although they've had some people from the FBI and Homeland Security saying the radiation levels aren't all that high and people shouldn't panic."

Kalakar nodded. Was this a catastrophe? He couldn't decide, couldn't focus.

"You're not responsible for this, are you?"

Kalakar turned on the man. "My plans are none of your concern. You have one job and one job only. It is all I and Allah ask of you."

The slender man blinked and nodded. "My apologies. Of course. I am here to serve Allah."

Kalakar softened his response. He needed John Seddiqi, but John didn't need to know what was really going on, and he did not trust John's tenuous—at best—commitment to jihad. No, John was an unwitting tool and it would be better if he just thought he was providing some innocuous information and offering his house as a place to stay quietly for a few days. Kalakar rested his hand on John's shoulder. "I appreciate your hospitality, John. I really do." He waved at the TV. "As for this event in Dallas, I don't know anything about it. It's a terrible thing. And so senseless."

Kalakar thought of what this premature explosion might mean to his plan. So many things had already gone wrong. He said, "You should go to bed, my friend. Get some sleep. You have a busy day at work tomorrow."

John nodded, swallowing hard. "Of course."

Kalakar patted him on the shoulder. "Go, go to bed. Kiss your daughter goodnight, go to sleep with your good wife. Don't worry about this." He gestured again at the TV. "This is Allah's will."

John hesitated before replying. "May Allah be praised."

After John headed for his bedroom, Kalakar scowled at the television set. He had much thinking to do. Would the explosion in Dallas change his plans? Certainly it would convince the Americans that the plan was really going to happen. But it worried him that he had not had time to edit the files on the computers in Islamabad.

As he watched, CNN cut to Vice President Newman, who was in Atlanta. The distinguished politician said, "This further reinforces why we must focus on domestic defense and homeland security. Although information is still coming in, I'm just grateful that there appears to be few if any fatalities. I encourage all Dallas residents to stay calm and listen to the authorities and follow their directions on how best to keep your families safe."

A reporter said, "Does this change your itinerary for the next two days, Mr. Vice President?"

Newman, looking properly grave, said, "Of course not. We can't let these sorts of attacks frighten the American voter or prevent the democratic electoral process from happening. I will continue with my election schedule and be visiting Dallas, as well as many other cities around the country, between now and Tuesday."

Kalakar smiled. "Allah is great," he said. "Praise Allah."

CHAPTER 15

Greg Popovitch directed Derek to a parking lot outside Pier 35, a Marina del Rey facility hosting larger boats. Derek felt immediately at home. He lived at Bayman's Marina near Baltimore on the Chesapeake Bay. He loved boats.

Popovitch stared through the windshield of the bucar for a moment. "This is a really bad idea, Derek."

"Get out of the fucking car, Greg."

"I want my piece back."

"I want peace on earth and goodwill toward men. Doesn't mean I'm going to get it."

Popovitch clenched his jaw and shook his head. "You know, you can threaten me all you want. You might smack me in the face, hell, you might even shoot me in the leg. I understand, Derek—you can be a real bastard and you're trying to convince me that cooperating will be less painful. I've had the training, I've been on both ends of this. But the two of us going over and confronting Ishaq Mukhtar unarmed is suicide. Give me my guns back, dammit."

After a moment's consideration, Derek handed over the Walther. He studied Popovitch, who checked it and slid it into the pocket of his warm-up jacket. Derek said, "They're going to search us, aren't they?"

Popovitch nodded.

"So why do you really want the gun?"

They climbed out of the car. Resting his hands on the roof of the bucar, Popovitch said, "What kind of message do you think it sends if you're armed to the teeth and I'm not, particularly since I'm here with a nice fat lip, thanks to you? It tells them that I can't be trusted and neither can you. But if we walk in there like two pros, on equal footing, Mukhtar will hopefully consider this a possible business deal and not shoot us both just for showing up without an appointment."

"Okay, Greg. Let's play it your way. Where are we going?"

Popovitch led the way. Out on the docks of the marina, Derek glanced around. The boats here weren't boats, they were yachts. Beautiful works of ocean-going art that were probably custom-built and cost millions of dollars. "Which one?"

With a wave of his hand, Popovitch said, "The trideck Trinity over there."

Derek looked to where Popovitch waved and whistled. "Baby!"

Popovitch nodded in agreement. "It ain't no rowboat, that's for damned sure. One hundred and fifty-six feet, crews twelve, has a cruising speed of twenty-two knots."

"You seem to know a lot about it."

"Mukhtar loves to talk about this boat and you might say I've got some boat envy going on."

"Yeah," Derek said, walking forward, studying the sleek lines of the yacht. "Me, too."

They were stopped by a burly, dark-skinned guy with close-cropped black hair and a nose like a falcon's beak. "No farther," he said. His voice was heavy and slow, deeply accented. Derek had no difficulty identifying the bulge on the guy's hip or the glittery look in his eyes.

"We need to speak with Mr. Mukhtar," Popovitch said.

The guard focused on Popovitch, drew a walkie-talkie to his lips and spoke in deliberate Arabic. Derek caught "Popovitch" but couldn't translate any of the rest.

The guard said, "Mr. Mukhtar wants to know what this is about. He says it is late."

"Tell him there's a possible last-minute business deal he will probably be interested in."

The guard stared at Popovitch, spoke again into the radio, gaze drifting to Derek. After a moment, he handed the walkie-talkie to Popovitch. "Mr. Mukhtar wishes to speak with you."

Popovitch arched his eyebrows at Derek, took the radio, and said, "Ishaq, it's Greg Popovitch. Sorry to show up so late and unannounced."

"Who is that with you, Greg?"

Popovitch looked at Derek for a moment before he pushed the talk button. "His name is Derek Stillwater. He's with Homeland Security."

The guard tensed, moving toward Derek. Derek flashed him a warning look, but the guard kept coming, reaching for his gun. Derek didn't let him get the gun out of its holster. He caught the guard's crotch with his left hand—gently. "Take it easy or I'm going to clench my fist."

The guard didn't move.

"Jesus." Popovitch said into the radio, "This isn't a bust, it's informational."

Derek said, "Tell him I love his boat."

Popovitch rolled his eyes. He held the radio away from his body. "Are you fucking nuts?"

"Tell him I live on a boat."

Popovitch said, "Ishaq, he wants me to tell you that he lives on a boat."

The walkie-talkie buzzed. Mukhtar said, "What kind?"

"Sixty-foot Chris-Craft Constellation. Built in 1961."

Popovitch eyed Derek. After a moment he relayed the information to Mukhtar. Mukhtar replied, "Come on up. Leave your weapons with Bulus and come aboard."

Derek let go of Bulus's testicles and handed over the confiscated .38 and his Colt. Popovitch handed over his Walther. Bulus said, "Hands on your heads."

"Hey, no hard feelings." Derek assumed the position.

Bulus didn't comment, but his pat down was a little more aggressive than Derek thought was necessary. Once Bulus decided they were clean, he waved them down the dock.

At the top of the gangplank stood another burly Arab wearing white pants, white shirt, and a navy blazer. His appearance didn't quite scream "thug" the way Bulus's did, but there was little disguising his purpose. He directed them to place their hands on top of their heads again, which they did. He patted them down, and ran a handheld metal detector over them, confiscating Derek's knife and car keys and satellite phone.

"Boy, you guys know how to make a fellow seem welcome," Derek said.

This new guard didn't respond except to say, "Follow me, please."

Derek admired the boat as they moved from the lower deck up two staircases to the skylounge. Teak, mahogany, gleaming fiberglass. Derek wasn't an art expert by any stretch of the imagination, but he thought he recognized a Cezanne hanging on the wall. In the skylounge, with a great view of the harbor, waited another armed guard. Dressed like his two partners in white slacks and a blue blazer, he had accessorized with an Uzi. Seated in a comfortable chair sipping from a glass of wine was the person Derek assumed was Ishaq Mukhtar.

Mukhtar remained seated. He gestured with a thick hand adorned with bejeweled rings. "Greg, this is quite unusual. Everything okay?"

Derek stepped forward. "I made him bring me here. I need your help."

Mukhtar studied Derek. "Mr. Stillwater? Or should I say Agent Stillwater?"

Popovitch said, "Actually, he's a professor. So Dr. Derek Stillwater."

Mukhtar nodded, expression politely interested. "And what are you a professor of, Doctor?"

"Biochemistry, basically."

"Interesting."

"Tell him," Popovitch said.

Derek nodded. "I'm a troubleshooter for the Department of Homeland Security. My specialty is biological and chemical terrorism."

"For it or against it?" Mukhtar burst into bubbling laughter at his own joke. He was a large man, scalp shaved, his goatee white and thick. Not fat, he was solid, and tailored his clothes carefully to minimize the impression he might enjoy food and drink too much.

"Preventing it," Derek said.

"Of course. This is certainly not—"

Derek interrupted. "If I may, Mr. Mukhtar. We have intelligence that suggests there's going to be a major terrorist attack here in L.A. on election day."

"There has been one in Dallas, apparently."

Derek nodded and continued. "And there's a possibility that it will involve a small nuclear weapon."

Mukhtar's eyes widened. "I see. Most interesting. So why come to me?"

Popovitch said, "If something like this came into the area, I imagine you would have heard of it."

The Arab's eyes closed momentarily. His expression changed and he waved a hand at his two security guards. "I'm insulted. Escort them out, please."

Derek stepped forward. "Please, just a name. Somewhere to go next. You can't want something like this to happen here."

Mukhtar's voice was cold. "Get out. Get them out of here. Now."

The two guards stepped forward. Derek jabbed his elbow into the Uzi guard's throat, caught the gun barrel with his other hand and kicked the man's feet out from under him. To his relief, Popovitch spun and took out the other guard with a one-two combination. Popovitch reached down and withdrew the guard's handgun.

Derek kept the Uzi pointed at the two guards. "You gave a reference for Abdul Mohammad when you sent him to Greg. How did you know him?"

Mukhtar's face darkened an angry plum. "You are a guest on my—"

Derek stomped over to the man and said, "I need your help. You can volunteer the information or I can use every method I can think of to get it out of you, which will not exclude arrest, torture, or blowing up your fucking boat."

Popovitch said, "Unfortunately, Ishaq, he's not kidding."

"How dare you bring him to me."

Popovitch snorted. "Like I had a choice."

Derek leaned forward and pressed the Uzi against Mukhtar's right knee. "I hope this is on single shot. I'd hate to blow your leg off by accident."

The Arab didn't flinch. He just glared at him. "What do you need to know?"

"How did you know Abdul Mohammad?"

"I received a phone call from a business acquaintance."

"Who?"

Mukhtar's face shifted from anger to a crafty calculation. "And what do I receive for this privileged information?"

"Two useful limbs."

"And if you torture and kill me and I tell you nothing, what then?"

"I'll find somebody else to annoy. You, on the other hand, will have had a really bad day."

"Twenty thousand," Popovitch said.

Mukhtar glanced over. "What was that?"

"Derek will arrange twenty thousand dollars into whatever account you want."

With an elaborate shrug, Mukhtar said, "That is not much money for the information I might have."

Derek pressed down with the Uzi. "Consider it the cherry on top of being able to walk. Think of it as a way of saving face."

Mukhtar nodded. "Very well. I received a phone call from a business acquaintance, Faiz Hasan Chughtai. He told me that a friend of his, this Abdul Mohammad, would need an introduction to someone who could get particularly hard to acquire items. I agreed."

"Did he say what particularly hard to acquire items he was looking for?"

"No."

Derek stepped back. On the floor the guard he had taken the Uzi from coughed. Popovitch said, "How do we get in touch with Chughtai?"

Mukhtar said, "So you can attack him?"

"Not if he cooperates," Derek said.

"And what is this worth…?" Mukhtar trailed off at the look on Derek's face. "Yes, of course. I have already seen the type of currency you—"

A noise behind them caught their attention. Derek spun, Uzi to his shoulder. Bulus and another guard were rushing through the door, machine guns raised. Derek dropped to the ground, firing as he rolled. He cut down Bulus in a swath of scarlet.

One of the guards on the ground rolled toward Derek, batting the Uzi from his hands. His big hands went around Derek's throat. Derek heard the pop, pop, pop above him of returning gunfire. The world grew dark.

Stiffening his hand, Derek drove his fingers into the man's throat. The grip on his neck loosened momentarily, and he tried to roll away, but the man tightened his hands again. Spots formed in front of Derek's eyes.

There was a louder pop and Derek felt something warm and wet splash over him. The man collapsed on top of him. He rolled out from under the guard to see Popovitch standing back, surveying the skylounge. The smuggler's arm was soaked in blood. Looking down at himself, Derek realized he was drenched in blood and gore as well.

Popovitch looked at him. "That got kind of ugly."

The four bodyguards were all dead. So was Mukhtar. Derek said, "This kind of went to hell, didn't it?"

"It's what you're good at, Derek. Let's go see if we can find this Chughtai before the cops show up."

Derek rubbed his neck, looking around at the carnage. "I want my gun and stuff back."

Popovitch pointed at Bulus. "He's got the guns. The asshole over there's probably got your phone and knife. Wipe down anything you touched and let's get the hell out of here."

Derek nodded, used a silk tablecloth to wipe off anything he may have touched, retrieved his belongings, and ran off the yacht after Popovitch. He dug a spare set of clothes from one of his Go Packs and handed Popovitch a first-aid kit. Popovitch sat in the bucar and studied the wound to his bicep. "Hurts like hell, but it's not very deep."

Derek stripped, changed clothes, and bundled the bloody clothing to be discarded at a distant location. Not for the first time he wondered if he really was one of the good guys. Sometimes it was hard to tell. He said, "Thanks for saving my life."

Popovitch cleaned and bandaged his wound. "I hate to say this, Derek, but this is the most fun I've had in a long time."

CHAPTER 16

Cassandra O'Reilly pulled up in front of the Federal Building where Shelly Pimpuntikar stood waiting. She noticed that Shelly had added something to her wardrobe—the full head scarf worn by Muslim women called the hijab.

Shelly climbed in, dropping her briefcase by her feet. O'Reilly said, "Why the hijab?"

Shelly adjusted it. It was black and she wore it loosely over her hair. "If we're going to talk to an imam, trust me, we'll have better luck if we cover our hair. I have one for you. It'll help."

O'Reilly bristled. "Unlikely." She pulled away from the curb. "Did you get an address for this imam?"

"Yes. Both of the mosque and his home address. I suggest we try his home first." She glanced at her watch. "It's almost one thirty in the morning. And I think you should wear the head covering anyway, as a sign of respect. He's likely to have a conservative attitude about women and by at least showing this small amount—"

"I'm not Muslim."

Shelly sighed. "I'm from Pakistan, where the hijab is not generally as important to Muslim women. And I do not, as a rule, wear it." She held out a black scarf to O'Reilly. "But it will help."

O'Reilly took it and dropped it on the armrest between them. She pointed to the bucar's GPS. "Plug the address in."

"The mosque is in Los Angeles, but his home is in Pasadena. I suggest we go to Pasadena."

They traveled in silence for several miles. Shelly finally said, "Have you heard from Derek?"

"Yes."

"I expected to be working with him. That was our—"

"Things changed."

"The explosion in Dallas. Does that seem unusual to you?"

O'Reilly glared at her.

Shelly backpedaled. "I mean, it was premature. There was nobody there. The latest report is there may have been one person on the scene."

"Maybe some part of the sleeper cell accidentally set it off and got himself killed in the process."

"Okay. Yes, I can see that as a possibility."

"Good. Did you and, what's-her-name, Birch? Did you and Agent Birch get anything useful out of all that data gathering?"

"Not yet. Although Pasadena would be one of the areas with high concentrations of Muslim groups, and it cross-references well with other factors like *hawaladars* and Western Union offices."

O'Reilly clenched her jaw and concentrated on her driving. She wished Pimpuntikar would shut up. She recognized the truth of what the woman was saying, just as she recognized the truth of what Derek had said about bringing a man or Shelly along to talk to the imam. It didn't help. She couldn't get her mind off Dallas.

Shelly, after a moment of silence, asked, "What about the rest of the team? Have you heard from them?"

"Everybody's pursuing their own angles. Look, what shouldn't I say or do in talking to this imam?"

"Well, it depends. I asked for a file on him after you called, but it's pretty thin. They had heard of him, but the file wasn't all that extensive. He appears to be a Sunni imam, which has a different connotation than a Shi'a imam. If he's really Sunni, then he's basically a leader of prayers versus the person who gives the sermons at the mosque, who in the Sunni tradition is the sheikh. Of course, the name is Ibrahim Sheik Muhammad, so I think it's safe to consider him a spiritual and religious and cultural leader out of this particular mosque. But since there's a connection to al-Qaeda, which is traditionally—"

O'Reilly scowled at her. "This is a long ways from answering my question."

Shelly colored and looked down at her hands. "Perhaps you should just be yourself."

"Fine."

They drove in uncomfortable silence until they found the house they were looking for. Even by Pasadena standards, it looked fairly luxurious, a three- or four-acre estate surrounded by a solid stone fence, gated, the property hidden by full-growth willow, palm, eucalyptus, and evergreens. The house itself was Mediterranean in style with white adobe walls and a red clay roof.

An iron gate blocked the drive. O'Reilly reached out to the keypad and pushed the call button, holding it a second or two longer than completely necessary.

They waited. O'Reilly punched the button again and held it down even longer this time.

A third time got a reaction. O'Reilly gazed up at the video camera built into the console. A thick voice said, "Who is it? Do you know what time it is?"

"Yes sir," O'Reilly said. She held her identification toward the camera lens. "I'm Agent Cassandra O'Reilly with the Office of the Director of National Intelligence. I'm accompanied by Agent Shelly Pimpuntikar with the Federal Bureau of Investigation. We need to speak with you."

A burst of static was followed by the same voice, sounding significantly more awake now and considerably edgier. "I'm sure this can wait until morning. Feel free to contact my attorney and we can set something up—"

"Mister Muhammad—"

Shelly made a throat-clearing sound, but O'Reilly ignored her and continued. "Did we just wake you up?"

"It's almost two in the morning. Of course you woke me up!"

"Then I suggest you take a moment to turn on your TV set, go to Fox or CNN and watch for a moment or two, then get back with us. We'll be waiting here."

"What is all this about? What are you talking about?"

"Please, just go and turn on your TV, sir."

"Oh, very well."

Shelly said, "I suggest you address him as Imam."

O'Reilly gave Shelly a hard little smile. "I will address him as I would any other individual in the United States. As mister, miss, misses, sir or ma'am. As Doctor or any other title, including Reverend or Father. But first he's going to have to introduce himself to me as Imam Muhammad, which is one way for us to begin a dialogue."

The intercom squawked. "I know nothing of the events in Dallas."

O'Reilly leaned forward. "Sir, we still need to speak with you. You're not under arrest. But we believe you may be able to help us."

Silence. Finally, "Very well."

With a loud clank the gate whirred open. O'Reilly drove ahead, following the curving path of the paved drive, stopping in front of a four-car garage. She maneuvered the bucar so she could pull directly out toward the gate. Leading Shelly, they went to the front of the home and were met by a tall, heavyset man, sleep still in his eyes, right hand tugging at his long gray beard.

"Your identification, please."

They supplied it. He gazed at Shelly for a long moment, lips pursed in disapproval. Without comment he returned their credentials and stepped aside. "Come inside, please. May I get you something to drink?"

"No, thank you."

Shelly shook her head as well.

The imam led them through the lavishly appointed home into an office overlooking a carefully cultivated rose garden. Spotlights lit up the crimson flowers even in the middle of the night. The walls were lined with books. The desk was made of cherry and appeared handcrafted. The imam sat down behind it, gesturing to two chairs.

"Please, be seated. As I said before, I know nothing about the events in Dallas." He pulled his robes around him as if he were cold.

O'Reilly asked, "Do you know somebody who goes by the name Kalakar?" She watched him closely for any reaction.

The imam stared off into space. "No, should I?"

"He's an al-Qaeda operative from Pakistan, who may be in the Los Angeles area planning a terrorist attack in the next two days."

"Perhaps he was in Dallas instead."

"And maybe he's heading here. If he were, would he get in touch with you?"

Imam Muhammad looked exasperated. "I am a Muslim cleric in the Los Angeles area. It's always possible. Am I aiding and abetting terrorists? Of course not! What is this all about?"

"We understand you are sympathetic to al-Qaeda."

The imam shook his head, closing his eyes. Opening them, he focused on Shelly. "Are you a Muslim?"

Shelly nodded.

"And are you sympathetic to al-Qaeda?"

"I do not condone their behavior."

Imam Muhammad perked up. "That is not what I asked. Are you sympathetic to al-Qaeda?"

"They wish for a version of Islam that never existed and never will. They declare a war that does not exist—"

"It does exist," Imam Muhammad said, waving a finger at her. "It does exist. There is a war of values between East and West, between crusaders and Islam—"

Shelly's voice was sharp. "We are not crusaders and this is not a Crusade. You cannot equate the United States' response to nine eleven and the murder of three thousand innocent citizens with a war of values. The Prophet would not have condoned attacks on innocents. That is not Islam!"

"Do not presume to know the mind of the Prophet, woman!" The imam raised his voice and in a tone that indicated he was quoting from the Qur'an, said, "'Permission to fight is granted to those who are being persecuted, since injustice has befallen them, and Allah is certainly able to support them.'"

Shelly, voice angry, said, "'If they resort to peace, so shall you, and put your trust in Allah. He is the Hearer, the Omniscient.'"

O'Reilly made a "T" with her two hands. "All right. Time out. I'm not here to referee a theological argument. Imam Muhammad, please, we need your help. Will you help us?"

The imam squinted at her, turning away from Shelly. He nodded thoughtfully, his expression as fake as a $29.95 Rolex. "Of course. I am always willing to assist the authorities."

I bet, thought O'Reilly. "Do you know of someone named Kalakar?"

"I do not."

"If someone were to come to this area and needed a place to stay, where would they go?"

"Perhaps a Holiday Inn," said the imam.

"If they wanted to stay with someone supporting them, providing a place to sleep, transportation, food, who comes to mind?"

Imam Muhammad tapped his fingertips together, pondering his hands in his lap. "No, I'm sorry, I can't—"

Shelly leaped to her feet and slapped her hands down on the imam's desk. "You are obstructing an FBI investigation. You are being purposefully unhelpful. Many thousands of lives are at stake and you sit there like some sort of pig and—"

The imam leapt to his feet, roaring. "You are calling me a pig? Get out! Get out of my house! How dare you! Get out of this house this instant, you infidel! You are no Muslim! You are unclean. You defile my home! Get out! Now!"

"We're not done with you!" Shelly shouted, slapping the desk again. "We'll come back with warrants and we'll tear your house apart. We'll investigate every corner of your life—"

O'Reilly tugged at Shelly's arm. "Time to go."

The imam rushed around his desk and pushed them. "Get out! How dare you! If you want to talk to me, you will have to go through my attorney! Get out! Get out now!"

The two women allowed the imam to herd them out the door. O'Reilly could barely contain her anger, but wasn't sure whether to direct it at the imam or at Shelly. The FBI agent had blown their entire interview.

Walking to the bucar, O'Reilly said, "Nice going. We got exactly squat out of that."

Shelly said nothing, slipping into the passenger seat.

O'Reilly drove down the drive. Once they were off the imam's property, Shelly reached into her briefcase. She drew out what looked like a radio receiver. "Just drive down the block and pull over."

"What? Are you out of your—"

Shelly held up the device. "I planted a couple bugs in his office. That's why I did all the desk pounding. I wanted to get one under the edge of the desk."

O'Reilly's breath caught in her chest. "You—"

"I really thought you'd go after this guy. That seemed more your style. I wanted him all riled up, that's why I went head-to-head with him. I didn't expect you to be so civil."

Feeling her face burn red, O'Reilly pulled the bucar to a halt beneath a eucalyptus tree and turned off the engine. Shelly turned up the gain on the radio receiver. There were the sounds of rustling and muttering. Finally there was the click of a telephone being picked up and numbers being punched in.

"Ali, the FBI and someone else, I think it was the Office of the Director of National Intelligence— Yes, they were just here, questioning me about Kalakar. What happened in Dallas?"

O'Reilly and Shelly listened to silence. O'Reilly really wished she knew what "Ali" was saying on the other end of the line. After a moment, the imam said, "They're pretty hot on him, then. Can you warn him?"

More silence. Finally, "Yes. Good. All right. Allah is wise."

There was the sound of the phone being set down, followed by the sounds of the imam leaving the room.

"That's a little helpful," O'Reilly said, "but we don't know who he—"

Shelly had her hand up, telling her to wait. She dialed a number on her cell phone. "Helen, he just got off the phone—okay, yes. Just a second."

Taking a notepad from a pocket, she said, "Go ahead." Shelly scribbled information on the notepad. "Thanks. You're terrific."

She clicked off and put away the phone.

O'Reilly raised an eyebrow. "What?"

"Before we left, I asked Helen to get some taps on the imam's phones. I knew we wouldn't have much time and it might be impossible to get actual recordings, but with the attacks in Dallas, we should have been able to at least put taps on his phones to record who he was calling and who he was receiving calls from."

"And—"

Shelly checked the notepad. "He called somebody named Ali Tafir, who has a home address in Century City."

O'Reilly fired up the engine. She shook her head. "You know, I like your style."

CHAPTER 17

Derek pulled the bucar into the drive of a beach house in Malibu. He said, "I hope this is worth it, Greg. It's a hell of a ways out of our way."

Popovitch climbed out. "You need to clean off the blood. I need some caffeine. And frankly, you're the asshole that shot out the window of the car. Let's switch to something that at least has windows."

He walked toward the front door. Derek followed. Once inside, Popovitch addressed a keyboard, tapping numbers into it.

"You have a ten-digit PIN?" Derek asked.

"I have a few enemies." The screen above the keyboard glowed green:

DEACTIVATED.

"Hard to believe, a law-abiding citizen such as yourself."

Derek started past Popovitch, but the gunrunner caught his arm. "Hang on."

He pulled open a closet door to their left, pushed aside some jackets to reveal a small metal door. Popovitch pulled it open to reveal a flat screen and another keyboard. Popovitch tapped a few numbers and pressed his right hand flat against the screen, which glowed white for a few seconds before going dark. Across the screen it said:

WELCOME, MR. POPOVITCH.

"You have a palm scanner."

Popovitch nodded.

"Anything else?"

"Sort of." Popovitch led him into the house, which had a wide-open floor plan. The brown leather sectionals, plasma TV, and glass-topped end tables were completely dwarfed by a wall of glass facing the Pacific Ocean. Derek was sure that during the day it would provide a stunning vista of blue on blue.

Popovitch turned to the kitchen, where another plasma TV was attached to the wall. Pulling out a drawer to reveal a keyboard, he tapped keys and the plasma TV lit up with a computer desktop. Tapping more keys, he brought up digital surveillance feeds. Scanning the readouts, he said, "Good. Nothing unusual."

"A little paranoid?"

"It's not paranoia, Derek. It's my lovely reality. I'll get some coffee going. The bathroom's down there on the left. Help yourself."

Not 100 percent sure he could trust Greg, but convinced he had no choice, Derek headed for the bathroom, locking himself in. He kept his gun close, balanced on the toilet seat, and took a fast, hot shower. When he got out, feeling a little more alert, he found himself a mug of black coffee in the kitchen and hunted down Popovitch in a back room that had been converted to a sort of office/den. A laptop sat on a big oak desk. Behind Popovitch stood a bookshelf dominated by books on foreign policy and guides to weapons. Written, Derek noticed, in half a dozen languages.

Popovitch held a cell phone to his ear, bare feet up on the desk. Derek thought it was interesting that the room had no windows. He suspected Greg actually did do some of his business from this room—and probably had it swept for bugs on a regular basis.

"Hey, Len, I've got something going. What's the word on a guy, Faiz Hasan Chughtai?"

Derek noticed a couple framed photographs on the desk, facing Greg. He reached out and turned them around. One showed Greg and a dark-haired woman with an olive complexion, her eyes large and almond-shaped, quite beautiful. Greg, still talking, reached over and twisted the photograph around and out of Derek's hands, expression annoyed.

"You've heard *what* about Mukhtar? Really? Well, the man did play things fast and loose, didn't he? Yeah, no shit. Now, what about Chughtai?"

Derek turned around another photograph. It was of a group of men in military uniforms standing in front of an Abrams tank, M-15s in their arms, cigarettes in their mouths. A cocky group of soldiers, off to play war. He knew that Greg, like himself, had been in the first Gulf War,

Desert Storm. Replacing it, he looked at the last photograph, which was of a young Greg Popovitch in a suit receiving a diploma from a man in another suit. They were both smiling at the camera, a typical grip-and-grin. The man looked vaguely familiar, but Derek couldn't quite place him.

Popovitch clicked off and took the photograph out of Derek's hand. "Graduation day. Recognize him?"

"Yes, but I don't know who he is."

Popovitch seemed amused by that. "Robert Michael Gates. Director of the CIA from, oh, let's see, ninety-one to sometime in ninety-three, I think. You know they actually give you diplomas and have a little sort of commencement ceremony when you graduate from spy school? Weird fuckin' world, isn't it?"

Popovitch leaned back, pulled a pack of cigarettes out of a desk drawer, and lit up with a cheap red Bic. He blew out a plume of smoke.

"Who's the woman?" Derek asked.

Popovitch fiddled with the Bic for a moment, not looking at Derek. Finally he said, "That beautiful woman was my wife. Lily Popovitch. Her maiden name was Lily Rabine and I met her when I was doing some work in Israel. I would have given it all up for her, Derek. I almost did. Then some Palestinian fuck decided to take a bus ride while wearing a suicide vest."

His expression was flat and angry. He reached over and took a gulp of steaming coffee. "I was all ready to go back to D.C. and try for a normal life. I was considering State, or maybe stay at Langley in some analytical position. I sure as hell knew the Middle East." He shrugged, clicking a flame on the Bic, letting it go out, clicking it to life again. "Life takes funny turns."

"I'm sorry, Greg. I never knew."

Popovitch shrugged. "I'll tell you what, she'd be pleased I'm helping you." He picked up the phone again. "Couple more calls. By the way, word is out that somebody hit Mukhtar."

He hit another button on the phone and said, "Bruce? It's Greg— yeah, yeah, I heard. Hey, I'm looking for a guy—"

Derek leaned back in his chair and closed his eyes, only half listening to Popovitch. This odd business of theirs had a way of screwing up personal lives. For a time he had been married to an Army physician,

Simona Ebbotts, but his travel and hers had kept them apart so much, they had divorced more or less amicably. There had been women since, but nobody like Simona.

"Just—Bruce. Someone I need to touch base with. Someone I can't talk about."

Derek drifted off.

In the dream he was ten years old. He and his brother and his parents had been living in Sierra Leone. Derek's parents had been doctors for a Methodist missionary group, traveling around the world. The political situation had gone totally to hell in SL and they had been choppered out as rebels overran the mission.

In the dream Derek ran toward one of the big helicopters, the rotors roaring overhead like thunder, those big soldiers with their huge guns waving them on, leading them out.

The dream shifted, as dreams do, to Irina Khournikova, standing at the airport at St. Bart's, kissing him goodbye. When he looked back at her, he saw Simona.

He woke up abruptly, Greg saying his name. "I think we've got a lead on this guy. He's got a place in Venice."

CHAPTER 18

FBI agent Dale Hutchins leaned back in the chair in the Pakistan National Police Bureau interrogation room. He didn't want to admit it, but he was tired. His shoulder ached, his ass hurt, and his head pounded. His injuries were proving to be more difficult to bounce back from than he'd anticipated.

Getting old, he thought with some irony. He was thirty-eight, but at the moment felt about sixty.

He thought of the explosion in Dallas. The news was all over Islamabad, although CNN and the BBC didn't have much detail. A call to Sam at the office had indicated they were on high alert in the States, and it seemed to confirm some of the data found on the laptops. The only thing really clear was that nobody had a handle on things yet.

The door opened and two Pakistani uniformed guards brought in the prisoner. Firdos followed them in. The prisoner wore a drab gray jumpsuit and sandals, hands manacled with a waist-chain, ankles secured with shackles. Head down, he shuffled to the table. The guards pushed him down and secured his wrists and legs to the chair.

Firdos nodded and spoke in rapid Urdu to the guards, who left the three of them alone in the room.

Firdos sat in a chair opposite the prisoner, the small wooden table between them. He said, "Agent Hutchins, this is Abdul Fareed. Abdul Fareed, this is Special Agent Hutchins with the American Federal Bureau of Investigation."

Fareed looked up, but said nothing. His beard was tangled and his dark eyes blazed with rage.

"Do you speak English?" Hutchins asked.

Fareed said nothing.

Firdos nodded. "He does."

Hutchins said, "How are they treating you? Getting enough to eat? Are your religious dietary needs being met?"

Fareed glanced over at Firdos and back to Hutchins, still not responding.

Firdos had warned him that Fareed had been uncommunicative. Hutchins wasn't terribly surprised. He was trying to build rapport, but didn't know if he was going to have the time. He said, "A dirty bomb went off in Dallas just a couple hours ago. Have you heard that?"

Firdos shot him a startled look. It was standard operating procedure to not provide prisoners with information concerning the outside world relevant to their investigations.

Fareed's eyes widened. "A couple hours ago?" His voice sounded rusty as if from lack of use.

Hutchins nodded. "Yes, around ten o'clock in the evening in Dallas."

A complicated mix of emotions flashed across Fareed's face. "Good. I hope it killed many infidels."

"Actually," Hutchins said, "we don't think it killed anybody. Well, that's not true. There appears to be one body. Hasn't been identified yet. It could be Kalakar."

Fareed twitched. "He's not in—" He trailed off, scowling, staring at the floor.

"He's not in Dallas?" Hutchins asked. "Where is Kalakar, then? Is he in Washington, D.C.?"

Fareed refused to speak, continuing to stare at the tabletop in front of him.

Firdos spoke. "If you cooperate with us, we might be able to get you some exercise time. Or perhaps better food rations. But you'll have to cooperate with us."

Still the terrorist refused to speak.

Hutchins watched Fareed closely. "If he's not in Dallas, is he in Chicago?"

Still nothing.

"Los Angeles?"

Was that a flicker of the eye? He wasn't sure.

"How about New York?"

Nothing.

Hutchins leaned forward. He gestured at his arm in the sling. "Know how I got this? I was there in the apartment. One of my men picked up a laptop computer and it exploded. I was standing next to him. I got lucky. I was injured, but I'll be fine."

"You should have died. Right along with your infidel partner."

Calmly, Hutchins said, "Allah did not wish for me to die. Allah kept me alive so I could question you. Allah kept me alive so I can stop Kalakar from murdering innocent people. My being alive is Allah's will. My stopping your plan is Allah's will."

"You are an infidel. An agent of the Great Satan." Fareed stared at him, mouth twisted in a sneer. "Don't speak to me of Allah. You know nothing of Allah's will."

"I know Allah let me live for a reason."

"To bear witness to the destruction of the infidels. Allah is great. Allah is wise."

"Allah seems to have a different plan than you do. The bomb in Dallas wasn't supposed to go off this soon, was it?"

Was there a flicker of doubt on Fareed's face? Hutchins thought so. He continued. "Allah set that bomb off early. Allah is actively working against your plan. It is Allah's will—" Hutchins edged forward, voice suddenly soft, but forceful. "It is Allah's will that you cooperate with us to stop this plan. Help us. Please help us."

Fareed looked away.

The silence stretched out like a road leading into the desert. Hutchins wanted Fareed to think about things. Carrot and stick. He personally didn't believe the stick worked with al-Qaeda zealots. Then again, neither did the carrot. But after a stick, sometimes a carrot can work with anybody.

Firdos interrupted the silence. "Who is Kalakar? Does he have a name?"

No response.

Firdos looked at Hutchins, shrugging. Hutchins said, "I'm a little confused about something. Maybe you can clear things up."

Fareed didn't respond. Hutchins said to Firdos, "Could you please translate that for me. I want to make sure he understands what I'm saying."

Firdos rattled off the question in Urdu. Fareed kept his gaze on the table in front of him.

With Firdos translating, Hutchins continued. "Just before our raid, Kalakar received a telephone call. Correct?"

No response.

"We know he did. Kalakar must have told everybody that he had to go out. From what we can tell, he slipped out the back door of the apartment complex and went through a couple loose boards of that fence by the shopping center."

Hutchins waited for Firdos's translation to catch up.

"We guess he had a vehicle there. Now, we're pretty sure that someone called, alerting Kalakar that we were going to raid the apartment. Yet he sacrificed all of you there. He left you to be arrested. He left you to be killed. Why in the world would you protect him when he betrayed you?"

Fareed blinked. Looking up at Hutchins, Fareed said, "We willingly sacrifice ourselves for the jihad. We will be honored by Allah."

Their eyes locked. Fareed did not look away. Hutchins, slowly, carefully, asked, "Did you and your brothers plan to die in that apartment?"

Fareed blinked again and looked down at his hands.

"Was part of the plan for you and your friends to die in the apartment so we would think the raid was a success?"

A twitch of one eye.

"Did you die so Kalakar could go free? Or did he sacrifice you? Was that part of the plan he didn't share with you?"

No response.

Hutchins asked a few more questions, then Firdos tried talking to him, but he refused to speak. Hutchins, tired, finally said, "Well, that's it. Let's go. Tell them Fareed wasn't helpful. Again."

Fareed looked up momentarily and for the first time Hutchins thought he saw fear in the man's eyes. "What will they do to you, Fareed? How do they treat prisoners who don't cooperate?"

Nothing.

Firdos said, "I will talk to the guards and see what punishments they give prisoners who do not cooperate. I know it can be pretty bad in there. But then—"

Hutchins waited.

Firdos let it go. He got to his feet and knocked on the door. The guards came in. Firdos spoke to them for a moment. Dale got to his feet to leave.

Fareed, voice desperate, said, "I...please...if...I can tell you..."

They waited.

Hutchins shrugged. "Guess it's time to go."

Fareed's voice cracked. "His name. I can give you his real name."

Firdos gestured for the guards to leave the room again. He and Hutchins sat back down. Hutchins wondered if Fareed's pump was primed. Was he ready to spill everything?

For everybody's sake, he hoped so.

CHAPTER 19

Derek and Popovitch tooled south on the PCH heading roughly in the direction of Venice. There was the slightest hint in the east that the sun would be rising soon. They had abandoned the bucar in favor of Popovitch's black Range Rover.

"I've always wanted to ask you," Popovitch was saying, "what the hell you were thinking back in Iraq when you attacked those Iraqi guards and broke into that drug manufacturing facility. I mean, you didn't really think they were going to just let you in, did you?"

Derek smiled, despite himself. The UNSCOM inspection team had been playing hide-the-weapons-of-mass-destruction with the Iraqis for months. There were procedures involved, requests for information, site applications—it was bureaucratic bullshit, but that was the way of the U.N. The Iraqis always complained that members of the UNSCOM team were CIA agents or even spies for other countries, which was basically not true.

But the inspections teams were in communication with representatives of the CIA and other intelligence agencies, which is where Derek had come in contact with Popovitch. The UNSCOM team didn't report findings to the CIA or anybody but the U.N., but they would go to their contacts and say, "Any idea where you think we should look next?" Which is when Popovitch had suggested they check the State Drug Agency in Samarra.

Derek and his team had put in the official request, but the Iraqis, as usual, started giving them the Iraqi Shuffle. In truth, Derek didn't have the patience and diplomatic tendencies required for that kind of work. He had taken his team, walked to the SDA's front door with his Colt in his hand, stuck it in the face of one of the guards, kicked another guard in the balls, and pushed into the facility.

He had been thrown out at gunpoint and berated by the head of the Iraqi UNSCOM operation. Overall, it had been totally counterproductive.

Derek said, "I may have been considering a change in career at that point."

"I gotta tell you, though, we all pretty much stood up and cheered when we heard about it."

"Bought me a few drinks, too, as I recall."

"Yeah. Well, UNSCOM was being a little too civil. Iraq lost the fuckin' war, after all."

"Our approach to the Middle East, Iraq included, has been screwed up for—"

Derek's phone buzzed, interrupting his foreign policy diatribe before he could really get going on it. "Stillwater."

"Derek, it's Jim. Any progress?"

Secretary Johnston. Derek said, "Some leads. Nothing solid yet."

"The reason I called, actually, is we just got information from Pakistan. The FBI contingent there got a name for Kalakar. We've put together a thin profile, and it's being e-mailed to you now. They'll keep digging and update you as we get more. We're also sending his photograph to all law enforcement agencies in the country. We're debating whether to take it directly to the media."

"Tipping your hand."

"The stakes are too high. His name is Miraj Khan. And he was once an art history professor at Quaid-i-Azam University in Islamabad."

"That explains the Kalakar nickname."

"At least partly. All right, Derek. How are things going with O'Reilly?"

"We're not exactly working together at the moment."

Johnston's sigh came over the phone loud and clear. "Derek, we set these START teams—"

"You either trust me or you don't, Jim."

More silence. "All right. Watch your back."

Derek clicked off the phone, reached into the backseat, and pulled his tablet computer out of one of his Go Packs. Popovitch said, "What're you doing?"

"Checking my e-mail."

"In the car?"

Derek smiled. "We've got the latest in satellite technology, Greg."

The computer came up and he retrieved his e-mail. He held up the computer so Popovitch could see the image of Kalakar. In the photograph Kalakar was probably in his mid-thirties, but it had been taken almost ten years earlier. He wore a thick black beard, had a thin, narrow face, and a dark complexion.

Derek read through the file, and as Secretary Johnston had said, it was thin. Miraj Khan earned his Ph.D. in art history at Oxford and returned to Islamabad to teach. His specialty was the history of Muslim art. He had been fired from the university five years ago for unspecified reasons. No friends or relatives had been located yet.

It was really thin.

"Where are we?" he asked.

"Closing in on Venice."

After a couple more minutes of driving, Popovitch pulled off onto what appeared to be a residential street. Mostly houses, an occasional apartment building. It lacked the funky character of the heart of Venice.

Derek said, "This is still Venice?"

Popovitch nodded. "Pretty close to Mar Vista, at this stage of the game." He said, "Yeah, I think this is it."

He pulled into the driveway of a pink stucco bungalow. It was the middle of the night, the neighborhood was dark, only illuminated by the occasional porch light and a distant street light. Derek could see just well enough to know that the lawn had seen better days, but the house itself looked to be in good shape.

Derek checked his gun and climbed out. "I'll follow your lead."

Popovitch nodded. "Of course you will." He seemed to be looking at something behind Derek.

Instincts flashing, Derek spun to see Popovitch's two thugs sprinting from the shadows, guns drawn. The big guy, Jeb, came right up to Derek, pushing the gun right toward him. "Hands on your head, asshole."

Derek shot Popovitch a look. "You son of a—"

Jeb smashed his gun against the side of Derek's head. Pain exploded in his jaw. He bounced back, leaping for Jeb, but Larry pressed his gun against the back of Derek's neck. "Easy."

Popovitch stepped forward and lifted Derek's gun out of his pocket, quickly patted him down and took the knife, too. "This treasure hunt is all well and good, Derek, but you interrupted an important business deal and I'm going to complete it." To Larry he said, "Valentin agree to the new location?"

"Yep."

Popovitch checked his watch. "Good. Right on schedule. Let's go inside, Derek."

"I'm not going—"

Larry kicked him in the back of the leg, and Derek fell to his knees on the scraggly grass. Larry kicked him in the kidney. "Get up."

Popovitch said, "Derek, take it easy. Larry, if you keep kicking him he won't be able to get up at all."

"I saved your ass, you know," Derek said, grimacing in pain. He thought he'd be pissing blood for a week if he lived through the next fifteen minutes. "The LAPD had you staked out. In fact, do you trust these two guys? Either one of them could be undercover cops."

Popovitch clucked his tongue. "Nice try, Derek. Come on. Get to your feet. Let's go inside."

Derek awkwardly stood up and followed Greg into the pink stucco bungalow. It was sparsely furnished. Popovitch pointed him to an oak captain's chair in the kitchen. "Sit."

Popovitch turned to Larry and said, "There's two bags in the Rover. Go get them for me."

Larry left. Popovitch said, "Here's the truth, Derek. I don't know anything about a nuke here in L.A. My gut says there isn't one. But my gut has been wrong before. And now that I know there might be one, I'm not going to play the fucking hero and wait around for it to go off. I'm going to complete this deal, which will bring me about eight mill in profit, and catch the first flight out of ground zero. Good luck."

"You're a chickenshit."

Popovitch glanced at Jeb and gave him a nod. Popovitch backhanded Derek with the Colt. Derek had a sense it was coming, but was half a beat too slow. Pain exploded in his jaw. He and the captain's chair crashed to the floor. Derek rolled with the fall and was on his feet, but Jeb had his gun out and ready.

"I owed you that one, Derek."

"So we're even." He spit out bloody saliva. *Good*, he thought. *Could be worse.* "Just run away."

Popovitch shrugged. "I always look out for my ass first, Derek. Oh, I think Jeb has something for you."

Jeb spun Derek around, swinging hard. Derek trapped Jeb's fist with his forearms and quickly shuffled forward, elbows pistoning into the big man's ribs. He followed up with a hard knee to the groin and a fist to the nose. Jeb went down like a house of cards.

Derek turned. Popovitch had two guns aimed at him. "Pick up the fucking chair and sit down." He rolled his eyes. "Jesus, Jeb. What do I keep you around for?"

"He got the—"

Popovitch shot the big man in the head. Derek held perfectly still.

Popovitch sighed. "See what you made me do, Derek? Good help is so hard to find. Not that he was all that good."

Derek said nothing. He was afraid that anything he said might set Popovitch off.

"Sit down on the fucking chair."

Derek picked up the captain's chair and sat in it. He tried to avoid the image of the big man's blood, bone, and brains spattered on the blue vinyl tile floor.

Popovitch said, "Hands behind the chair."

Derek complied. Popovitch walked behind him and secured his wrists to the oak slats of the captain's chair with what felt like plastic ties, what the cops called plasti-cuffs.

Larry walked in a moment later with Derek's Go Packs. His gaze fixed on Jeb's lifeless body. "What the fuck?"

"Shut up."

Popovitch dropped Derek's gun, knife, and sat phone on the kitchen island. "Don't try to pin this bullshit on me, Derek. If you've got any blow-back in mind, I'll tell the cops all about Mukhtar and your involvement with that."

Larry's eyes grew wide. "You're going to leave him alive? What are you, crazy?"

Popovitch squinted at Larry. "We're doing this my way. Go out and wait in the—"

Larry pulled his own gun and shot Popovitch in the gut. Popovitch dropped to the floor, arms pressed against his stomach. He gasped, a high-pitched moan of rage and pain.

"You fuck!" Larry shrieked. "You goddamned fuck! You couldn't leave well enough alone. You had to go along with this asshole." He fired twice more and Popovitch lay still. He was beyond pain now.

Sweat beaded up on Derek's forehead. Tied to the chair, he said, "You need to get out now, Larry. Just walk out the door, grab the Rover and go."

"You! You're the reason for all this!" Larry raised his gun and aimed it right at Derek's head. "You're dead!"

"I'm a federal agent, Larry." Derek tried to keep his voice level and calm, to convince Larry he was on the level, to try and infuse his voice with the idea that Larry should stay calm and think. I'm in this for you, buddy. I'm only thinking of you.

"If you kill me, every government agency in the country will come after you. The LAPD knows you were with Greg and Jeb. They know who you are. They'll come right after you and hunt you down and I guarantee you, you'll never make it to prison."

"You fuck! You fucking bastard!" Larry paced around the room, hands tangling in his reddish-brown hair, blue eyes wild. "What am I going to do? I should just kill you!"

"You don't want to do that. It's too risky for you. You didn't kill Jeb. And Greg was going to kill you. It was self-defense. But if you kill me, that's murder. So just leave. Complete the deal with Valentin. Take the money and run. Go now."

"Jesus. Valentin." He stared at his watch. "Dammit. I can't just— Jesus."

His eyes seemed to light up. Derek thought, *Uh-oh*. His heart pounded in his chest. *This can't be good.*

Larry jogged out of the kitchen. Derek heard a door slam, then Larry appeared a moment later, a red plastic six-gallon container in his hand. He popped the top and Derek smelled the acrid stench of gasoline.

Larry poured the gasoline over Greg and Jeb, then over the carpeted floor, the couch, and La-Z-boy in the living room. Derek prayed to whatever gods might listen, *not on me, please, not on me.*

Larry upturned the container over Derek's head, but only a little gasoline dribbled out. He cursed in impotent rage and flung it away. He backhanded Derek, twice, screaming, "You're going to die! Motherfucker, you are dead!"

Larry dug into his pocket, pulled out a lighter, clicked it alight and tossed it onto the sofa. Flames roared instantly to life. "So long, motherfucker."

Larry walked out the door.

CHAPTER 20

Agent Dale Hutchins and Firdos Khan Moin stepped into the office of Dr. Mizafa Rizvi, Chairman of the History Department at Quaid-i-Azam University. Rizvi was a short, broad-shouldered man with neat dark hair parted on the left. He dressed casually in a light blue dress shirt and khaki slacks. Hutchins thought he looked like a clerk at Blockbuster.

Firdos said, "Thank you for seeing us, Doctor. This must, of course, remain confidential."

Rizvi ducked his head in assent. "Whatever I can do. This is about—"

Firdos held up a photograph. "A former faculty member in this department, Dr. Miraj Khan."

Leaning back in his chair, Rizvi folded his hands over his lap. Almost to himself he murmured, "So, it finally happened."

"What finally happened?" Hutchins said.

Rizvi focused on him. "Miraj got in trouble. I always thought it was going to happen."

"Why is that?"

Shrugging, Rizvi said, "The world over, there are academics who are radicals. But the world over, radical academics tend to spew their rhetoric to college students, but do not actually put their beliefs into action."

"And which was Miraj Khan?" Firdos asked.

Rizvi hesitated. "May I inquire what this is about?"

Hutchins interjected, "Based on your knowledge of Miraj Khan, what do you think it would be about?"

Cocking his head, Rizvi said, "You were introduced to me as being with the FBI. The American Federal Bureau of Investigation is primarily in Pakistan—for better or worse—to investigate terrorists. So you must believe that Dr. Khan is a terrorist. Is he?"

"Perhaps you can tell me," Hutchins said.

Rizvi seemed amused by the way the conversation was going. Hutchins wasn't. He didn't think Firdos was either, based on the impassive expression on his face. Rizvi said, "Miraj was a specialist in Islamic art—the history of Islamic art. Our history program here focuses on Pakistani and Asian history. We do not have an art program, per se, but we do have a focus on Islamic history, especially as it pertains to Asia, and that was Miraj's area of expertise."

The history professor glanced at a wall of bookshelves. Hutchins followed his gaze, but didn't think Rizvi was actually looking at any book in particular. He thought Rizvi was gathering his thoughts. He noticed photographs of Rizvi on the Great Wall of China, in front of The Forbidden City, on a junk off what was probably Hong Kong.

Rizvi continued. "Miraj had impeccable credentials. I believe he earned his master's degree here, went to Iraq for his doctorate, and read at Oxford for a year afterward. I believe that is the case. I would have to look at his records to confirm that. Nonetheless, he made many friends in Iraq who were later killed in the first Gulf War." He turned to Hutchins. "I believe it was called Desert Storm, correct?"

Hutchins nodded.

"He was not a supporter of Saddam Hussein, but he was a supporter of Osama bin Laden. Of that I am certain. He may have even met the sheikh during his college years in the Middle East. He traveled extensively for his doctorate, looking at many of the art treasures in Saudi and Iraq and Afghanistan."

"Why was he fired?" Firdos asked.

Rizvi clucked his tongue and shook his head. "He was not fired, exactly. He was laid off. The university went through one of its economic cycles, as they always seem to do. Our program had been expanding, but we were forced to prioritize, and art history was one of the areas we—" He looked slightly embarrassed, then shrugged. "Very well. Art history was one of the areas I did not feel was relevant to our program, given the economic contraction. So Miraj was let go, as were two other professors."

"How did he take that?" Hutchins asked.

"Poorly. He was quite threatening. He took it very personally."

"Did anything come of it?"

"No."

Firdos said, "What happened to him? Do you know where he went?"

"I heard that he went to Afghanistan to work at the Kabul Museum, such as it was after the Taliban had their way with things. Then, after that, I heard nothing."

With a personal history like that, Hutchins thought, it shouldn't be a surprise that Miraj Khan became radicalized. Al-Qaeda had many people who were educated and middle to upper class who became leaders in the organization. Unemployment and poverty were breeding grounds, but misplaced idealism was the fertilizer.

"Would it surprise you to find that Miraj Khan was a member of al-Qaeda?" Firdos asked.

Rizvi shook his head. "Not at all. He was quite a powerful personality, brilliant in his way, highly educated. His religious—tendencies—were conservative and not very tolerant. And—"

Hutchins waited.

Rizvi said, "I know he spent several years in the Army."

Moin said, "Army or National Guard?"

"Army, I believe. I'm not certain, but I believe he was in the Army. He seemed to know a great deal about infantry weapons, things like ground-to-air missiles and rifles and bombs. I don't remember specifics except he volunteered when he was sixteen years old. That I do remember. That's the earliest you can join."

Firdos said to Hutchins, "But you can't be deployed until you're eighteen." He turned his attention back to Rizvi. "Do you know how long he was in the Army?"

"I'm sorry, no."

They questioned him for a while longer, but it was clear he had provided them with all he knew. They thanked him and left. Walking back to Firdos's car, Hutchins said, "It would be very interesting to find out where and when he was deployed, if he was deployed."

Firdos clearly had something different on his mind. "I think it would be very interesting to know who he served with and under during his years in the military."

"Why?"

Turning to him, Firdos's expression was troubled. "I served in the

Navy. I still have friends from that time. Those friends are from all levels and corners of Pakistan society. Some are farmers, some are shopkeepers, some are policemen, some are politicians, and some are still in the military, but much higher up."

He was quiet a moment. "It's possible the men he served with are part of his support group here in Pakistan. Believe me when I say this, that not all people in Pakistan are happy to see Americans here. And not all people in Pakistan are happy with President Tarkani's support of the global war on terror and his opposition to al-Qaeda."

Hutchins met his gaze. Firdos had something specific on his mind, but Hutchins had no idea what it was. Perhaps the Pakistani wanted more evidence before he voiced his suspicions. "You're saying?"

"I am saying that we should be careful."

CHAPTER 21

The flames roared to life, hungrily eating the furniture, the carpeting, and reaching for the ceilings and walls. Derek shifted his weight forward. His feet hit the ground and he stood up, gripped the chair rungs awkwardly and swung it as hard as he could against the kitchen island.

The vibration nearly snapped his wrists, but the chair didn't break. Damned oak chair.

Sweat broke out over his entire body and was immediately dried by the flames.

As Derek watched, the flames found his Go Packs and devoured them. Heat blasted through the house in rippling waves.

He shuffled around the kitchen island. His gun, his sat phone, and his knife rested on its granite surface.

Greg Popovitch's body caught on fire. The skin reddened, then blackened, his features obliterated.

He turned away. It felt like his hair was on fire. Frantically he leaned over the island and got his mouth on the knife. He bit back a howl as the metal burned his lips. Straightening up, he dropped the Emerson knife to the floor and knelt beside it, no easy feat with your wrists strapped to the rungs of a captain's chair.

The air was easier to breathe down here, but not by much. It was still hot, and he hoped the fire wasn't hot enough to cause flashover—so hot that everything caught on fire from the heat itself.

He laid down on the floor, thunking awkwardly onto his side. Derek felt like a turtle struggling to flip over. He was nose to nose with Jed, whose features seemed to be melting in the flames that rose from his clothes and skin.

Derek concentrated, twisting. He still couldn't reach the knife.

He started rocking himself in the chair, levering his legs beneath him. His clothing begin to smolder. He was no longer sweating. His eyes felt parched, his skin papery and hot.

Derek nearly flipped over the chair, but lost his traction and fell. His back screamed at the assault.

Again! His shoes scrabbled for purchase on the vinyl tile floor, which was starting to melt from the heat of the flames. He coughed. The smoke was marginally thinner close to the floor, but he knew that the vapors emitted by burning vinyl and plastic were toxic. A coughing fit racked his body and he lost his balance again. This time his head snapped against the high back of the chair. Red and black starbursts exploded before his eyes.

He roared in anger and frustration, legs pumping, feet sliding, and the chair tilted sideways and onto its back. His hands were now inches from the floor, trapped in the curve of the chairback.

Now he really felt like a turtle—a roasted turtle.

Twisting and bending, he looked down to locate the knife. It was about a foot from his hands.

He tried rocking the chair, but it didn't seem to get him anywhere. His arms could slide up and down the chair rails, but he was still too far from the knife. The flames went fwoof! and the curtains caught fire in the living room.

Derek tried to take in a breath, but the air was so hot it felt like inhaling lava. He gasped, coughing, afraid he wouldn't be able to stop. The chair was smoldering.

Feeling like a contortionist, he slammed his feet down onto the floor, heels striking the ground. His back arched. Using all his strength, he pressed his heels down hard and strained his thigh muscles. The chair slid a couple inches.

Again!

Closer.

Again! His back screamed in agony, but his fingers closed on the Emerson knife. He found the button and popped the blade out. Switching directions, he sliced through the plastic flexi-cuffs like they were mozzarella cheese.

Free!

He rolled to his feet, grabbed his sat phone and gun, which were so hot he almost dropped them.

The flames roared around him.

He picked up the chair with one hand and flung it at the rear windows. The glass shattered. Air blasted into the house, fueling the fire that exploded around him. His shirt caught fire.

Derek plunged after the chair, rolling on the dry California grass. His hands pounded at his hair, at his shirt, rolling, rolling.

Finally, flames extinguished, a few yards from the inferno, he struggled to his feet, gulped in cool morning air, and staggered away.

Not far away he heard the wail of sirens. He didn't want to be around for that. He walked steadily west, figuring if he didn't find a place to clean up first, he'd at least hit the ocean eventually.

Derek walked through middle-class subdivisions. Inside the homes kids were getting ready for school, eating Cap'n Crunch and drinking orange juice. Mothers and fathers were eating Raisin Bran and drinking coffee and wondering how they would make it through their workweek. Sometimes he resented their ordinariness, how blithely they went about their comfortable, safe lives, unaware of the danger that people like him faced daily so they could sleep well at night.

He didn't know how long he walked. His entire body ached. The sun rose off his right shoulder, and the day started to heat up. Cars began hitting the roads in force. Finally, he looked up to see a river of white sand bordering the blue of the ocean.

On a park bench a homeless man, looking like a pile of refuse, was curled up on one end. Nearby was a public restroom. He ignored the street guy and pushed his way into the restroom. The face staring back at him from the mirror didn't look so great. His normally wavy brown hair was blackened and charred in spots. His eyebrows were almost completely missing. His face was unusually red as if he'd been sunburned.

He cautiously touched his face. It was hot to the touch. His hands, he noticed, were worse. They were blistered from burns. His shirt was blackened and torn, holes scorched through it. His shoes looked odd, as if the rubber had melted.

Derek cupped his hands and took a drink of water. A little more cautiously he pressed the cool water to his face. It felt wonderful.

He tried to clean himself up as best he could, but in the end, understood that he would be hard-pressed to continue before getting a change of clothes, some first aid for his hands, and possibly some kind of antiburn lotion for his face. He was also hungry in a physical way that was mitigated somewhat by his aches and pains and general feeling of crap-piness. The machine had to be fed, even if the person didn't feel much like eating.

With a sigh he pulled out his sat phone. When he checked, though, there was no power. He fussed with it for a few minutes before deciding it had been damaged by the fire. In disgust, he went searching for a real rarity—a pay phone.

He found one two blocks away in front of an open-air deli that hadn't opened yet. It took two phone calls before he got hold of Cassandra O'Reilly.

"I need help," he said. "It's a long story, but I need you to pick me up at the Windward Plaza at Venice Beach."

O'Reilly was quiet for a long time, then, "What happened to your voice? It's sort of—"

"It's a long story, Sandy. Just please come. And if you've got a first-aid kit, that would be good, too. I'll be waiting for you."

He hung up and plodded back toward the beach. The homeless guy had woken up and moved on. Derek took his seat on the bench, listening to the ocean and watching the seagulls fly overhead.

CHAPTER 22

Cassandra O'Reilly and Shelly Pimpuntikar reluctantly left their surveillance post outside a high-rise apartment building on Wilshire Boulevard in Century City. They had not found Ali Tafir to be at home, nor had they found him particularly easy to locate. The brown glass high-rise had well-trained security who had informed them that Mr. Tafir had left the building in the last hour. When they had pressed the guard about where Mr. Tafir had gone, he had assured them that he did not know, and if he did, he wouldn't have provided that information without a warrant or subpoena.

So they had found a parking spot on Wilshire with a view of the building's front entrance and decided to wait. Cassandra was convinced it was a waste of time. They wouldn't even recognize Tafir if he came up and knocked on their car window.

The man had no criminal record and no files existed on him at FBI or in any of the other criminal databases Shelly had checked. Shelly had asked Helen Birch to get a couple people digging into the guy's past, at least finding out where he worked and what he did for a living. They had decided to give it a couple hours and were just debating what to do next when Derek's cryptic phone call came.

Pulling away from the curb, O'Reilly set sail for Venice Beach, wondering how in hell Derek had ended up there. She didn't like how he sounded, as if his throat had been scraped raw. What had happened to him over the last few hours?

And a more disquieting thought: "What happened to him over the last few years?"

"Who?" Shelly asked.

Mired in rush hour traffic, it was a few seconds before O'Reilly realized that Shelly was talking to her. "What? I was just thinking out loud, I guess."

"Wondering what happened to Derek over the last few years?"

"Well, closer to fifteen, actually. Never mind."

O'Reilly could feel Shelly's gaze on her. She met her eyes and said, "Really. Never mind. What's the update on Dallas?"

Shelly had just gotten off the phone with her supervisor in D.C. "One fatality, but they haven't identified it yet. Or even really confirmed it, although it's clear someone was at ground zero. The bomb was a lot smaller than anybody expected, and they think it might have been ANFO mixed with medical waste. The radiation levels are really low."

O'Reilly frowned. ANFO stood for ammonium nitrate and fuel oil, the same mixture that had been used in the Oklahoma City bombing. But in that case, Tim McVeigh had filled a Ryder truck full of the material, enough to almost destroy the building. "It must have been very small, then. That's weird. Did you get any specifics on the radiation levels?"

"No. That's just not my area."

But it was O'Reilly's. She had three degrees, including a Ph.D. in nuclear physics. In addition to her years with the IAEA, she had worked with the CIA as well as for the Department of Energy's intelligence division. She remained on a NEST team—Nuclear Emergency Search Team.

She wasn't at the moment convinced that al-Qaeda had access to a nuclear device. She was even less convinced they could have gotten one into the country. And she was rather doubtful that if al-Qaeda did have one, that they would detonate it in Los Angeles, when New York City or Washington, D.C. would be significantly more devastating, both politically and in terms of fatalities.

But as she knew, you didn't prepare for what you thought the enemy might do, you prepared for what they could do.

It took them a while to fight their way through traffic, but after forty-five minutes, O'Reilly found a parking spot near the beach and she and Shelly trotted to where Derek had said he would be. They found him curled up on a park bench, asleep.

Shelly gasped and O'Reilly felt her stomach do a slow flip-flop at his appearance. What the hell had happened?

Derek stirred, opened his eyes and groaned as he sat up. "Morning."

"Derek, what's going on?"

Derek shook his head, blew out air, and said, "I fell asleep."

O'Reilly's blood pressure spiked. "Dammit, Derek. What have you been doing all night?"

He eyed her with suspicion and exasperation. O'Reilly thought, *Oh, here we go again.*

So she was surprised when he looked at Shelly and said, "Why don't you take a walk on the beach. Or better yet, I'm going to need some clothes and a cell phone. How about I give you my sizes and you try to find me some jeans and a T-shirt. That work?"

Shelly frowned, her posture changing. O'Reilly saw that Shelly didn't like being excluded from whatever Derek had to say.

Derek did too. He sighed. "Shelly, unless you want to spend a great deal of time testifying under oath before Congress, why don't you go shopping."

Oh shit, thought O'Reilly. She raised an eyebrow at the FBI agent. "I'll decide whether or not to fill you in," she said.

Shelly said, "What are your sizes?"

Derek told her. O'Reilly followed Shelly back to the bucar and retrieved her own Go Pack, which contained a first-aid kit. She said to Shelly, "Figure out where the nearest emergency room is around here, too. And pick us up some food. And lots of coffee."

Shelly hesitated.

O'Reilly said, "No, Shelly, I'm not making you the gofer. Just let me get a handle on this situation, okay?"

Shoulders hunched in anger, Shelly agreed, climbed in the bucar, and drove off. O'Reilly returned to the bench. There were some early morning joggers and beachcombers in the area. Derek was leaning forward, head in his hands, elbows on his knees.

She said, "I hope you're kidding, but you're probably not."

He shook his head, but didn't look up at her.

She said, "Take off your shirt. And tell me what you've been doing since we parted ways last night."

He said, "First off, that cop we ran into outside Bongos? They had Greg under surveillance. So they played me a tape—"

As he talked, he struggled out of his shirt. She noticed he was having problems with his hands, but concentrated on the shirt first. These burns didn't seem too bad, although "too bad" was a relative thing. "Do these hurt?"

"Yes, they hurt!"

"Good. No nerve endings were destroyed."

"A fucking silver lining, O'Reilly."

"Hang on. I'll be right back." She jogged over to the rest room, wet down paper towels with cool water, and returned to Derek. She gently patted the burns on his back and right side, which seemed to be the extent of the burns on his body besides his hands. She didn't want to deal with the hands just yet.

He winced, but otherwise kept quiet. "You've got more scars than I remember," she said.

"As Indiana Jones said, 'It's not the years, it's the mileage.'"

"Keep talking," she said. "Tell me what happened."

"Maybe I should keep this to myself. I don't think you'll find Congressional hearings much fun."

"You've had your share over the years."

"Unfortunately. At least the majority have been closed-door sessions with intelligence committees. Anyway, I decided Greg knew more than he was telling me."

"Clearly."

"So I kidnapped him."

O'Reilly closed her eyes, sat back, and hung her head. She pressed her palms to her face for a moment. When she looked up, Derek was watching her. "No comment?" he said.

"Was he any help?"

"Sort of."

"Then no comment. I'm going to put some bandages on these burns. It looks like there are three spots. Probably first degree, but none of them are more than about two or three inches around."

He went on talking and she taped sterile gauze bandages over the burns. Taking a bottle of water from her Go Pack, she handed him a couple pain pills, which he took gratefully.

"These are just Tylenol. I've got some Tylenol Threes, but the codeine might knock you out."

"Not to mention give me constipation and loss of interest in sex."

"You still have your sense of humor, no matter how misplaced."

"Yeah," he said, carefully flexing his hands. "Give me the Tylenol Threes just in case."

"Keep talking, but let me see your hands."

He slowly held his hands out for her, palms up. As he talked she studied them. Like the burns on his back and side, they seemed relatively mild—no charring, just redness and blisters. But they were more extensive than the burns on his torso.

She interrupted him to suggest that when Shelly returned they take him to a hospital. He didn't move, his hands remaining motionless in hers.

What he said also surprised her. He said, "Tell me about your children."

She sighed. "You're changing the subject."

"Tell me the names and ages of your children, then I'll tell you the rest of my story."

Her heart beat a little too hard in her chest and she could feel her stomach muscles tightening. Derek had managed to find the one area that could tear her apart. "Adam is ten. Lisbeth is eight," she said.

"A boy and a girl," he murmured. "In Dallas?"

She nodded.

"And you live in D.C.?"

"I don't think this is the time, Derek. Yes, Rick has full custody. I visit them as often as I can. Now, tell me the rest."

He did. She kept her emotions under wraps. What Derek had done was reckless, but she also understood that with the entire FBI, Homeland Security, and local cops looking for Kalakar, the START teams needed to be creative if they were going to be able to justify their existence.

She was about to ask him if he had at least gotten any useful information when Shelly sped up in the bucar, double-parked, and came running toward them. Even from a distance O'Reilly could see that her complexion had turned a pasty gray.

When she got to them she blurted, "I just got a call and it's all over the news. A bomb went off in Chicago."

CHAPTER 23

Derek took the fresh clothing Shelly had purchased and changed in the public restroom, tossing his old, scorched clothes into a trashcan. The running shoes were cheap, but fit well enough, and she had been smart enough to pick up socks and a pack of boxer shorts for him. The shirt was a solid blue dress shirt, but she had bought a larger size so he could wear it untucked to cover his gun.

When he went to check his Colt and attach its holster to his belt, his hands were so stiff and sore that he fumbled the gun and dropped it on the restroom floor.

Derek stared at the gun at his feet and clenched his jaw. O'Reilly and Shelly did not need to know about that. He gingerly picked up the gun and methodically checked it, slid it back into its holster, and attached it to his belt.

Shelly had also picked up some burn medication, which he smeared on his face and hands. It helped.

He found the two women in the car, the radio turned to a news station, both on their sat phones.

Early in the morning in Chicago, an as-yet-unidentified male of Middle Eastern ethnicity had attempted to enter Chicago's City Hall on LaSalle. An alert security guard had observed that the man seemed to be wearing something bulky beneath his jacket. When he attempted to stop the man, the man reached inside his coat.

The guard, jittery because of the terror threats and the explosion in Dallas, drew down on the man, demanding he put his hands on his head. The man instead hit the detonator to his suicide vest.

The guard had survived, although he was in the hospital with injuries. There had been no other victims. This was due to the fact the attack took place at 5:30 a.m. central time. Derek thought that was a little strange.

Derek drank a cup of coffee and nibbled at a breakfast burrito, listening to the radio report. Shelly got off the phone and turned to him. "You look better. How do you feel?"

"I'm hanging in there." He felt like he'd been stuffed into a microwave oven on high then beaten with a shovel, but decided to keep that assessment to himself.

O'Reilly clicked off her phone and turned around as well. "You up to working?"

Derek nodded.

Shelly said, "We should really take you to a hospital."

Derek met O'Reilly's gaze. Something flickered between the two of them, an understanding, perhaps, of the situation. A war with terrorists had been ongoing for some time—far longer than September 11, 2001—but at times the battles became more intense. There was a battle going on now and it wasn't in Afghanistan or Iraq or Spain or London or Indonesia. It was here, in the United States. Dallas and Chicago and Washington, D.C. and New York City and Los Angeles were the battlefields, and Derek wasn't leaving the battlefield unless he was carried out in a body bag.

"I'll be fine."

Before Shelly could protest, O'Reilly said, "We've got two leads. One is Ali Tafir. I've got a work address on him now and a little background. I suggest we track him down first."

"Unless you want to drop me off at Greg's place and get the other bucar. We could split up on this."

O'Reilly shook her head. "Let's not waste time. We can deal with that later."

"What's Tafir do?" Shelly asked.

"He's a businessman," O'Reilly said. "The Compass Organization."

"What's that?" Derek asked.

"Import/export. He's a big deal down at the Port of Los Angeles."

Shelly said, "In other words, if somebody wanted to get something into the U.S., he might be able to take care of that."

O'Reilly nodded. "That's what I was thinking."

CHAPTER 24

Kalakar rose early, said his morning prayers, and joined John Seddiqi and his wife, Ghazala, in the kitchen. Ghazala was very quiet, as she should be, thought Kalakar. He sensed, though, that she did not approve of his presence. Their daughter, Malika, was in the bathroom brushing her teeth, getting ready for school.

For his part, Kalakar felt exhilarated. Today was the day the plan really went into effect. Today—

John, voice quiet, said, "There was a suicide bomber in Chicago. It was on the news."

Kalakar nodded. He thought Ghazala's shoulders tensed. He said, "And did this bomber kill many infidels?"

"According to the news, just himself. It was very early in the morning. Nobody was there except a security guard, who was injured."

"All praise to Allah."

Ghazala dropped a spatula. It bounced off the stove and onto the floor. She bent to pick it up and took it to the sink and washed it off. Kalakar watched her closely, but she kept her back to him.

John looked ill. Kalakar reached over and held his hand. "All praise to Allah, John."

"Allah is great," John intoned without fervor and energy.

Kalakar nodded. There was not much more he expected from John. Kalakar's bags were packed and in his truck. He was ready to complete his mission and disappear. All he needed from John now was a single telephone call with valuable information. He held up his cell phone and tapped it for John to see. Rising to his feet, he said, "I will leave now. Thank you for your hospitality. May Allah bestow blessings upon your house."

John nodded. "And on you."

When Ghazala did not respond, Kalakar left. He had bought a used Chevy pickup truck with four-wheel drive and a truck cap on it. It was parked to one side of John's driveway. John and his family lived in a ranch house in Inglewood. The yard was small, but well tended and John and his wife seemed content there. Kalakar did not have much patience for people like John, who took their wealth and comfort for granted and failed to see that the crusaders stole that wealth and comfort from the rest of the world.

Clambering into the truck, Kalakar pulled out and drove for thirty minutes through increasingly heavy traffic until he hit Culver City. After driving in wider and wider circles and doubling back to make certain he wasn't being followed, he pulled into the entrance of Bel Vista Toro Self-Storage.

Kalakar used his electronic card to activate the gate, which whirred open. He drove through, turned left, then right, slowly driving down the rows to the unit that had been rented six months earlier for him by one of his contacts.

He backed the pickup to the corrugated steel door, shut off the engine, and used his key to unlock it, rolling it upward with a rusty rattle.

Inside the storage bin, which was ten feet wide and twelve feet deep, rested a single wooden crate six feet long and one foot by one foot. The outside of the crate indicated it was the property of Coldwater Productions in Hollywood, California. The labels claimed it contained movie props.

Taking a crowbar out of the back of the truck, he pried open the box. Inside was another container, more like a suitcase. Kalakar knew full well what was inside, but couldn't resist from opening it as well.

Flipping the container open he looked with fondness at the contents.

The technical name was a MANPAD, which stood for Man Portable Air Defense System.

Specifically, the container held an FIM-92A Stinger missile, capable of shooting down a low-flying jet.

Kalakar closed the case and loaded the missile into the back of the truck. Now all he needed to know was which of the presidential nominees was flying to Los Angeles today, what time, and what their flight path would be. And he had John for that.

CHAPTER 25

Unlike the bucar Derek had left at Greg Popovitch's Malibu beach house, O'Reilly's car had a GPS. Which was good, Derek soon realized as they entered the San Pedro area where the Port of Los Angeles was located. Finding their way around without it would have been tricky.

He had been there once before when he first came onboard with Homeland Security. His job then had been to take a tour and offer supposedly educated counsel on how to make the port safe from terrorism threats. It was the first time he had been called to the White House, when Secretary Johnston still had his office in the West Wing.

Johnston had held up Derek's report and said, "Derek, I'm not sure this is useful."

The report had been a single page. It had said:

> There's no fucking way to secure the Port of Los Angeles.
> Bend over and kiss your ass goodbye.
> Derek Stillwater, Ph.D.

The Port of Los Angeles was the busiest port in the U.S. and the eighth busiest port in the world. It sprawled out over a total of 7,500 acres, 3,300 of those acres involving water. The Port of Los Angeles had forty-three miles of waterfront.

Derek had then picked up a piece of paper and scrawled some calculations on it for Secretary Johnston. A TEU was the basic unit ports used to determine what their capacity was. A single TEU was a cargo container twenty feet long, eight feet wide, and eight feet and six inches high. The Port of Los Angeles handled 7.5 million TEUs annually, which Derek then calculated as over 205,000 TEUs every single day.

"Look at it this way, Jim," he'd said. "We've got the rough equivalent of a quarter million semis, any single one of them which could be jammed full of explosives, coming into an area bigger than most cities every single day."

"Yes, Derek, but—"

"And I'm a goddamned specialist in biological and chemical terrorism, Jim, and any one of the 16,000 people employed directly in the port or the million people around the country employed in work related to the Port of Los Angeles, could be carrying a plastic test tube the size of my little finger containing enough plague bacteria to wipe out the entire planet. So my professional evaluation is that securing the port is impossible."

Gazing out the bucar's window, Derek was more convinced of his evaluation than ever. Warehouses, loading areas, docks, cranes, cargo terminals, ships, office buildings, railroad tracks, trains, trucks, as well as tourists heading for one of the fifteen cruise lines that operated out of the port. The Port of Los Angeles was like a large city whose single purpose was to move freight.

People griped about how porous the U.S.–Mexican border was, but so were the controlled commercial ports. There was so much freight moving in and out every day, churning the U.S. and world economies, that there was no way you could inspect every single container and person coming in or out.

In the front passenger seat Shelly breathed a heavy sigh. Derek laughed. "Impressive, isn't it?"

"I didn't realize. I've read about it, but to be here—"

Off to their left a crane unloaded boxcar-sized containers—hundreds of them—off a freighter and onto the dock. Derek knew that each of those containers undoubtedly held hundreds of cardboard or wooden boxes on palettes containing blue jeans from Taiwan or engine gaskets from India or piston rings from Brazil.

Or dirty bombs from Pakistan.

O'Reilly tapped her finger to the screen of the GPS. "Okay, almost there."

Easier said than done, though; their route was slowed by caravans of passing trucks and multiple trains on a number of individual tracks hauling freight. They finally found The Compass Organization close to the docks. It was a drab, utilitarian two-story building adjacent to a row of corrugated steel warehouses. There must have been a dozen of the warehouses affiliated with The Compass Organization. The steel doors were all rolled up and a fleet of trucks were constantly coming and going.

They parked the bucar and went into the office. It looked like any other office building. A dozen people either on telephones or computers worked at counters and desks. Anyone not sitting was walking back and forth on errands. The office hummed with activity.

A flinty-looking black woman in a gray business suit walked over. "May I help you?"

Shelly held up her credentials. "FBI. We're here to speak with Mr. Tafir."

The woman reached out and took Shelly's ID, studying it. She looked to O'Reilly and Derek. "May I see your identification, please."

They complied. Already Derek had a bad feeling. This woman was either used to officials coming by, or she was stalling. She knew how to control the pace of things, that much was certain.

"Homeland Security," she said. "That's not unusual, but we generally work with Taylor Zerbe."

"I'm from the D.C. office."

She handed back his ID and studied O'Reilly's. "And I can't say I've ever had dealings with anybody from the Office of the Director of National Intelligence. What is this about?"

"Why don't you stop stalling and take us to see Mr. Tafir," O'Reilly said. "This is about national security."

The woman sighed. "I'm Lora Worth, the manager here, and you're going to have to be more specific."

O'Reilly said, "We're here to see Ali Tafir. It's urgent."

Worth raised an eyebrow. "And as I said earlier, I'm the manager. What is this about?"

O'Reilly took a step toward Worth, probably intending to be physically threatening, but Worth didn't budge. O'Reilly said, "You are obstructing a federal investigation—"

"O'Reilly, isn't it?" said Worth. "Agent O'Reilly, if you have a subpoena or a search warrant, this would be a good time to present it to me. Otherwise, you really need to tell me why you're here. Mr. Tafir is very busy. As you can tell by just looking around you, we're all very busy. The entire Port of Los Angeles is busy today, as we are every other day of the year. We comply with everything the FBI and Homeland Security and INS and the FTC and the Department of Transportation throw at us, and I would be glad to provide you with a desk and all the paperwork we create complying with government regulations, but—"

Derek didn't hear any more because he turned on his heel and walked out. He didn't know if Worth was dragging her feet on purpose. He had a suspicion she wasn't. He had the idea that she was a control freak in a very busy job and what she had just said about complying with the government regulations had the ring of truth to it.

Standing outside, he watched trucks go in and out of the warehouses. He was debating his next move when O'Reilly appeared next to him.

"Shelly's going to talk to Tafir," she said. "Hang on." She went to her own Go Pack in the trunk of the bucar and retrieved a small briefcase. Opening it, she handed him a device slightly smaller than a shoebox. It was heavy enough to hurt his hands, but he bit back his grimace and made do. "Geiger counter," she said.

She pulled out another device that looked like a blow dryer with a PDA mounted on top. "Scintillation counter. Let's go. Warehouse to warehouse. And just so you know, this isn't like finding a needle in a haystack. It's like finding a needle in a needle stack." She abruptly smiled. It was a grim smile, but a smile nonetheless. "Actually, my favorite analogy so far has been that it's like finding a drop of vodka in a rainstorm. In other words, it's a waste of time, but we do it anyway."

"Pretty much my job description."

At the nearest warehouse, O'Reilly flashed her badge and walked past the hard-hatted warehouse supervisor. She said, "We don't need to go box to box—"

"Good thing," Derek said. The warehouse was cavernous, filled with thousands of crates and trucks; a half dozen forklift trucks loaded crates onto trucks. As they watched, a truck pulled up to the rear gates and began unloading more crates.

"—because these are NEST quality gear. High sensitivity. Just wander around a bit—"

"—and try not to get run over."

A burly man in denim and steel-toed boots was waving at them to step back. When they did, a truck backed out of the warehouse. The air smelled of exhaust and was filled with alarms sounding from reversing trucks, the roar of engines, and the thud and clanks of cranes and boxes being moved out.

He followed O'Reilly, watching the meter on the Geiger counter, but it remained in normal levels. O'Reilly explained that U-235, which would be used in a real nuclear bomb, probably wouldn't show up unless they were right on top of it. But maybe they'd get lucky.

And we've got to do something, thought Derek, *besides stand around talking to cranky office managers.*

With a shrug, they finished their first sweep and moved to the next warehouse. More of the same.

They were entering the third warehouse when Lora Worth, Shelly Pimputnikar, and a tall, broad-shouldered man in khakis and a brown shirt wearing a hard hat, waved them down. The man was Ali Tafir. His dark eyes were angry, his mouth twisted in a snarl beneath a thick mustache.

"Hey, what the hell you think you're doing? You can't just run around here. You'll get yourself killed. Know what that would do to my insurance rates? Look, look, look, I cooperate with all you guys, I allow inspections, I fill out all your paperwork. You—" He pointed at Derek. "You're the guy from Homeland, right? I work all the time with Taylor Zerbe. What, the right hand doesn't know what the left is doing? Don't you guys ever talk to each other? You get Taylor on the phone. He'll tell you. Call him."

O'Reilly said, "Mr. Tafir, we have reason to—"

An explosion nearly knocked them off their feet. They all spun toward the source of the detonation. The explosion hadn't come from any of Tafir's warehouses, but from north of where they stood. Already they could see a large black cloud of smoke rising toward the sky.

Derek checked the Geiger counter readout, but it hadn't budged. It wasn't nuclear and it probably wasn't a dirty bomb. But whatever it was, it had been big.

"Sorry to trouble you, Mr. Tafir," O'Reilly said, and turned and ran back toward the bucar. Shelly and Derek sprinted alongside her.

CHAPTER 26

Mary Lynn Travnikar stood on the top deck of the *Alaskan Princess*, gripping the rail with one hand while she waved enthusiastically with the other. Down on the ground, what seemed like miles down, which was why she was holding the rail so tight, were her two daughters and their families. They had sent her and her husband Donald on this Alaskan cruise for a fiftieth wedding anniversary gift.

It was their first cruise. She wanted to take in everything. Don, who was standing just behind her, mostly wanted to find the nearest bar, order a Bloody Mary, and then locate the casino.

Mary Lynn squinted against the bright sunshine. A warm breeze blew her short, curly silver hair around her head. She wanted to see it all. She wanted to experience everything. She was seventy-one years old and she doubted she'd ever be on another cruise. It was another thing to check off on her life wish list. As she waved, her daughters and grandsons waved back, then turned and headed toward the car. Feeling slightly disappointed that they weren't waiting for the ship to actually leave port, she turned to Donald and said, "Isn't this fun?"

"Yeah. Let's get a drink."

She gave him a playful slap on the shoulder. "You'll have the entire trip to play blackjack, Donny. And it's too early in the morning to go to the bar. I want to watch us leave. Let's go over to the other side of the boat. I want to look out at the port. Isn't it amazing?"

Donny shrugged. Mary knew Donny was thrilled to death, but he had played the grumpy old fart for so long that he couldn't quite break out of that role. She thought that was the problem with getting older. Sometimes you acted a certain way because that's what people expected of you—the motherly grandma, the grumpy grandpa, the dutiful wife, the loving mother, the dedicated employee—and before you knew it, that's what you were, whether you wanted to be or not.

She caught his hand. How long had it been since they'd held hands? His eyes widened a little at her touch. I'll show you, she thought. I'll re- mind you tonight in our cabin just why you married me in the first place. "C'mon, big boy. Let's go look out at the ocean. This is an adventure."

He allowed himself to be dragged to the other side of the boat, which wasn't nearly as crowded as the rails alongside the docks. They stood next to each other and looked out at the main channel. Another cruise ship was just leaving the mouth of the channel into the Pacific. Coming in the other direction was a freighter flying the flag of China.

She had been right. Donny was more interested in the ships and the harbor than he had been in waving at his daughters, sons-in-law, and grandchildren. She noticed the faraway look in his eyes when he looked at ships. She wondered if all men felt that way, if embedded in their DNA was a memory of ships and the sea. Did all little boys want to be pirates and sailors?

She pointed at a few smaller boats that were buzzing through the channel. "I would think they wouldn't let pleasure boats in here. They might get run over by a freighter or something."

Donny leaned forward. "Particularly that one there." He pointed. "I'm not sure it's even staying in the—what're they doing?"

The white cabin cruiser, which had been racing up the channel, sud- denly changed course right toward them. With a far-off buzz of a boat engine revving, the cruiser suddenly leapt forward, shooting a beeline directly at the stern of the *Alaskan Princess*.

"Are they crazy?"

"I don't—"

The cabin cruiser struck the *Alaskan Princess* at full speed. Mary and Donny felt a slight tremor run through the big ship at the impact. They had just time to look at each other in concern when the smaller boat exploded, tearing a huge rent through the port stern side of the *Alaskan Princess*, and sending steel, aluminum, fiberglass, mahogany, and glass shrapnel blasting upward and outward, destroying everything—and everyone—in its path.

CHAPTER 27

Derek, O'Reilly, and Shelly found it wasn't easy getting to the site of the explosion. The World Cruise Center was on the other side of the port, easily five miles if they could have gone in a straight line, which they couldn't do. They had to drive all the way around a number of canals and basins, and by the time they arrived, fire trucks and ambulances and other emergency vehicles were already in place.

Climbing out of the car, they took a moment to just stare. A large white cruise ship was sinking into the harbor as flames licked at its hull and black clouds of smoke billowed into the pale blue morning sky.

O'Reilly's phone buzzed. "Yes, we're already here. Where are you? Really? Okay, we're—yes. Okay."

She clicked off and shook her head. "Givenchy and Welch are here somewhere."

Shelly pointed and waved as the two START agents appeared out of the crowd and walked toward them. Givenchy was the first to speak. "We were here when it went off."

Welch nodded. "We were fuckin' useless. We were four hours behind these guys. We followed down a lead that there were some guys loading barrels of something onto a pleasure boat, a cabin cruiser, and it might be explosives. How about you guys?" He took in Derek's appearance for the first time. "Jesus, Stillwater. What the hell happened to you?"

"Long story." He gestured at O'Reilly, who told the two agents about being at The Compass Organization on the other side of the port when the explosion occurred.

"So it was a suicide bombing?" O'Reilly asked.

Givenchy nodded. "Big time. From what we've been able to tell, these guys loaded a thirty-two-foot cabin cruiser full of ANFO, piloted it up the main channel, and drove it full speed into a cruise ship headed for Alaska."

Shelly said, "How many dead?"

Givenchy shook his head. His Texan drawl was more pronounced than usual. "No solid numbers. It could've been worse, but the boat was getting ready to sail. All those people lined up on deck. They're the ones who got killed, those on the starboard aft rail and anybody in their cabins on that side of the boat. I would say dozens. We offered to help, but by the time we got close enough, they had things under control. The ship crew was well trained and so was the port's fire and rescue."

O'Reilly leaned back against the bucar, appearing defeated. "So that gives us Dallas, Chicago, and L.A. We can look at New York and D.C. now. I guess we call in and see if they want us to come home."

Derek turned from watching the smoke. The ship was listing, but not sinking. Besides, the port was only about forty feet deep at the docks. Even if the hull had been completely breached the ship would have just sunk into the mud.

He wondered why the suicide bombers hadn't waited for the boat to get out to sea, where more would have died. Or maybe that wouldn't have been quite as spectacular. He'd had a similar thought about the 9/11 World Trade and Pentagon attacks. If they had taken place a couple hours later, they would have been more deadly than they were. Derek supposed that was one of the downfalls of his experiences with terrorism—he always thought things could be worse.

And of course, today they had managed to pretty much shut down the Port of Los Angeles. Even if they got it up and running again in twenty-four hours, millions of dollars would be lost.

Derek said, "Who owned the boat?"

Welch said, "What?"

Derek turned. "Who owned the boat? The one they drove into the cruise ship. Who owned it?"

Welch frowned. Reaching into his jacket pocket, he pulled out a notebook, flipped pages and said, "It was a Thompson St. Tropez. The Hull Identification Number was TMS38947D998. Owner of record was—"

Givenchy interrupted. "According to the harbormaster, it was some sort of corporate ownership. Berth was paid for by a law firm in L.A. Jamieson, Perzada, Suliemann and Hill. Entertainment lawyers."

Derek recognized the name. It was the firm in the Avco Center on Wilshire, three blocks from the Federal Building, where the Pakistani Consulate was located. They had employed a courier named Abdul Mohammad who had been around a few weeks earlier feeling out Greg Popovitch about whether or not he could acquire a suitcase nuke for him. And now he was dead.

And a boat owned by the same firm had been used in a suicide bombing.

Derek didn't say anything. In truth, he was feeling pretty lousy. He walked over to the bucar, opened the door, and sat down. The rest of the team talked among themselves. Derek watched O'Reilly walk away from them and make a phone call. He wondered what she was thinking. He got the impression that leading a START had been important to her. She'd always been ambitious that way. He wondered what her title was at the ODNI, if maybe she had plans for running an intelligence agency someday, or ending up in the bureaucracy at CIA.

After a few minutes, she walked back and said, "We've been called in."

Everybody nodded, unsurprised.

She said, "I'll meet you back at the Federal Building, then I'll see about heading back to D.C. I'm sure we'll have some reports to write." Her gaze flickered toward Derek. "Oh. Hey, Shelly, I'm going to take Derek back to his bucar. Why don't you ride with Givenchy and Welch."

Shelly nodded. She retrieved her Go Pack and computer from O'Reilly's bucar and followed the other agents back into the crowds. O'Reilly settled into the driver's seat, her fingers tapping on the wheel.

"Back to Malibu, I guess."

Derek grunted. His mind was elsewhere.

She looked at him, gaze sharp. "What're you thinking?"

He stared at the cruise ship. Helicopters beat the air overhead, circling. Finally, "Anything about these attacks seem odd to you?"

She followed his gaze. "This one was pretty effective."

"Yeah, but Dallas was a screwup. Even if it had gone off during the election tomorrow, everything we've seen so far suggests that as a dirty bomb it wasn't more than a—"

"What?"

He murmured, "—a distraction. It all feels like a distraction. And Chicago, that was a joke. You don't do a suicide bombing at an abandoned building."

"Maybe he lost his nerve. Maybe he got confused. Maybe—"

"Maybe this whole deal is screwy."

O'Reilly sighed. "We've been recalled. We're going to get flown back to D.C., write up our reports, and if—"

Derek shook his head. "I'm not going back. I'm not done here yet. There are too many loose ends."

After a moment O'Reilly said, "What do you want to do first?"

"I want to go back and talk to Ali Tafir. It was kind of convenient that during this explosion his witnesses were three federal agents, wasn't it? And I'd really like to see if there's some connection between Tafir and this law firm at the Avco Center. That's where I want to start."

O'Reilly fired up the bucar. "Then let's do that."

Shelly Pimpuntikar appeared in front of them, a frown on her face. She walked back and flung open the rear door and slid in. "Just what I figured. You two are going to continue the investigation. Okay, I'm in. Where are we going?"

O'Reilly and Derek shared a look. Derek grinned. "What about Givenchy and Welch?"

"They want to stay here and make sure the scene gets investigated properly. They're pissed that they didn't avoid this. They were awfully close." Shelly deepened her voice and added a Texas accent, giving a very effective impression of Agent Givenchy. "'I may 'ave fucked the dog today, but that don't mean I gotta like it. I can at least clean up afterward.'"

"Colorful," Derek said.

O'Reilly said, "I'm beginning to think that as a START leader I'm a total failure."

Nodding, Derek said, "Call Welch and tell them you ordered them to stay here and we're going to keep looking at our loose ends. That way your ass is covered."

She agreed. "I've never thought of you as a guy who worried much about covering his ass."

Derek smiled. "I'm not in prison and I'm not dead."

"Yet," Shelly said.

"Yet," Derek agreed. "The day's still young."

CHAPTER 28

It was almost noon by the time they finally made it back to The Compass
Organization. A long day, Derek thought, dragging himself out of the car.
Shelly and O'Reilly went to talk to people working in the warehouse.
Derek had convinced them to let him talk to Ali Tafir alone.

He pushed through the door and it was only seconds before the office
manager strode toward him. "I don't know why you're back here, but—"

Derek walked past her without speaking. Shelly had told him Tafir's
office was on the second floor in the back. He beelined toward the stairs,
the woman yapping at his heels.

"Hey, you can't just walk in here like this."

Derek's reply was to flip out his Homeland Security badge and keep
on walking. She trotted after him.

"I'm going to call Taylor Zerbe. You have no right to come in here
like this."

Derek made a tapping gesture with his index finger. "Ring him."

On the second floor, he strode through a door into a large office
whose windows overlooked the rear of the port. From this vantage it was
mostly train tracks, cranes, and warehouses. Tafir sat behind a maple
veneer desk, feet up on its surface, phone pressed to his ear.

"I understand, but we're going to have to reschedule everything.
We've still got freight coming in here and we're still shipping freight out
unless they lock that down, too. If they don't, we'll have empty warehouses by tomorrow morning."

He looked up at Derek and held up one finger. The office manager
hovered at his shoulder. Derek waited patiently. He wouldn't wait for-
ever, though. Finally Tafir hung up and the woman said, "He barged right
in here—"

"It's okay. I'll talk to him. Thanks."

She left, leaving an aura of annoyance and irritation in her wake. Tafir took his feet off his desk and gestured at a chair in front of him. "You're from Homeland, but I didn't catch your name."

"Dr. Derek Stillwater."

He proffered a hand and introduced himself. Derek held up his bandaged hands with an apologetic look.

Tafiar frowned. "So?" His hands splayed out in a "what now?" gesture.

"Quite a mess," Derek said.

Tafir cocked his head. "You're here for small talk? Yeah, Doctor. It's quite a mess. I don't know any details. Someone tried to blow up a cruise ship. So why come to me? That's miles from here and now that they're shutting the port down for at least twenty-four hours, I've got to totally reschedule for days and weeks. So I'm kind of busy. What do you want?"

"I want to know what your involvement with the explosion was." He supposed he could have put that more gracefully, but he wanted to see Tafir's reaction.

Tafir blinked. He flung a hand toward the window. "That explosion? What're you talking about? I'm not involved at all."

"Tell me about your relationship with Ibrahim Sheik Muhammad."

Tafir's expression went black. "What? I don't *have* a relationship with him. Why? What does he have to do with me and—" He trailed off and Derek noted that his expression went from angry to worried.

"Mr. Tafir?"

Tafir's voice was soft. "What's going on here? Why do you think I had something to do with—" He waved toward the smoke on the horizon.

"Do you?"

"No!"

"Do you have a relationship with Sheik Muhammad?"

"Like I said, I don't."

"But you know him."

"Do I? Not directly. I think Ibrahim Sheik Muhammad is a pain in the ass. A dangerous pain in the ass. Look, I'm a Muslim, sure, and I understand that you Homeland guys and the FBI all are suspicious of a Muslim working in import/export, but I'm an American citizen, okay? I don't support al-Qaeda or any of that crap."

"You said you don't have anything to do directly with Ibrahim Sheik Muhammad. You have an indirect relationship?"

Tafir sighed and his expression now was one of profound frustration. "I know him. I disapprove. My—" Again, his voice trailed off and his eyebrows knitted together in worry. "Why are you asking about this?"

"Mr. Tafir, you received a telephone call from Ibrahim Sheik Muhammad around two o'clock this morning."

"I most certainly did not."

Derek raised an eyebrow. To his reluctant dismay, he wished O'Reilly and Shelly were with him right now. He leaned back in his chair, letting the silence build. Finally he said, "We know that Ibrahim Sheik Muhammad did in fact call your home in Century City around two o'clock and spoke to Ali—"

"I wasn't at home. I've been here most of the night."

Derek paused. "You can verify that?"

"Of course. I'll call—"

Derek waved him off. Later. He said, "Why would the boss work midnights?"

"Because this business runs twenty-four seven and sometimes I like to be here at night to make sure I know who in hell works for me."

"Sheik Muhammad did call your number this morning and he did talk to someone named Ali. You're saying—"

Suddenly, alarm on his face, Tafir pulled out a cell phone and punched a button. After a moment he said, "Rana, let me talk to Aleem. What do you mean he's not there? Where is he?"

Derek had no difficulty reading the current expression on Tafir's face. Alarm had given away to fear, maybe even panic. He'd also switched into a language Derek guessed was Urdu. Tafir clicked off the phone and punched another number. He stared at the phone, pushed more buttons, pressed it to his ear. He ran a hand through his hair. Sweat broke out on his face, a light sheen on his forehead.

"Mr. Tafir? What's wrong?"

When Tafir clicked off the phone a final time, his hands were trembling. Slowly he swiveled to face the window. He stood up and walked to the glass, hands pressed against it, looking toward the cruise ship and the smoke still billowing from the explosion.

"Mr. Tafir?"

Tafir turned and ran out of the office. Derek took off after him.

CHAPTER 29

In the parking lot, Tafir jumped into a silver Mercedes and roared off. Derek glanced around frantically and saw Shelly and O'Reilly running toward him. O'Reilly shouted, "What did you do?" Her tone was accusatory, but Derek ignored it.

"Let's go. I think he's going home."

They jumped into the bucar and tore off after Tafir. It soon became obvious that home was exactly where Tafir was headed. Derek explained the phone call that had set Tafir off. "I think it's a family member. A son, maybe."

Shelly was immediately on the phone to Helen Birch back at FBI headquarters. "What do we have on Tafir's family?"

She listened and asked a few more questions, then hung up. "Two children. A nineteen-year-old son named Aleem and a fifteen-year-old daughter named Bibi. His wife's name is Rana. He wasn't lying to you, either. He's an American citizen. All of them are. The children were born here in the U.S."

"I wonder if the son, Aleem, has a relationship with Ibrahim Sheik Mohammad," O'Reilly said, staying close behind Tafir's Mercedes.

"I would bet on it," Shelly said.

Tafir drove his car into his building's underground garage. Shelly and Derek jumped out and ran to the building to intercept him while O'Reilly found a place to park.

The security guard at the lobby was no more willing to let them pass than the one in the middle of the night had been. Derek scowled and paced while Shelly said, "We're here about Mr. Tafir. Can you confirm when Mr. Tafir left the building last night?"

The guard, a moon-faced African-American in a black uniform complete with badge, shook his head. "I came on shift at eight this morning."

"Do you have the phone number for the guard who was here at night?"

"Billy? Nuh-uh. Can't give that out. What's this all about?"

Rolling his eyes and shaking his head, Derek walked past him toward the elevator doors. The guard reached out for Derek. "Sir, you can't go up unless—"

Derek brushed past him and jabbed the button. The guard came round the desk. "Sir, you need—"

With one quick and fluid motion, Derek snatched the guard's gun from his holster. The guard looked more than startled. Fear spread across his face like a visible stain. His hands came up to his sides, almost in surrender, but not quite. "Sir—"

Derek held up his Homeland Security ID. "I'm going up. You're welcome to accompany me. When Mr. Tafir sees me, he'll let me in. But this is a matter of national security and you can do this easy or hard, but either way, I'm going up."

"Sir, I don't want to lose my job."

The elevator bonged and the doors opened. Derek stepped in. "Are you coming?"

The guard hesitated. The elevator doors began to close. Derek set the gun down outside the elevator just as the doors shut.

He rode to the penthouse. Apparently there was a lot of money in import/exports. The elevator, one of two, opened onto a small lobby with four penthouse doors. He was debating which door belonged to Tafir when the second elevator opened behind him and Tafir burst into the hallway. The man barely noticed Derek. He rushed past him and flung open the far door on the right. Derek was quick enough to slip in behind him.

"Rana! Rana! Where are you?"

A beautiful, dark-haired woman in a white silk blouse and charcoal slacks appeared. She was tall and slender and could have been a model. Derek was slightly startled at the woman's looks, which were elegant and exotic. Her gaze shifted uneasily between Tafir and Derek. "What's wrong? I heard about the explosion at the docks. Are you all right?"

Tafir caught her by the elbows. "Where is Aleem?"

"I don't know. He wasn't here when I got up this morning. Did you try calling him?"

"His cell turned over to voice mail. Where's he supposed to be today?"

She looked bewildered. "School, as usual." She looked at Derek. "Hello. I'm Rana Tafir."

"Derek Stillwater, ma'am."

Tafir gritted his teeth. "He's with Homeland Security. They think this whole explosion mess has something to do with Ibrahim Sheik Muhammad."

Rana paled. "And you think Aleem had something to do with it?"

"I don't know," Tafir said. "Aleem thought the Sheik was wonderful. I forbid him to have anything more to do with him, but—"

A knock at the door interrupted his thoughts. Tafir spun and answered it. Shelly, O'Reilly, and the security guard stood in the hallway.

The security guard said, "Mr. Tafir, I'm very sorry—"

Tafir waved him off. "Go back downstairs, Nick. It's okay."

To the women Rana said, "And who are you?"

Shelly and O'Reilly introduced themselves. Rana held her left hand to her chest, as if feeling for a heartbeat. She seemed slightly breathless. Derek said, "Mrs. Tafir, perhaps it would be best if we all sat down. Where is your daughter?"

"How do you know about my daughter?" Tafir demanded.

Derek met his gaze. "You've got to be kidding?"

Tafir's fists clenched. "I don't like that. I don't like it at all."

"It's simple, Mr. Tafir. You ended up in our headlights so we checked you out. And before this is through, I'm sure the Bureau, Homeland Security, and everybody else involved will find out significantly more about you and your family than even you know. Hopefully it's all a misunderstanding." But Derek didn't think it was.

Rana interrupted. "Please, have a seat in the living room. Can I get everyone coffee?"

"That would be excellent, ma'am," Derek said. "Thank you very much." To Ali Tafir he said, "Do you have a photograph of your son? His name is Aleem, right?"

Tafir stared at him. "Why? Why do you want a photograph of him?"

Rana listened intently. She had not left for the kitchen yet.

O'Reilly said, "Please, Mr. Tafir, let's sit down."

Rana walked toward the kitchen and Tafir reluctantly led them into a sunken area facing a wall of windows overlooking Century City. It was a dazzling skyline, with the early afternoon sun flickering off glass high-rises.

Shelly said, "Tell us about your son, Mr. Tafir. Where does he go to school?"

Tafir glared at her. "He's a freshman at UCLA. Business major." He glanced toward the kitchen. His wife was visible, fussing with the cof-feemaker, clearly listening.

"What does he have to do with Ibrahim Sheik Muhammad?" Shelly asked.

"That bastard is all over the universities trying to recruit Muslims to his madrasah. As far as I'm concerned, he's an al-Qaeda recruiter. He pours hatred into these kids' heads."

From the kitchen came the clatter of cups and saucers and the gur-gle of the coffeemaker. A moment later, Rana Tafir appeared carrying a silver tray with five coffee mugs, cream and sugar. She set it on the long, rectangular smoked-glass coffee table and passed out the mugs before sitting beside her husband.

Derek took a sip of his coffee and decided it was excellent and that he desperately needed it. He still felt lousy and his face and hands ached. He wondered if it was too early to take more Tylenol, figured what the hell, and swallowed a couple tablets.

Shelly continued her questioning. "What did Aleem find compelling about the Sheik's message?"

Tafir's hands shook, but Derek thought from rage, not fear. "Aleem thinks this—" He waved his hands around at the opulent surroundings. "—is a waste, a sin, something that Allah would frown upon. He thinks we should live like paupers. He doesn't understand that all this that I earned from hard work and luck—Allah's blessings—support thirty-five families at the company, pays for their health insurance and their retirement, that I give money to charities and to my mosque, that I have relatives back in Pakistan that I provide for. All he thinks is that we live too comfortably, that no Muslim should live well until they can all live well."

Rana said, "Aleem is an idealist. He is very sensitive, and when non-Muslims show hatred for Muslims, he takes it very personally. He was devastated by the wars in Afghanistan and Iraq. He takes it very personally, as if they're attacking him."

"Don't defend him. He's wrong and I've told him so."

Derek thought: *good to know that Muslim families are just as fucked up as everybody else's.*

He briefly thought of his missionary parents' reactions when he joined the Army. It had taken him years to look back on that with any sense of humor.

He focused back on the Tafirs.

Shelly said, "Does Aleem have a job or an allowance?"

Derek turned to look at her, puzzled as to where she was going with that question. O'Reilly seemed curious as well.

"He worked for me at Compass if I could get him down there. Plus he's got money. I guess you'd call it an allowance. Why?"

"What did he do with the money?" Shelly asked.

Tafir shrugged. "How would I know? Whatever college kids spend their money on. Music and girls and—"

Rana said, "He donated most of it to Sheik Muhammad's madrasah."

Tafir turned to her. "He what! How do you know that?"

"I asked him."

Derek said, "I'd like to look at his bedroom."

Tafir said, "You got a warrant?"

"No."

"Ali, please. Let him look."

Tafir's mouth was a harsh flat line. His arms folded across his chest. "What are you looking for?"

Derek shrugged. "Why don't you and I go in the bedroom and see what there is to see. Agents O'Reilly and Pimpuntikar can talk to your wife."

Man to man, woman to woman, Derek thought. But he didn't think Rana Tafir was the problem. Ali Tafir was, and he thought fear was putting the man's back up as much as anything else. Tafir, he thought, would benefit from doing something, anything, just as long as he was in motion.

"Fine." Tafir jumped to his feet and strode off down the hallway. Derek nipped along at his heels.

Aleem's bedroom was spacious, with a big-screen plasma TV, an

MP3 speaker system, a king-sized bed, and several shelves built of oak holding a dozen books and hundreds of DVDs, both movies and music. Rolled out on the floor next to the opulent bed was an embroidered prayer rug. A door led to a full bath.

Tafir said, "See? What did you expect? The materials for a bomb?"

What caught Derek's attention was a sealed padded envelope lying on the top of the computer desk. It was labeled: MOTHER.

Quietly Derek said, "I think he left something for your wife."

Tafir blinked, lunged toward the desk, and picked up the envelope, tearing it open. It was a CD in a jewel case.

He glanced around, then said, "Come on. I've got a computer in my office."

Tafir pivoted on his heels and cut across the hallway into a smaller room that was set up as a home office. It was almost a cliché'd "man's man" kind of room, Derek thought. Leather-bound furniture, dark wood, the ever-present plasma-screen TV.

Tafir booted up the computer, tapping a foot nervously on the thick plush carpeting.

It occurred to Derek that the package should probably have been opened by Rana Tafir, not Ali. However, because he wanted to see what was on the disk, he kept his mouth shut.

Once the computer was up and running, Tafir dropped the disk into the drive and clicked the mouse to get it running.

Derek came around the desk so he could watch the screen. After a moment a headshot appeared of a handsome young man who looked more like his mother than his father. So handsome he was almost pretty, with thick black hair, large brown eyes, and long eyelashes.

The shot zoomed back slightly until Aleem Tafir was seen from the waist up. In one hand he held what Derek thought was probably a remote control for a digital video camera. Aleem sat on the computer chair in his bedroom.

"Mother, I'm sorry for any pain my death may cause you."

Tafir's face went white.

"By the time you watch this, I will be with Allah, having struck a blow for all of Islam, in the name of the Prophet. Know that I love you always."

CHAPTER 30

In Washington, D.C., Homeland Security Agent Jeff Ayers, leader of START Team Alpha, studied the storage unit facility from the darkened windows of a panel van. He didn't have a terrific vantage point from where he watched through binoculars, but he had two men inside, ready to go.

Ayers and his team had been assigned Washington, D.C. The capital was already a high-security zone, so they had merely stepped up their investigations, focusing on the Pakistani calling himself Kalakar.

Within six hours a report had come in from the National Security Agency. Their ECHELON system, a highly sophisticated eavesdropping and computer network associated with the UKUSA Alliance, a loose affiliation among English-speaking Intelligence organizations—Canada, U.S., U.K., Australia, and New Zealand-—had sorted through a few billion e-mails and phone calls with the name Kalakar in them, and come up with three exchanges between a cell phone in Los Angeles that was no longer active and a cell phone in Washington, D.C. that belonged to Tim Safa.

Ayers had promptly set up a net around Safa, a college student at George Washington University. Digging into his finances, they quickly discovered he had rented a storage unit six months earlier.

What Ayers wanted to do was get into the storage unit and figure out what was in there.

Unfortunately, before his team could do so, their surveillance unit had indicated Safa was on the move, picking up two other men. They appeared to be heading toward the storage facility.

Ayers had raced to get in place by the storage center before Safa and his people arrived. Half his team was following Safa. The voice of Jim Zay crackled in his ear.

"Alpha, this is Zeta. Target is leaving Benning Road onto H Street, heading west."

Into his microphone, Ayers said, "Zeta, this is Alpha. Benning onto H Street, heading west. Confirm. Describe the vehicle."

They weren't far away.

Zay's voice: "Gray Dodge Ram pickup. D.C. plate: X78-LU7. Just passed H Street and Eleventh Street. Still proceeding west. Three subjects in vehicle."

Into the microphone, Ayers said: "Copy, Zeta."

Within minutes he spotted the pickup truck. It turned into the storage unit facility. Through binoculars, Ayers watched Safa punch numbers into a keypad. The gate rolled back and they drove in.

He radioed his team members already in the facility.

"Gamma, this is Alpha. They're coming through the gate now."

The voice of Tony Gallagher rang through his earpiece. "Affirmative. Gamma monitoring."

"As soon as they open it," Ayers said. "I want a report."

"Affirmative. Stopping now."

Ayers fired up the engine of the van and pulled into the storage facility. He'd had just enough recon time so he knew where their unit was. He pulled toward the end of the row at the back so when the timing was right he could block their potential exit in that direction with the van.

"Zeta here. We've got the front."

Ayers said, "Affirmative. Gamma?"

"They've stopped. They're waiting. Someone's out—"

Ayers's heart beat hard in his chest. Gamma reported: "They've pulled the truck into the garage. It's a large unit."

"Go!" Ayers shouted. "Now! Go!"

He stomped on the gas and pulled the panel van into the middle of the mouth of the alley. At the far end he saw that Jim Zay and Bill Hayen had pulled their Ford Taurus into the alley and were sprinting toward the storage unit, MP5s at the ready. From two corners Gallagher and LaFontaine rushed toward the container. They were the closest.

Running, Ayers heard shouts and the sound of gunfire. Gallagher and LaFontaine dived to the pavement and returned fire.

And then the entire world erupted into flame.

CHAPTER 31

Derek settled in next to Sandra O'Reilly and slumped into the passenger seat. He rested his forearm over his eyes.

O'Reilly said, "You don't look so hot."

"Compared to how I feel, I look great."

"Maybe you should take a break. I can drop you back at the Federal Building and—"

"No, just drive around a bit."

They had left Shelly at the Tafir's townhouse. Another FBI agent was on the way to take official statements and gather evidence—like the suicide video. In addition, Shelly indicated she wanted to get as much financial data on Aleem and his parents as she possibly could.

O'Reilly said, "There's the Fox backlot."

Derek opened his eyes long enough to look, but didn't comment. He wasn't feeling much like a tourist. After a moment he asked, "Do you have your original report? The one they pulled from the computers they got in Pakistan?"

"Sure. It's in my briefcase."

Looking over his shoulder, he reached back and snagged the briefcase. Dropping it on his lap, he opened it. On the inside of the lid was a photograph of two children in a clear plastic frame. He studied it for a moment. The daughter, in particular, resembled Sandy.

"Nice looking kids," he said.

"Thank you." Her jaw was tense and so was her voice.

"It must be hard, not living nearby."

She said nothing. She pulled onto Santa Monica Boulevard and headed toward the ocean. Finally she said, "We all have to live with the decisions we make. And I'm not talking about this with you."

"I'm not talking about this," Derek reflected, and *"I'm not talking about this with you"* were two very different things.

He nodded and focused on rereading the report. When he looked up, they were in Santa Monica. Glancing out the window, he smiled at topiary shaped like dinosaurs. Santa Monica, in particular, seemed very "California" to him. Part of it was the palm trees, but the rest was the architecture and the attitude. It might be an old-fashioned California attitude, but it worked for him.

He said, "You notice that almost all of the information we got off the computers so far has been inaccurate?"

O'Reilly didn't say anything for a long time. Derek bristled. "Look, if you don't want to work with me, take me out to Malibu, and I'll pick up the other bucar."

She flashed him a sidelong look. "You can be a real dickhead, Derek."

"Thank you. Coming from you—Jesus, like I give a shit. We either work together or we don't, but this is bullshit the way we're going right now. I'd rather work alone."

"Now that sounds like the Derek I knew in Iraq." She pulled the bucar into a parking lot near the Santa Monica Pier. "Let's take a walk," she said.

He climbed out after her. She led him onto the pier. She seemed distracted. Curious, he didn't say anything. Finally, on the beach, she took off her shoes. "Come on."

He took off his cheap Kmart shoes and socks and followed her. The sand felt good. Warm.

But he was puzzled. This was very un-Sandra-like. She walked down to the waterline and stopped above the waves, looking out at the Pacific Ocean. After a few seconds she said, "I met Rob here. Well, it was our first date. I knew him from school."

"I didn't know you were a California girl."

She nodded, wrapped her arms around herself. "Born and bred. UCLA for undergrad. I was a physics major."

Derek didn't comment. He waited. She turned and set off down the beach. He paced alongside her.

She said, "You never talked about yourself in Iraq. Where did you grow up?"

"Everywhere and nowhere."

She waited. He sighed. "My parents were missionary doctors. I grew up all over the world. Even before Iraq, I got kicked out of a number of Third and Fourth World hellholes. Congo. Sierra Leone. West Africa. Parts of the Amazon. Sri Lanka."

"You don't strike me as being very religious."

He laughed softly. She stopped walking and looked at him. "What's so funny?"

"My ex-wife asked me once if my brother, David, was religious. He's a physician with Doctors Without Borders. He's in Congo. I told her no, David's religion was medicine. She told me my religion was counter-terrorism."

"Is it?"

Derek shrugged. He knew his marriage to Simona hadn't survived his obsession with it.

She stood and contemplated him. He met her gaze without flinching. Finally she said, "I'm not really a counterterrorism expert, Derek. You know, that, right?"

He nodded.

"I'm a counterintelligence expert. But since nine eleven the CIA shifted away from CI to CT. I'm trying to find my place in this new world. That's why I leapt at the chance to go to ODNI. I also think all the focus on CT is only going to lead us back to the need for CI."

He thought she was right, but counterintelligence wasn't his area of expertise. He believed that the long-term solution to preventing continued terrorist attacks was through intelligence and politics. History had proven this time and again, with the IRA, with Baader-Meinhof, with most successful counterterrorism efforts. Neither were his fortes, though. He didn't have the patience for CI or the taste for politics.

He had spent years trying to educate politicians on ways to minimize terrorists, but intelligence gathering and political change were not as attractive to politicians as going to war against an enemy with no borders or rules of engagement.

She said, "The computer files said there were going to be attacks in five cities. They were focusing on election day. You know how nebulous intelligence can be. These files were very unspecific."

"Election day is tomorrow. But so far we've had one explosion last night and two attacks the day before. Doesn't that bother you?"

"It confirms that there is at least some truth to those files. Maybe Kalakar decided to accelerate the attacks because he knew we got the computer files."

"Why not change them altogether? If they're not targeted at polling stations on election day, why not activate them as soon as the raid went down?"

She turned to stare at him. "What are you getting at, Derek?"

"What I'm getting at is that I think these computer files the Bureau picked up in Pakistan are bullshit."

"You can't deny there have been attacks in three of the five locations indicated in those computer files."

"But there's no accuracy in the times. And the Chicago attack was just plain weird."

"So a suicide bomber chickened out and decided that he was okay with killing himself but didn't want to take a bunch of innocent people with him. That's not unprecedented, Derek. There have been instances of suicide bombers who altered their original plans so fewer people died."

Derek frowned. "It's a—"

O'Reilly's phone buzzed. Holding up her hand, she answered it. She listened intently, nodding, and said, "Yes. We're still working. Okay. Yes."

She clicked off. "There's been a major explosion in Washington, D.C. START Alpha was tracking a potential bogie to a storage facility only a couple blocks from the White House. They got into a firefight and the bad guys set off their explosion. Alpha's dead. All of them."

Derek's heart sank. "What type of explosion?"

"Looks like a truck full of ANFO. At least eight dead—the three terrorists and all five members of Alpha Team. It took out almost the entire facility."

Derek's brain raced. It was a day early, but that could just be because they were caught. The Dallas explosion was weird and might have been accidentally set off as well. The Chicago attack could have been a terrorist who panicked. And from everything they could tell, their own investigation had sparked the earlier attack here in Los Angeles.

"What do they want us to do?"

"They want us to report in to the Federal Building. And you're supposed to contact Secretary Johnston."

Derek thought about it. If everything in the computer records was somewhat accurate, their job was done. The local FBI and Homeland Security office could sort things out, follow-up on the Tafirs, collect whatever evidence they could from the cruise ship, bring Ibrahim Sheik Muhammad in for questioning, and follow up any loose ends. They would be focusing all their efforts on New York City, trying to prevent the last and final attack.

He held out his hand for the phone.

She handed it to him. He dialed Secretary Johnston's direct number.

Johnston's wood rasp voice said, "Derek? Where the hell have you been?"

"Long story. I'll have to get a phone so I can stay in touch."

"You've heard about the attack here in D.C.?"

"Yes sir."

"It's all gone tits-up, Derek. Maybe we can prevent the New York attack. Report in at the Federal Building, write up your report, and come on home."

Derek hesitated. His gaze locked with O'Reilly. "Jim, you trust my instincts, right?"

There was silence, then Johnston asked, "What's on your mind?"

"I have a gut feeling, Jim. A gut feeling that there's more going on than we think. I want to talk to somebody who was in that raid in Pakistan. Do you think you could arrange that?"

Johnston said, "I can do that. At this phone number?"

"Yes."

"Okay. I'll be back to you in the next half hour."

Derek clicked off and returned the phone to O'Reilly. She asked, "What are you thinking?"

"I'm thinking that we're not done yet. And neither is Kalakar."

She stared at him. Finally, she shook her head. "No, Derek. I'm following orders. I'm going back to the FBI. I'm done working with you."

"Then drive me to Greg's place so I have a car."

Her expression was opaque, unreadable. The waves washed ashore, receded, came ashore again. Metronomic and timeless. She nodded and walked back toward her bucar.

CHAPTER 32

John Seddiqi studied the computer monitors in front of him. Triangles and lines and computer readouts indicated where most of the airplanes in California, Nevada, and Colorado were at any given moment. He was in the air traffic control tower at LAX and Vice President Newman's plane was coming into the Los Angeles airspace now. The atmosphere of the ATC center was one of intense professionalism.

Sweat beaded up on his forehead. Seddiqi couldn't forget his argument with his wife this morning after Kalakar had left.

She had turned the moment he was gone and asked, "What did you agree to do for him?"

"Nothing. It's none of your business."

He should have known better. Ghazala Seddiqi was a good wife, a good Muslim, but she was strong minded and outspoken. Hands on hips, she had said, "It is my business, John. I have a bad feeling about him. He wants you to do something bad. What does he want you to do?"

"Nothing. Nothing. Leave it alone."

She walked across the kitchen and sat down across from him. "You're afraid of him. Has he threatened you? What's wrong, John?"

"He's just a friend of my cousin Shaukat, in Pakistan. He needed to stay with us a few days. And now he's gone. It's nothing."

But in truth, Kalakar felt like a threat to him. He did not know exactly what the man had planned, but John was certain it was something bad. And now there had been that suicide bomb explosion in the Port of Los Angeles. So far there were twenty-one dead.

Had Kalakar been involved in that?

Had Kalakar been on the boat that plowed into the cruise ship? Was he dead?

Despite himself, John hoped he was. Then this would all be over.

But he didn't think so. John suspected that Kalakar was connected in some fashion with al-Qaeda, although he didn't believe his cousin Shaukat was. The whole thing confused him.

He knew that Kalakar had something big planned for Los Angeles. That it somehow involved either Vice President Newman or Governor Stark's visits to Los Angeles for tomorrow's election.

Glancing at the monitor, John noted that Vice President Newman's plane would be routed through the northern approach.

His job was to phone Kalakar with the approach and GPS coordinates on the ground so Kalakar could identify the plane.

John didn't know why this was important. He couldn't imagine what Kalakar would be able to do with this information.

John had been educated in air traffic control during his stint in the Pakistan Air Force. His cousin, Shaukat Seddiqi, had asked him to host Kalakar for a couple weeks and do whatever he asked.

John was sympathetic to al-Qaeda, although he felt their attacks on civilians were getting out of control. He was a good Muslim, however, and he felt that Americans—and probably all westerners—just didn't understand the legitimate complaints of the Muslim world. Americans, he thought, were oblivious to the effects of their actions—that they were a relatively small proportion of the people on Earth, but squandered a disproportionate amount of the planet's gifts—oil, food, water, natural resources. And they aligned themselves with governments and leaders who were evil and oppressive just so they could maintain those natural resources.

But John did not have sympathy for the terrorist tactics. He thought the 9/11 attacks were evil and misguided.

He fingered the phone in his pocket. He was supposed to call Kalakar.

He thought of Ghazala. He thought of his daughter. He shook his head.

He would not call.

And as he thought that, his phone rang. He answered it. "Seddiqi."

It was Kalakar. "What's going on, John? You haven't called me yet. The news reports say Vice President Newman's doing a rally in L.A. in ninety minutes. Where is he?"

Glancing nervously around the control tower, John said, "I can't talk now." And hung up.

He broke out into a sweat. His stomach churned. He set his jaw and thought, *I will not cooperate with you, Kalakar.*

CHAPTER 33

Kalakar clenched the cell phone in his fist. If John Seddiqi had been in the truck with him at that moment, he would have snapped the man's neck with his bare hands. Waves of fury washed over him. This entire operation was falling to pieces. From the very beginning, when the Pakistani National Police and the FBI raided the apartment prematurely, he had been playing catch-up, trying to improvise an operation that had been planned for months.

Kalakar glared around him. He was parked near the Observatory in Griffith Park, the white building all shiny and clean against the washed-out blue of the L.A. sky. He wanted to scream. He wanted badly to hurt someone, to break and destroy something.

Controlling his rage, he pressed his fingers to his temples, rubbing away the headache that was starting there. The first problem had been the premature raid. But the raid itself had been expected and part of the plan. The biggest problem with the raid had been that although the three laptops had been booby-trapped—one to go off, one to possibly go off, and one to fail—Kalakar had not yet finalized the data on the hard drives. The Los Angeles location was not supposed to be included on the hard drives.

The multiple attacks around the country were, ultimately, planned to be diversions away from the main event, the downing of either of the presidential nominees' planes as they flew into Los Angeles. This would throw the U.S. government into a panic; the traditional rollover of power would be disrupted.

Al-Qaeda would directly affect the election of the next president of the United States.

But everything was going wrong.

The Dallas bomb had been set off prematurely. As a result, Kalakar had decided to push ahead most of his planned attacks.

He did not know exactly what had happened in Washington, D.C. It sounded like his team there had been caught by the authorities and committed suicide with the bombs.

The Chicago attacker had lost his nerve.

The only attack that had gone according to plan was the attack on the cruise ship. It had been in the planning stages for a long time and, in fact, had not been planned for this week. But with the U.S. government tearing apart L.A. to prevent an attack, Kalakar needed them to think the attack had already gone down. He had sent a message off to Ibrahim Sheik Muhammad, ordering him to give Aleem Tafir and his people the go-ahead.

Now everyone would be looking to New York City.

Los Angeles would be wide open for the prime attack on the presidential candidates.

Except John Seddiqi was balking.

Think, think, think.

He knew Vice President Newman was in Los Angeles today.

And Governor Stark would be in Los Angeles tomorrow morning for a rally on election day.

Kalakar looked at his watch. It was 3:00 pm on Monday. Stark would fly into LAX around 8:00 or 8:30 tomorrow morning, on Tuesday. He had less than fifteen hours to put together another operation.

Putting the truck into gear, he headed out of Griffith Park and back toward Inglewood. Seddiqi was going to cooperate. Kalakar was going to guarantee it.

CHAPTER 34

As O'Reilly drove toward Malibu, Derek leaned back and closed his eyes. He tried to not think, letting his subconscious mind work through everything that had happened. His iPod had been destroyed in his Go Pack in the fire, otherwise he'd plug in and listen to music. That usually helped him.

He felt jittery and ill, like he had drunk a gallon of Turkish coffee. His gut told him he was missing something, something big.

Derek opened his eyes and asked for O'Reilly's phone.

"Why?"

"It's a simple request, O'Reilly. But if you must know the truth, I'm going to order a pizza. You like anchovies?"

She glared at him. He glared right back. Finally she turned over the phone and he dialed Secretary Johnston, whose first response was, "I'm still working on Pakistan, Derek. Show a little fucking patience."

Derek laughed. "That's not what I wanted. Isn't Stark or Newman coming into L.A. today?"

Johnston's voice was throatier and rougher than usual. "Newman's there right now."

"Where?"

"Century Plaza Hotel, then over to the UCLA campus, then flying up to Sacramento to speak at the Capitol Building, then down to San Francisco. Why?"

"I don't know. I was just thinking. What about Stark?"

"He's coming into L.A. tomorrow morning. He's a little weak in California, so he's spending more time there."

"Send us an itinerary, would you? For both of them."

"Is this your gut feeling again, Derek?"

"I don't know. Maybe."

"I'll e-mail it to—"

"My regular account."

"Will do."

He clicked off and Derek said, "Pretty tough to disrupt these things, though. The Secret Service is all over them." *But not impossible*, he thought.

O'Reilly seemed to be following his train of thought. "Hard to guard against a suicide attack."

Derek nodded.

He drifted off a bit, waking as O'Reilly pulled into the drive of Popovitch's beach house. She muttered, "Nice place."

"I imagine it'll be up for sale soon if you're in the market."

"Asshole."

Derek crawled out of the car, slapping his pocket to make sure he still had the keys to the junky bucar he had left in Greg's driveway. "Bye O'Reilly. Been the same old pleasure."

"Stop somewhere and pick up a damned phone, Derek. Then keep me posted."

He shot her a mocking salute. "Yes sir, ma'am. I work at the pleasure of my leader, Commandant O'Reilly."

O'Reilly paused, as if she had something to say, shook her head, reversed with a squeal of tires, and pulled out of the driveway.

Derek turned and studied the house. Here was the thing: he didn't just want to get back here for the bucar. He wanted to get inside the house. Greg Popovitch knew all the low-lifes and bad guys up and down the entire West Coast. Somewhere in Greg's house there were records and contact information. Derek wanted it.

And in order to get it, he was going to have to do some B&E and he doubted O'Reilly was going to cooperate. Better to get rid of her.

Now, though, he needed to contend with Greg's alarm system, which was a significant deterrent if he didn't want the alarm company to call the cops on him. If he could find a work-around, good; if he couldn't, he'd do a smash-and-grab and get the hell out of Dodge.

The first thing he did was hop in the bucar, fire it up, and turn it around so it was nosed toward the exit.

The second thing he did was find a patch of fine beach sand—it was blowing all over the place—and pocketed it.

The third thing Derek did was approach the door. It was solid enough, but—

He jumped forward and kicked out, driving his weight into the door right by the knob. With a shriek of tearing wood, the door imploded inward.

Derek stepped to the keyboard, remembering that Popovitch had a ten-digit password. He had one chance to get this right. He typed in: L-I-L-Y-R-A-B-I-N-E.

The small screen read: DEACTIVATED.

Derek breathed out in relief. That had been easy enough.

Now, the hard part. He prayed for a small miracle.

Turning, he opened the closet, pushed aside the jackets, and yanked open the small metal door to inspect the palm scanner. Reaching in his pocket, he took out a fistful of beach sand and gently blew it at the screen. A ghostly outline of a palm appeared.

He tapped the keyboard menu, heart slamming in his chest. Derek didn't know how sophisticated Greg's palm scanner was. At a CIA training course Derek had watched someone fool a palm scanner using melted Gummy Bears. But many of the higher-end scanners didn't scan for fingerprints. They scanned for the blood vessels and capillaries in the palm beneath the skin. Some even took the temperature of the hand to verify that it wasn't some sort of fake.

After what seemed like an eternity, the screen said:

WELCOME, MR. POPOVITCH.

He was in. He hoped he hadn't used up his miracles for the day. Derek closed the battered door behind him, walked into the kitchen, and went about making a pot of coffee.

He needed a Go Pack to replace his things. Hunting through the house, he found a nylon backpack. Good enough. Scrounging through the kitchen he packed away a couple water bottles, medicines from the bathroom for a makeshift first-aid kit, a box of ammunition that would work for his Colt, and some energy bars. He found an iPod sitting on an end table. Picking it up, he clicked it on, curious to see what sorts of things Greg listened to. Lot of classic rock, country, and a little bit of jazz. He added the iPod to the backpack. What the hell. Greg didn't need it anymore.

Derek didn't know if Greg's clothes would fit him or not. The shoes didn't, but the jeans did, so he took a couple pairs, snagging a few T-shirts and sweatshirts as well.

Pouring a large mug of coffee, Derek entered Greg's office. He figured Greg had a lot of safeguards on the computer to prevent hacking.

Opening all the drawers of the desk, he looked for a list of passwords. One of the banes of modern existence was everybody's need to maintain a constantly shifting series of PIN numbers and passwords. Most people either made one they could remember and never changed it, or wrote them down. One study done by a computer security group found that the number one choice for passwords in the United States, used by over 70 percent of those quizzed, was PASSWORD. The number two choice was PASSWORD1. Another study indicated 12345678 was a common password. From there it went to a combination of birthdays, children's names, and social security numbers.

Having broken into the house using Greg's late wife's maiden name, he doubted he would get so lucky on the computer.

Pawing through the drawers, he found a checkbook, pens, pencils and a lot of useless office detritus. He also found four small leather-bound books. Curious, he flipped through them. They were diaries. This seemed very un-Greg-like. Derek quickly realized they were old. They were labeled with four consecutive years: 1990, 1991, 1992, and 1993.

Paging through the 1991 book, he saw it was an account of Greg's time in Iraq. Frowning, he caught mention of his name. He read the account in Greg's broad, loopy handwriting.

I see Stillwater and O'Reilly have got a thing going. I doubt he even knows she's married. I give Stillwater a couple more months before he gets fed up with weapon hunting. Doesn't seem to have the patience for it. His ying with O'Reilly probably won't last that long, though. I had a go at her myself. She's kind of fun in the sack, but I don't trust her. She's manipulative. God only knows what she must think she's going to get out of Stillwater.

Well, Derek reflected, Greg had sure had insights about O'Reilly. He put the diaries back in the drawer. Morbid curiosity urged him to hunt through it looking for mention of himself, but he knew he wasn't likely to find anything he would be happy reading.

Finally, Derek leaned over and turned on Greg's computer. As he'd expected, it was password protected. He tried typing in LILYRABINE, but that didn't get him anywhere. He tried a few other combinations, but none worked, which didn't surprise him much. Greg must have known that if the cops or Feds got hold of his computer, it wouldn't have taken them long to crack the password. He'd had a PDA on him, which was now a charcoal briquette. He wondered if all of Greg's contact information had gone up in flames.

Something caught his attention. He didn't know if it was a sixth sense, or maybe he just heard the car pull into the driveway. Derek rushed from the office to the front of the house. A white panel van was pulling into the driveway. It was followed by a black Chevy Caprice. Shit. It looked like the L.A. cops were here.

Pulling the backpack over his shoulder, he went out to meet them.

Detective Stephen Connelly stepped out of the Chevy, a grimace crossing his dark features. "Returning to the scene of the crime, Stillwater?"

Connelly's fellow cops climbed out of the van. It was not a cheery group. Derek was pretty accustomed to that kind of reception from local law enforcement. Connelly waved at them to stay where they were. He walked toward Derek. "We're not too happy with you, Stillwater."

"What do you want? I'm a little busy here. You know there's already been a terrorist attack in L.A.—"

"Yeah, you guys are doing a great job of stopping them I see." Connelly studied Derek. "Nice job with Popovitch and his buddy. You set that house on fire? You shoot Popovitch after you fuckin' kidnapped him?"

Derek shook his head. "I didn't set any fire."

"I only have to take one look at your face to see you were involved with that fire. Even if you didn't kill Popovitch or Smith, you're a witness. You left a goddamned crime scene."

"I don't know what you're talking about."

"The fuck you don't." Connelly got in Derek's face. "I tried to co-operate with you. I helped you find Popovitch. You blew this whole operation, Valentin's still running around loose—"

"We've got bigger issues to—"

Connelly jabbed Derek in the chest with his finger. "No, we do not! There's a right way and a wrong way to handle this kind of shit, and you're doing it the wrong way."

"Poke me again and—"

"Or what, Stillwater? I'm taking you in for questioning. I'm going to sit you in a box and make you wait around for me. And maybe we'll forget you for a day or two." He thumped Derek in the chest.

Derek caught Connelly's arm, levered it backward, and dumped the L.A. detective on his ass. The other two cops raced toward them. The bucar was blocked in. Derek spun, sprinted around the side of the Malibu house, and suddenly found himself in midair. Popovitch's beach house rested on the top of a high, steep bluff above the Pacific Ocean.

"Sssshhhhiiiiiiitttttttt!"

He dropped into the scrub and sand on the side of the bluff, tried to stop his fall, and tumbled. Derek dug into the hillside with his heels and hands, trying to keep from rolling all the way to the bottom of the bluff. Each time he hit the ground, a cloud of dirt and dust churned upward, surrounding him. It got in his eyes and his nose and mouth, blinding and choking him.

Heart thudding, frantically scrabbling at the rocks and brush, Derek was able to stop from somersaulting to the bottom, but he wasn't able to stop completely. In a barely controlled fall, he lunged from bush to bush and rock to rock, gaining speed. Thirty feet from the sandy beach he lost his balance and fell, spinning the remaining distance to the sand, where he thudded to a halt.

I am so fucking stupid, he thought.

Dizzy, sore, and more than a little angry at himself, Derek lay there for a moment, then sat up and looked back up the bluff. At the top, Connelly and his two cop buddies stood looking down at him.

Connelly shouted, "Climb back up here so I can kick your ass back down!"

Well, Derek thought, *I guess that answers my next question.* He stood up, brushed dirt off his clothes, flipped Connelly and company the bird, and set off down the beach. He guessed he was on his own for a while.

CHAPTER 35

Agent Shelly Pimpuntikar sat in Aleem Tafir's desk chair, gazing out the window at the Century City skyline. Beyond the bedroom she could hear the sounds of grief, of anger, of mourning. Rana Tafir was in tears and had gone into her bedroom and shut the door. Ali Tafir had stalked around the penthouse as if looking for something to kill, before getting on the phone and making arrangements for a relative to pick up the daughter, Bibi, at school. Then he had gone into his office to call the office manager at his company.

She wondered if their marriage would survive this. Families were sometimes fragile things, destroyed by divorce, death, illness, or just the pressure cooker of modern life exaggerating everybody's flaws and weaknesses. She wondered if Ali would blame his wife for being too soft on their son. She wondered if Rana would blame Ali for not being understanding and supportive.

Overall, Shelly thought she liked spreadsheets better than all this raw emotion.

Both Ali and Rana Tafir had accepted her presence there, but she had been more than a little surprised that O'Reilly and Stillwater were leaving her there alone. Well, not Stillwater. He was so clearly not a team player, she couldn't imagine why anybody had envisioned he would work well on a START team. O'Reilly, who was a certifiable control freak, allowing her to work alone—that surprised her. And made her suspect that O'Reilly was just getting rid of her and didn't think she could make any real contribution to the START team.

She crossed the hallway and knocked softly on Ali Tafir's office door. "Yeah?"

She pushed the door open and stood in the doorway. Ali Tafir looked up, his expression clouded, eyes haunted.

"I have some questions I need to ask."

"Go ahead."

"Do you follow Shariah in terms of money?" She referred to Islamic economic guidelines.

He made a face. "You mean do I take out loans and pay interest?"

She nodded. In Islamic law, paying interest, or *riba*, was prohibited, condemned as usury. There were other similar prohibitions—investment in businesses that were unlawful, such as those that sold pork or alcohol or that produced pornography or gossip. Shelly wondered if a Muslim had ever owned a southern barbeque joint. The thought made her smile, but not in a very happy sort of way.

"Yeah, I've got loans. Look at this place. You think I paid cash for it?"

"Did you go through an Islamic bank?"

Islamic banks, at least in theory, did not charge interest. What they typically did was buy the property, then sell it back to the customer at an inflated rate. The customer could buy it in installments. It was part of Fiqh al-Muamalat. From Shelly's point of view, it seemed an awful lot like paying interest, but calling it something else. She also understood that many religious beliefs that had survived for hundreds or thousands of years did so for different reasons than what they were originally created for. Often they remained because by following them, you were reminded of your religious affiliation. Not: I am Muslim, therefore I don't take out loans, but: I don't take out loans, it reminds me I am Muslim.

Tafir shook his head. "None of that crap. Sorry, if that offends you."

She wasn't offended. She was relieved.

"Did your son have a credit card?"

"Yeah. Why?"

"Who received his bills?"

"He did. He was a grown-up, at least I thought he was." Tears welled in his eyes. His voice cracked. "He got an allowance from me, he worked for me from time to time, and I made it clear he needed to handle his own expenses, including the gas in his car and the insurance for it. He had a Visa card and he paid his own bills. Gave him some freedom. Seems like a stupid idea now. Look what he went and did."

She nodded. "I'm going to need your credit card account numbers, as well as various banking and checking accounts."

"What? Why?"

Keeping her expression neutral, she said, "Mr. Tafir, I want you to understand that we are not treating you as a suspect. But your son was apparently a major player in a terrorist attack. The FBI will be looking into all aspects of your son's life, which will include you and your wife's personal and financial history. It will be much quicker and easier if you just provide me with the information I need, rather than require me to obtain subpoenas and get it anyway."

He stared at her, then reached over to a filing cabinet, rifled through the files, and pulled out five files. "It's all in here. Just copy what you need. You'll have to get Aleem's somewhere else. I assume they're in his bedroom somewhere."

Shelly hesitated. Softly, "Mr. Tafir, I think your wife needs you right now. I think she needs to know you don't blame her for this."

He looked shocked, but didn't respond.

She took the paperwork and returned to Aleem's room. A few moments later she heard Ali walk into his bedroom, followed by the murmur of voices. With a pleased nod, Shelly did a quick search of Aleem's desk and found several credit card and checking account statements. Scanning through Aleem's most recent credit card statements, she felt her heart beating hard against her ribcage. There was some very interesting information here.

She slipped Aleem's statements into her briefcase, writing out a receipt. Sifting through Ali and Rana's files, she wrote down the relevant numbers, but didn't intend to take them with her.

A knock at the penthouse's door brought a wave of relief. She followed Ali to the door, where a pair of L.A. field office FBI agents awaited. She introduced herself and turned over the files and the Tafirs for their safekeeping.

She said, "Did you come in two cars?"

Jon David Burkheither, one of the agents, nodded. "You needed one of them, right?"

She nodded. He handed her keys and told her where it was. Grabbing them, she bid farewell to the Tafirs and headed down to the street.

CHAPTER 36

Derek trudged along the beach. He'd moved beyond the bluffs and now most of the multimillion-dollar beach shacks—he just knew the owners thought of them that way—were right on the beach. From time to time they were fenced off and he was forced to take off his shoes and socks and roll up his jeans and wade through the surf until he could get back to quasi-public beach. He was expecting the local cops or LAPD to come corner him at any time, but so far he hadn't seen any signs of law enforcement.

"Hey there, stranger."

Lost in thought, Derek looked over. A woman was sunbathing in a tiny orange bikini on a lounge chair, a paperback in one hand, a martini glass in the other. An Igloo cooler rested in the sand between her chair and an empty lounge chair. She was blonde and tanned and smiling, all of which Derek found tremendously appealing.

"Hi," he said. She was maybe in her twenties, maybe in her thirties, or maybe even a very well-maintained forties.

"You look like you could use a drink. Have a seat."

He raised an eyebrow. He had heard rumors that parts of Malibu were friendly like this, but he'd never really believed it. He wandered over and sat in the lounge chair next to her. She opened the cooler and pulled out an iced bottle of gin and an iced bottle of vermouth. "Martini?" she asked.

"I appear to have died and gone to heaven."

She had a lovely smile. And a lovely everything else. He concentrated on her smile. For a moment Derek wondered if he should throw in the towel and just spend the rest of the day right here.

"And you appear to have been out in the sun too long." She stared at him. "Or are those burns?"

"Burns. It's been a bad day."

"I've never seen you before. I know most of the beachcombers around here." She smiled and held out a hand. "I'm Marion Gilette."

He took her hand. "Derek Stillwater."

Pouring him a martini, she dropped an olive in the glass. She studied him. "There's a story here, I'm sure. Want to tell?"

He sipped the martini, which tasted like liquid steel, and felt like a sledgehammer to the back of his skull.

"I'm with Homeland Security."

"For real?"

He nodded and sampled more martini. "For real." He contemplated the olive in the martini, then drank some more. "What do you do, Marion?"

"Real estate."

"Ah. Would you be interested in driving me to the nearest car rental place? I'd be glad to pay you."

She sat up. "You don't have a car?"

"Like I said, it's a long story."

She studied him. "Do you have any identification, proving you're who you say you are?"

He smiled slightly and retrieved his wallet and showed her his HS badge. She read aloud. "Dr. Derek Stillwater. Medical doctor?"

"Ph.D."

"In what?"

Derek drank some more. Almost done with it, he thought. Wonder if I should drink another before I go on my way. Probably wouldn't be a good idea to get hammered right at this particular moment. He wondered, also, if Marion Gillette would give him her phone number, so that when he was done with all this nonsense he could take her out for dinner, or something like that.

"Biochemistry and microbiology," he said finally.

"You must be smart."

He sighed. "If I was smart I'd be selling real estate so I could own a place on the beach in Malibu instead of falling off cliffs and getting shot at."

Her laugh was warm and genuine. "Good point. What do you do for Homeland Security?"

"Hunt bad guys."

"It looks like you found some today."

"Yeah, but they were the wrong ones. Some days are like that."

"I bet. When do you want to go?"

"As soon as I finish this martini." He drank it down.

"You wouldn't have a business card, would you?"

She gestured to her bikini. "Not on me."

"Yeah," he said dryly. "I can see that."

"Why, you interested in buying a house?"

He grinned. "Something like that."

It took Derek two hours to rent a car and then visit a store that sold computers and cell phones. He walked out of the store with a laptop and cellular phone. He'd already downloaded all the software he needed in order to access the Internet using a cellular card. He sat in the rental car, a black Nissan Pathfinder, and checked his e-mail account. Secretary Johnston had sent him the itineraries for Vice President Newman and Governor Stark.

There was also a note for him to call ASAP.

Using the new phone, he obliged.

"What the fuck have you been doing, Derek? The LAPD contacted me personally to demand I turn you over to them for questioning."

"It's a, uh, small misunderstanding."

"With you it's never a small misunderstanding. It usually borders on an international incident."

Derek bristled. "You'll be glad to know I'm alive, Jim. Burned, bruised, but alive. Greg Popovitch, however, is dead. Shot by one of his own people, then set on fire. I was handcuffed to a chair at the time, so really, Jim, why don't you tell the LAPD to kiss your ass. And while you're at it, you can kiss mine."

To Derek's surprise, Jim Johnston's laugh bellowed over the phone. "I was beginning to worry about you, Derek. Ever since you got back from your leave of absence you've been acting like a company man, towing the line, being cooperative. Glad to hear you're returning to your old self."

"Fuck you, Jim. I'm having a shitty day."

Johnston still sounded amused. "I've got the phone number of two of the FBI agents involved in the raid in Pakistan. Sam Sherwood's the head of the CT unit, and he's probably worth talking to, but Sherwood says the point man on the follow-up is an agent named Dale Hutchins. Apparently he got in the way of one of the booby-trapped laptops, but he's back on the job as of today, and he's up-to-date on the investigation." Johnston rattled off a pair of international numbers.

Derek jotted them down.

"Before you go, Derek, I want to warn you. Apparently, Cassandra O'Reilly went to the FBI after dropping you off. They complained to her about you and to the LAPD. She pretty much fed you to them. The SAC gave me a call as well. Also, my guy in L.A.—"

"Taylor Zerbe?"

"Yeah, he's been informed that cooperating with you would hurt his relationship with the bureau."

"Haven't even met the man. Is there a bottom line here?"

"Yes, Derek, there is. You're on your own. O'Reilly has essentially kicked you off the START team and the FBI agrees with her. It's probably her way of distancing herself from you. Don't bother going back to the Federal Building."

"Are you calling me in?"

Johnston snorted. "Would you come in?"

"No."

"So we understand each other."

Back working alone, Derek thought. *What I do best*. "I think we do, Jim."

"Good. Keep me posted."

"No plausible deniability?"

"I'm out of work no matter who wins the election. So I'm not worried about keeping my job. I'd just rather not spend my retirement in congressional hearings, understand? On the other hand, you've got my full backing. Always do."

"Thanks, Jim."

"I'm counting on you, Derek. Figure out what the hell's going on and stop them."

"And I'll try not to get killed in the process."

"That, too. Good luck."

CHAPTER 37

Kalakar idled his truck outside the Oak Street Elementary School in Inglewood. He did not approve of the Seddiqis' decision to send their daughter to a public school. Particularly this one, which appeared to be made up of Africans and Hispanics. Why didn't they send their daughter to a Muslim school? He thought it was a sign of betrayal on their part, an indication that they had become more Western than Muslim, more American than Pakistani.

He searched the crowd of children for Malika Seddiqi. She should have stood out among all the other children. She would be one of very few—if any—children wearing a hijab, a headscarf.

But he wasn't spotting her.

His sense of frustration grew. He was well trained enough to know that few operations went exactly according to plan, and the more complex they were, the more likely they were to change. Still, this plan had started disintegrating before it even got started and had been gaining speed as the pieces flew off ever since.

What if John or Ghazala had taken their daughter out of school? What if after he left them, John packed his family into a car and headed out of town?

Scowling, he glared at the children climbing into school buses and those who were streaming from the school, being met by parents, or heading home on their own. There were shouts and screams and excited chatter. It reminded him of his own childhood at school, always in a rush to get out of the classroom and play football—Americans called it soccer—with his friends. So long ago. *Children*, he thought, *were the same everywhere.*

He knew that Malika walked the four blocks home. Sometimes

Ghazala walked her to school, but mostly she met one of her friends, a Hispanic girl named Dominica, and they walked together.

There!

He spotted Malika. She wore jeans and a T-shirt and a headscarf. He frowned at the jeans and T-shirt.

Climbing out of the truck, he trotted over to where Malika and her friend Dominica were heading down Oak Street together. "Malika," he called.

She turned to look at him. "Hello, Mr. Kalakar."

"Your mom and dad asked me to pick you up at school today, honey," he said.

"I can walk," she said. She was a slim, pretty girl with big brown eyes. Very serious and very smart, she seemed entirely too American to Kalakar.

"But your mom's not home, Malika. Come on. No arguing." He kept his voice gentle.

Dominica, her hair black and long and straight, wearing a denim miniskirt and a T-shirt, piped up, "Malika can come to my house, then."

Kalakar thought Dominica was dressed like a whore. A mouthy, bitchy whore. "Her mother specifically told me to bring her home. We're going to go see your mother. Come on."

Doubtful, Malika walked along with him. Dominica, hands on hips, said, "I don't think you should go with him, Mal."

Malika seemed doubtful, too. "I . . . I think it's okay, Dom. He's a friend of my dad's."

"But you should have a note or something. Your mom should have called the school and told them someone else was picking you up today."

Kalakar couldn't believe what a hassle this was turning out to be. He wished the little bitch would shut up. He reached out to take Malika's hand, aware that some of the parents were starting to pay attention to this little minidrama playing out here. Maybe he should have waited for them to get closer to home, away from the school.

"Your mom was a little busy. There's been an emergency."

"An emergency?" Malika's eyes grew wide. "What kind of emergency?"

"I really think it would be better if she told you about it herself,

Malika. Please, we don't want to be late. Tell your friend goodbye and get in the truck."

"Is it Daddy? Did something happen to Daddy?"

"Malika, please, just get in the truck. Your mother is waiting for us."

Malika gave Dominica a last, backward glance, then popped her friend a quick wave and followed Kalakar across the street. She jumped into the front seat and he hurried into the driver's seat, fired up the engine, and got out of there fast before anything else could go wrong.

In his rearview mirror he saw Dominica staring after them. The intensity of her gaze made him a little uneasy, but he put it out of his mind. After all, she was only ten years old. What trouble could a ten-year-old girl be?

CHAPTER 38

Derek decided he had better get back into L.A. and pay a visit to the law offices of Jamieson, Perzada, Suliemann and Hill in the Avco Center on Wilshire. It seemed a lot like walking back into the lion's den—it was right by the Federal Building—but he couldn't just ignore it. An awful lot of leads seemed to point toward the entertainment attorneys. They employed someone who had been asking around about suitcase nukes. They owned a boat that had been used in a terrorist attack.

He went online and pulled up a website for them. Glancing at his watch, he noted it was almost five o'clock. There was no way he would be able to get back into downtown in anything resembling a reasonable time frame.

Plan B involved calling the two FBI agents in Pakistan.

Instead, he searched his memory and made a call. Shelly Pimpuntikar picked up.

"Oh good. I remembered your number right. It's Derek."

"Where are you?"

"Look, I don't know if you've heard, but I gather I'm officially off the START team. I'm going to—"

"I'm on my way to Culver City."

"What? Who are you with?"

"I'm by myself."

Derek sat up straight. "Shelly, you don't have any field experience. You really should do fieldwork with a partner. Someone to watch your back. What's in Culver City?

"Coming from you? Seems like a laugh."

"Shelly—"

"Derek, if you're really off the team, I shouldn't even be talking to you."

"Fine. At least call Cassandra."

"I don't need her permission—or yours—to follow a lead."

He sighed. So much for a well-organized START team. "What's in Culver City?"

"Aleem Tafir rented a storage garage in Culver City. I'm headed over to check on it now."

With alarm Derek thought of the bomb that went off in the storage facility in Washington, D.C. And that had been an entire experienced START team. "Wait, wait for—"

"I'm almost there. Bye, Derek."

She clicked off. Frantic, Derek plugged into the net, Googling for Culver City storage facilities. Heart sinking, he discovered there were eight of them.

Turning to the rental car's GPS unit, he started stabbing in the addresses, planning the fastest routes to each one. As soon as he was done, he stomped on the gas, hoping he got lucky and intercepted Shelly before she got in trouble.

CHAPTER 39

When Shelly Pimpuntikar was ten years old, her parents took her to see the movie, *The Untouchables*, starring Kevin Costner, Sean Connery, and Robert DeNiro. It planted the idea of becoming an FBI agent in her mind, although her parents did little to encourage the notion. Her father was a physician, her mother a veterinarian, and they fully expected their only child to pursue some sort of science field, preferably medicine.

But it became clear early on that Shelly's head for numbers was going to lead her into business or accounting or, her parents hoped, physics or mathematics or computer science. Because her parents made it so obvious they didn't support a career in law enforcement, Shelly took what she sometimes thought of as the path of least resistance, and earned a degree in accounting. She became a CPA and took a job at KPML, a large accounting firm in Chicago. She became one of the star players in their forensics division, tracking down mishandled or missing funds.

On September 11, 2001, Shelly, like many others, found herself questioning her background and path in life. She thought someone with her particular set of skills and experience would be a valuable asset in trying to prevent another terror attack. She understood that those three operations hadn't occurred in a vacuum; they had been well-funded and there had to be a money trail.

So she applied to the FBI. Fresh from the raw wounds of the 9/11 attacks, uncertain of the nature of the enemy, the FBI was not quite ready for a female Muslim FBI agent.

Furious, Shelly left her lucrative job at KPML and returned to school, earning a dual master's degree in economics and history with a focus on Islamic financial law and, specifically, *hawaladars*. She completed her degrees, applied to the FBI, and was hired, although her initial placement wasn't as a special agent, but as support staff for an organized-crime unit in New York City.

It had taken several more years of constant applications before she was transferred to special agent status in the finint division. Mostly she was expected to stay in the office and crunch numbers, but Shelly had more ambitions that that, perhaps remembering the movie character of Agent Oscar Wallace, the FBI agent from accounting who realized they could bring Al Capone down via tax evasion charges.

Shelly checked her gun and pulled her bucar into the parking lot of Bel Vista Toro Self-Storage. Her cell phone rang. She glanced at it and noted that it was Derek again. She ignored it, letting it turn over to voice mail. He was going to be patronizing and lecture her on proper procedure, but from what she had seen, the man was a cowboy who never spent any time following proper procedures. Besides, all she was going to do was check things out.

She walked into the office, a small trailer-like structure whose sole occupant looked like he was interested in leaving for the day. He was leaning back in a creaky old office chair covered with cracked green leather, a small color TV playing soundlessly in one corner. In one hand he had a cell phone and from what she could tell, he was either playing some sort of video game on it or looking at pictures of some sort. Maybe twenty-five, his head was shaved bald, and his goatee was black. He barely glanced at her.

"Just about closed for the day," he said. "We've got a couple boxes open for rent, though."

She held up her badge. "I'm with the FBI. I'm afraid I'll need a little bit more of your attention than this."

The expression on his face didn't change much, but he looked at her. One hand swept over the shaved scalp. "Yeah?"

She stood at the counter and cocked her head. "You rented a storage locker to a man named Aleem Tafir."

The guy shrugged. Bulging biceps and a potbelly pushed at his blue shirt. "Okay."

Shelly felt the fabric of her patience fray just a little bit. "I would like you to verify this for me, please."

He clicked a couple keys on his cell phone and dropped it in his shirt pocket. Acting as if she was asking for a lung or a kidney, he hauled himself to his feet, pointedly looking at his watch as he did so. As if in slow motion, he shuffled over to the computer on the counter.

"What's that last name again?"

"Tafir," she said.

Frowning, he tapped at the keys. He scratched at the goatee, wiped a finger across one eye. "Nope."

She craned to look around at the screen. "T-A-F-I-R," she said. "Not T-A-Y-F-U-R."

"Huh. Spell that again?"

She did. He tapped away. "Al—how you pronounce that first name?"

"Aleem."

"Raghead, right?"

She blinked. "He is Pakistani. I don't believe 'raghead' refers to Pakistanis."

"Whatever. Yeah. He rents a box. Started in June, pays by the month. Visa."

"What number is the box?"

Her slow-mo pal blinked like a turtle. "Number?"

"Yes. What is the identification and location of the storage unit?"

"Oh." He stared at the computer screen. He frowned, tongue poking at the inside of his cheek. "You're with the FBI, you said?"

"Yes."

"I see that ID now?"

With a barely concealed sigh, Shelly handed him her FBI credentials. He took it and stared at it. "Yeah. How you pronounce that last name?"

"Pimpuntikar."

"Pimp-yer-car?" His expression showed blank expectancy. Maybe he wasn't as stupid as he came off, Shelly thought. He seemed to enjoy yanking her chain. Or maybe he was just bored.

"Close enough," she said.

"You got a warrant or something?"

"No," she said. "But if you think we need one just to get the number of the storage unit, I'll have to take you down to the Federal Building in downtown L.A. while I write one up and then hunt up a judge. Should take a couple hours. You've got plenty of time, though, right?" She was bluffing, but it was a good bluff.

He stared at her, mouth half open. After a moment in which she swore she could hear the rusty gears in his head clank and grind, he said, "Unit eighty-three. It's toward the back. If you want to enter—" He reached beneath the counter and Shelly tensed, hand darting toward her gun. He pulled out what looked like a white credit card—an electronic keycard. "—just use this. Drop it in the mail slot when you leave."

She took the keycard from him. "You're leaving?"

"My shift is over. Time to go home."

"And does someone work the next shift?"

"No. We just have someone here during the day in case someone wants to rent a unit."

She raised the keycard. "Thanks. You've been very helpful."

He shrugged.

She walked over to the gate and used the keycard. The gate ground open and she walked through, looking for unit 83.

CHAPTER 40

Derek careened into the parking lot of Palm's Self Storage. A stoop-shouldered woman in her sixties was locking the door of the office. She looked as if a stiff breeze could blow her away. He rushed over. "Did someone just stop in here?"

The woman, her white hair looking like it had been cut with a butcher knife, shook her head. "Been dead today. You lookin' for someone?"

"A woman. She's coming to one of the Culver City self-storage places. She's FBI."

"You FBI?"

He flashed his ID. "Homeland Security."

"Haven't seen anybody in an hour or two. Sorry. What's this about?"

Without answering, he returned to his rental, jabbing the number for Shelly's cell. He gritted his teeth when it shifted him over to voice mail. Dammit, Shelly. "Shelly, it's Derek. I've got a bad feeling. I trust my intuition. Don't go in there without me. Call me."

And the feeling was really bad. He knew he could be just as wrong as anybody else, but he paid attention to his instincts. His instincts told him something was wrong, seriously wrong.

Jumping into the Nissan, he checked the list on the GPS. Three down. Five more to go. The next stop was called Bel Vista Toro Self-Storage. He screeched out of the parking lot, blood roaring in his ears.

CHAPTER 41

The little girl, Malika Seddiqi, wouldn't shut her mouth. Kalakar was doing the best he could to keep her relaxed, but she was pestering him with questions:

Where are we going?
Is my Mommy okay?
Is it my Daddy?
What's going on?

She was persistent. He tried to reassure her. Kalakar knew the time would come when she would realize exactly what the situation was, but he was trying to delay that as long as possible, certain it would create its own set of problems. So his answers were: I'm taking you to your mother. She's the one that asked me to pick you up at school. I think your father is just fine (although I'm mighty angry with him, child, and you can blame him for your current predicament), and I think it would be better for your mother to tell you.

When he pulled into the entrance of the Bel Vista Toro Self-Storage facility, Malika said, "My mother's here?"

"No, honey. I just need to stop here and drop something off." It was going to be a headache enough trying to keep the girl quiet. He might have to rent a motel room and tie her up and gag her. He didn't want to take the risk of driving around L.A. for the next fifteen or sixteen hours with a Stinger missile in the back of his pickup truck. He didn't want to get pulled over by a cop or any other fluke of bad luck that might happen to scramble his careful plans more than they already were.

He noted the Grand Marquis in the parking area, but was too distracted by the girl to think much of it. He pulled the keycard from his pocket and activated the gate.

"What are you dropping off?"

"Just some things I don't want to carry around with me."

"What?"

Kalakar sighed and shot the little girl an annoyed look. Maybe he should tie and gag her and leave her in the storage unit; except he was going to need her to leverage her father into helping him. "Do your parents ever tell you you talk too much?"

"Daddy says asking questions is good. Mommy does, too. She says I have an active mind."

"And an active mouth."

The little girl pouted. "Don't you like me?"

Kalakar closed his eyes for a moment. "Of course I like you, Malika. But I've got a lot on my mind right now and you're kind of distracting me."

"Why are you here?"

"I told you—"

"No, here in the United States. Daddy says you're an old friend, but he doesn't act like he knows you very well."

And doesn't act like he likes me very much, Kalakar thought.

"I've just got some business to do, and your parents let me stay with them a while to save money."

He pulled the truck up to his rented unit and clambered out. Malika slithered out and came around to his side of the truck. He snapped his fingers at her. "Get back in the truck."

"Why? I've never seen one of these places before. I want to see."

"There's nothing to see. Now get back in the truck."

She crossed her arms over her narrow chest and scowled at him. She looked exactly like her mother at that moment and he wanted to do nothing more than slap that petulant expression off her face. But he would not strike this girl. If he could not control a ten-year-old girl without resorting to violence, he wasn't much of a mujahedin.

"You're not the boss of me."

He modulated his voice so he would sound angry without shouting. "Malika, get back in that truck right this instant or I will tell your mother what a bad girl you've been."

"I have not!"

"Now."

"No."

164 | MARK TERRY

"Malika—"

A woman appeared around the corner of the shed. She was medium height wearing a blue suit and looked Pakistani, perhaps Indian. She aimed a handgun at him. "Freeze, FBI. Hands where I can—"

Kalakar ducked behind the truck, drawing his own weapon. He jumped up and fired over the hood.

The FBI agent returned fire.

Malika screamed, turned, and ran.

Kalakar dropped to the ground next to the truck. Peering underneath, he saw the agent's feet and lower legs. She was moving for cover.

Taking careful aim, he fired from under the truck. The agent screamed and fell.

Jumping to his feet, he sprinted around the end of the truck. The FBI agent was on the ground. Her face was contorted in pain. Kalakar fired.

The FBI agent's body jumped. She groaned, fought to hold her gun steady, and fired back at him.

A burning sensation cut along Kalakar's right side.

Glancing over his shoulder, he saw that Malika was almost to the gate.

The FBI agent was struggling to aim her gun at him. He raised his own with difficulty. Pain shot through his ribs and up to his shoulder. Jaw tense, struggling against the wound and the pain, he fired. The FBI agent's body went limp.

Kalakar rushed back to the truck, jumped in, and roared after Malika. She was trying to scramble up over the fence without much success. He lunged out of the truck.

"No! No! Leave me alone!" she screamed. "Go away! Go away!"

He snagged the back of her shirt and dragged her back to the truck. She clawed at him. "You're not my Daddy! Help! Help me!"

He struck her with the gun in his hand. Her head snapped backward and she slumped to the ground. Kalakar picked her up and flung her into the truck like a rag doll. *Stupid little bitch*, he thought. *Look what you made me do. Stupid little bitch.*

He climbed back in the truck, keyed his way out of the facility, and drove away.

CHAPTER 42

The first thing Derek noticed as he approached the Bel Vista Toro Self-Stage facility was the black Grand Marquis parked in the lot outside the facility's office. A Grand Marquis screamed law enforcement. He didn't know if someone fresh from Pakistan would realize it, but to any American bad guy, they might as well have a light rack and big sign saying COP written on the side.

A lot of other things registered on his radar screen as he drove up, but only from the periphery. Traffic was only moderate here. He saw a Ford F150 with a man and a little girl drive by. The little girl seemed to be crying. The office was locked and closed for the day. A motorcycle roared by, its female rider helmetless, long red hair blowing in the wind. It was starting to cloud over, the sunny blue California sky turning over to a chillier November evening, the sun starting to set early.

A hundred other things bombarded his senses, but he pushed them away, screeching into the parking lot and pulling in next to the Grand Marquis. He took a quick peek in the window and recognized Shelly's briefcase.

Spinning, he scanned the facility. He stepped over to the gate, saw it was locked and required a keycard to enter.

He pulled his cell phone and redialed Shelly's number. Faintly, he thought he heard the ringing of a phone. After a couple rings it clicked over to voice mail. The distant ringing of a cell phone ended as well.

Derek's heart thumped against his ribs. He strained to hear something other than traffic noise as wind ruffled his hair.

He clambered over the fence, casting a glance toward the security camera mounted on a pole nearby.

Dropping to the pavement, he dialed Shelly's number again. This time he definitely heard the phone ringing. He sprinted in the direction of the sound.

As he rounded the corner, he spied the crumpled figure of Shelly Pimpuntikar. Racing toward her, he bent down. Blood soaked her clothes, seeping onto the pavement beneath her.

Pressing fingers to her throat, he felt for a pulse, relief sweeping through him as he felt it. She moaned and opened her eyes. "Der-ek?"

"Yeah. Hang on."

He quickly dialed 911. His voice sounded harsh and angry as he spoke rapidly into the phone. "Officer down. I repeat, officer down. I have an FBI agent, victim of gunshot wounds, at the Bel Vista Toro Self-Storage facility in Culver City."

"Your name, sir."

"I'm with Homeland Security. Get an ambulance here ASAP. Female FBI agent with multiple gunshot wounds."

"Sir—"

"I'll leave the line open," Derek said.

Leaning over, Derek grabbed hold of the sleeve of Shelly's suit coat at the collar, and pulled. With a tearing sound, the cloth ripped. He pulled off the sleeve, pulled open her coat to look for the wounds.

There was no difficulty finding them. She had been shot three times. Once in the lower left leg. One bullet had struck her lower stomach. The other bullet struck her upper right shoulder. He folded the sleeve and pressed it down on the stomach wound. It quickly became saturated with scarlet.

Using his knife, he stripped Shelly's coat into tatters, creating makeshift compresses on the shoulder and stomach wounds. His hands were bright with blood. The unmistakable scent of blood, coppery and hot, slammed against his nasal plates.

Fifty-two bodies dead—

Derek flinched, shaking his head, forcing the flashback away.

Digging up graves in Pakistan, bodies rotted, the buzz of flies, the muffled sounds of digging broken by the chunk of metal striking bone—

Sweat beaded up on his forehead. Not now!

He checked her pulse. Nothing.

"Shelly! Stay with me!"

Sirens shrieked in the distance.

She moaned. "Girl . . ." she breathed.

"What? Stay with me, Shelly. The ambulances are on the way. Hang in there."

"Little . . . girl . . ."

"Little girl?" What was she talking about? He took another wad of cloth and pressed it down on the stomach wound. His stomach did a low, threatening roll. He stared at the wound, closed his eyes, pressed down. The leg was bad, the shoulder was bad, but the gut wound was really, really—

He forced the thoughts from his mind. It wasn't time to give up hope.

The sirens grew louder.

Shelly's voice was a whispery croak. "Kal . . . a . . . kar . . ."

"What about him?" *Come on, Shelly. Stay awake.* He brushed a lock of her dark hair out of her face, but she didn't seem to notice.

"Had . . . a . . . girl . . ."

Derek flashed on the Ford F150 that had driven by him as he showed up. A little girl had been crying in the passenger seat. "He had a little girl with him?"

"Y-y-yesssss." A sibilant bit of her life escaping with the word.

"Good, Shelly. That's just great. Now hold on, the ambulance is almost here. You hold on."

The sirens were loud. "Over here!" Derek shouted. "We're over here!" He thought there was a panicked rawness to his voice and didn't like it.

A moment later a uniformed cop ran up, gun drawn. He took one look at Shelly and shouted into the radio pinned to his collar. Derek pawed through the remnants of Shelly's coat and through her pants pockets and came up with the white key card. He tossed it to the cop, who sprinted off toward the gate.

"Was Kalakar in a Ford pickup truck?" he asked.

Shelly didn't respond. Her eyes were open, but she seemed to be looking off into space. "Dammit, Shelly! Stay with me. You're going to make it. Stay with me!" He pressed his fingers to her throat. Nothing.

"Shelly!"

There. A pulse. Weak, but there.

The white-and-red ambulance wheeled up to them and two paramedics jumped out. One, a woman, eased Derek aside. They immediately went to work.

Derek stepped back, watching her. He blinked. The cop stepped toward him, but Derek held up a finger. He held up the cell phone, trying to remember O'Reilly's sat phone number. His mind was a blank.

The female paramedic looked at him. "Are you Derek?"

He nodded, hurrying over.

"She asked for you."

Derek knelt down by her. Shelly's eyes blinked open.

"I'm here, Shelly. Right here." He reached out and took her hand, squeezed. "Everything's going to be all right." He ignored the look the two paramedics shot each other as he said that.

"Girl . . ."

"Yes," Derek said. "Kalakar had a little girl with him. I saw her."

Shelly seemed to struggle to speak. Her mouth opened and no sound came out. The male paramedic said, "We're going to lift her onto a stretcher and get her to the hospital now."

Derek nodded.

They deftly lifted Shelly onto the gurney, clicked it up, and were rolling it toward the ambulance, when Shelly said, "Girl . . . name . . ."

"What? The girl's name?" He squeezed Shelly's hand, but she didn't respond. She was sending him a message, telling him something, but it seemed to be sapping all of her energy.

"Mmmmmm."

Derek looked at the paramedics, who shrugged. "Shelly?"

But Shelly was out. They loaded her into the back of the ambulance, and with siren wailing, sped out of the facility. Derek stared after it, mind buzzing.

CHAPTER 43

The cop lumbered toward him. Derek held up his hands. "Wait, wait, wait!"

The cop, who looked like he used to play college football, scowled at him, obsidian eyes suspicious. Cop eyes, Derek thought.

"What?" The cop started toward him again. Built like a refrigerator, his skin was the color of burned toast.

"Don't move! Don't move!"

The cop cocked his head. "What's this about, Agent Stillwater?"

Derek's eyes narrowed. He scanned the ground. "Are detectives coming?"

"Yeah. What's this about?" He took a step toward Derek.

"No. Stay right there. Right there."

Derek studied the facility, then the pavement, and said. "Don't move. Have you notified the FBI?"

"No sir."

"I don't remember the phone number, but call the FBI Field Office here and tell them Special Agent Shelly Pimpuntikar was in a shooting. Ask to speak with Agent Cassandra O'Reilly. She's not FBI, but she's federal. Tell her they need to get here ASAP. We need a crime-scene team."

"Sir—"

Derek pointed to a spot about five feet in front and to the left of where the cop stood. "Does that look like blood to you?"

The cop looked to where he pointed. His eyebrows raised above his dark eyes. "You think she nailed her assailant?"

Derek nodded. "Make those calls, please."

When the two Culver City detectives showed up, Derek cooperated. He knew he wouldn't have to cooperate for long. It took thirty minutes before O'Reilly arrived with an FBI team. The FBI SAC, Jeremy Black, showed up as well and informed the local cops the scene was theirs. Because it involved the shooting of an FBI agent, even the locals knew they didn't stand a chance in hell of fighting them on it.

Black was tall and broad-shouldered and pissed off. He got into Derek's personal space and slammed the flat of his palm against Derek's chest. "You're a fucking menace, Stillwater."

"The only reason Shelly's alive is because of me. So you can stick your attitude up your ass. Kalakar was here. He rented a storage unit. And I think Shelly shot him. Also—"

He looked past Black to O'Reilly, whose face was a pale gray mask. "I think you need to take control of the video cameras here. Now. I think we got Kalakar and his truck on video."

O'Reilly's eyes grew wide and she spun to take in the video cameras. She strode off without a word. Black shouted after her, "It's the bureau's, O'Reilly. Remember our conversation."

She waved her hand at him, but didn't hesitate or pause.

Black stared at Derek for a moment. "Run me through it, then I want you to go back to the FO and write up a statement. Then get on the first flight out of LAX back to wherever the fuck you came from."

"That's not your call."

Black's glare could cut tempered steel. "Listen to me closely, Stillwater. This START team bullshit has been a waste of time and resources. We didn't need you coming here, and you sure didn't do us any good, did you? We've got a nice little body count over at the port and we've got a wounded agent and then we've got you wandering all over town causing trouble with the locals. I have contacted the director in D.C. and informed him that the L.A. START team is done. I'm pulling the FBI out of the team and I'm sending the non-bureau personnel home—that means you and O'Reilly and Givenchy. Welch can stay if he wants to."

Derek shrugged. "It's still not your call. I answer to Secretary Johnston."

Black's face had the look of a thunderhead. "I've given you all the slack I intend to, Stillwater. The LAPD wants you for questioning. I don't answer to them, and I'm not sad Popovitch is off the playing field. But I'm being real generous by suggesting you go back to the FO, write up your report, and catch the first flight back to D.C. Otherwise, you're going to be spending a lot longer time here than I think either one of us wants you to. You understand me?"

"Loud and clear."

Derek turned and walked to his car. Black just gave him a "Get Out Of Jail Free" card, but it was temporary and he'd better use it while he could.

He climbed in the car and fired up the engine. Suddenly the door opened and Cassandra O'Reilly threw her Go Packs into the back seat. She settled into the passenger seat.

Derek cocked his head. "What do you want?"

"We're working together. The START team is history and so is any cooperation I'm going to get from Black or the Bureau. But we're not done yet and, frankly, I'm pissed off. So drive."

"Where to?"

"Jesus, Derek. Anywhere but here."

CHAPTER 44

Ghazala Seddiqi was vacuuming her living room carpet and waiting for Malika to come home from school when the phone rang. She thought it was probably Alicia Rodriguez, Dominica's mother, telling her that Malika was over at her house. Those two, Malika and Dominica, were as thick as thieves. Malika was just as likely to be at Dominica's as Dominica was to be here. Ghazala liked Dominica. She liked her energy, her spark, her sassiness. She liked her Americanness.

Shutting off the vacuum, she picked up the phone. Her spine went stiff and her heart pumped a little faster as she recognized the voice.

"Hello Ghazala. This is Kalakar."

Biting back her anger, Ghazala said, "John is not here. He's still at work."

"I know that. He's not answering my calls. As soon as I hang up, I want you to call your husband and tell him he has to take my calls."

"I don't understand. If John doesn't want to talk to you, I think that's a good thing."

"I know that, Ghazala. But I have your daughter."

"What?"

Ghazala felt a ripple of terror wash over her. She did not know exactly who Kalakar was, but she had a pretty good idea of what he was. "Let me talk to her. Now."

"That's a good idea. Just a moment."

Ghazala heard rustling and then her daughter's voice. "Mommy?"

"Malika, honey. Are you all right?"

"I'm—I'm—"

Kalakar took the phone away from the little girl, his voice louder, flat. The flatness somehow struck Ghazala as the worse thing, the unemotional, cold way he was talking to her. "Your daughter is fine, Ghazala, and she will remain fine just as long as John cooperates with me. We had an agreement and he broke off his end of our arrangement. He has one opportunity to save your daughter—"

"What do you mean, save my daughter?" Ghazala clutched the phone as if it were a life preserver, but she felt as if she were falling away, the real world spiraling beyond her reach while she dropped into a whirlpool of fear. "What do you mean? Don't you hurt her! Don't you hurt her!"

Kalakar's voice continued in that cold, flat way. "You call John and tell him I will be calling him in a few minutes."

The phone line went dead. Ghazala's breathing was ragged. She thought she might pass out. Clutching the edge of the kitchen counter, she swayed, chest burning, blood roaring in her ears. With trembling hands she dialed John's cell phone by heart. When he answered, she blurted, "Kalakar took Malika! He took her! What did you do?"

CHAPTER 45

Derek stared at O'Reilly. "Get out. I'm not working with you."

"Oh, grow up, Derek."

"You hung me out to dry—"

"You're wanted by the LAPD for questioning, you've assaulted an officer, you've—"

"Get out of the fucking car."

"Turn the damned key, put your right foot on the gas pedal, and let's get the hell out of here before Black decides to lock you up for the week."

It was probably good advice, although Derek would have been happier following it without her company. It was also clear she wasn't leaving without making a scene. Without further complaint, he aimed the rental car toward downtown L.A. It was so solidly rush hour that they promptly slowed to a crawl. He figured that was probably a good thing, in that he was soon going to have to either tell O'Reilly where he was going or kick her ass out of the Nissan.

She said, "We're fired, in case you hadn't heard."

Derek shrugged. "You were fired; I quit."

She snorted. "Trust me, Derek. You were fired."

He shrugged.

O'Reilly said, "Maybe we should get over to the hospital. Do you know where they took her?"

"I heard someone mention Brotman, but I'm not sure. Not much we can do for her."

"Seems a little cold. Don't act like you don't care. I saw your face when I showed up."

Staring through the windshield at the traffic congealing around him, Derek said, "I'd be glad to drop you off at the hospital." Turning to her, he added, "In fact, it would give me great pleasure and satisfaction to drop you off at the hospital —preferably without stopping the car or slowing down."

He felt the intensity of her gaze on him. Finally, "You're an asshole, Stillwater."

"You're the one who jumped in the car uninvited. Feel free to jump back out."

She clenched her fists. "I'm sure in school your teachers said you didn't work or play well with others."

"I went to missionary schools run by religious zealots in Third World hellholes all over the planet. There was no satisfying them no matter what I did, but it did give me insight into the kind of mind that would kill civilians because they think God wants them to."

He tightened his grip on the steering wheel. "And by the way, O'Reilly, fuck you."

O'Reilly was silent for a moment, which relieved Derek. His little rant had taken him to a place he really didn't care to go.

Finally she said, "Where are you going?"

"The Avco Center."

O'Reilly stared out her window for a moment before turning to him. "The law firm. And the guy asking Popovitch about a suitcase nuke. Right?"

"Got it in one."

She glanced at her watch. "You think someone will be there? It's late."

Derek's smile was grim. "I was sort of hoping no one would be there. Of course, in the world according to John Grisham, there's always some young and ambitious attorney working late, so it's possible there will be somebody there."

"A couple federal employees breaking and entering. Seems to me there's a bad historical precedent." Yet O'Reilly didn't sound very upset about this.

Derek said, "G. Gordon Liddy became famous. Wrote books, went on talk shows, opened his own school, got his own radio program."

"Went to prison first."

Derek dipped his head. "Yeah, there's a potential downside."

"So we don't get caught."

He glanced at her. "That would be part one of my plan. Don't get caught."

"What's part two?"

"Haven't figured that out yet."

CHAPTER 46

John Seddiqi was on his way home from LAX when he received the call from Kalakar. His fingers groped for the call button on his phone and his voice sounded strained and weak to his ears. He hated the desperation in his voice, wishing he sounded tougher. For his daughter, he needed to be strong.

"Have you lost your—"

"John. Listen." Kalakar's accented English was low and calm.

"I want to talk to Malika. Right now."

"You're in no position to make demands, John. You do understand that you have no options, correct?"

"I'm not talking to you. I'm not going to speak with you until I first talk to Malika."

"John, you're not listening. You need to listen to me."

A horn wailed. John realized he wasn't paying attention to his driving. He had drifted into oncoming traffic. Heart leaping in his chest, he jerked the wheel. Sweat drenched his shirt. John was a good traffic controller. A traffic controller needed to be able to process complex information and stay calm. A traffic controller needed to think and not panic. He tried to switch on the focus and concentration that served him on the job, but this was his daughter here, this was his daughter's life at risk.

He took a deep breath, felt his heart calm. "I'm listening."

"Malika is going to be just fine if you do what I ask you to do. First, you need to go home and make sure your wife behaves."

"Behaves?"

"Yes, John. Your wife is unpredictable. She does not obey you the way a good Muslim woman should. When you get home, you need to make absolutely certain she calls no one. E-mails no one. Make absolutely sure she does not panic and bring in the police or the FBI. This will get your daughter killed. Do you understand me, John?"

John swallowed. His throat felt like sandpaper.

"John?"

"Yes," he croaked.

"What do you understand? Tell me."

"No police. No FBI."

"Good. Very good. We had an arrangement. A deal. You promised me, John, and you broke that promise. I no longer trust you, which is why I have your daughter with me. You love your daughter, don't you, John?"

"Let me talk to her."

"In time, John. In time. Here are your instructions. You are to go directly home. Keep your wife calm. You will go to work as usual tomorrow morning. Governor Stark has a rally in the morning. His plane will be flying in early. As soon as you have their flight path, you will call me with the time and location and GPS coordinates of where I will be able to have early visual contact. Do you understand me, John?"

"I don't—"

"Do you understand me, John?"

"I—I—yes, I understand you."

"Tell me what you understand, John."

"As soon as I have the flight path for Governor Stark's plane, I'm to call you and tell you the time, location, and coordinates of where you will first be able to see the plane."

"Good, John. And that is all. Once I have done what I came here to do, I will return your daughter to you unharmed. Are we clear on that, John? I will not return her after you make your call. I will return her after I have accomplished my mission. That means that your information must be accurate and reliable. It means that you must continue what you are doing and not alert law enforcement or anyone else what is about to happen."

"I don't know what you're going to do. I don't understand how this information is useful to you."

"You don't need to know, John."

"If I knew what you were going to do, maybe there's something I could do to help now."

"No, John. There isn't. You'll do what I ask. No more. No less. Understand me? No more. No less."

"Yes. I understand."

"Be sure that you do."

John swallowed. "I want to talk to Malika."

"Of course."

Traffic sped by. John realized he had unconsciously slowed as he concentrated on the phone call. He eased his foot down on the gas, sliding back into the stream of traffic.

"Daddy?"

"Malika? Are you okay?"

"Y-yes. But I'm scared."

"It'll be okay, honey. Do what Mr. Kalakar tells you to do and you'll be home tomorrow."

"Tomorrow?"

"Yes, honey."

"I want to come home now."

Her voice quavered with fear, tearing at his heart. "I want you home now, too, honey, but we have to do what Mr. Kalakar wants and everything will be all right. Okay?"

Silence. John strained his ears for background noise, but heard nothing. "Okay, honey?" he repeated.

Kalakar's voice came back on the phone. "You see, John? Your daughter is just fine. And she'll stay fine just as long as you cooperate and do what you're told to do. Keep your cell phone charged. I'll contact you again before tomorrow."

"Okay. Yes. Don't hurt her."

"If you do what is asked of you, your daughter will be returned unharmed. But John?"

John felt his throat close. Something about Kalakar's tone, his words, promised a threat. "Yes?"

"Fail me, John, and I'll mail your daughter to you in pieces."

CHAPTER 47

Derek and O'Reilly's concerns about entering the Avco Center turned out to be unfounded. The twelve-story office building was open and all they had to do was sign in at the desk. Confusing the issue somewhat, a nearby theater was called the AMC Avco Center. There apparently was a movie premier playing there tonight, and crowds were already starting to gather, complete with red carpet and limousines.

Parking several blocks away, they walked into the building. O'Reilly flashed her credentials to the security guard and scribbled something un-readable on the sign-in sheet. The guard wasn't paying much attention. Earbuds from an iPod were plugged in and so was he, bopping along to some hip-hop tune of recent vintage.

They slipped into the elevator and punched the button for the eleventh floor. Derek noted that the Pakistan Consulate was on the top floor, twelve. He wondered, not for the first time, about the connection between Kalakar, who was Pakistani, the Pakistan Consulate, and the law firm of Jamieson, Perzada, Sulieman and Hill. There were plenty of other businesses in the Avco Center, and it was in downtown L.A., so it was possible it was only a coincidence. Derek wasn't a big believer in coinci-dence, although he generally followed the axiom: it's not a coincidence unless it is.

They got off on the eleventh floor and walked the length of the hall-way, checking to see who was here and who was not. In addition to the offices of Jamieson, Perzada, Sulieman and Hill, which took up most of the floor, there was a commercial real estate office and the offices of a medical-billing firm. If there was anybody still in the offices, it wasn't ob-vious. The floor seemed dead.

The plaque beside the law office's door said:

Jamieson, Perzada, Sulieman and Hill
Attorneys at Law
International Entertainment, Representation, Contracts

Derek murmured, "*Sssshhhoooooowwww bizness.*" He reached out and tried the door. Sure enough, locked. So much for the World According to John Grisham. Derek wondered if he'd ever written about Hollywood lawyers. Maybe not.

O'Reilly pulled a handful of picks from her pocket. "Stand back, unless you want to do it."

"You're going to use picks?"

"Yes. Why? Were you planning on kicking the door down?"

"No. I usually use a power rake."

"Noisy. This is quiet. And elegant."

She went to work on the locks. The reason Derek used a power rake, sometimes called an electronic lock pick, for his occasional B&E in the name of national security, was he couldn't pick locks worth a damn. It was a skill he'd never mastered.

In less than a minute O'Reilly had the door open. Derek cocked his head. "Nice."

"I've got skills."

"Apparently."

"After you."

"I guess I've got skills, too. I make a good target in case there's someone inside there."

"Lead with your strengths, Derek."

He slipped inside the door. The lobby lights were still on. It was large and square with leather chairs and glass coffee tables, the walls covered with photographs of celebrities, many of whom Derek recognized, many that he didn't. On one wall were photographs of the partners and staff. Derek studied them.

He said, "I'm going to check out Lawrence Perzada's office. You suppose Lawrence is his real first name?"

O'Reilly checked the photograph. Lawrence Perzada was clearly Pakistani or Indian. She said, "Might be Americanized. I'm going to hunt around and see if I can find personnel records, see what we can find out about Abdul Mohammed. Although it's doubtful there'll be a line on his résumé saying, 'procurer of suitcase nukes.'"

Derek nodded. The lobby transitioned into an open space of cubicles. He guessed it was for junior attorneys, paralegals, and secretaries. Off to the right angled a hallway that appeared to be conference rooms, mailroom, and storage. To the left another hallway seemed to host offices. He went left. O'Reilly went right.

Three doors down an office with a closed door had a single plaque saying:

Lawrence Perzada, Esq., Partner
International Entertainment

Derek considered that for a moment. Hollywood films were international. They were distributed throughout the world, often shot throughout the world with actors from around the world. When a film was shot on location in Morocco or Egypt or Russia or England or Pakistan, often at least part of the crew—the gaffers, best boys, key grips, and all the other esoterica of filmmaking—was hired from the countries where they were shooting.

And vice versa, he supposed—international films got distributed or shot in the U.S. as well. An attorney with expertise in this area would be invaluable to the film industry.

He checked the door and found it unlocked. He stepped into a plush office with windows looking west. Derek spied a tiny sliver of the Pacific Ocean, but mostly he saw skyline, lit up. It was a good, if not exactly spectacular, view.

Flicking on the office light, he studied the room. Large maple desk cluttered with manila file folders. A large computer monitor. A butter-colored leather chair. Two client chairs and at one end of the office, a seating arrangement of glass coffee table, two chairs, and a sofa. A vase of lilies rested on the coffee table.

A door led to a private bathroom complete with shower. A small closet revealed a blue suit, a pair of shoes, socks, three white dress shirts, and two ties. Backup business clothes.

The wall was covered with photographs. From what Derek could tell, they were of Perzada with a variety of movie notables: Mel Gibson,

Angelina Jolie, George Lucas and Steven Spielberg, George Clooney, and a bevy of people Derek didn't recognize.

He sat down at the desk, booted up the computer, and while it warmed up, studied a massive old-fashioned Rolodex. Derek began to go through it, card by card, starting with *A*.

Most of the cards seemed to be contacts in the international film business. There were directors and producers and attorneys and distributors and technical crews and caterers and hiring organizations in a variety of countries: Pakistan, India, Russia, England, France, China, Germany, Poland—the list went on. Nothing really caught his eye until the letter *C*.

Chughtai, Faiz Hasan.

Under the name was a telephone number and the notation: Vice Consul, Pakistan, L.A.

Derek blinked. He found a blank Rolodex card and scribbled down the information. He proceeded through the Rolodex, but nothing else struck him. He was about to focus on the computer when O'Reilly appeared at the door. "Anything?"

He told her what he had discovered.

"Shit. That's bad. Diplomatic immunity and all that bullshit."

"It definitely makes things more complicated. You find anything?"

"Not really. I found some personnel records and there's a file for Abdul Mohammed, but there's nothing useful in it. I made a copy of it."

Derek held out his hand. She gave it to him. "Want me to take a look at the computer?"

Derek nodded. He crossed over to the leather sofa and read through the employment history of Abdul Mohammed. Apparently he had graduated high school in Pakistan, joined the Army where he served for three years. He then rattled around Pakistan for a few years, working as a laborer, truck driver, carpenter, and then, a two-year period of unemployment. A year ago he came to the U.S. under a temporary work visa and was hired under the recommendation of Lawrence Perzada and brought into the mailroom at the firm.

There was a single evaluation written by someone named Gerald Koughman, saying Abdul's work performance was "adequate" and noting frequent absences. A note suggested that Abdul Mohammed's strong suit was his willingness to do whatever was asked of him, hinting that Abdul was more of a gofer than anything else. He apparently worked in the mailroom, ran errands, did a little bit of light chauffeuring when needed, and otherwise was an unspectacular employee.

O'Reilly had photocopied a photograph that had been included in the file. It showed a swarthy man with a round face, close-cropped black hair, and dark, sunken eyes. There was something not quite right about his expression, a blankness or dullness, but Derek couldn't decide if that was the bad reproduction or something inherent in the man.

He finished reading and watched O'Reilly frowning at the computer. Standing, he began studying the photographs on the wall. Lawrence Perzada had been around the world for his job, apparently. He stood with an actor that seemed familiar to Derek from The Mummy movies, the Egyptian pyramids in the background. Another photograph shaking hands with someone who looked like Brad Pitt, but it was a fuzzy photograph. Someplace in Mexico, maybe?

He moved on and suddenly froze. The air felt icy in his chest.

The photograph before him was different than most of the others. It was of six men in olive-colored military uniforms. They stood in a row, rifles in their arms. Studying the photograph, Derek identified Perzada, much younger, second from the right. On his right, big arm draped over Perzada's shoulder, was Abdul Muhammed. Studying Muhammed's face, Derek noted the big grin but also the odd vapid expression. He wondered if Muhammed had been learning disabled or had some other disability.

But it was the man on the far left that had caught his attention.

Kalakar, otherwise known as Miraj Mohammad Khan.

Derek carefully took the photograph off the wall. "O'Reilly, you got a digital camera?"

She glanced up from the computer. "On my phone. Why?"

He walked over, removing the photograph from the frame. He laid it on the desk. She gaped at it.

"We need a really clear photograph here. We need to send this to our people in Pakistan and get IDs on these people ASAP."

CHAPTER 48

FBI Agent Dale Hutchins sat at his kitchen table watching the news on TV and drinking coffee. His wife, Teh, was still showering, getting ready for work at the U.S. Embassy. He hadn't had a good night's sleep. His mind was very much on the various attacks ongoing in the United States. The attacks in the U.S. were at the top of the TV news cycle, but not a lot of hard information was offered. From what he understood, there had been four, with a fifth still being anticipated in New York City.

It made him feel like their raid on the cell's apartment and the subsequent death of the new guy, Jason Barnes, had been a waste.

He also hadn't slept well because his body ached, and because he had received what seemed like one of the most bizarre telephone calls of his entire career. It had woken him up from his restless sleep at four in the morning. It had been the officious sounding voice of a woman with a Brooklyn accent saying, "Agent Dale Hutchins? Please wait for a direct phone call from U.S. Secretary of Homeland Security James Johnston."

He jerked upright in bed, confused and a little alarmed. He had struggled to pull his shit together, but felt like he wasn't doing a very good job of it. His ass ached, his vision was blurry, and his mouth tasted like the cat had used it as a litter box. After a moment the rough voice of Secretary Johnston came on the line. "Agent Hutchins, Sam Sherwood tells me you're the man to talk to regarding the raid on the apartment a few weeks ago."

"Uh, yes sir."

"I'm sorry for this call. It's what, about four in the morning there?"

Peering at the digital alarm clock, Hutchins nodded. He was sitting on the edge of his bed in his boxer shorts. Teh muttered in her sleep and rolled over. She was used to phone calls at odd hours, and was able to sleep through them. "Yes sir. What can I do for you, sir?"

"I've got one of my troubleshooters working with a START team in Los Angeles. He's got an idea that this attack in the port earlier is some sort of ruse or something, and he wants to speak with you personally about the raid."

"Sir?" Hutchins was confused, and it wasn't just because it was four a.m.

Johnston's sigh sailed over the phone line. "The troubleshooter's name is Dr. Derek Stillwater. He'll call you. Maybe. He's got your cell number, too. Derek's a bit of a maverick, but he's got excellent instincts and Homeland Security would greatly appreciate your cooperation on this. Agent Sherwood assures me you're the man. And in case you were wondering, Agent Hutchins, I have discussed this with the director."

"Okay, sir. Do you know when, uh, Agent Stillwater will call?"

Johnston snorted or laughed or something, Hutchins wasn't sure which. "I wish I did, Agent Hutchins. Derek's rather unpredictable. I don't know exactly what his concerns are, but like I said, I trust him, so thank you for your cooperation."

"I'll do everything I can, sir."

"I know you will, and again thank you."

Secretary Johnston had hung up and Hutchins had sat there blinking at the phone like an owl, wondering what kind of juice this Derek Stillwater had to get the secretary himself on the phone to an agent in Pakistan?

And now, three hours later, still no word from Dr. Derek Stillwater. The name had been vaguely familiar to Hutchins. He logged onto the FBI database and quickly realized why. Stillwater had a mixed relationship with the bureau. He had been under investigation for collusion with a terrorist group, and for the alleged murder of a Russian national. Later, he had been involved with a high-level cover-up. Congressional hearings had been called behind closed doors, but he had done something heroic and impossible at the G8 Summit debacle where terrorists had infiltrated the summit and kidnapped twenty world leaders, so apparently Stillwater had been cleared of whatever charges had been leveled at him.

Tehreema appeared, and like he always did when he saw her, Dale thought she was the most beautiful woman in the world. She brushed her long black hair away from her face and said, "You look tired. Bad night?"

His cell phone chirped. Holding up a hand to his wife, he answered it, identifying himself. The voice was strong, American, a little ironic, and seemed excited. "Hutchins, this is Derek Stillwater, with Homeland Security. I—"

"Secretary Johnston called to tell me you might be calling—" Hutchins couldn't help himself. He added, "—over three hours ago."

"Yeah. Sorry. Some things came up. Look, you have an e-mail address?"

"Of course."

"I'm going to e-mail you a photograph right now. Tell me when you get it."

Hutchins, puzzled, rattled off his e-mail address. Tehreema shot him a quizzical look and he shrugged.

Stillwater: "Okay, we've sent it now. Hopefully it'll get there in a couple minutes. It's a photograph of six guys in the Pakistan Army. One of them is Kalakar. One of them is an entertainment attorney out here in L.A. One of them is a guy named Abdul Mohammed. He's dead, murdered. He was working in the lawyer's office, but he came to our attention and the LAPD's attention because he was wandering around trying to convince somebody to acquire a suitcase nuke for him."

"What!"

"As far as we can tell, he never even came close to getting one. There's something— I get the impression Abdul Mohammed was a little slow. Retarded or something, or learning disabled. Something. Just an impression. He was sort of a gofer for this attorney, whose name is Perzada. Anyway, we need you to see if you can identify the three other men in the photograph. Find out who they are, where they are, what they're doing now. Find family members, anybody who might be in the U.S."

"Okay." Hutchins headed for the spare bedroom where they kept a computer. He clicked it on, impatiently waiting for the system to boot. When the system came up, he accessed the Internet and checked his e-mail. The file hadn't arrived yet.

"Stillwater," he said. "I need contact information for you."

Stillwater rattled it off.

"I understand there's already been an L.A. attack."

"Yeah, but Kalakar's still running around. He shot an FBI agent just a couple hours ago."

"You're sure it was him?"

"Positive. And this is weird, but he had a little girl, maybe ten years old, with him. When I saw them she was crying."

"You saw them?"

"Yeah."

"Weird."

"Yeah. You've apparently found out more about Kalakar than anybody else. Does he have a daughter?"

"Not as far as I know. We'll dig a little deeper on that. But you think he'd be dragging his daughter around on something like this?"

"You wouldn't think so, but al-Qaeda isn't that predictable. They've done some strange shit."

"Yeah, I hear that." Hutchins checked the e-mail again. This time the file had appeared. He clicked on the attachment and studied the photograph. He recognized Kalakar. He didn't recognize the two men tagged as Perzada and Muhammed. There was something oddly familiar about one of the other men, but he didn't know why.

"I got the photograph. Any idea when it was taken?"

"None. Except you've got the dates Kalakar was in the service, right?"

"Right. That'll narrow it down. Hey, Stillwater."

"What?"

"I've been working with a local cop on this, Firdos Moin. He was just saying yesterday that there was some sort of military connection here. I'll show this to him. We'll get right on it."

"Thanks."

"And Stillwater, watch your ass, all right?"

"Thanks." He clicked off.

Tehreema stood over Hutchin's shoulder, looking at the photograph. "Who are those men?"

Dale pointed at Kalakar and explained who he was. Tehreema pointed at another man. "He looks familiar."

"To me, too."

She tapped the computer screen. "And this guy, that's Faiz Chughtai. He's Vice Consul in Los Angeles. A lot younger than he is now, but I recognize him. I met him at an embassy party several years ago."

"One down, two to go, then. Thanks honey." He burned the image to a disk, dumped it to a flash drive just in case, kissed Tehreema goodbye, and headed into the office. On the way, he called Frito to tell him he needed him at the office ASAP.

CHAPTER 49

The Brotman Medical Center in Culver City was surrounded by satellite news vans. Derek and O'Reilly shot each other worried looks. The media had to be there because of Shelly. Finding a parking space, they slipped into the emergency room, and were instantly caught by their former START partner, Jon Welch. Welch's face looked gray. He was leaning against a wall, looking down a hallway as the bureau SAC, Black, held a press conference.

He blinked at the two of them. "Thought you guys were decommissioned and sent home."

Derek shrugged.

Welch's mouth twitched in response, not quite a smile. "Yeah, I figured. Dog with a fucking bone. You hear about Shelly?"

"I was the one who called the EMTs," Derek said.

Welch met his gaze. After a moment he shook his head. "She died on the table, man. I'm sorry."

O'Reilly made a little sound, a grunt, a gasp, a cry, something. Derek felt his stomach roll. A wave of black rage swept through him. And guilt. He had promised to take care of her and it hadn't happened. If only—

"Ah, shit."

Derek reached out and put his arm over O'Reilly's shoulder. For a moment she leaned into him. He murmured, "Sorry. Sorry, sorry, sorry. Dammit."

Welch said, "Shit bad luck, Sandy. I know you're taking heat for this op, but far as I can tell, there isn't a START in the bunch that's done any good. Givenchy and I fucked up good. We were only a couple hours behind those pricks at the port."

O'Reilly stood up straight, moving away from Derek's embrace. "I know, Jon. You guys did your best under the circumstances. Damn. Shelly—"

Welch nodded. "She's Bureau. She's family. We're on it now. Everybody's looking for Kalakar." He focused on Derek. "Ford F150. Color?"

"Red."

"Year?"

Derek shrugged. "Recent. Had a cap on the back. They find anything in the storage unit?"

"Wooden crate, empty."

"How big?"

Welch shrugged. "About six feet long, foot or two square. Could've been damned near anything in it. Label on the box connects it to a movie production company that's nothing more than a UPS Store mailbox. We've got people on it. Lab guys are all over it. No signs of radiation whatsoever, much to everyone's relief, but we still don't know what was in it." His gaze shifted down the hallway. "Looks like Black's press moment's over. You guys might want to get out of here before he sees you, if I understand the politics right."

Derek held out his hand. "Thanks, Jon."

Welch shook it. "Good luck."

Derek, behind the wheel of the rented Pathfinder, said, "This sucks."

O'Reilly nodded. "I liked Shelly. She surprised me. She was all over—" She trailed off, lost in thought.

Derek cocked his head. "What? She was all over what?"

"Who. Not what."

With a sigh, Derek splayed his hands. "Hello? Remember me? What are you talking about?"

Slowly O'Reilly said, "She was all over Ibrahim Sheik Muhammad. You know, Derek, he's someone we might want to talk to again. That or try and talk to Lawrence Perzada. Everything's intersected with the two of them."

"Any idea where Perzada lives?"

She shook her head. She pulled out her laptop and tried to find a home address for the attorney, but not surprisingly it wasn't listed. Derek just drove, pulling through the window of a fast-food chain selling quasi-

Mexican food. They ordered some burritos and Cokes. He headed vaguely in the direction of Pasadena, but at the moment they had no real destination.

O'Reilly shut the laptop. "No luck on the net. There are ways to dig up that information through official channels, but since we already know where Ibrahim Sheik Muhammad lives, let's go talk to him again."

Derek nodded and asked for directions.

CHAPTER 50

It didn't take Kalakar long to decide that kidnapping the little girl had been a bad idea. A very bad idea.

From the simplest point of view, he wasn't very accustomed to children. He had an older brother, but they had not spoken in years. His brother was married and had three children, whom he had never met. His brother Sayid, a successful chef in Islamabad, was not a supporter of al-Qaeda. Sayid was, in Kalakar's eyes, an infidel, a Muslim who had given up his religion; who had turned his back on Allah.

Kalakar had been in love really only once in his entire life, with a woman in Afghanistan, but she had died during a skirmish between the Taliban and U.S. troops. Before her death Kalakar almost considered marrying her and returning to Pakistan to pursue the quiet life of an art history professor. His future had balanced on a knife's blade before fragments from a mortar had killed his beloved Farishta. Kalakar had fallen, or been pushed, into this life, this hatred of the Americans, into his belief in the glory of the jihad.

But sometimes he thought of Farishta and the life that he might have had, of the children he and Farishta would have raised in the light of Islam.

The first problem with Malika was she wouldn't be quiet. She had cried and screamed as they left the storage facility. He would not admit it to her—didn't want to admit it to himself—but when he had struck her and she had collapsed, he thought he had killed her. And he had felt relief. He had thought: *now I won't have to deal with the little brat any more.*

He had hated himself for that. He was not a child killer. He was a soldier of Islam, a jihadist.

Once she stopped crying and screaming, Malika had shifted into a sullen pout, which unfortunately only lasted a few minutes as Kalakar drove around Los Angeles considering his options. Once she had adjusted to the new reality, she had started badgering him with questions about the woman he had shot, about the box in the back of the truck, about why he was keeping her from her parents, about why he had lied to her.

He had finally glared at her and said, "Shut up or I'll hit you again."

She stuck out her lip, crossed her arms over her thin chest, and said nothing, tears leaking from her eyes. But at least she had shut up.

For a while.

"I have to pee."

He jerked his head. "What?"

"I have to pee. I have to go to the bathroom."

Kalakar ground his teeth. What was he going to do with her? He didn't even want to think about the risk of checking into a motel for the night. He would have to tie and gag her and someone would see them go into the hotel. It was a huge risk.

The operation had not made room for this kind of improvisation.

"Hold it," he said.

"I have to go now."

He sighed and started looking for a gas station. When he finally found one he thought would be suitable, he pulled up as close to the rest rooms as he possibly could. He took her arm and squeezed, enough to hurt her a little, to make sure she was paying attention. Making his voice hard and threatening, he said, "If you scream, if you bring any attention to yourself, I will kill you. Do you understand me? I will take the gun and shoot you in the head. If you cooperate with me, you'll be back with your parents by lunchtime tomorrow. But if you become a problem, I will kill you."

She began to cry. He shook her gently, but hard enough to get her attention. "You must calm down. Get control of yourself."

She cried harder, clutching her school backpack.

Kalakar blinked. He wanted to hit her. He wanted to shake her hard and bash her head against the window. Why was she making this so difficult?

Softening his voice, he said, "Malika, you need to be strong. Do you understand? We are on a mission from Allah and you are part of Allah's plan. You must be strong."

She hiccupped, clearly puzzled, but stopped crying, or at least stopped the edgy hysterics.

Kalakar stepped out of the truck and came around to her side. He opened her door and escorted her to the restroom. Opening the door, he looked inside at the filthy space and scowled. Disgusting. There was no outside window, only a vent fan.

"Go," he said.

She bit her lip. "I'm not going with you in here."

He glared at her. "If you have to go, you'll go."

She crossed her hands over her chest. "Pervert. I'm going to scream and the police will come and lock you up. I'll scream that you're not my daddy and that you've kidnapped me and are trying to rape me."

Dear Allah, please help me! Kalakar begged.

"If you lock the door I will kick it in," he said. He closed the door and stood waiting outside. What was he going to do?

Flipping open his cell phone, he paused, trying to decide if this was a major mistake. But what choice did he have?

"It's Kalakar," he said when the phone was picked up. "I have a problem. I need a place to stay for the night that's safe and secure and I need a new vehicle. We need to meet."

"How about—"

"Don't say it. The same location we met before. At eighty thirty."

The voice on the phone hesitated. "Okay. Yes, that will work. Eight thirty."

"Good."

Kalakar hung up. He knocked on the bathroom door. "Hurry up in there."

Malika's voice said, "I'm going as fast as I can."

It made Kalakar smile, despite himself.

CHAPTER 51

Jon Welch, back at Brotman Medical Center, carried a box of Shelly Pimpuntikar's belongings out to his car. He had volunteered to catalog her personal belongings and to make sure they were delivered to her parents. SAC Black was going to call her parents—and he wouldn't be surprised if the director made a call as well—but Welch had collected her gun, her briefcase, her cell phone, her car keys, and purse and was going to make sure they got to her parents. They deserved that at the very least.

Sitting in his car in the parking lot of the medical center, he carefully checked everything. Placing Shelly's briefcase on the seat next to him, he flipped it open. He took in its contents: tons of paper, yellow legal pads, pens, a pocket calculator, file folders, maps, extra ammunition for her handgun, a PDA, and what looked like a small radio. He picked it up, curious, not completely sure what it was. It didn't look like a cell phone or a BlackBerry. Welch clicked the switch to on.

Static burst from the tiny speaker, followed by voices. They weren't speaking in English. He wasn't sure if it was Urdu or Arabic or Farsi. What the hell?

After a moment, he was able to separate out two distinct voices, both men. Suddenly a phone rang.

One voice, deeper, accented, clicked a button. "Hello?"

Apparently they had put the phone on speaker. A heavily accented voice said, "It's Kalakar. I have a problem. I need a place to stay for the night that's safe and secure and I need a new vehicle. We need to meet."

Welch's heart beat in his chest. What was this?

The first man's voice said: "How about—"

Kalakar cut him off. "Don't say it. The same location we met before. At eight thirty."

There was a pause in the conversation during which Welch heard rustling sounds, as if the two men in the room were moving around. Finally the first man said: "Okay. Yes, that will work. Eight thirty."

Kalakar: "Good."

Welch heard a clack as the phone was disconnected. Silence for a moment, then the two men began to speak to each other in whatever language they had been speaking in and Welch felt like smashing the radio receiver beneath his heel.

Ears straining, he heard the conversation come to an end and what sounded like the two men leaving the room.

Welch checked his Timex. It was 7:21. He reached for his phone.

CHAPTER 52

Derek was driving when O'Reilly's phone rang. He heard her listen for a moment then say, "Jesus. That's a bug she put in the office of Ibrahim Sheik Muhammad in Pasadena."

Derek raised an eyebrow.

After a longer moment during which O'Reilly listened to the caller: "No, Jon, it's not fucking legal. But the person who placed it there's dead. That's a gray area— Really? Eight thirty?"

She pulled out a notebook and rattled off an address. "Yes. Meet us there."

She clicked off and told Derek, "The imam's meeting Kalakar somewhere at eighty thirty." Reaching over to the Pathfinder's GPS, she typed in the address.

"Shelly bugged this guy's office? Illegally?"

O'Reilly related the story. Derek laughed. "Everybody's on my case for the way I bend the rules—"

"—more like disregard them."

"—and you're a damned accessory to a major breach in privacy that was conducted by an FBI agent." He shook his head, amused, but only a little.

She described the phone call Jon Welch had overheard. Derek nodded. "He knows somebody saw the truck. He's ditching it. But—"

His eyes on the GPS unit, Derek took a turn. "What?" O'Reilly asked.

"Kalakar's improvising."

She thought about it. Finally, she said, "Maybe just because he didn't expect to run into Shelly."

"Maybe. Maybe something else. Like the little girl."

"You think he's hauling a daughter around with him? Or what?"

"I have no clue."

It was the first time Derek had seen the imam's home. Even by Pasadena standards—or maybe especially by Pasadena standards—he was impressed.

As they drove by the front gate, the gate ground open, and a black Mercedes SUV pulled out of the drive. O'Reilly turned her head away.

"That's them," she said. "The guy in the passenger seat is the imam."

"Got it." Derek kept driving, watching the Mercedes in the rearview mirror. His heart sank. What the hell?

As Imam Ibrahim Sheik Muhammad and Sayid Zaheer Abbas approached the gate, the imam saw a Nissan Pathfinder with two people in the front seat pass slowly by. On any given day the imam was paranoid; even if he weren't a supporter of al-Qaeda he believed the Americans kept an eye on him because he was Pakistani and because he was an imam. So he paid attention to his surroundings—even more so in the last twenty-four hours, especially after the port attack and after his middle-of-the-night visit from the FBI and the ODNI.

And he was absolutely certain that the ODNI bitch, the blonde, was in the passenger seat of the Pathfinder. He reached out and caught Sayid's elbow. "Stop. Stop. Stop the car."

Sayid hit the brakes hard. Both men jerked against their shoulder harnesses.

"What is it?"

"Did you see that Pathfinder? The black one?"

Sayid shrugged.

Sheik Muhammad stroked his beard, thinking. "You have your cell phone on you?"

"Of course."

"Stay right here. Right here." He slipped out of the Mercedes and ran—ran! How long had it been since he had actually run? His heart beat hard in his chest and his knees protested and he felt awkward and old. He let himself into his garage and climbed into his other vehicle, a white Cadillac, and headed down toward the gate. On his phone he clicked

Sayid's number. "That Pathfinder has federal agents in it. They will follow one of us. We have to lose them. Stay in touch."

"Yes."

"Go."

They weren't coming out, Derek thought. What the hell was going on? He slid the Pathfinder to the curb, eyes fixed on the rearview mirror.

O'Reilly turned to watch out the rear window. "You think they saw us?"

Derek shrugged. He didn't know what to think. There was no reason to believe the imam knew him, but he'd probably remember the blonde female federal agent who woke him up in the middle of the night.

"Huh," he said, eyes wide in surprise.

The Mercedes nosed out of the driveway and rolled in their direction. Derek waited, ready to follow.

"What the hell?" O'Reilly sounded a little bit freaked out.

The white Cadillac pulled out after the black Mercedes and turned in the opposite direction.

The Mercedes passed them and O'Reilly said, "That's the driver. Go after the Cadillac! Go! Shit! Go!"

Derek spun the wheel and goosed the gas, did a U-turn and chased after the white Cadillac.

CHAPTER 53

Dale Hutchins sat back in his chair at the FBI office in Islamabad and sipped black coffee out of a blue FBI mug. It was hot and strong. One of the other agents had brought in some specialty coffee, not one of those froufrou flavors like mocha-vanilla-caramel-bean, but a rich premium roast of some sort, and he was hooked. He shifted in his chair, then stood up to pace. His butt hurt this morning—probably from extended car travel and desk duty the day before.

He had uploaded the image into his work computer and was staring at it, trying to scratch the itch in his brain that told him he should know who one of those men was.

Firdos strode in, a smile on his face. Firdos wore khaki slacks and a white dress shirt, no tie. His dark skin contrasted sharply with the starched, crisp whiteness of the shirt. "Hang on," he said, gesturing to the mug in his hand. "Is that Bernie's coffee?"

With a grin, Hutchins nodded.

With a rueful shake of his head, Firdos said, "I'm addicted," and aimed for the break room and the Braun coffee maker.

Two minutes later Firdos was back. "You're not sitting down."

"A little sore today. This job is literally a pain in the ass."

Firdos laughed. "Indeed. What's all the fuss?"

Hutchins brought up the image on the computer. He tapped the computer screen, pointing at each image as he introduced them. "Kalakar. An entertainment lawyer now in L.A. named Perzada. A now-dead guy named Abdul Mohammed who was asking around about a suit-case nuke before someone slashed his throat. Now this guy looks sort of familiar but—"

Firdos, face twisted in concern, glanced over his shoulder to make sure no one was watching, then reached out and snapped off the monitor. "Who's seen this?"

Hutchins, coffee mug halfway to his mouth, said, "Frito, you're scaring me."

"Delete this off your office computer. Now. Do you have backup?"

"Yes. What the—"

Firdos gestured at the computer. "Do it. Quickly."

More than a little confused, Dale sat down with a wince and turned the monitor back on, deleted the image from his office computer and pulled the flash drive from the UBS port. Turning, he said, "Frito, what's—"

Firdos snatched the flash drive from his hand and turned on his heel. "Come on. Let's get out of here. We have to talk somewhere private."

Hutchins and Firdos walked between giant beds of roses at the Rose and Jasmine Garden. Bumblebees floated by. Hutchins spotted hummingbirds flitting among the flowers. The air was heavy with the mixed scent of roses and jasmine. Three years ago he had proposed to Tehreema here.

The setting was pleasant, but he was puzzled and getting a little angry. Firdos hadn't said a word. He'd led him to his car and driven in a haphazard route through the city, doubling back, constantly checking his rearview mirror. Hutchins was no fool. Firdos was either trying to lose a tail or make sure they weren't under surveillance.

But from whom? Every time he'd asked a question, Firdos had shushed him.

Finally Firdos stopped by a particularly beautiful bed of yellow roses. "Where did you get that photograph?"

Hutchins told him. Firdos nodded, but his gaze flicked past him. Watchful. Paranoid?

"Firdos! What's going on?"

"The man you recognize is a young General Bilal Sharif."

It all came together. Hutchins cursed. "Oh, man."

Firdos nodded. President Tarkani might very well run the country and the military, but his primary adversary, both politically and in the military, was General Bilal Sharif. Sharif was a conservative Muslim who did not support Tarkani's cooperation with the U.S. after 9/11. But Sharif was too popular within the country for Tarkani to do anything overt about Sharif.

Glancing around again, Firdos said, "You know that we believe Sharif has been behind some of the assassination attacks on Tarkani. Indirectly."

"Yes." It was a given within the bureau that the attempts on Tarkani's life had been linked to political opposition within the government, not just by terrorists actively working within Pakistan.

Firdos raised his fist. It contained the flash drive. "Bilal Sharif was in the 16SP Artillery Regiment. I will try to identify the last man, but I must do it very, very carefully. You understand?"

Hutchins understood all too well. Pakistan could be a volatile country, particularly when you became mired in the quicksand that was internal politics within the military. Firdos's paranoia was justified.

Firdos clapped him on the shoulder. He began to walk back to his car. "I'll drop you off at your office. Please, don't start making inquiries about this. Word would get back to Sharif. If he is somehow connected to Kalakar, it would be very dangerous for both of us."

"You be careful, too."

Firdos nodded. He looked sad. He shook his head. "Bad business, my friend. Let's hope it's just a coincidence."

But he didn't look like he believed it.

CHAPTER 54

The smell was strong and familiar: rotting bodies. Derek gripped the steering wheel of the Nissan, knuckles going white. "Shit."

O'Reilly flashed him a sharp look. "What?"

He shook his head. Derek had lived with panic attacks for a long time, since the 1990s. Their triggers were unpredictable—he could go through periods of intense stress and not have any incident, and then have an attack while kayaking on Chesapeake Bay or working out at the gym. Although the triggers were inconsistent, the attacks weren't. They typically began with a sensory flashback, usually the odor of rotting bodies.

He had a large supply of images in his memory to support the smell: Kurds gassed to death by Saddam Hussein's soldiers in northern Iraq; digging up graves under cover of night in Pakistan; battlefield dead in Iraq; mass killings in Baltimore and Detroit and Colorado.

Derek blinked back the memories and struggled to bring his heart rate down. *Not now*, he thought.

O'Reilly gripped his bicep. "What's wrong?"

He struggled for air. Sweat beaded on his forehead. "Nothing. Where the hell is he going?"

Ibrahim Sheik Muhammad in the white Cadillac was turning off Del Mar Boulevard onto Orange Grove Boulevard. Trying to ignore his body and mind's rebellions, Derek glimpsed the black SUV in the rearview. "Damn, we've got a tail." At least, he thought so. It was tough tailing somebody in the dark.

O'Reilly got on the phone. "Jon, where are you?"

After a moment's silence, she said, "We're coming up on the Pasadena Museum of History. We're being followed. That's fine, but can you get in behind him? Good. I'll keep the line open."

To Derek she said, "Concentrate on Sheik Muhammad."

• • •

Sheik Muhammad, talking into his cell phone to his assistant Sayid Zaheer Abbas, said, "That's them, in the Nissan Pathfinder, right?"

"Yes. They did a U-turn and followed you."

Sheik Muhammad cursed. He thought for a moment. "I'll just drive around for a while. Let me think of something to do."

"I'll be here."

Jon Welch, in a Ford Taurus supplied by the local bureau, roared onto Fair Oaks and sped north. He hoped to intercept them on Walnut Street by the Old Pasadena Courtyard by Marriot if they turned onto Walnut; if they kept going on Orange Grove he could try to follow or intercept farther north.

Welch, sweating lightly in his summer-weight suit, felt like he had joined a play toward the end of the second act. He had thought O'Reilly was a totally by-the-book agent, so he was shocked to find that she and Shelly had been playing cowboy. But he'd be damned happy to defend their actions if they could be the ones to snatch Kalakar.

O'Reilly's voice in his ear: "Jon, he's turning east onto Walnut Street."

"I'm on it."

Derek's fingers felt stripped of flesh, as if only his bones clung to the steering wheel. His heartbeat hammered in his ears.

O'Reilly's voice seemed distant. "Derek? Are you all right?"

"Water?"

She scrounged through her Go Pack and handed him a bottle of water. Unscrewing the cap, he took a deep gulp, feeling a little better. As the white Cadillac turned the corner by the Pasadena Museum of History, Derek said, "We're blown."

"Just drive. We can always drag him in for questioning if we have to."

The Pasadena Museum of History was in a beautiful white mansion, Edwardian in design, on about two acres of manicured grass, palms, and ornamental trees. The grounds were flooded with dramatic lighting: the building appeared to glow. Sheik Muhammad seemed to be heading toward Old Pasadena, or perhaps the Playhouse District. Traffic was dense and slow.

O'Reilly studied a map on the GPS. "Stay on him. We're coming up on a big junction where one thirty-four crosses two ten. He's got a lot of options there."

Derek nodded. He sucked in deep breaths, trying to calm his nerves. His stomach churned.

Sayid Abbas, behind the Pathfinder, heard Sheik Muhammad say, "I'm getting on the two ten north. Follow me on. We've got to get rid of these people. I can't miss this meeting with Kalakar. Here's what I want you to do."

Sayid Abbas listened, nodding. When the imam was finished, Abbas leaned over and snapped open his briefcase, which lay on the passenger seat. He slid out his pride and joy, a Brugger & Thomet MP-9. It was considered to be the most compact machine pistol in the world, only thirty centimeters long with its stock collapsed.

Derek watched the imam's white Cadillac turn onto the ramp to the 210 and followed. Behind him, the Mercedes turned onto the ramp as well.

O'Reilly was on the phone, giving Jon Welch directions. The imam got in the right lane heading north, took it up to sixty-five miles per hour and stayed there. Clouds were starting to roll in from the west and night had completely fallen. Derek knew it would be hard to track the car in the dark.

He also had a bad feeling about things. To O'Reilly he said, "Tell Welch to get his ass in gear. I think—"

Sayid Abbas stomped on the gas. The Mercedes's V-8 engine chuckled with throaty power and the SUV surged ahead. Within moments he was alongside the Nissan Pathfinder. The driver glanced over at him. The passenger, a blonde woman, was talking.

Sayid Abbas floored it. The Mercedes SUV roared forward. He pulled ahead of the Pathfinder, then cut in, slamming his brakes.

Derek didn't finish his thoughts. The black SUV was alongside him. Glancing over, he saw the driver staring at him. Then the Mercedes leapt ahead.

O'Reilly said, "What the—"

Sweat rolled down Derek's forehead. A high-pitched tone whined in his ears. He fought to focus on the now and push aside his panic attack. He felt slow and unresponsive. Something was going—

He slammed his foot to the floorboards, brakes shrieking like a wounded animal. O'Reilly cursed, clutching the armrest. Derek's elbows locked, fighting the steering wheel, the black SUV skidding to a halt in front of them.

Jerking the wheel, he slid onto the shoulder. Behind him the sound of horns and brakes squealed.

They hit the guardrail. The Pathfinder shuddered and groaned. The sound of metal on metal split the air.

O'Reilly started to say something, but Derek reached out, caught her by the collar and slammed her sideways and down, leaning on top of her.

"Derek—"

The windshield exploded above their heads. Squares of safety glass filled the car, falling on their shoulders. The rattle of automatic weapons fire chattered around them. The SUV seemed filled with buzzing wasps.

Derek reached for his gun. "We've got to get out of here."

O'Reilly, still sprawled on the seat, kicked out at her door. "We're up against the guardrail. It'll have to be on your side."

Which was the side facing the shooter.

"Out the back! Hurry! I'll cover! On three. One." He gripped the door handle with his left hand, his Colt in his right. "Two."

Now out of the Mercedes, Sayid Abbas tossed aside the empty clip and slammed in another. The MP-9 could fire two hundred rounds a minute. The Pathfinder's windows were blown out, the front grill and hood and front left quarter-panel pocked with bullet holes. He doubted they were still alive. Yet—

Derek said, "Three!" and kicked the door open. He rolled out, slamming to the hard ground littered with safety glass. He vaguely heard O'Reilly scrambling over the seats into the back of the Pathfinder.

Continuing to roll, he aimed at the shooter, firing his Colt. The screech of tires rent the air.

•   •   •

Jon Welch blasted the Ford Taurus up and onto the 210. The cell phone pressed to his ear, he heard O'Reilly's voice cut out, followed by what sounded like a small explosion, cursing, then bumping and thumping as the phone fell—then the ominous sound of gunfire, like firecrackers over the cell phone connection.

The 210 looked like a parking lot. People were even climbing out of their vehicles to see what was going on. "Fucking idiots!" he snarled and veered over to the shoulder and began to weave around traffic.

Derek was certain he had hit the shooter. The dark-skinned man had bucked backward as if struck by a bullet. But Derek hadn't killed him. He was still coming.

Continuing his roll, Derek came up on his feet, firing as he ran. Behind him he heard more gunfire: O'Reilly, out of the Pathfinder.

The shooter seemed to take a deep breath. He was a good thirty-five feet away. It wasn't that easy to hit a moving target in the dark at that distance with a handgun, but Derek was sure he had hit him at least once. But the shooter was still upright, bringing the machine pistol around.

O'Reilly screamed, "Get down! Derek—"

Derek felt something clip his skull, followed almost simultaneously by the roar of gunfire. He was falling—

Sayid Abbas swept the barrel of the MP-9 toward the Pathfinder. The door exploded outward and he saw movement. But he also saw something toward the back of the vehicle. He couldn't hear the rounds being fired at him over the sound of his machine pistol, but he felt something strike his left shoulder and he jolted backward.

In the glow of distant headlights, he saw moisture on his shirt. Touching his chest, he felt hot, sticky liquid. He had been shot.

Turning his attention back to the Pathfinder, he sprayed the car again. Another shot struck him. He dropped to his knees. He felt cold. Weak. Pain radiated from his shoulder, from his hip. He glimpsed the driver of the Pathfinder, rolling onto his feet.

Struggling to bring the MP-9 around, he let off a burst. He could barely control the gun. The recoil forced his arm upward. He tried to drag in air. *Praise be Allah*, he thought. "Allah is great," he muttered.

The rumble of an engine caught his attention. Turning, he saw the headlights of a fast-moving car veer off the shoulder and race directly toward him.

O'Reilly saw Derek fall. She sprinted out from her cover behind the Pathfinder toward him. The shooter fired again, just one burst, and something bit at her arm. She staggered, returned fire, kept going. Off to her left headlights approached fast. It was going to run over both her and Derek.

"Derek!"

He didn't budge. He was crumpled in the road.

Springing toward him, she caught him by the shoulder and heaving with all her strength, rolled backward, bringing Derek's limp body with her.

The car, a Ford Taurus, clipped her and sent her and Derek tumbling to the pavement. The shooter, on his knees, raised his gun and fired a long burst directly into the Ford. It didn't stop the Taurus. It plowed right into the shooter, driving him back into the side of the black Mercedes SUV, crushing him between the two vehicles with a low-pitched crunch.

O'Reilly clutched Derek to her. There was blood everywhere, but she wasn't sure where it was coming from. He groaned. Alive!

She shook him gently. "Derek! Derek, speak to me!"

He opened his eyes and held a hand to his head. She saw the blood was coming from a groove in his scalp, just over his left brow. "You got lucky," she said.

"Ah, yeah, I guess." He struggled to sit up, then rested on one elbow. He closed his eyes. "Bad day."

"Sit tight." In the distance sirens rose into the air. Good. She gripped her Beretta and slowly approached the two cars. Five feet away, she saw that the shooter, a man of Pakistani or Arab descent in a blue suit, was crushed between the two vehicles, clearly dead.

Peering into the Ford Taurus, she tried to figure out who was behind the wheel. A figure was slumped forward, illuminated only by the dashboard lights, surrounded by the white billowing form of the car's airbag. She tugged at the passenger door. It opened and the interior dome light clicked on. She let out a gasp that sounded like air leaving a tire. It was Jon Welch. But the shooter's last fusillade had hit its mark. The FBI agent was dead.

CHAPTER 55

The EMTs treated Derek and O'Reilly in the back of the ambulance. They insisted that O'Reilly go to the hospital. Her wound wasn't life threatening, but it was more than a gouge, which is what Derek's head trauma was. They were more concerned about Derek's burns, and wanted him to go to the hospital for treatment as well. They were also concerned that the lucky shot to his head may have caused a minor concussion.

A parade of cops and FBI agents had spoken to them, but Derek was waiting for the other shoe to drop. FBI SAC Black stalked toward the ambulance. "Come out here, Stillwater."

With a sigh, Derek slid out onto the expressway. Above, news and traffic helicopters swarmed like bees. The press was everywhere, being held back by a legion of cops. Their camera lights blazed, turning the crime scene from night to artificial day.

Detective Stephen Connelly slipped out from behind the FBI SAC and before Derek could react, slipped handcuffs around Derek's left wrist.

"Ah, shit. That's not necessary."

Connelly looked sour. "You jumped off a fucking cliff to avoid talking to me. I've had enough chasing your bullshit. Hold up your right hand."

Special Agent-in-Charge Black's expression was as hard as concrete. "Do it or I'll shoot you myself. I've lost two agents today thanks to you."

Derek pulled away. "Don't try to pin their deaths on me, Black. I had nothing to do with it."

Black reached out and caught Derek by the throat. He was a big man with big hands. He squeezed hard enough to get Derek's attention. "I don't like you, Still—"

Derek yanked the other end of the cuff from Connelly's hand, spun it around and clicked it shut around the FBI SAC's wrist. Before Black could react, Derek reached in the agent's coat and gripped his gun, preventing him from reaching for it. He drove his knee into the FBI agent's ribs, bending him over.

Then Derek's world exploded into reds and yellows, then black.

Derek woke up in the back of a Grand Marquis. His hands were cuffed behind him. He was crumpled awkwardly on the seat. Struggling to a sitting position, he noted Detective Connelly in the driver's seat. He couldn't be sure, but he thought they were heading downtown.

Connelly held up three fingers. "How many fingers do you see?"

"Six."

Connelly barked a laugh. "You're a pain in the ass, Stillwater. You know that?"

"Yeah. What'd you hit me with?"

"Sap."

"Standard issue, huh?"

"What do you care? You assault the SAC. You got off easy. He was ready to put a round in your stupid head."

"I would argue that he assaulted me and I was just defending myself."

"If I hadn't stepped in you might be explaining your point of view to a judge."

"I guess I should thank you, huh?"

"You can thank me if you want. But it's just delaying matters. The bureau is going to have their turn with you. I convinced Black I would only need you for a couple hours, and then I would personally deliver you to him at his office."

"You're aware that this terrorist is still out there?"

"Yep." He pulled into a parking lot behind the Police Administration Building or PAB, LAPD headquarters. Connelly came around to the back door and opened it. "I brought you here to talk about Greg Popovitch. I'm very tempted to spend some time discussing Ishaq Mukhtar and a big shooting that went down on his boat at the marina, but it's not my case. You know anything about that, Stillwater? The reason I ask is, when we were going through Popovitch's things, we found Mukhtar's name and contact info in Popovitch's computer."

"Never heard of him." Derek met Connelly's gaze, but he felt something flutter in his chest. It would be bad to be connected to that mess.

"Uh-huh."

Connelly reached in, caught Derek's collar and dragged him from the car, intentionally slamming his head into the edge of the door. Derek grayed out for a moment and sagged against the Grand Marquis. "Nice. You're an amateur, Connelly. Anybody told you that lately?"

Connelly buried his fist in Derek's stomach. Derek folded and collapsed to the pavement, wretching.

Connelly leaned down. "It would be a shame if you never made it into interrogation."

Derek gasped out: "I'd like to make a phone call."

"I bet you would. For the record, I owe you that. We're even. Sort of."

Connelly reached down, caught the handcuff chain and yanked Derek to his feet by the cuffs. Derek's shoulders protested, but he decided it might be better to avoid getting beat up again today. Connelly led him into the PAB, into an elevator and up to the fifth floor. He left him in an interrogation room. On the detective's way out the door, Derek said, "You going to take the cuffs off?"

"No."

"I could use a drink. I prefer Diet Coke. Strong coffee would be good, too."

"Fuck you."

"I want to make a phone call."

"I'll be back."

And the door shut.

Derek almost felt relieved.

Derek couldn't tell what time it was or how much time had passed. He wished he'd noticed the car clock before Connelly had hauled him out of it. When about ten minutes had gone by and Connelly hadn't returned, he sighed, slipped to the edge of the molded plastic chair and tried to relax. He kicked off his shoes and consciously tried to relax his body, from the top of his head to the tip of his toes.

He took a deep breath and slipped his hands beneath his butt, beneath his thighs to behind his knees.

Now was the tricky part.

Staying relaxed, he leaned forward and slipped the handcuff chains beneath his left foot.

So far, so good. He was all tangled up like a bent hanger, but he was halfway there.

Deep breath, letting it out, he completed the task.

Now his hands were cuffed in front of him. He could check the time. It was 11:15. Later than he had thought.

Connelly pushed the door open and stared at him. "That was sort of impressive for a guy your size. Yoga?"

"Once upon a time. Mostly just martial arts."

"Kung fu, huh."

"Mixed. Plus, I'm getting older. I get a little creaky if I don't stay limber."

"I hear that. The mileage adds up."

Derek held up his wrists. "I'm not going anywhere, Connelly. Unlock me."

Connelly fished the key out of his pocket and unclasped the cuffs, pocketing them. "Coffee?"

"Please."

"Sugar? Cream? Or what passes for it?"

"Black."

Connelly disappeared and returned a few minutes later with two Styrofoam cups. Handing one to Derek, he seated himself on the opposite side of the Formica table, which wobbled alarmingly.

Derek took a sip. "How's O'Reilly?"

"No word. She took a shot to the upper shoulder. Might require anything from stitches to minor surgery. Frankly, from what I saw of that scene, you two are the luckiest sons of bitches on the planet."

Derek shook his head. "If Welch hadn't run over the shooter—what's his name, Abbas?—I'd be playing a harp right now."

"Or wielding a pitchfork, from what I can see. So, you feel guilty for being such a fuck-up then? You been getting people killed all day. You get Popovitch killed the same way?"

Derek took a gulp of the steaming, nasty-tasting coffee, felt the caffeine surge through his veins. After a moment he said, "Nice segue. Guess the foreplay's over and we're on to the questioning, huh?"

Connelly leaned forward and dropped a manila folder in front of Derek. "You might say that."

Derek cautiously flipped open the folder. In it were a dozen glossy photographs apparently lifted from a security camera. He recognized the Culver City storage facility. The first photograph showed a little girl in jeans, a T-shirt, and a headscarf, running. Her mouth was open and she looked terrified. Her eyes were wide, her expression panicked. Derek tried to remain cool, but he could feel the fear coming off her in waves.

The next photograph showed her closer to the camera. In this one she was looking over her shoulder. Behind her the front of a pickup truck was visible.

In the next photograph the truck was right behind her and a man was climbing from the driver's side. Derek studied the image. It was Kalakar. No doubt about it. No hat. Short-cropped dark hair. Dark features, mustache. He wore a long-sleeved denim shirt, jeans, and boots. There was a stain of some sort on the shirt—probably blood. He looked determined.

The little girl had spun to face him, but was blurry in the image, as if she was continuing to spin. Her fear was palpable.

Derek turned to the final photograph. In it, Kalakar had caught the little girl. He had just completed what looked like a backhand to her face. Her head was turned to the side, her expression one of shock and fear and pain. It was obvious from the way her body was tilting that the blow had knocked her off her feet. The photograph had caught her before she hit the ground.

Derek slid the photographs back in the folder and shot Connelly a questioning look. The detective leaned forward. "You could try saying thank you."

"Thank you. Where'd you get these?"

"A friend. The FBI's being stingy with what they distribute. Nobody's sure what to make of this little girl. Is she a relative of Kalakar? Was she with Agent Pimpuntikar? Was she in the wrong place at the wrong time? We don't fuckin' know."

"She wasn't with Agent Pimpuntikar," Derek said. "I talked to Shelly before she got there and she was alone. I'm sure of it."

"You think she's Kalakar's daughter? Or he's a pedophile or something?"

Derek shook his head. "I don't think so. And he's supposed to be al-Qaeda. Bringing along a daughter, especially one that young, would be very atypical."

"So wrong place at the wrong time."

Derek reopened the folder and studied the photograph. His brain was spinning like a tornado. "Or," he said slowly, "she's a hostage."

Connelly craned his neck, thinking about it. "A kidnapping. This Kalakar's got a lot on his plate. Why would he kidnap some kid? He a pervert?"

Derek shook his head and rolled his eyes. "Get off the pedophilia thing. If that were it, he probably would have run her over right there. He's in a storage facility getting whatever the hell he's getting—"

"—yeah, about that—"

"—and he's surprised by an FBI agent, there's a shootout, the agent dies, Kalakar maybe gets wounded, the girl runs from him. He chases her down, which makes sense, but why hit her and throw her back in the truck? I saw them just moment's later. The girl was alive, conscious, and crying. Something else is going on."

Connelly shrugged his shoulders, as if trying to loosen up. Finally, he said, "Kidnapping. Why take a hostage? Money?"

Leaning back in his cheap molded-plastic chair, Derek thought for a moment. "Not money, I don't think. Information? Maybe he's holding her to apply pressure to someone."

"For what?"

"I wish I knew."

Connelly nodded and jumped to his feet. "Hang tight. I've got somebody I want you to meet."

It was thirty minutes before the door opened again and Connelly walked through. Accompanying him was a heavyset woman with long, curly red hair, a fleshy face, and bifocals. Her age was hard to figure. The long hair made it tricky, but Derek guessed she was in her late forties. She was one of those heavy women with a big bust that appealed to a certain type of man; she wasn't unattractive, but she looked like she'd seen a bit more of the real world than was healthy. She was in a khaki suit and looked tired and more than a little annoyed.

"Derek Stillwater, Homeland Security, this is Betty Andine, Juvenile Crimes."

Derek shook hands with the woman. She had the manila folder. She dropped it in front of him on the table and flipped it open. There was an additional photograph. It was a close-up of the little girl. She pointed to it. "How good a likeness is this?"

Derek shrugged. "Good, I guess. The expression makes it hard to tell."

"This Kalakar, he's Pakistani, right?"

"Yes."

"And the girl probably is, too."

Derek studied the photograph again and shrugged. "I can't tell. Why do you think so?"

"The headscarf. She's Muslim, but she's otherwise dressed modern. There's a lot of variation and it's not a given, but Pakistani Muslim girls and women aren't quite as rigid as the Arabs and some Persians about following the dress code. Otherwise it's a guess."

Derek nodded. "Okay."

"How old?"

"I'm not the best judge, but I figured ten, maybe nine or eleven."

"You're a good judge. That's my guess, too." Betty Andine stood up straight. "I think I might be able to identify this little girl if she goes to school in a twenty-five mile radius of that storage facility."

"Really?"

"Really. But I got a couple questions for you."

Derek splayed his hands. "Go ahead."

"Why's the bureau keeping quiet about this? Why don't they have her face on TV? The guy, he's the terrorist behind the boat bombing at the port, right? Why aren't they all over her? They're showing his photograph on TV, but not hers."

Derek considered that piece of information. "Because," he said slowly, "someone might think that if they identify the girl, Kalakar will think she's a liability and kill her. So they don't want to tip him to that. There's something about the girl—"

Betty Andine waited. Derek shook his head, the thoughts slow to coalesce. "The bureau's afraid he'll kill her if he knows they're looking for her."

"Go on. You said there's something about the girl."

"This is a guess."

"I'm open-minded."

"I don't know if the bureau thinks this or not, but my gut says there's something about this girl that's key to Kalakar's final plan. Otherwise he wouldn't keep her alive and he wouldn't have taken her with him. And, although I think we'd better find out fast what that is, I suspect Kalakar definitely doesn't want us to know."

Betty Andine glanced at Connelly, who shrugged. She said, "I'll be in touch. We'll be subtle, but I think we'll figure something out."

"Thanks."

She nodded as if she was annoyed with him, and left the interrogation room. Connelly sat back down at the table.

Derek said, "Thanks, but I don't get your role in this."

Connelly's face creased in a grin. "I wouldn't mind being involved in collaring Kalakar, let me tell you. And I'm not a big fan of the bureau. They don't want LAPD involved in this, so they're stonewalling. I got the photos from a friend at the bureau. I'm working this with you."

Derek digested that. Connelly wanted to make a big headline bust. A career move. "Okay."

Connelly leaned forward. "But first, let's talk about Greg Popovitch. Tell me exactly what went down in that house in Venice."

CHAPTER 56

Kalakar's truck was parked in a gravel turnout off one of the roads that meandered through Griffith Park. He and the little girl, Malika, stood quietly behind the trunk and boughs of a huge fir tree, the air redolent of sap and pine needles. His side hurt from where he had taken a bullet from the FBI agent. As far as he could tell it had gone through and hadn't hit anything vital. He had bandaged it, but it was still seeping blood. He found it a little bit hard to breathe and he was struggling to move and stay limber, but he was still functioning.

The girl stood next to him, shoulders slumped, quiet. She hadn't said much in the last thirty minutes. His threats were apparently effective.

Somewhere behind him, in the foothills, he heard the scurry of small animals. Squirrels, he supposed. Some coyotes, maybe. Occasionally he heard the hoot of an owl.

He was almost prepared to abandon this site when headlights glowed on the road and a white Cadillac appeared, rolling to a stop next to the Ford pickup. The engine shut down, the lights went off. After a moment, the interior lights flashed on and Kalakar verified that it was indeed Ibrahim Sheik Muhammad.

The little girl didn't move or make a sound.

Kalakar waited until the imam was out of the car. He gave Sheik Muhammad a moment, in case he was being followed, then, tugging on the girl's hand, stepped out of the woods.

The imam spun. "That you?"

"Who else?"

The imam seemed agitated. Even in the dim light, Kalakar thought the man looked pale, upset.

"Why didn't you complete your mission yesterday?"

Kalakar ignored the question. He said, "I said I needed a vehicle and a place to stay."

"Yes, I know. I have a house in Baldwin Park. It has a two-car garage. You can hide the truck in there. There's a Jeep Cherokee in the garage." Sheik Muhammad fished in his pocket and pulled out a set of keys and a card with an address written on it.

"Can they trace this to you?"

"Eventually, if they had reason to. But it's owned by one of my companies, and that company is protected by several shells. You'll be fine for twenty-four hours, probably much longer."

Kalakar nodded.

For the first time, the imam focused on the child. "Who is this?"

"None of your business."

Sheik Muhammad reached out and touched Kalakar's elbow, drawing him away from the little girl. Kalakar allowed himself to be pulled away. The imam said, "Everyone is looking for you. You know that, right? My house was being watched. I was followed, but Sayid took care of them."

Kalakar's heart thudded in his chest. "You're absolutely certain you have not been followed?"

Sheik Muhammad swallowed. Voice soft, he said, "I think Sayid is dead. He had a gunfight with your pursuers. He was a good soldier. A true jihadist. May Allah bless him."

"Allah is great," Kalakar responded.

The imam again studied the little girl. "She is part of your plan?"

"The less you know, the better."

"I don't understand how she could be part of your plan. Is she—" Sheik Muhammad hesitated. "For your needs?"

Kalakar felt disgust rise up in him. "I am a Muslim, imam. A jihadist. A soldier. I'm not a pervert. She is a necessary part of the plan."

He turned to the girl. "Come. We're leaving now."

"And tomorrow this will be over?" Sheik Muhammad asked. Kalakar thought there was fear in the imam's voice.

Kalakar nodded. The girl shuffled over toward him. Without warning, Kalakar pulled out his gun and fired it into Sheik Muhammad's face.

The imam went down like an imploding building. A small cloud of cordite faded in the breeze. All the background chatter of the woods, the scurry of animals, the click of crickets, and the flutter of birds, died.

The little girl's only reaction was a sharp intake of breath.

Kalakar reached for her hand. "Let's go."

That was when the little girl bolted for the trees.

When Malika Seddiqi had used the restroom at the gas station, she had decided it would be better to try and escape than to wait for whatever the bad man had planned. Kalakar kept telling her she must behave or he would hurt or kill her, and she believed him. But she also believed that when he had done whatever it was that he planned to do, she would be lucky to still be alive.

Malika was only ten, but she watched a lot of TV, especially with her friend Dominica. They even watched Oprah, and she remembered an episode of Oprah where they talked about what you should do if someone tried to kidnap you. Like: if they have a gun, it's better to run, because it's really hard to hit someone running at a distance with a gun. And: never let them get you in their vehicle, fight them on-site.

Malika guessed she'd screwed up on that one. She had been a little suspicious when Kalakar picked her up at school. He was her daddy's friend, sort of, but she knew her mother didn't like him at all.

So she had waited for the right moment. She wondered what Kim Possible would do. Kim Possible was a character in her favorite cartoon. Kim was a redheaded cheerleader and great student who was also a superhero. She could do anything. She refused to let anyone stop her.

Malika knew that Kim Possible was just a cartoon character, that the things she did with her friend Ron Stoppable were just made up. But still, she knew that Kim had an attitude: I can do anything.

Her mother had even watched the show with her. Her mother seemed to like Kim a lot.

So Malika knew that there would come a moment when Kalakar would be distracted, when there might be a policeman nearby, or there might be a chance to run, that there might be a hiding place nearby, and she needed to be ready.

She had wanted to warn the old man. She knew that Kalakar didn't trust him. She didn't know why she knew, but she could tell that Kalakar was growing impatient, that things weren't going well for him, that his plans weren't working the way he wanted them to.

But she was ready.

When Kalakar shot the old man, she had jumped, a little scream coming from her mouth, but in a way, she wasn't all that surprised. Her stomach hurt, though, and she felt sick. She wanted to cry, to throw up.

Can't, she thought. *You have to be ready.*

It would have been a good time to run, and she was angry at herself for not running right then. But as soon as Kalakar reached for her, she knew this was it. She was out of the truck, he didn't have a hold on her, it was dark, and the woods were right there.

So she ran, heading for the trees like a deer, light on her feet, bounding into the cover of darkness.

Behind her Kalakar swore and tore after her, his footsteps thudding in the dark.

Malika ran, dodging between trees so close together Kalakar could never follow. Low-hanging branches clawed at her. She felt something catch at her cheek. Pain slashed across her forehead and she was certain she was bleeding.

She kept running, stumbling over roots, through brush, the sounds of Kalakar crashing behind her slowly fading.

Malika stopped running, a stitch in her side, her breath hard in her chest. She strained her ears, listening for sounds of Kalakar. But he had stopped.

His voice then, drifted through the woods. "Malika, I will go back to your parents' house and hurt your mother if you don't come out."

Tears rolled down her face. She believed he might. But she also believed her father would be there. This had something to do with her father, and if Kalakar didn't have Malika, her father would not help Kalakar.

Slowly, as quietly as possible, she crawled into a clump of shrubs and huddled as close to the ground as she could. In her hand she clutched one of her homework pages, crumpled into a ball.

Waiting.

Kalakar seemed to melt out of the shadows. He caught her with both of his hands and shook her. She let out a scream, struggling, flailing with hands and feet.

"Not again," he said. "Let's go." He gripped her wrist like a handcuff and dragged her back toward the truck.

Malika had been dropping balled up papers with her name on them when she had an opportunity. She prayed to Allah that someone would find one.

CHAPTER 57

Derek studied the dregs at the bottom of his Styrofoam cup. He had gone through three cups of black coffee and, as far as he could tell, it was having no effect on him. Glancing at his watch, he noted that it was closing in on midnight and he was in need of some sleep. He considered saying so to Connelly, but figured the detective was trying to push him into screwing up and admitting to something besides really bad judgment.

Connelly, noting the time-check, mildly said, "Am I boring you?"

"A little bit."

Connelly's eyes grew big. "Well, fucking excuse me!"

Derek shrugged. "You asked." He had been, in his opinion, pretty cooperative. Of course, the LAPD detective wouldn't see it that way.

Connelly leaned forward and tried to look menacing. Derek thought Connelly should give up on menacing. He wasn't intimidated by Connelly. He was tired. His mind was on other things. He wondered about O'Reilly. He wondered what Kalakar was up to.

Connelly growled, "I think you're holding something back. If you don't cooperate, we're going to spend the night—"

Derek leaned back in his chair and yawned.

"—going over this."

Abruptly the door opened and Officer Betty Andine stepped in. "I've got five possibles. You guys coming?"

Connelly looked embarrassed. Derek smiled. "Sure."

Ghazala Seddiqi sat in her living room staring at the TV, which was playing the local news. She wasn't paying any attention to it. Her ears were tuned to the sound of the telephone, hoping, praying.

Yes, praying, praying constantly, begging Allah to deliver her daughter back to them.

John paced. When he had gotten home, she had lit into him, furious that he had brought this on their family. The argument had been like a brushfire: hot, explosive, and suddenly over. She had clung to him, sobbing into his chest while he patted her shoulder.

It wasn't completely his fault. He admitted to her that he didn't know what Kalakar had planned. All Kalakar wanted was the flight route and GPS coordinates along the route of Governor Stark's plane the next day. He was baffled as to what Kalakar could do with the information. Thinking of September 11 and the jihadists who had used airplanes as weapons, he speculated to Ghazala that maybe Kalakar was going to rent a small plane and crash it into the governor's plane.

She didn't know what to make of it either. She had commented that doing that seemed complicated and difficult. Wouldn't it be easier, she had asked, to just rent a small plane and fly it into the building where the governor was speaking?

John had shrugged.

She wondered if Kalakar had a missile, something he could use to shoot down the plane. John shook his head, saying those antiaircraft missiles were so tightly controlled that Homeland Security would have sent warnings out to ATC and the FAA. He said it was something everybody in the field was afraid of, but nobody believed they were on the loose. It was the most obvious idea, but the least likely, because the difficulties in actually getting hold of an antiaircraft missile seemed insurmountable.

The sound of the phone trilling was like an ice pick straight through her heart. Ghazala had expected Kalakar to call John's cell phone, not the home phone. John lunged for the phone. "Hello?"

She rushed to be next to him, hands twisting together.

John nodded. He gave Ghazala a glance, a "she's-okay" look. She clutched his arm, suddenly feeling the weight of the world bearing down on her. Her knees felt weak.

"I want to talk to her, Kalakar. Right now."

John's face brightened. "Malika, are you okay? Are you all right?"

Ghazala rushed down the hallway to the bedroom and picked up the extension. She heard her daughter's voice saying, "I'm really tired."

"Oh, honey," she cried. "It's Mama. I love you. Are you okay?"

"Mama! Mama! Yes, I'm—"

Ghazala heard shuffling and rustling over the phone and then

Kalakar came back on speaking in Urdu. "She will be fine, Ghazala. If your husband does what I ask."

"She'd better be," she shrilled into the phone. "You had just better—"

John's voice cut her off. "Ghazala. Enough. Kalakar and I need to talk. Hang up."

"Not until he promises me. Promise me. You will not harm my daughter. Vow it. On the Koran. In Allah's name. You will not harm my daughter."

There was only silence from the other end of the line. John said, "Ghazala, please."

"If John does what I ask, your daughter will not be harmed. Whether she stays safe is up to him."

John said, "Ghazala! Enough."

She bit her lip, thinking of John's warning, the one he didn't say, but was there nonetheless: don't provoke him, he's holding a gun to our daughter's head.

Feeling ill, she gently set down the phone and began to weep.

Derek and Connelly and Betty Andine walked out to Connelly's car in the parking lot of the PAB. It was 12:15 and Derek had voiced his thoughts: "We're going to drop in on these people's homes asking about their daughter this late at night?"

Connelly scowled at him in the harsh glare of the sodium lights. "You're the one who runs around acting like your hair's on fire, gotta do whatever you can to stop the next attack. What's a little door-to-door late at night?"

"We're going to scare the living shit out of these people."

Betty Andine stopped and turned to him. Her broad face was serious. "You have another suggestion?"

"No." He took a sip of the coffee he had brought with him.

Connelly unlocked his car and they climbed in. Derek took the backseat. He said, "I'm impressed with your detective work, Officer Andine, but can you maybe explain it to me?"

Connelly fired up the car and pulled from the lot. Andine turned to face him. "My squad and I try to have a very good, close relationship with schools in the area. I regularly meet the principals and counselors. I keep a database of them. I have their e-mail addresses and their cell phone numbers and their home numbers so I can contact them if I really need to. So we sorted out a list of possible elementary and middle schools in the region, then I got some officers making calls, offering to fax or e-mail the photographs of the girl. I got enough bodies working it that we had some hits."

Derek put the coffee in the cup holder and nodded. "Again, impressive." He was puzzled as to their motives. Cooperation was undoubtedly good, but he was surprised by it.

Andine seemed to sense his thoughts. She said, "That little girl doesn't make sense to me. But she's definitely terrified."

He nodded. He didn't know what to say. But finally it occurred to him that there was something he should say. "Thank you."

Andine smiled. "You're welcome."

Ghazala thought her heart might stop when the telephone rang. It was very late. It had to be Kalakar. What would he want now?

From the look on John's face, he was having the same thoughts. She saw that his hand shook as he picked up the phone. She ran for the other phone to listen in.

"Hello, Mr. Seddiqi?"

"Yes?"

Ghazala thought the voice was familiar, but couldn't place it right away.

"This is Lawrence Brennan, the principal at your daughter's school."

Ghazala put her hand on her chest, listening. What was this all about?

"Yes, Mr. Brennan. It's rather late."

Brennan continued on. "Yes, I'm sorry. This is a little unusual. I was contacted a short time ago by a police officer with the LAPD's Juvenile Crimes Unit. They had a photograph of a girl running away from someone. She looked terrified. They were trying to identify the girl and they had reason to believe she might have attended our school. I thought the girl looked like Malika."

Ghazala clutched the phone so hard she thought the plastic casing might break. Her brain was a whir of conflicting thoughts: Tried to run away? Terrified? The LAPD was looking for her?

John said, "Well, Mr. Brennan, thanks for calling, but Malika's just fine. She's in her bed sleeping right now."

Ghazala bit down on her hand. She wanted to scream. What did this mean?

"You're sure?"

"Quite sure. But thank you for letting us know. Have a good night."

The phone clicked off. John appeared at the bedroom door a moment later. His face was twisted with worry. "Throw some things in a bag. We're leaving right now."

She stared at him. "No," she said, shaking her head hard. "No. He'll call. Kalakar will call. We have to stay here in case he calls."

"The police might come to check on this. If they take me in for questioning, I won't be able to go to work. If I can't do that—"

Fear was like a living thing, a crab that burrowed inside you, lived under your skin, its pincers pinching and clicking and tearing at flesh. "But—"

"I'll change the message on the machine," John said. "Kalakar's got my cell phone number, too. Hurry. We have to get out of here."

CHAPTER 58

Cassandra O'Reilly pulled her car to a stop and sat there for a moment in the bath of flashing red and blue lights. She felt ill, seriously ill. She knew exhaustion was part of it. Too much travel, no sleep, too much stress, a bullet to her right shoulder. She had been lucky. The round tore a big chunk out of her trapezius, missed the bone, her neck, her carotid artery, her head, and any significant nerve.

Her shoulder was packed in gauze and she wore a sling to give it some rest. She was also downing Vicodin, which was alternately making her feel sleepy, high, or nauseated. The doctors had encouraged her to stay the night in the hospital. Her bosses in D.C. had told her to write up her report and come home. The various functionaries who had their fingers in the pie here in L.A. had told her to write up her report, go home, and don't come back.

Yet here she was, following up on a report that the body of Imam Ibrahim Sheik Muhammad had been found in a turnout in Griffith Park.

An L.A. County Sheriff's deputy trudged toward her. O'Reilly rolled down the window and held up her identification. The deputy brushed blonde hair out of her eyes and studied the identification. "National Intelligence. I guess you do learn something new every day."

"I need to talk to the detectives and see the body."

The deputy, who was probably in her thirties and looked like she was a wannabe actress, entirely too glamorous to be a cop, eyed her for a moment. "If I might say so, Agent, you don't look so good."

O'Reilly pushed open her car door, forcing the deputy to step backward. She wished she had a smart comment ready. For a moment, she swayed on her feet. The deputy reached out and braced her arm.

"Whoa, you been drinking?"

"I got shot a couple hours ago. How about you? You having a good day?"

She brushed past the deputy and walked toward the crime scene. Portable lights turned night into harsh, unforgiving day.

The sheriff's deputies worked the scene. A handful of investigators watched, one from the Sheriff's Department, two from LAPD. O'Reilly handed over identification and waited for the inevitable skepticism. She was surprised when the LAPD detective, an Asian who introduced himself as Peter Lee, said, "You were chasing this guy when that shootout happened, right?"

She nodded.

"Well, somebody shot him. Looks like point-blank. Any idea who did it?"

"Kalakar," she said, and explained.

Peter Lee nodded. "Go on and take a look, then."

He followed her over to where the forensic unit was working the scene. Peter Lee called out, "Hoshi. Got a second?"

A female investigator wearing a jumpsuit looked up from what she was doing and padded over. She looked Korean, young, pretty, her long dark hair pulled back off a face with high cheekbones. "I'm working here, Pete. What?"

Lee introduced O'Reilly to Officer Hoshi Sato. O'Reilly said, "Who found him?"

"LAPD patrol car on a routine drive-by. You want to talk to them?"

She shook her head. She didn't know what she wanted. "Mind if I look around?"

Sato shrugged. "It happened right here. There was another vehicle, probably a pickup—"

"Probably a Ford F150. Pretty good bet we know who the shooter is. Pakistani terrorist calls himself Kalakar, full name is Miraj Mohammad Khan."

"Ah. Okay. Thanks."

"But how do *you* know?"

"Tire tracks."

O'Reilly checked the ground. The turnout was dirt and gravel. It wasn't exactly muddy, but the ground was soft. She asked why the ground was so soft.

"Rained pretty hard a couple days ago. Still drying out here, I guess."

"So it's okay if I look around a bit?"

"We'll tell you when you get in the way."

I bet you will, O'Reilly thought.

O'Reilly returned to her car and retrieved a flashlight from her Go Pack. Returning to the scene, she walked around the perimeter of the white Cadillac and the crime scene. A crime-scene team and somebody she suspected was with the Medical Examiner's Office was processing the body of the imam. She tried to keep her distance.

She didn't know what she was looking for exactly. But the ground was soft enough to reveal footprints, and she was curious to see if she could identify footprints belonging to the little girl, whoever she was. Detective Lee let her wander around, but he was keeping an eye on her.

There had been so many people through the scene that footprints seemed obliterated. She called out. "Officer Sato, did you make casts or photographs of footprints? Were there any?"

Sato, looking frustrated by the interruption, said, "Yes. Besides the two patrol officers' footprints, we found two others beside the victim's. One's a child. The other is an adult."

"Where did you find them?"

Sato pointed to where a section of the turnout was cordoned off with yellow crime scene tape. O'Reilly walked over and studied the shuffle of prints in the mud. She reflected that in books and TV the footprints were always nice and neat, not overlapping. In real life, people couldn't stand still. Their own feet overlapped. They tapped their toes and rocked on their heels and rolled their feet and fidgeted around. That's what she saw here, but by careful study she could differentiate what she thought were three separate pairs of prints, one clearly smaller like a child's.

She contemplated the footprints, trying to imagine what had happened here. Scanning the ground wider, she moved in wide arcs around the scene. Peter Lee walked over and asked, "What are you doing?"

She shrugged. "Just trying to get a sense of things."

"You want to tell me what's going on? I just called the L.A. office here. They're a little surprised you're here."

She shrugged again. "I'm not quite ready to let go of Kalakar."

"Okay. Fine. But if you find anything, let me know. This is our crime scene. You don't have any jurisdiction over a murder here. You probably don't have jurisdiction over a murder anywhere."

"Sure," she said. She went back to her search, wondering if she could pick up more prints. Lee watched her for a moment before wandering away.

Toward the edge of the woods she thought she saw another small print. She crouched down, immediately wishing she hadn't. The world became gray for a moment, lit up by fireworks. She sucked in air and regained her equilibrium.

When she could focus, she saw that there were, indeed, footprints that looked like a kid's leading into the woods. Studying the footprints more closely, she tried to remember any of the basics she knew about tracking.

These footprints seemed to be quite a ways apart.

The little girl was running, O'Reilly thought. Running into the woods.

A little more study further substantiated this thought. Although the entire footprints were there, they were deep in the toe and very, very faint in the heel. The little girl had really been running hard.

Glancing around further, she thought she saw larger footprints nearby, also running.

She thought: the little girl ran away and Kalakar chased after her.

A chill swept over her, thinking of the little girl being chased into the woods by the terrorist.

What's your name, honey? How did you get mixed up in this?

Standing up, O'Reilly looked around. Nobody was paying her any heed. Flicking on the flashlight, she followed the footprints into the woods.

It became almost impossible right away. O'Reilly had to go very slowly and look for each print. The ground was harder here, rockier, and any footprints tended to be partials. She thought ruefully of every western she'd ever seen where the scout was able to track through desert and over rocks and through streams. She thought it was all a crock of shit.

Twenty feet in and she was about ready to give it up.

Think like a ten-year-old.

Crouching down, knocking a good eight to twelve inches off her own height, O'Reilly studied the woods. And she saw the way she would probably go, particularly if a grown man was chasing her. There were routes between tree trunks and beneath branches and through shrubbery that would be far easier for a little girl than for a man.

Pushing her way through the undergrowth carefully, O'Reilly swatted at mosquitoes that hadn't yet gotten the message that it was November. Behind her she could hear the cops talking. The red and blue lights glowed and flashed in her peripheral vision.

Glancing down, she saw a footprint. It was a beautiful, full, child's footprint, followed by another and another. The little girl had slowed down.

O'Reilly followed the tracks. They disappeared for a while among a bed of pine needles, but she picked them up again twenty feet farther on.

She also saw a larger set of footprints following her.

The footprints abruptly ended.

O'Reilly studied the tracks. The pine needles and dirt here looked disturbed, but not like it had been walked on.

It looked like—

It looked like maybe the girl had crawled here.

Cautiously, O'Reilly followed the tracks into a clump of shrubs.

Nothing.

Except—

It did look like someone had been there. The ground was matted, pressed down. Scanning around, she saw a larger footprint.

He found her, she thought.

The little girl ran and hid in the brush and he found her.

Heart beating in her chest, O'Reilly looked around, wondering if she was going to stumble onto the little girl's cooling corpse.

What she saw was something different.

A small ball of crumpled paper.

She reached down and picked it up from where it had been left.

A voice behind her said, "O'Reilly? You back here?"

It was Peter Lee, crashing around in the woods behind her. Heart hammering in her chest, she tucked the piece of paper into her pocket and called out, "I'm over here." She waved her flashlight around.

Lee stumbled over to where she stood. "What the hell are you doing?"

"I think the little girl ran away and hid back here. I was following her tracks."

Lee looked skeptical. "Show me."

She did, pointing out the tracks. O'Reilly described the potential scenario. He grunted, as if interested, but said, "I'm not sure that helps us much. So he found her and dragged her back to his truck and drove away. Probably more pissed off than before."

"I'm just following clues as I find them, Detective."

"Yeah. I see that. Anything else?"

"No."

"Okay. You coming back?"

She nodded. "Yes, I think I'm done here."

Back in her car, she drove away. Once she was out of sight, she pulled off to the side of the road, flipped on her interior light, and pinched the ball of paper from her pocket. She flattened it out and studied it.

It was a math assignment. Multiplication. Basic stuff: 8 x 9 = 72, the times tables. Third- or fourth-grade math. Twenty questions, all completed in pencil. Only one had been wrong. It was circled in red ink. There was a big red A printed at the top of the page and circled.

Had this been left in the woods on purpose?

O'Reilly studied the page, zeroing in on the name. Just a first name with the number 17 next to it, which she supposed was some sort of student number identification for the classroom. The name said: Malika S.

O'Reilly popped the car into drive and fished out her phone, dialing Derek Stillwater's number. God only knew where he was these days.

Okay, Malika S., she said. *We're looking for you, honey. Hold on.*

CHAPTER 59

Derek dozed in the back of Detective Connelly's Grand Marquis as they left Santa Monica and headed toward Culver City. The first family, the Farooqs, lived in a two-story colonial in a subdivision that was upwardly middle class. They hadn't been thrilled to receive a knock on their door so late at night from the LAPD asking about their daughter, Noor.

Officer Andine had handled the parents. Connelly and Derek had stood in the background trying to look unthreatening, although Derek was fairly sure that their presence had alarmed the Farooqs. Betty Andine had explained that they were trying to identify a girl who had been kidnapped and they were trying to confirm that their daughter, Noor, was not the missing girl. Was she home?

She was, they assured her.

Could I see her? Betty had asked.

They were obviously reluctant. She was sleeping, in bed, it was very late.

Betty suggested perhaps they had a family photograph. From what Derek could see, she was handling things significantly more tactfully than either he or Connelly would have. She was working very hard to put them at ease, to assure them that if their daughter was home, they had nothing to worry about.

They showed Betty a school picture. Derek stepped forward to peer over Betty's shoulder. Betty shook her head. "I don't think that's her."

"Me neither. Show them the photograph."

Reluctantly Betty gave the Farooqs the photograph of the little girl. They studied it for a moment before shaking their heads and handing it back. "That is not our daughter." Their expression was a mixture of relief and confusion.

"You see our problem, though?" Betty had said. "They do look a little bit alike."

The wife, whose name was Roshan, had waved for Betty to follow her into the house. A moment later Betty had returned, thanked the Farooqs for their time, apologized for any concern she may have caused them, and led Derek and Connelly back out to the car.

Now they were heading to Culver City, which had two possibles, a little girl named Abida Masood and a little girl named Parwin Younis. If those didn't pan out, there was a girl in Huntington Park and one in Inglewood.

Meanwhile, the last thirty-six hours or so were catching up to him, and no amount of coffee was keeping him awake. He dozed off, but not completely. A part of his brain was monitoring the murmured conversation between Connelly and Andine. He was all too aware that to all extents and purposes he was a prisoner of the LAPD and his future freedom might depend a great deal on what happened over the next couple hours.

He didn't completely trust their involvement. It seemed clear that Andine was Connelly's friend, but her motives for helping seemed to revolve around the little girl. She was whispering something to Connelly about how she was going to have a lot of explaining to do, and Connelly told her not to worry, she'd be a hero. Her reply was inaudible, but Derek got the impression she was telling him he was full of shit. Then he remembered nothing for a while.

His buzzing cell phone jerked him awake.

Connelly glanced over his shoulder. "What the hell's that?"

Forgot you gave it back to me, Derek thought, *didn't you?* Cell to his ear, Derek identified himself.

"Derek? It's Sandy. Are you all right? Where are you?"

"I'm fine. I'm working with the LAPD." *Sort of*, he thought. "What about you? Where are you? Are you okay?"

"Just a graze. But they found the body of Imam Ibrahim Sheik Muhammad."

This bit of news woke Derek up completely. "What? Where?"

"Griffith Park. And Derek—"

"Kalakar, right? It had to be."

"Yes. Almost positive. But Derek, I found something a little strange."

"What?"

She explained about following the footsteps and discovering the crumpled bit of math homework. "There's a name on it, Malika S. No last name—"

"Seddiqi," Derek said. "The name is Malika Seddiqi."

"How—"

He leaned forward and tapped Betty Andine on the shoulder. He gestured for the list. She handed it over and Derek reached up and snapped on the overhead light so he could read it. "Yes, Malika Seddiqi in Inglewood. We're on the way. Don't go knocking on the door, okay? Meet us down the street. We're in a black Grand Marquis. We'll meet you there."

He rattled off the address and clicked off. "We might actually have gotten a break."

It was well after midnight when they arrived at the Inglewood address. The house was dark, although a pair of lights shined from each side of the garage. Derek didn't think that meant much, considering how late it was. They studied the house for a moment. It was a ranch, sided with brick, and had a two-car garage. The lawn, though difficult to study clearly in the darkness, appeared well cared for. The neighborhood seemed a little older, prosperous, conservative.

Connelly said, "Where's your partner?"

"Maybe she got caught in traffic."

Andine shrugged and angled her way out of the car. "Let's go talk to these people."

Without waiting for Connelly or Derek, she trudged up the driveway and rang the doorbell. No response. After a moment's wait, she rang it again. Again, no response.

Derek watched a car roll down the street and stop in front of the house. It shut off and O'Reilly hurried over. He noted the arm in a sling and the general look of exhaustion on her face.

"Everybody keeps telling us to pack up and go home," he said.

"Fuck 'em."

He nodded, satisfied. Andine, meanwhile, continued to knock on the door. Nobody answered.

Andine looked at Connelly. "You want to discuss evidence and probable cause here?"

Connelly, Derek saw, didn't look very confident all of a sudden. He seemed to consider what Andine was saying and then decided he'd gone out far enough on the edge to lose his job if things didn't go right. "I need to think about that a bit."

Andine turned to look at O'Reilly. "You're National Intelligence?"

O'Reilly seemed puzzled. "Yes, Agent Cassandra O'Reilly. Who are you?"

Andine introduced herself.

O'Reilly's expression of puzzlement shifted over to one of skepticism. "Why are you involved?"

Andine jerked her head at Connelly. "Favor. What makes you think Malika Seddiqi is the girl in the photograph?"

O'Reilly didn't respond immediately. Derek thought, *uh-oh*. After a moment O'Reilly said, "A piece of paper, math homework, was found near a crime scene in Griffith Park—"

"What?" It was Connelly. "What are you talking about?"

"LAPD is processing a murder scene, Imam Ibrahim Sheik Muhammad."

"When was this?"

Derek sighed and edged away from the trio. Appearing as if he was just checking out the property, he glanced around the side of the house. Connelly was getting belligerent with O'Reilly, who was snapping back at him to mind his own business. Andine seemed lost in thought. Nobody was paying any attention to Derek.

He slipped around the side of the house, jumped the fence into the backyard, sprinted across the yard and over the back fence. Nearby he heard a dog barking. He heard Connelly curse and call his name. Hoping he didn't charge full-speed into some kid's play structure, he ran until he was several blocks away, then settled into the shadows beneath a slide in an elementary school playground. Checking his watch, he decided to give them half an hour. Then he would head back to the house.

CHAPTER 60

Connelly and O'Reilly were squabbling. Betty Andine sighed and reached into her purse and pulled out a pack of cigarettes. She slipped one between her lips and used a cheap plastic lighter to set it ablaze.

"Look, O'Reilly, I'll—"

Andine took in a heavy lungful of smoke and blew it out in a blue flume toward the porch light. In a matter-of-fact voice she said, "Stillwater just disappeared on you."

Connelly started, staring around. "What? Fuck! Stillwater!" He sprinted around the corner of the house, reappearing a moment later. He glared at O'Reilly. "What the hell is that guy's problem?"

O'Reilly cocked her head and laughed. "What, are you saying you politely invited him into an interrogation room and he came willingly? Come on, Connelly. You forced him to cooperate when he's in the middle of an operation, then you force your way into the middle of the op—"

"He blew my op! And so did you!"

"Yeah, and now Popovitch is dead and you can go focus on something—"

Andine brought her hands together in a T. "Time out. I've done enough today. I'm going home. C'mon, drive me back to the PAB. I'm off the clock and as far as I can tell, we've hit a dead end with the little girl. I'll swing by in the morning and see if anybody's home." She headed for Connelly's car.

Connelly stared at her, then turned back to O'Reilly, "When you see Stillwater, tell him we're not done."

O'Reilly rolled her eyes. "If we need you, we'll call you. Thanks for the help tracking down the Seddiqis."

"Fuck you." He stormed past her and fired up the Marquis with a roar.

O'Reilly sighed, walked back to her car, and waited for Derek to appear.

Agent Dale Hutchins was sitting at his desk, picking at a salad, rereading the files on Kalakar, when his phone rang. It was Tehreema. "Honey, turn on the TV."

Scrambling for a TV on the opposite side of the office, he said, "What's up? Is everything all right?"

Tehreema didn't sound particularly upset, but she did sound a bit annoyed. Through the glass walls of his office, Sherwood raised an eyebrow and stepped to the door to watch. Hutchins clicked on the TV and found the local station. The screen showed the U.S. Embassy compound surrounded by a crowd of what looked like a couple hundred protestors. They appeared to be mostly young men, possibly college students, typically bearded, some in western clothing, some in more traditional robes, many holding signs and chanting, some holding what Dale thought was probably the Koran.

He said into the phone, "I see it. How big is it really?"

"Big enough."

"What are they protesting?"

"U.S. presence in Pakistan, what else?"

"Not aimed at Tarkani?"

"Not specifically, from what we can tell. But any protest of the U.S. in Pakistan has to include Tarkani."

"Stay inside until it's over. Are the police there yet?" Watching the TV screen, it didn't look like the Pakistan cops had begun breaking things up. Maybe because it was focused on the U.S. Embassy. In the past, when it focused on Tarkani, the cops or the army broke things up pretty quickly.

"The embassy staffers have our instructions and SOPs, Dale."

"I know, but—"

"You worry too much."

"No," he said, teeth clenched. "I don't. If I could get you out of the embassy right this second, I would. These things sometimes get out of hand and you know it."

As he watched, the police riot cops moved in. The reporter ducked. The camera jostled in a dizzying jumble. A cloud of what Hutchins was sure was teargas hit the crowd.

Sherwood was at his side, studying the screen. His scowl said it all.
"I've got to go, honey."
"You be careful."
"I will."
She clicked off and Sherwood said, "She okay?"
Dale nodded. He watched the action unfold, the cops in their khaki pants, gray sweaters, and blue berets swinging batons. The Pakistani riot gear was different than that in the U.S., their helmets having wired plates like a catcher's mask. But the approach was the same: quell reaction quickly and brutally.
Sherwood said, "Timing's interesting."
"Protesting the U.S. election?"
Sherwood shrugged. "What's going on, Dale?"
Dale shot his boss a look. Sherwood glowered at him. "Something's up. Where's Frito?"
"Checking something out."
"Like what?"
Dale glanced around the unit and gestured to his boss's office. "Something we need to keep under wraps."
Sherwood frowned before leading him into his office and shutting the door. Sherwood slammed down in his chair and said, "You got a problem with some people in the office?"
"No, but this investigation into Kalakar took an odd hop from the U.S. side." He told Sherwood about the men in the photograph with Kalakar and how one of them was General Bilaf Sharif.
Sherwood scratched his jaw. He focused on the TV playing in the squad room for a moment. "Sharif's been very, very vocal about U.S. presence here. And he's probably Tarkani's biggest internal opponent."
Dale nodded. Sherwood tapped his fingers on his desk, thinking. "Right. As soon as you find out something else, let me know. But I think I'll make a call or two to Washington, let them know that things might be a little weirder than we thought."
"We've got to be careful."
Sherwood nodded, but his hand gestured to the TV playing images of a riot around the U.S. Embassy. "Let's start carefully putting together a report on Sharif and everything we know so far."

•   •   •

Derek snuck up behind O'Reilly's car, not even sure if she was awake. He was a little surprised she'd waited for him, if indeed that was what she was doing. He tried to make his approach obvious, but she didn't seem to be aware of his presence. Maybe she was asleep. He lightly tapped on the window and she jumped. *Yeah*, he thought. *She'd fallen asleep.*

She rolled down the window and said, "You waited long enough to come back."

"And here I am."

"You're a pain in the ass."

He stepped back so she could climb out of the car. She studied him. "I assume you're intending on breaking into the house."

"I was hoping your superior skills with a lock pick would come into play here."

With a sigh, she leaned back in, rummaged through her Go Pack and pulled out her lock picks. They walked to the front door and within minutes they were in.

"It would sure be embarrassing if Connelly showed up here with a warrant while we were inside," Derek said.

"Shut up." She turned on a light and they looked around the house. Derek pointed to a school photograph of Malika Seddiqi. "That's her."

"So now all we need to figure out is the connection between her and Kalakar."

First they did a quick run through the house to make sure they were alone, then Derek took the master bedroom and O'Reilly started in the kitchen. There was a desk in one corner of the master bedroom, the bottom right drawer used as a filing cabinet. Derek sat and went through everything he could find. The first clue was a group of check stubs that indicated John Seddiqi was employed by Los Angeles International Airport. That in itself was enough to interest Derek, but Derek couldn't know what Seddiqi did there from a check stub.

He continued searching and finally found a copy of a license showing that Seddiqi was an air traffic controller.

Derek settled back in the desk chair, staring off into space. O'Reilly appeared at the door. "I've got his cell phone number. If he and his wife, whose name is Ghazala, by the way, are out and about, if we're still on speaking terms with our bosses we might be able to get a track on the phone."

Derek rubbed his chin. "That'd be good. I've got a question for you. Does anybody have a clue what was in that storage unit in Culver City?"

"I don't think so. Why?"

Derek looked around the room. He waved a hand. "What would Kalakar need an air traffic controller for?"

"Seddiqi's an ATC?"

"Yeah, at LAX."

O'Reilly frowned. "That's—you think Seddiqi was providing some sort of flight information to Kalakar?"

"I wonder."

"But why?"

Derek shrugged. "The worst-case scenario is he intends to shoot a plane out of the air."

"You're—what about the little girl?"

"I don't know. Leverage?"

O'Reilly blinked. "We don't have much evidence."

"Babe, we don't have any evidence. But I think I'd better call Secretary Johnston and report in."

CHAPTER 61

Secretary James Johnston was still in his office when the call came through from Derek Stillwater. Derek was more than an employee, he was a friend, and Johnston had been worried about him. He always worried about Derek when he was in the field. There was no denying Derek's overall success rate, but the price he paid for that success was steep, and there was almost always fallout and blowback from his actions. Johnston had plans to retire when the new administration came in, and he was concerned that this latest operation of Derek's was going to tangle them up in after-action investigations for months. It wouldn't be the first time.

Johnston had loosened his tie, but was otherwise as ramrod straight and businesslike as ever. He had just finished touching base with the remaining START team in New York City, which was following leads on what everyone hoped would be the final attempted terrorist attack in this group's plan.

"Derek. What do you have to report?"

"What do you know about loose MANPADs?"

Johnston closed his eyes for a moment. MANPADS were an acronym for Man Portable Air Defense Systems, which was military jargon for shoulder-launched antiaircraft missiles. "I hope like hell you're joking."

"I wish, sir. But the fact is, this is nothing more than a guess."

Johnston felt a little bit of weight lift off his shoulders. A little, but not all. He respected Derek's intuition. "I'm not aware of any missing MANPADS in the U.S. That doesn't mean there aren't others from other countries. God knows Russia hasn't kept track of their hardware terribly well. As you probably know, they've even indicated they'd lost about ten thousand of them back in the eighties and nineties. But getting them into the U.S.? Very tricky."

"What about if someone in the international film business were to arrange one as, say, a movie prop, or something like that?"

Johnston was silent a second. He said, "I think you'd better tell me everything. And I mean *everything*."

Once he was off the phone, Derek leaned back in the passenger seat and looked at O'Reilly. "DHS has a special office looking at MANPADS. Johnston's going to call them in right now. He's also going to see about tracking Seddiqi via his cell phone."

"We could go to LAX and try to intercept him on his way there."

Derek nodded. He glanced at his watch. "Unless you have a few brilliant ideas, I need a couple hours sleep."

"Let's head over to LAX and check into a motel for a couple hours." O'Reilly turned the key and fired up the engine.

Ghazala Seddiqi followed her husband into the Super 8 Motel near LAX. She was exhausted, but most of that exhaustion came from terror. It felt to her as if the walls were closing in and her world was crumbling around her. She did not know what she or her husband might have done to bring Allah's disfavor on them like this. Did Allah really want her daughter to die?

She sent out a small prayer begging for mercy, asking Allah to care for her daughter.

John set his duffel bag down on the bed and turned to her. There was something in his expression she had never seen before. She believed her husband was, ultimately, a good man. Like many in the Muslim world, they had been appalled by the attacks on September 11. Like many in the Muslim world, they had been shocked when the United States invaded Iraq. As a conservative Muslim, Ghazala knew that Osama bin Laden and al-Qaeda did not have any particular relationship with Saddam Hussein. Hussein was from a different sect and was entirely too secular.

The United States' own actions in Iraq kicked open a door for al-Qaeda. The U.S. responded to the death of three thousand innocents on September 11 by destroying the lives of thousands and thousands of Muslim innocents in Afghanistan and Iraq, by forcing their way into Pakistan life and politics. It was heavy handed and shortsighted and it had forced a war where perhaps none had been needed.

Like many Muslims around the world, Ghazala and John had friends and relatives who had been killed or whose lives had been turned inside out by the U.S. invasions. It was this alone that had made John cooperate with his cousin's request to host and help Kalakar.

If only they had known how badly that decision would turn out.

John said, "I think you are very brave."

His words shocked and confused her. "What? What are you talking about?"

"I have been thinking about what Kalakar wants. What he plans to do. He says that if I provide him the information he wants, he will let Malika go unharmed. I'm not sure I believe him."

Ghazala felt her breath catch in her chest. "But—"

Her husband held up a hand, not commanding her silence, but requesting it. "Hear me out. I can't *not* give him what he wants. If this is a negotiation, I can't hold back the information or he'll kill her. I'm certain of it."

Ghazala felt frozen.

"So we need to change the conditions of the negotiation. So I want you to know that I think you are very brave. Because I've been thinking and I need you to do something. It will be very difficult and you will have to be strong. For Malika. For me. But I think you are."

"What? What do you want me to do?" She felt and heard the fear in her voice, bordering on panic.

"In a couple hours I can go into the tower. I'll be able to figure out which route Governor Stark's plane will be taking. Then I can give Kalakar the GPS coordinates he wants." John hesitated, licked his lips. "But before I call him, I'm going to call you. He won't get the coordinates from me. He has to get them from you. And you won't give them to him until he releases Malika to you."

His words frightened her so much she shook. It was a gamble, but also she saw it was the only way. The only leverage they had over Kalakar was the GPS coordinates. John, who she understood was indeed a very smart man, maybe a brilliant man, had been thinking. He was maybe not strong or brave—though she hoped he would be strong and brave for their daughter—but she did not doubt his intelligence.

John had plans to utilize those GPS coordinates to make sure they got their daughter back.

He reached into the duffel bag and pulled out a Thomas Guide. "I have a pretty good idea of where Kalakar will need to be. Not completely though. But I've been paying attention to the weather and I have a good idea which route the governor's plane is likely to take." He flipped the Thomas Guide open on the room's cheap desk and pointed. "We've got to make sure we get you there with plenty of time. So I think you should leave here in the next hour. I can catch the shuttle into the airport from the motel and report to work. But we have to work out exactly what you need to do."

She nodded her head.

John reached out and cupped her face. Voice soft, he said, "I love you, Ghazala. And I am so sorry for what has happened. I'm doing my best to get us out of this and to get Malika back safely."

"Perhaps," she said softly, "we should just call the police or the FBI."

He shook his head. "I thought about that. But their priority will be to capture Kalakar, not to get Malika back safely. That's *our* priority."

She nodded, fighting back tears.

"Can you be strong? For Malika?"

She nodded again.

"Good." He kissed her lightly, then dipped into the duffel bag again. He brought out a gun. It was the small revolver—she thought it was the Smith & Wesson .38 he had bought two years ago after someone had tried to carjack him on the way home from work. It had been an ugly, terrifying incident of random violence, all too common in Los Angeles, and he had bought the gun to keep in the car and in the house, although she hated it and was afraid of it.

"I want you to take this," he said. He looked into her eyes. "And if you have to, use it."

CHAPTER 62

Ghazala Seddiqi drove away from her husband into the gloom of a Los Angeles predawn. When he had kissed her goodbye there had been a finality to it that made her chest ache. Was it because she feared what was going to happen in the next few hours? Or was it because his commitment to Islam and his assistance to Kalakar had driven a wedge between them that she wasn't sure could be removed? How had they come to this horrible place in time?

Although John hadn't said so, she understood how precarious and dangerous things were for them right now. The authorities were looking for Kalakar. They were, for some unknown reason, looking for Malika.

Malika!

A sob seeped from her mouth and she clutched the steering wheel with hands slick with sweat, hoping, praying, begging Allah for her daughter's safe return. Her fear was so great it was almost paralyzing. What she needed to do was move, but she felt like she was frozen, strapped down by her fear for her daughter.

Clicking on the overhead lights for a moment, she double-checked the directions John had written out for her. She knew them by heart, they were engraved in her memory, but she kept checking to make sure she hadn't misread them or had forgotten some small but important detail. Even this early in the morning traffic was heavy, which is why she left so early. Getting lost would be fatal.

John was convinced the governor's plane would be coming in from the northeast. She was to drive north on the 405 and pick up the 10 in West L.A., travel east through Mid-City, South L.A., and Pico Union, picking up the 110 around Echo Park and Elysian Park, eventually finding California Route 2 and an entrance to Angeles National Forest.

She was to purchase an Adventure Pass at a ranger station and proceed to one of the parking lots he had picked out. John had said, "It's here that you'll meet Kalakar and trade Malika for the coordinates. Call me when you get there. I'll call you if Kalakar contacts me before then."

Ghazala had felt overwhelmed by it, but he assured her he had a plan, although he hadn't shared it with her. His holding anything back now made her temper flare and she had demanded he tell her what he intended to do. He had shaken his head and told her it would all depend on Kalakar's reaction and the eventual flight direction the ATC gave the governor's plane as it came into LAX. Then he had held her tight and whispered that he loved her and was counting on her, that Malika depended on her.

John had told her he wished he could be there instead, but he had to be able to verify the GPS data.

She had to trust John. Now all she needed to do was drive.

The airport security guy who was dealing with Derek and O'Reilly was named Trevor Lottke and Derek thought he was a dick. It's possible he wasn't, it was just that Lottke was totally unimpressed with their credentials, their story, and them. He had a bald head that reminded Derek of the moonrise, skin the color of ash, and about twenty-five too many pounds under his belt.

"I need you to run that by me again," he said. "You think somebody's going to try and shoot down the governor's plane as it flies into the airport. That what you're saying?"

"That's what we're afraid of," O'Reilly said.

Lottke leaned forward and planted his elbows on his desk. "I'm afraid of it, too, but you haven't told me much that sounds like evidence."

"We don't have much that *is* evidence," O'Reilly said. "Look, wouldn't it be better to be safe than sorry?"

Lottke studied her for a moment. "That shoulder hurt?"

"Yes. What's that got to do with anything?"

"Get you some Tylenol or something? Every time you move it you wince. Figure it must be hurting you."

"Thanks for your offer, but I've got some medication."

Lottke nodded. He turned his attention to Derek. "I spoke to your guy."

"You spoke to Secretary Johnston?"

Lottke laughed. "Yeah, right. I called up the Secretary of Homeland Security in the middle of the night. No, I—"

"I gave you his number."

"I know you did and I appreciate that. But we have protocols here for security. First, I needed to verify that you two are who you say you are. And as you might've guessed, you do check out. The problem is—"

A knock on the door interrupted Lottke's speech. He called out, "C'mon in."

It opened and two men in navy blue suits appeared. Derek didn't know who they were, but he could guess.

The blond suit with the thin, angular face, held up his identification. "Agent William Smith, FBI."

"Got it in one," Derek said. Everyone ignored him.

Smith's partner was older with a gray crew cut. There was something about him that suggested he had a long history in the military. Derek thought that the guy looked about fifty-five but might be closer to sixty-five. Whatever his age, he looked like he was in fantastic shape and didn't take much bullshit from anybody. "Agent Taylor Zerbe, Department of Homeland Security." He grinned at Derek. "I know you by reputation. And it ain't good."

John Seddiqi took a quick shower and shaved. He pulled on fresh clothes, knotted his tie, and walked to the motel parking lot to catch the shuttle bus that would take him into LAX. He found it interesting, the way his mind was alternately churning and blank. Disconcerting, because he was accustomed to working under stress. But not personal stress, he supposed. He hoped he was not sending his wife to her death. But he could think of no other way to change the equation with Kalakar. He knew that if he gave Kalakar the coordinates and Kalakar did whatever it was he was going to do, he had no incentive to set Malika free. In fact, he might have great incentive to kill her.

John was just trying to wrest some of Kalakar's leverage away from him.

May Allah be with us, he prayed.

CHAPTER 63

Leaning against the wall in the airport security room, Agent Taylor Zerbe said, "I know you've got the secretary's ear, but there are ways to do things so you don't make all our lives harder. I just got off the phone with Secretary Johnston, and he insists I should listen to you."

Derek said, "Good. We need—"

Zerbe raised a hand so Derek would stop. "I've also been talking to the bureau, the ODNI, and the LAPD. And it seems you two are actually supposed to be either on your way back to D.C. or in a holding cell at the PAB."

He leveled his gaze on Derek. "I share that with you so you don't start thinking I'm as stupid as you apparently think everybody else is. Got that? So tell me your story."

So Derek did. Fifteen minutes later Zerbe raised an eyebrow and said, "That's it?"

"What do you mean, 'that's it?' That's enough!"

Zerbe sighed. "Good work identifying the girl. Of course, since you didn't actually talk to the parents, it's still not proven. And as to how you found out that John Seddiqi worked at LAX ATC, I'm a little fuzzy on that. You want to explain it to me?"

"I made some calls."

"Uh-huh. You didn't by any chance go into the house without a warrant, did you?"

"Of course not." Derek met his gaze and gave him his full-out honest look. "Are you going to let us out of here or not?"

Zerbe crossed his arms over his chest. "Haven't decided yet."

Agent Smith said, "If I call LAPD and ask for an inventory of evidence of the crime scene in Griffith Park is there going to be any evidence listed that fits the description of a piece of a third grader's math homework?"

It was O'Reilly's turn. She said, "Why don't you call them and ask?"

Smith stared her down. "In time, Agent O'Reilly. In time." He shot Zerbe a look.

Lottke said, "So if I got this right, you two came in here with a bunch of illegally acquired 'evidence,'—" He used his fingers to make "quote" marks in the air when he said evidence. "That adds up to what sounds to me to be a wild-assed guess. That right?"

Neither Derek nor O'Reilly said a word. Zerbe nodded. "That about sums it up."

"So what are you going to do?" Lottke demanded.

Zerbe shrugged. "With your permission, we're going to go over to the ATC tower and talk to Mr. Seddiqi when he comes into work. Then I'll decide whether or not to lock up Dr. Stillwater and Dr. O'Reilly."

"Or push them in front of a moving train," Agent Smith said.

"Or that," Zerbe agreed. "Might be a lot fewer headaches that way."

Governor Stark and Donna Price rode in the back of a limousine to the Denver airport while Secret Service Agent Frank Long sat in the front passenger seat sipping coffee. They were discussing the Secret Service's opinion of Secretary Johnston's suggested change in itinerary. The mountains were behind them in the darkness as they drove through the neon and fluorescent lights of suburban Aurora, Colorado.

"Here's the thing, Governor. This warning isn't very well substantiated. I've talked to the director personally, who has full access to Secretary Johnston's data on this. It is wildly circumstantial, and although Secretary Johnston respects the source's opinion, the director finds him to be a bit of an alarmist—to say the least."

Stark said, "Who's the source?"

Donna noted that Governor Stark didn't seem tired. He seemed energized by finally reaching election day. She had handed him the overnight polls putting him three percentage points ahead of Vice President Newman. She knew he could practically taste the presidency, it was so close.

Long said, "It's one of his troubleshooters, a Dr. Derek Stillwater. His expertise is biological and chemical terrorism."

"But he's got an opinion on a MANPAD? A little outside his area of expertise, isn't it?"

Long frowned and Donna wondered what he was thinking. Long had been with the Secret Service for nineteen years and was considered a seasoned pro. It was hard to figure what was going on in his head though. Maybe that was from years of protecting presidents and visiting world leaders.

Delicately, Long said, "He's an expert on terrorism and I'm aware of his reputation as well as his track record, which is admirable."

"So your recommendation?"

Long said, "Would you consider skipping California—"

Both Price and Governor Stark exploded. "Absolutely not!"

Long nodded. Donna Price realized the agent wasn't surprised by their reaction. Long said, "We could fly into a different airport than LAX, which would add some unpredictability to our flight plan. It won't delay us more than a few minutes."

"What do you suggest?" Governor Stark asked.

Donna interrupted. "How much of a delay?"

"No more than thirty minutes. I suggest that instead of flying into LAX, we fly into Ontario Airport and take cars into the rally in L.A. It's an easy fix, and if there actually is someone near LAX with an antiaircraft missile, they'll be in the wrong place. Hopefully the bureau and local cops will be on their toes, assuming there's a real threat."

Governor Stark nodded. "Very well. Our pilot can make up the time to keep us on schedule?"

"Absolutely."

"Go ahead then."

John Seddiqi arrived at the air traffic control tower at six-thirty, early for work. He clocked in, grabbed a cup of coffee, and went about checking all the various weather information before anybody noticed he was there. Tapping away at a computer, he pulled up information regarding Governor Stark's flight, which was being shifted from LAX to Ontario.

Frowning, John pulled up a map and looked at the Governor's flight plan. With a sigh of relief, he realized it would make no difference. He didn't know why the change of destination, but until they entered into

LAX airspace, their flight was essentially the same and would fly along the route he expected.

He made some simple calculations and nodded his head.

"Hey, John, good morning. You're here early."

John quickly changed the computer monitor screen so his boss, Bruce Abelson, wouldn't see what he had been looking at. "Thought I'd pick up some overtime, if it's okay."

Abelson was a slim, wiry man with round wire-rimmed glasses that magnified his blue eyes. He looked geeky, which he was, but John thought he was a good boss. "Sure, I guess that'd be okay. Hey, did security catch you on the way in?"

An icy hand gripped John's chest. "What?"

Abelson frowned. "Uh, Trevor Lottke, he was calling about you, said some federal agents wanted to talk to you. He mentioned something about your daughter. Everything okay?"

"Huh," John said, acid flooding his stomach and throat. "Far as I know. Must be a misunderstanding. I'll go and call him right away."

"Sure. No problem."

John turned to leave the tower. Abelson called after him. "John?"

He turned. "Yeah?"

"You sure everything's okay?"

John shrugged. "Far as I know. I'm sure it'll be nothing. I'll see you after I get this all cleared up."

He walked normally until he was out the door, then he sprinted for the stairs. He had the information he needed. All he had to do was trade it for his daughter.

CHAPTER 64

Ghazala pulled into the parking lot her husband had identified. Although the sun had been rising while she was driving on the L.A. expressways, once in Angeles National Forest, it was hidden by the San Gabriel Mountains. She read signs pointing toward Mt. Wilson, Mt. Zion, and Mt. Harvard through twilight.

She took a peek at her cell phone and felt a surge of relief that the small screen showed service. She'd been worried that once in the park with its mountains and winding roads there would be no contact and John's plan would fall to pieces, and any hope for Malika's safe return with it.

Ghazala climbed out of the car, stretched, and walked to a nearby restroom facility. It was rustic, only pit toilets and a hand pump. She couldn't hide her distaste, but reminded herself that this was about her daughter. She used the facilities, then pumped and drank the icy water.

Again she looked at the cell phone, thinking, *John, where are you?*

John Seddiqi fled the LAX air traffic control tower, quickly making his way to the nearest terminal building and flagging down a taxi. The driver was young, maybe college age, with skin like coal and an attitude like steel wool. His accent was hard to pinpoint. Jamaican? Cuban? John wasn't sure.

"Where you wanna go?"

John hadn't thought this through completely. All he knew was he needed to stay on the move. He didn't understand how the authorities had connected him to Kalakar so quickly. Had Kalakar been caught? Had he led them to John?

Or had Kalakar done something to Malika, killed her and left her body somewhere?

He refused to think of that, refused to believe. Could not believe it.

No, he didn't know how the Americans had made the connection, but he knew if he wanted his daughter returned safely he had to stay ahead of them.

John started to give the cab driver his home address, thinking he would pick up his other vehicle and meet Ghazala in the park, when his cell phone rang.

"Yes?"

The cab driver turned in his seat, impatiently gesturing at the meter.

John held up his hand, telling him to wait. The driver scowled and turned forward, watching a few early morning passengers walking out of the Delta terminal.

It was Kalakar. "John, have you left for work yet?"

"I'm already there. I've had a change of plans. I already have what you need."

A moment's silence filled the air. "Why the change of plans?"

John's brain buzzed. How to handle this? He had thought it through a million different ways, but now that he had Kalakar on the phone, it was harder than he had thought. An image of his daughter filled his mind, and hardened his resolve.

"Because of Malika. Here's the plan."

The cab driver turned around and glared. "You goin' somewhere or not? I start meter now or not?"

John held up his hand. He needed to concentrate on Kalakar.

"I've got what you want, but I'm not going to just turn it over to you."

"You're gambling with your daughter's life, John."

"I'm thinking of her."

The cab driver turned back to him. "You go somewhere? What you problem, mon? Gimme where go or get outta my car."

"Problem, John?"

John kicked open the cab door, walking away from the car. The cabbie flung up his hands, swearing at him.

"No problem. It's as simple as this. You take Malika to Angeles National Forest. That'll put you in the right—"

Kalakar was furious. "Are you out of your mind? What game are you playing?"

John clenched his fist. He saw that the cab driver was still staring at him. Turning away, he said, "You take Malika there, Kalakar. You take her to this location. Are you listening?"

"I'm not going to—"

"You do as I say or you don't get the coordinates you need. Understand me? I want proof that Malika's okay before I give you anything. Do *you* understand *me*?"

Kalakar was silent for a long moment. John's stomach clenched. He thought he had blown it. He thought Kalakar wasn't going to negotiate, that he had just signed his own daughter's death certificate. His guts roiled and he thought he was going to be sick right there. Nausea swept over him.

Kalakar finally said, "Tell me where, John."

John's chest heaved. He was almost panting, his tension was so severe. He coughed out the directions to the parking lot in Angeles National Forest. He told Kalakar to repeat them back to him.

Kalakar did. "Then what?"

"Ghazala will be there. You turn Malika over to Ghazala and call me. I will give you the GPS coordinates you need. Then you're on your own."

"If you try to screw me, John, I'll kill your daughter, your wife, and then come after you. I will make all of your deaths slow and excruciating. Are we clear on this? If there are cops there or the coordinates you give me—"

John took a deep breath. "You'd better get on the road, Kalakar. The governor's plane is already in the air." He clicked off the phone, bent over, and vomited on the sidewalk.

Trevor Lottke led all of them through a maze of corridors to an elevator that took them up to the air traffic control tower. Derek couldn't help himself: the air traffic control tower at LAX was iconic and he'd always wondered what it looked like inside. He wasn't disappointed. Windows gave three hundred and sixty degree views of the airport, all its terminals and runways. More than a dozen controllers stood or sat at computers. There was a constant buzz of conversation as they talked to planes. Managers walked around tracking what the controllers were doing.

As Derek watched, a 747 rumbled down a runway and roared into the air.

A thin blond man hustled over and was introduced as Bruce Abelson. Lottke said, "These folks are with the FBI, Homeland Security, and the Office of the Director of National Intelligence. They need to speak to John Seddiqi. When does his shift start?"

Abelson cocked an eyebrow. "Pretty soon, but he came in here just a little while ago." He glanced around. "I don't see him though. That's odd. He was checking something on the computer, said he hoped to work some overtime, help us out."

Derek said, "Which computer? Can you check what he was doing?"

Abelson shrugged. "Over here." He led them to an open computer monitor. "In fact, I told him you were asking about him, Trevor. He got a little jumpy."

I bet he did, Derek thought. "When was this?"

"Just a few minutes ago."

Abelson tapped some keys, looking for a user history. After a moment he said, "Looks like he was checking a specific flight. Flight, hmmm— That's Governor Stark's plane. I see they're not flying into LAX—"

Agent Zerbe said, "God dammit!" He spun on Lottke. "Let's go find this guy."

He ran out of the air traffic control tower with Lottke and Smith behind him. O'Reilly hurried after them, but slowed when Derek didn't follow. Derek said to Abelson, "Take a look at the flight path of the governor's plane, would you?"

Abelson studied him for a second. "I didn't get who you are?"

Derek introduced himself. "There are hints a terrorist might be targeting the governor's plane, possibly with a surface-to-air missile."

"Are you shitting me?"

"It's not confirmed. But there's a possibility John was providing the terrorist with the flight path and time information."

Abelson paled, if that was possible. He already had milk white skin. Turning, he tapped at the computer screen and brought up a flight path. "This is the probable flight. It's subject to change, but here it is."

Derek was no stranger to maps, but this was an incomprehensible mess. He hesitated. "Let's say you had a portable missile. You wanted to shoot the plane down and you need visual confirmation. Where would you set up?"

"What's the range?"

Derek turned to O'Reilly, who said, "Half mile to a little under five miles."

"So it would have to be on landing or takeoff."

"I don't think so," Derek said. "Then why get flight path data?"

Abelson studied the computer screen. "Out in the suburbs somewhere?"

"Maybe someplace high."

"Up in the mountains," Abelson murmured. "Hmmm." His finger followed a track on the computer screen. "Lot of mountains here. Timing could be a problem, but if it was me, I'd get set up in the mountains around Mt. Wilson or Mt. Zion. Mt. Wilson's got the observatory and all that up there, so there's a lot of cleared space, not many trees And if I knew exactly what time the plane was coming through, I'd have a pretty clear visual field and Mt. Wilson, for instance, is about fifty-eight hundred feet, and planes coming into LAX or even Ontario, which is where the governor's plane is coming in—"

But Abelson was speaking to himself, because Derek and O'Reilly were on their way out the door.

CHAPTER 65

Out on the street, Derek studied their surroundings. He felt ever so slightly like a wolf sniffing the air for prey. They had just missed John Seddiqi, and it was like he could still scent him, he was that close. The man still might be around. He might be walking to his car, taking a shuttle. He wouldn't be far away.

They were near the Delta terminal, the air traffic control tower was in front of them. A jet shrieked and lunged into the sky. A black cab driver was standing outside his taxi shouting something unintelligible at a receding cab. That wasn't particularly unusual. But Derek was trained to connect the dots, to notice the oddities and place them in context. And he trusted his instincts.

O'Reilly said, "So what? We've narrowed it down to what?, a few million square miles?"

Derek ignored her. He ran over to the irate cab driver, who was shouting, "Mo' fucka! You get in my cab, waste ma time, then—"

Derek flashed his identification. "What's the problem?"

"Some mo' fucka gets in my car to talk on his phone, then jump out and puke, mon, then swear at me and run and jump into another cab. It not right. It jus' not right!"

The man's accent was odd. Not quite Jamaican, maybe Louisiana, maybe someplace more exotic like West Africa. Derek said, "What did he look like?"

"What? What you want, mon?"

"What did this guy look like?"

O'Reilly caught up. Her phone was in her hand and she said, "They triangulated on his cell signal, but it's moving. They're scrambling to get a lock on it, but things are moving slow and there's some bureaucratic hassles—"

"Where?"

"Who the woman? Who you?" The cab driver was flailing his arms and Derek wondered if he was schizophrenic. He was a nut. But then again, this was L.A.

O'Reilly ignored the cab driver. "Here. Just a couple minutes ago. But they've lost the signal. Probably turned the phone off."

Derek focused on the cab driver. "What did he look like? Was he Pakistani?"

"Dat o' Injen. Yeah, prob'ly. Dark hair, dress like businessman— white shirt and tie. Very tense. Talking strange on da phone."

"Strange how?"

"Upset, but tryin' to be a tough mon."

Derek stared where the cabbie had been shouting only moments before. "What did he say? Did he—"

"He never give directions to me. He jump out of car. Then hang up and vomit." He mimed bending over and vomiting in case Derek didn't understand. He pointed to the spot near the curb where the proof of the action was still evident.

Derek reached in his pocket and pulled out a roll of bills. He held them where the driver could see them. "Could you hear him on the phone?"

"Yuh. He in back of car most of the time."

Derek peeled off a twenty and held it up. "Any idea who he was talking to?"

The driver eyed the bill. "No. Not really. But not a friend."

"Any names?" O'Reilly asked.

"No, well, I don't know. Funny words. Maybe he talk some of time in Pakistani or Indian."

"You sure?"

"Sometimes. Sometimes in English. They funny words, like 'Cal-ico,' like da cat."

Calico? Derek thought. "Kalakar."

"Maybe."

"What else?"

He shrugged. "Mallory, maybe."

"Malika?"

"Maybe."

Bingo. Derek gave him the twenty and tugged out another. "Where was he going?"

"Don't know, mon. He give directions, but I'm not—" He trailed off.

"Yes?"

"National Forest. Off Route 5. He tol' man to meet someone there. At leas' I think it a someone. Could be, like, deer, no, gazelle. That I re-member, thinking we have gazelle in National Forest? In California? Didn't know that."

"Ghazala," Derek said.

"Maybe."

"What else?"

"Dat all, mon. Jus'—he say to trade something for Mallory—Malika, I guess. I don't know what a Malika is."

"Trade for what?"

"Don't know. He say, maybe, I dunno, he don't say."

Derek handed over the twenty. "Anything else? And I mean any-thing."

The driver thought, eyes on the money in Derek's hand. Finally, "I think he give directions. He talk about a parking lot in the forest."

Derek held up an additional twenty.

The driver licked his lips. "He say something a red box. I remember him say something about a red box, but did not think that made sense."

"A red box? Any idea—"

O'Reilly snatched the money from Derek's hand and flung it at the cabbie. "Come on, I know where they're going."

She sprinted toward where they had left the car, Derek at her heels.

CHAPTER 66

JOHN F. KENNEDY INTERNATIONAL AIRPORT, NEW YORK

There were four of them. Each of them was dressed for travel—slacks and polo shirts with a carry-on bag. They approached John F. Kennedy International Airport in New York almost simultaneously. It was election day and it was nine thirty in the morning on the east coast.

Each of the men drove up to a different terminal. There were nine terminals at JFK. One man went to Terminal 8 where American Airlines was located; another to Terminal 7, where United Airlines ran their operation; yet another hit Terminal 5, where JetBlue operated. Terminals 1, 2, 3, and 4 were all international flights. They had debated hitting all four international terminals, but they didn't have the manpower, and security was higher at the international terminals. Still, they needed to make their presence known at the international terminals, so Yusef Abdulla selected Terminal 4, the largest of the international terminals, which included service by El Al and Israir.

Each man entered his respective terminal at nearly the same time, bypassed ticketing, and headed for the security screening area. As expected, the lines were long, hundreds of people with their carry-on luggage shuffling toward the metal detectors and bomb sniffers.

Each man waited until they were deep in a crowd of people. Yusef Abdulla checked his watch. He said a prayer, set his carry-on bag down on the ground, and tapped out a phone number.

Yusef's three fellow martyrs at Terminals 5, 7, and 8 did exactly the same thing at almost identical times.

Each carry-on bag held approximately five pounds of Semtex plastic explosive. The detonators were hooked to the circuit board from a cell phone. Surrounding the Semtex were galvanized roofing nails.

The lucky ones never knew what hit them.

CHAPTER 67

Scrambling into the passenger side of O'Reilly's bucar, acceleration pressed Derek against the seat when she fired up the engine and peeled out of the parking lot. "Where are we going?"

"Red Box Road." She nodded at the GPS. "Get it programmed in. We're heading for Mt. Wilson. You take Red Box Road to the observatory entrance on the top of Mt. Wilson."

Derek began fussing with the GPS device. "You knew this off the top of your head?"

"I grew up around here, remember? Whenever people visit you in L.A. you have fairly standard tourist things to hit: Disneyland, Universal Studios, the beach, maybe the Reagan Library, Huntington Gardens—"

"And Mt. Wilson."

"Depends, but yes. And I used to hike around there a lot, too."

"It makes sense."

Once Derek got the GPS working, he called Secretary Johnston. Or tried to. The secretary's line was busy. He left a message. "It's Derek. We're pretty sure Kalakar is heading for Mt. Wilson here in L.A. and has the flight path of Governor Stark's plane. Contact the governor and get them to abort this trip completely. And we need backup. O'Reilly and I are on our way."

He hung up. "Who else?"

"Did you get Zerbe's number?"

"No. I'll call the local Homeland office."

He tried that number as well, but it was busy too. He left a message then he said, "I'll dial the local bureau, but they're sure as hell not going to talk to me."

He dialed and handed the phone to O'Reilly. She held it to her ear.

After a moment she said, "This is Agent Cassandra O'Reilly, ODNI. We have a serious lead on the location of Kalakar." She rattled off the information, asking for backup and suggesting they clear any air traffic near the Angeles National Forest.

"Strange," she said. "Nobody answered and it went over to voice mail. I'll—"

Derek interrupted by jabbing on the radio and hunting around for a news station. He picked up KCRW, a Los Angeles National Public Radio affiliate. The announcer was saying: ". . . four separate explosions, believed to be the work of suicide bombers. They are at four different terminals at JFK—"

The sounds of sirens in the background could be heard and momentarily blotted out what the reporter was saying. "...still have no casualty numbers, although initial reports have said in the hundreds. There has been no statement from the Homeland Security Secretary or the president yet, although—wait—"

More sirens and a babble of voices.

The reporter came back on. "We are speaking with Nadine Robert of Manhattan. You were inside the terminal?"

A woman's high-pitched, nervous voice came on. "Yes, I was catching a flight to Boston. We had gotten through ticketing and were heading for the security line when there was a huge noise, an explosion. I was knocked off my feet by the blast." She stopped and sniffed and it was clear she was fighting back tears. "There was a fire and so many dead bodies. I've never seen anything like it."

"So you believe the explosion took place in the security line?"

"Yes. Everybody was all lined up. You know what it's like. We're all shuffling through queues waiting to take off our shoes, you know, and hand over our boarding passes. The bomb could have been—"

Another voice, male, said, "You could have a bomb in your carry-on bag or your briefcase or your laptop case, walk right into the airport, if you've got your boarding pass preprinted nobody will check or stop you until you hit security."

"And you are, sir?"

"Jeremy Wainright."

"From?"

"Brooklyn."

"And when the explosion—wait, we're cutting to a press conference."

Derek turned to O'Reilly, who was driving fast, weaving in and around L.A. rush-hour traffic. Traffic was the usual L.A. mess and she was doing reasonably well, but Derek could feel the passing seconds dropping on his head like Chinese water torture.

A different reporter's voice came on. "From Washington D.C. this is Gerald Bennett with National Public Radio. Homeland Security Secretary James Johnston is to make a statement and field questions in just a moment. As reported earlier, after two days of attacks across the United States, a dirty bomb in Dallas, a suicide bomb in Chicago, a truck bomb in Washington, D.C., and an explosion on a cruise ship in Los Angeles apparently caused by a boat filled with explosives, there has been a major attack at JFK Airport in New York City. Here's Secretary James Johnston, Homeland Security."

Derek listened to Johnston's familiar raspy voice come over the radio: "As I'm sure you are aware, we have just received a report of a fifth terrorist attack, this one at John F. Kennedy International Airport. At approximately nine thirty a.m. eastern time four separate explosions occurred nearly simultaneously at four different terminals. Each explosion took place near the security checkpoints. Each explosion killed dozens of people and wounded hundreds. The victims are still being—"

CHAPTER 68

Kalakar headed into the parking lot where John had told him to meet Ghazala. He had traded the Ford F150 for the imam's safe house vehicle, a black Jeep Cherokee, transferring the missile to the back. He would have been far angrier had he not been listening to the news on the way there. Malika, who sat as docile as a doll in the front seat, hands duct-taped together in front of her, said, "You made them do that, didn't you?"

He turned his gaze on her. "What's that?"

She gestured awkwardly at the radio. "Those people who hurt all those people. You made them do that."

"That's a little simple and there's no reason for you to be asking questions like that."

"I'm not simple," she said. "You're a bad man who hurts people. Why do you hurt people?"

Kalakar's face flushed. His voice was very rough and he tried to be reasonable. "There is a war. In war you fight for what you believe in. Unfortunately, people get hurt in a war."

"I don't believe you," she said. "I think you hurt people because you like to hurt people. It makes you feel more important than them. You're just a bully. We talk about bullies in school and how to deal with them."

He glared at her. "And did you learn how to deal with someone like me?"

It annoyed him that she didn't turn away, cry, or even drop her gaze. She stared back at him, her eyes large, brown almost black, and somehow penetrating. "I think you will be punished. That's what happens to bad men."

"I think it's time to shut up if you want to see your parents alive."

That worked. Now, pulling into the lot, he said, "You will do exactly as I tell you to or your mother will be hurt. Do you understand me?"

She nodded her head.

"I want to hear you say it."

"I understand."

"Good."

He parked a good fifty feet away from Ghazala. As he drove in, the woman had climbed out of her car. She wore a *kamiz*, the loose pants and tunics of Islamic women in Pakistan. Her hair was covered—loosely, he noted with distaste—by a scarf. A purse hung over her shoulder, which she clutched to her.

To Malika he said, "I will come around and open the door for you. Do not move." He held up his handgun. "Understand?"

"Yes," she said, voice small.

He stepped out of the Jeep and slowly walked around the back to Malika's door. Ghazala seemed uncertain what to do. First she started toward him, then stopped, waiting.

He opened the door for Malika. "Step out. Don't go to your mother. Don't run away. Don't speak. Understand?"

"Yes."

She stepped out of the Jeep and stood by him. Kalakar took out his cell phone and placed a call to John. When he answered, he said, "I'm at the park, John. Ghazala is here. I'm going to hang up so you can call Ghazala."

He clicked off and put a hand on the little girl's shoulder. She flinched at his touch. "Sshhhh," he said. "We're almost done."

Ghazala was petrified with fear. It was only the sight of her daughter, her hands cruelly duct-taped together in front of her, that kept her in control. A flair of anger spiked through her. How dare he!, this monster that had abused their hospitality.

The cell phone rang. She answered it.

"It's John. Kalakar says he's there."

"He is."

"And Malika?"

"She's here, too."

"How close are you?"

"Forty, maybe fifty feet."

"Tell him to let Malika come to you."

"John—"

"Go ahead. Don't hang up."

Taking a deep breath, she called out, "Send Malika over to me."

Ghazala's heart nearly stopped when Kalakar shook his head. "I don't think so, Ghazala. She stays right here with me until John tells me the time and coordinates."

She told John what Kalakar had said.

"Stay calm. He wants the information. Say: 'John says that as soon as Malika is safe he'll call you with the time and coordinates.' Go ahead."

"John says that as soon as Malika is safe you'll get the time and co-ordinates."

"John's got a problem. He's not here. I am and I have a gun pointed at your daughter's head. Tell him I want the damned information right now."

"John—"

"I heard him. Walk toward him."

"John?"

"Do you have the gun?"

"John, I can't do this."

"Do you have the gun?"

"Yes. But—"

"Put your hand on it in your purse. It's loaded. All you have to do is point and pull the trigger."

"John—"

"Do it."

She closed her eyes. Opened them. Kalakar was watching her closely. She unzipped her purse and dipped her hand inside it. She had a flash of what she hoped was inspiration. She said, "I have it here. Written down. Once Malika is safe, I'll drop it on the ground and you can get it."

Kalakar laughed. "Walk halfway here, drop it on the ground, I'll come out and look at it. If it's what you say it is, I'll let your daughter go."

He had called her bluff. She felt lightheaded. What was she going to do? She held the phone to her ear. "John?"

"I heard. Tell him to call me or give you his number so I can call him."

"John—" But the phone was dead.

She yelled, "Call John."

●　　●　　●

Kalakar didn't like the way this was going. There was no way they were going to come to an agreement on this. He needed the information and didn't trust John or Ghazala to give it to him if their daughter was safe.

He nudged Malika forward. "We're meeting your mother halfway."

They walked forward, slowly, one step at a time. Kalakar's movements were slow. The pain in his ribs was like being poked by a knife with every step. Kalakar dialed John's cell. "I don't like this game, John. And the stakes are too high for you. Don't play it. You have to trust me to play fair."

"You kidnapped my daughter and threatened her life. Why would I trust you? You have to earn trust now. Do it by letting her go."

"John, you need to listen to me. I have your daughter. I have a gun to her head. If I run out of patience, your daughter is dead. Then I will kill your wife. If I miss this deadline, I will track you down and kill you. Do you understand me?"

"Yes. You've threatened me with that before. So this is how a jihadist works in the real world, Kalakar? This is Mohammed's great plan for his people? Kidnap and murder children?"

"Don't go there, John. We're not having a religious discussion right now. We're talking about—"

"You have twenty-five minutes, Kalakar."

Kalakar's heart skipped a beat. He glanced at his watch. It was 7:05. "Stop wasting time, then. Tell me the rest and I'll—"

"I just gave you half the information, Kalakar. I need a show of faith on your end. Can you meet us halfway?"

Kalakar noted that Ghazala was walking slowly toward them. Her hand was deep in the purse and he didn't believe that John had written the coordinates down and given them to his wife. Why was her hand in the purse? Did she have a gun?

"John," Kalakar asked. "Do you own a gun?"

There was momentary silence on the line and Kalakar knew instantly. He dropped the cell phone, swung an arm around Malika, picking her up off her feet. He jammed the handgun against the side of her head. "Slowly take out the gun, Ghazala. Take it out and drop it on the ground. Do it or Malika is dead! Do it now!"

Malika struggled in his arms. She kicked and thrashed and shrieked,

"Mother! Mama!"

He whipped the barrel of his gun against her skull. She screamed louder, but didn't struggle.

Ghazala screamed. "Malika!"

"Drop the gun or she's dead!"

"Mama!"

Ghazala dropped her phone. It fell to the ground, chirping like a baby bird that had fallen from its nest.

She reached into the purse.

Kalakar adjusted his grip on Malika. "Slowly."

Ghazala slowly pulled the gun out, holding it in her hand.

"Drop it to the ground."

The fear and panic on her face was wonderfully satisfying to Kalakar.

Ghazala hesitated.

He jabbed Malika with his gun again. "Drop it."

She dropped it.

"Pick up the phone and answer it."

Slowly, Ghazala bent and picked up the cell phone. She flipped it open. "John? He made me drop the gun."

Kalakar said, "Ask him to listen carefully."

Ghazala said, "He says to listen carefully."

Kalakar shifted position and shot Ghazala. A look of bewilderment and shock crossed her face as she fell to the ground.

"Mama! You killed my Mama!"

Malika struggled and kicked and flailed. He hit her with the barrel of the gun, harder this time. She slumped, dead weight under his one arm. He dropped her like a bag of bones to the ground, stepped quickly to Ghazala, who was struggling for air, hand pressed to her side, blood seeping around her fingers.

Kalakar picked up the phone. "I've shot your wife. And I'll shoot your daughter if you don't tell me the coordinates right now."

CHAPTER 69

O'Reilly revved the bucar's engine, screeching around nearly stalled traffic. Derek took the bubble flasher from the floor of the car and reached out and attached it to the roof. It didn't help much, but at least traffic knew they were coming.

He returned to working the phone without any luck. He tried the main switchboard at the Department of Homeland Security and was flipped over to voice mail. Finally, frustrated, he looked at his limited list of phone numbers and dialed Detective Connelly's cell phone.

A sleepy-sounding Connelly said, "Yeah? What is it?"

"It's Derek Stillwater—"

"What do you want, you psycho?"

"We know where Kalakar is headed and we know what he's going to do, but because of the attacks at JFK we're having problems getting hold of anybody."

"You've got a problem with credibility, too, Stillwater. Everybody thinks you're full of shit. Including me."

"Then you're not paying attention to my track record." Before Connelly could respond, Derek told him everything he could.

Connelly grunted. "I'll see what I can do."

Derek clicked off, reached into the backseat, and retrieved O'Reilly's Go Packs. She glanced over. "What're you doing?"

Rummaging through the packs, he came up with a Llama Max-I, three magazines loaded with .45-caliber ammunition, and a box of .45 rounds.

"That's my backup gun," she said. "Stick it in my jacket pocket."

He did. Not bothering to ask permission, he took out his own gun, a Colt M1911, released the magazine, and began reloading it with the .45-caliber shells.

Glancing over, O'Reilly said, "I didn't think the military used those any more. Didn't they stop around 1985? You weren't in that early, were you?"

"Not quite. Marine Force Recon and Delta still use them, I've heard."

"Those guys are all walking-talking armories. They'd carry howitzers if they could."

"I used the Beretta just like everyone else when I was in the service. This was a gift and I've always been comfortable with it."

"Who gave it to you?"

He frowned. "General Johnston."

"What a sentimental guy."

"Yeah. He made me promise not to shoot myself in the foot with it."

"I wonder if he was speaking metaphorically."

Derek nodded. "He was."

John Seddiqi had made all of his phone calls while in a cab driving toward his house. Most of the conversation had been in Urdu so the cab driver wouldn't understand. John was almost hysterical with fear. The words caught in this throat. His stomach churned. The driver, puzzled, kept glancing at him in the rearview mirror, dark eyes concerned.

Kalakar repeated, "John, give me the information or your daughter is dead right now."

The cabbie pulled up in front of John's house. John flung some money at him and lunged out of the cab. Without a word the driver pulled away.

Into the phone, John said, "I need to talk to Malika. I want to—"

From around the back of the house sprinted four men in tactical gear, HOMELAND SECURITY printed on the back of their blue jackets. They all carried assault rifles, expressions serious, attitudes grim.

Spinning away from them, John blurted to Kalakar: "Go to the Mt. Wilson Observatory. Stark's jet will fly just to the east at 7:30. It's not a commercial airliner. It's a Gulfstream III, a—"

One of the Homeland guys, tall, thick, and blond, plucked the phone out of his hand, demanding to know who was on the other end. Another agent caught John by the hair and slammed him to the ground, knee on his spine. Yet another swung John's arms up behind him and cuffed his wrists. It was all done with a frightening efficiency. What shocked John most was their silence. They didn't say a word. They were as fast, silent, and as effective as attacking sharks.

A black Chevy Suburban motored up and Agent Zerbe climbed out of the passenger seat. "Get that phone to the lab ASAP. We want to know who he was talking to and where he is. Go!"

Zerbe crouched next to John. His voice was patient, but there was an undertone of threat. "Okay, Mr. Seddiqi. Time to talk."

Governor William Stark leaned back in his leather recliner on board the Gulfstream III his campaign was using and stared out the window. As far as he could tell, they were either in California or northern Nevada. After an early morning stop in Chicago where he shared breakfast with some party high rollers followed by a short rally at Northwestern University, he and his team headed for California.

Donna Price, voice shrill with anger, snarled into the phone. "We want an update—yes, I know things are in flux, but—" She clicked off. "No update."

The Governor smiled slightly, thinking that Donna was having a meltdown, that her obsessive-compulsive control-freak tendencies that served her so well as his campaign manager were going to kill her if anything else went wrong. Stark admired her, respected her, needed her. Sometimes, he thought, she was a little scary, which could sometimes be a good thing in government. She'd make a good chief of staff. "I'm sure they'll inform us as soon as there's something to know."

"They're shutting down JFK and rerouting the entire eastern seaboard."

Stark's grin was wry. "Bet Newman's having a fit about that. Wasn't he concentrating on the South and East today?"

"He was, but I imagine they're going to have to do something different. We might have to, as well."

"Let's just get through the California rallies, then get me home to vote."

Bill Lamb, one of their staffers, walked up, phone in hand, big smile on his face. "Just got off the phone with the pollsters on the East Coast. Exit polls have you up by four points!"

"Four! That's fantastic!"

Stark couldn't hide his elation, but said, "It's a long day. A lot can happen. Best not to get too excited."

Kalakar knew something had gone very wrong. A voice that wasn't John Seddiqi's said, "Hello? Who is this?"

Kalakar shut off the phone, peeled back the battery compartment, ripped out the battery and tossed it aside. They wouldn't be able to trace his location now.

Turning, he nudged Malika, who was crumpled to the ground, dazed, but otherwise fine. Her mother lay bleeding to death on the ground a dozen feet away. He considered either leaving Malika there with Ghazala or putting a bullet in both of their heads and heading for Mt. Wilson. He had seen the signs nearby. It was going to be tight. Damn that bastard for forcing him to play it so close.

He decided that Malika might still come in handy, as insurance if nothing else. Kalakar reached down and dragged her to her feet. Her face was twisted in fear and hatred. "Mama! You killed Mama!"

Half dragging her, he walked her over to the Jeep Cherokee and tossed her into the front seat. Climbing in, he raced off, eyes on the clock. Time was running out.

CHAPTER 70

Derek gasped and clutched the door handle. O'Reilly, concentrating on her driving, said, "Shut up."

Red Box Road was not meant for a mad dash sprint in a car. It was narrow and steep, winding up the side of the mountain toward the summit of Mt. Wilson. The bucar was struggling with the grade, but O'Reilly was pushing it as hard as she could. She had it up to eighty-five miles an hour, but the twists and turns were such that she was skidding around the bends, tires screeching.

He tried his cell phone again, only to note that at this elevation he had no signal. Mt. Wilson was the site of dozens of antennae, but for some reason he didn't currently have a signal. Shaking his head he said, "We might be alone."

"Shut up." She struggled with the wheel as the bucar screeched across the yellow line, angling toward the drop-off.

Derek said, "I might be a little fatalistic, but I don't have a death wish."

"Shut. The. Fuck. Up."

Derek decided it was probably good advice. If his estimates were correct, they were only about a mile from the top of the mountain. There had been no sign of Kalakar. They didn't even know what vehicle he was driving. He hoped they were wrong. He also hoped that somebody— Connelly, Zerbe, Johnston, anyone—had gotten through to Governor Stark and called him off. That would solve a lot of problems.

Around the last bend appeared the entrance to the Mt. Wilson Observatory. Barely visible through the trees was a white dome. There were a couple cars there, but this early in the morning he didn't know if they belonged to tourists, hikers, observatory staff or, perhaps, Kalakar, shoulder-fired missile in tow.

O'Reilly braked to a halt and jumped out of the car. She checked both guns and said, "Eyes wide open, Stillwater. Let's go."

Michael Hoban was a National Park ranger, one of not nearly enough who were stationed in the Angeles National Forest. Part of his early morning job was to drive around the various tourist and parking sites and check to make sure that the vehicles had Adventure Pass stickers on their cars. It was just routine, right up there with pulling over drunk drivers, helping change tires, calling tow trucks for drivers whose cars couldn't handle the steep mountain grades, or rescuing hikers whose ambitions had outstripped their physical fitness.

Pulling into the lot, the first thing he noticed was the Ford Explorer parked near the restrooms. This was more of a picnic area of sorts than a hiking spot. In truth, it was a bigger area for kids to come and make out— or he supposed "make out" was old-fashioned; today they just had sex, skipped the smooching entirely and called it "hooking up." The evening shift spent a lot of their time chasing kids out of the woods, although the sex wasn't as big a deal as the drinking and the drug use.

Hoban screeched to a stop when he saw the woman lying in the parking lot. She was dressed in some sort of foreign clothing—Arab or Middle Eastern, something. Not quite robes, but definitely not western. And she looked—

He slammed to a halt and ran over to her. Then he saw the blood. Her hands were pressed to her stomach, which was soaked with blood. So much blood—

Radio to his lips, he called for emergency medical services. Sprinting back to his Jeep, he grabbed the first-aid kit, thinking, *There's nothing in here that's going to help. She's been shot, for God sakes!*

Kneeling next to her, he went to work. The woman opened her eyes and seemed to take him in for a moment, before her eyes sank shut. From her mouth came a moan and something that sounded like "Malika."

What the hell's a Malika? he wondered.

Dragging a fully armed Stinger missile at the same time he was trying to keep an eye on a ten-year-old girl was more difficult than Kalakar anticipated. The terrain was no help either. After ditching the truck back in the parking lot, Kalakar had hauled the Stinger out of its crate and cut the duct tape off the little girls' arms, warning her that if she tried to run, he would shoot her. No warning; no second chance. He didn't like having her loose, but she was his insurance policy in case things went to hell.

The missile weighed about thirty-five pounds. It was about five feet long. They were a mile high. The air was thin and smoggy. Kalakar was strong, but his wounds, the altitude, and the weight of the missile were exhausting him. His heart struggled in his chest and the air felt thin and insubstantial in his lungs.

The observatory was really a complex with several telescopes and what looked like water towers, but were actually solar telescopes. Kalakar had never been here and under other circumstances would have been fascinated by all the technology. Right now he had other things on his mind. He needed to get into the open where he could see to the north and northwest. At the moment they were hustling along a mountain path. Malika hadn't said a word.

Kalakar glanced at his watch. The governor's plane would be flying over in only a few minutes. He picked up his pace, moving as fast as he could along the path.

O'Reilly and Derek scanned the area. Derek said, "My guess is north and northwest. Which is—"

Pointing, O'Reilly said, "Let's go." She took off at a jog. Derek raced after her as best he could. They were both walking wounded, beat up, shot, burned, and operating on caffeine and adrenaline. They found themselves on a hiking path that wound through the trees, the multiple telescopes, antennae, and buildings of the Mt. Wilson Observatory visible over and between the trees.

After about a minute of jogging, they broke out into a clearing. The view was tremendous. They could see for miles and miles, an entire mountain range visible below their feet.

A hundred yards away, near the edge of a steep drop-off, stood two people. A man and a girl.

Derek pointed, "Look!"

Maybe a mile or two away a small jet was flying over the mountains, heading roughly southwest. Simultaneously they sprinted toward Kalakar and Malika.

CHAPTER 71

Kalakar set the case for the Stinger missile on the hard rocky ground and clicked it open. Despite his pain and exhaustion he was flooded with adrenaline, almost joyful at the near completion of his mission. Finally!

He focused on the Stinger, setting it up. It didn't take long. For a moment he lost track of his environment—of the incoming jet, of Malika. It was going to be a warm day, very clear with little of the usual brown L.A. smog. A breeze of about ten miles per hour rustled the trees. It was just him and the missile, preparing to change destiny.

Malika said, "What are you doing?"

He glanced up. He couldn't help it. He smiled at her. "What I came to this country to do."

"I don't—"

"Sshhh, little one. We're almost done."

He shouldered the missile launcher and pointed it toward where he had last seen Governor Stark's jet. In Pakistan when he was in the military, and later in Afghanistan as a Taliban fighter, he had used a variety of MANPADs, including the Stinger. It wasn't difficult to use, although visually sighting in on a moving target could be a little tricky. The launcher had an IFF antenna that locked in on the target, buzzing when it was locked.

Kalakar, with a sort of grim amusement, remembered that IFF stood for identification, friend or foe.

He brought the launcher around, waiting for the IFF to lock in on the Gulfstream III.

"Is that a missile?" Malika asked.

"Yes," he said tersely.

"You're going to shoot down that jet?"

"You need to stop talk—"

The launcher buzzed. It had locked in on the governor's jet.

The little girl stepped toward him. He barely saw her movement out of the corner of his eye. Kalakar felt a sharp, intense pain and bent over, gagging. The little bitch had kicked him in the crotch and was now sprinting toward the tree line, screaming her head off.

And he saw two people, a man and a woman, rushing toward him, guns drawn.

Onboard the governor's jet, Donna Price and Governor Stark were going over his script for the rally in L.A. when the copilot appeared in the cabin. He was a clean-cut ex-Air Force pilot turned commercial pilot, maybe thirty, clean shaven except for a thick mustache. His face looked the color of bleached bone. Even as he spoke, they could feel the movement of the jet as they turned.

"Sir, we've just been contacted by Homeland Security. We're moving out of this airspace *now*. They're pretty certain a terrorist has a Stinger missile and is in these mountains with it. Please fasten your seatbelt and—"

Price jumped to her feet. "We absolutely are not turning around. The governor has to make that rally. We've already changed our plans—"

The copilot stared her blankly, then turned back toward the cabin. "It's not up for discussion, ma'am. Fasten your seat belt."

"You don't have the authority—"

"Yes, ma'am, I do. And unless you plan on flying—" The copilot's eyes grew wide. Suddenly he lunged forward toward the cockpit as the plane lurched and went into a steep dive, accelerating.

Derek saw Malika kick Kalakar. *Good girl!*

Kalakar stumbled, dropped the Stinger and spun, crouched over. It was clear to Derek that Kalakar had seen them. But they were still about forty yards away. Probably less than a mile away he could see the jet.

Still running, O'Reilly raised her gun and fired at Kalakar. Derek knew she didn't stand a chance in hell of hitting him from this distance, but maybe distraction was enough. If they could just keep him away from the missile until the plane was out of range, all they would have to do was take down the terrorist.

Kalakar returned fire. Derek heard the zing of a bullet passing nearby.

The terrorist adjusted his aim to fire at the little girl. Seeing it, O'Reilly shouted, "Get the girl!"

Derek cut off at an angle to intercept Malika, who was sprinting more or less toward them. He fired toward Kalakar and with some satisfaction, thought he had hit him.

Kalakar stumbled. He felt as if he had been punched in the shoulder. Looking down, he saw blood seeping into his shirt. He'd been shot. Again!

Raising his other hand, he fired at the man, twice, three times—

Spinning, he fired off a round at the woman, who tumbled to the ground. Got her!

Kalakar thought that Allah must be helping him, giving him time to complete his mission. Kneeling, he snagged up the Stinger and slung it over his good shoulder, gritting his teeth at the pain. He searched the sky for the jet. To his dismay, it was turning away from him, heading for a ridge of mountains.

Setting his feet, he aimed the Stinger toward the jet. It was growing distant, a speck. He prayed, "*Ash-hadu an laa ilaaha illallaah.*" I bear witness that there is no god but Allah.

"*Allahu Akbar.*" God is great.

The IFF seeker buzzed. Locked on! Kalakar fired the missile.

The launch rocket blasted the missile from the launcher, flying out into the air. A moment later the launch rocket dropped away and the solid rocket booster kicked in with a roar. The missile streaked toward the jet.

"*Allahu Akbar.*" Turning around, Kalakar saw that the woman was closing in on him. He raised his gun and fired. The woman spun. Kalakar thought, *I hit her. She's down.*

He shifted his attention to the man, who was off to his left, lying on the ground. Blood soaked the man's shirt, but he was still alive. The man was shouting at Malika, "Run! Run back and get help! Go! Now!"

Kalakar turned, tried to raise his gun in both hands, but his left arm wouldn't cooperate. His own wounds were weakening him. He hadn't even realized how much blood he had lost. He lifted it with his right arm and aimed. He squeezed the trigger.

CHAPTER 72

Derek felt like he had been pinned to the ground with a giant nail. He had been shot in the back. Falling forward on the ground, he tried to roll over and get back to his feet, but the pain blasting through his body was so intense that he laid where he was, struggling for breath.

And couldn't. He couldn't breathe. And he couldn't get up.

The little girl, Malika, stopped, turning to look at him, eyes big and brown and frightened. "Are you—"

"Run," he shouted, struggling to suck air into his lungs. "Run back and get help! Go! Now!"

She turned and jack-rabbited toward the tree line.

With a monstrous groan, Derek rolled onto his side. Pain radiated out from his back and chest. The difficulty breathing and the pain suggested he possibly had a collapsed lung. Looking down, he didn't see any blood on his chest. The bullet hadn't gone through. He supposed that was a good thought, although he wondered where the slug was. Was it edging toward his heart? Lodged in a lung? Next to an artery?

Struggling to stay conscious, he tried to locate Kalakar and O'Reilly. Where were they?

Then he heard the whoosh and roar of the missile being launched and thought: *We were too late.*

When Kalakar fired at O'Reilly for the last time, she spun, throwing herself to the ground. She had felt the bullet as it bit at her neck. She felt something wet and realized she was bleeding. Pressing her fingers to her neck, she thought, *I got lucky. Half an inch to the left and I'd be dead. That's the second time I've been lucky today.*

Kalakar must have thought she was dead or injured enough not to be dangerous. He ignored her, going after Derek, who was on the ground, alive, but hurt. O'Reilly lunged to her feet, gun raised. She fired. The bullet struck Kalakar in the shoulder. He reeled, staggered, then returned fire, aiming for the little girl, although she was nearly to the trees. O'Reilly fired again.

Kalakar bent double, arms bent over his gut. Blood soaked his shirt. He dropped slowly to his knees and toppled over onto his side.

O'Reilly approached cautiously, gun held carefully in her left hand. Her right arm was still in its sling. Kalakar still clutched his handgun. He seemed to be muttering to himself. Praying, she thought.

"Drop the gun," she said.

His gaze shifted. He said, *"Allahu Akbar."*

"Drop the gun," she repeated.

He suddenly twisted, brought the gun up and fired. O'Reilly felt the jolt through her chest. She fell backward to the ground. Tried to get up, tried to move. Only eight or nine feet away she saw Kalakar lying there on the ground, eyes dark, a smile on his face, muttering a prayer.

O'Reilly, with her last bit of consciousness, brought her gun around and aimed it at Kalakar. She saw his eyes grow wide in shock.

She emptied the weapon.

Captain Charles Windham was already moving the Gulfstream III out of the area when his radar showed an incoming object. Windham had flown F14s in Iraq in '91 and he didn't need a refresher course on Stinger missiles. They flew 1,400 knots per hour and the Gulfstream topped out at 490. They couldn't outrun it. Their only hope was evasion.

He spun the Gulfstream onto its left wing, throttled up to full speed, simultaneously going into a steep dive toward the trees. He could hear the screams of his passengers. His copilot, Jim Moore, flopped into the seat next to him and craned to look out the windows. "Two o'clock!"

Windham kicked the Gulfstream up and over the nearest mountain ridge, skimming the trees and boulders. He dived deeply down the side of the mountain, crossing past a road, dropping the jet into a valley filled with shadows. The Gulfstream's wingspan was seventy-seven feet, ten inches.

"Still on our six and closing."

This early in the morning on this side of the mountains it was almost like the middle of the night, the sun behind the trees. His visual status was a disaster.

And Windham saw that the valley ended. Another mountain, a sheer granite cliff face.

"Hang on!"

Gripping his armrest, staring out the window at the dark trees swooping by, Governor Stark thought: *so this is terror.*

Windham jerked the controls, kicked the pedals, and tried to get the Gulfstream to behave like a fighter jet. The sheer rock wall disappeared from view as the Gulfstream swung to the right, wings biting at the thin mountain air. It was a maneuver the commercial jet was not built for and he wondered if it would hold together.

In a screamingly steep, angular climb, Jim Moore shouted, "We're clear. We're clear."

A reverberating sound could be heard from behind and below them as the Stinger missile slammed into the cliff face.

Bringing the jet out of its climb, Windham used his sleeve to wipe the sweat off his face. "Better go check on our guests."

Moore patted him on the shoulder. "That was some fancy flying, Captain." He walked back to tell the governor and his staff that they were safe. Glancing out the window, he saw a Medivac helicopter roaring into a lower section of the park and an LAPD helicopter dropping onto the ground near the Mt. Wilson Observatory.

Wonder what the hell happened over there?

The LAPD helicopter landed near where Derek lay. He came to just long enough to see Detective Connelly jump out, gun drawn, and run over to-ward him. Connelly said, "You're alive. Hang on, man. We'll get you to the hospital."

"Find the . . . little . . . girl."

"Got it. Got it. I'm going to check on O'Reilly."

"Connelly—"

"What?"

But Derek was no longer conscious.

CHAPTER 73

It was almost midnight in Islamabad and Dale Hutchins was tired. His butt ached, his shoulder hurt, and the tension was like an electrical current applied to his nuts. He and his boss, Sam Sherwood, were at the U.S. Embassy with Ambassador Miller Kallendar, the CIA station chief, and a handful of State Department people whose exact names and job titles remained a mystery.

They were joined by Firdos Moin and his boss. Their task was to explain to the Pakistani government and the U.S. Embassy the course of their investigation into Kalakar's movements in Pakistan and his support by members of the Pakistani government. Hutchins wasn't really happy that his name was being attached to a document that had the potential to destroy relations between the U.S. and Pakistan. He understood the blame game played by government bureaucrats, and as the lowest ranking U.S. official in the room, he knew where most of the shit was likely to land. Most worrying to Hutchins was the presence of Khalil-ui Mouseff, an advisor to Pakistan's leader, President Tarkani. Mouseff was the Pakistani equivalent of the United States' National Security Advisor.

Firdos and Hutchins made their report and everybody listened intently, then peppered them with questions.

Silence now fell over the group. Finally, Advisor Khalil-ui Mouseff, a burly, dark-skinned Pakistani with a thick mustache, cleared his throat. His voice was a deep rumble. "If I may sum up: General Bilal Sharif and Colonel Shaukat Seddiqi were behind a complicated plan to support an al-Qaeda cell here in Islamabad that organized the various attacks that occurred in the United States over the last several days."

He stared at Hutchins, his gaze accusing and skeptical. Hutchins wanted to punch the guy in the face, but controlled his impulse and nodded. "Yes, that's correct."

286 | MARK TERRY

"And if I understand all this correctly, General Sharif is responsible for getting a Stinger missile into the hands of a terrorist whose given name is Miraj Mohammad Khan, but who went by the name of Kalakar."

"Correct."

"And Khan and Seddiqi and Sharif all served in a unit together many years ago—"

"As well as with several people in the United States, Lawrence Perzada and Abdul Mohammed, who were involved in the plan. Perzada was in the international film business in Los Angeles and was responsible for procuring whatever props movie people needed, and transporting them to where they were needed. Abdul Mohammed was a sort of gofer."

Mouseff looked puzzled. Ambassador Kallendar said, "An errand boy."

"Ah. I see."

"They used their film prop business to transport the missile into the U.S., disguising it as a movie prop," Hutchins said.

Advisor Khalil-ui Mouseff said with a shake of his head, "It is very complicated. Very confusing. And Abdul Mohammed, this errand boy, what became of him?"

"Murdered several weeks ago. The Los Angeles Police Department was investigating him just prior to his death because he seemed to be making the rounds of illegal weapons merchants in California attempting to acquire a suitcase nuke." Hutchins had been growing increasingly impatient with all the reiteration and the skeptical tone Mouseff used. "You know what a fucking suitcase nuke is?"

Sherwood rested a hand on Hutchins's arm.

The Pakistani advisor studied Hutchins for a long moment. Hutchins didn't drop his gaze. Hutchins wondered if he was about to be kicked out of the room; or out of the country.

Ambassador Kallendar interrupted with a sigh. "Mr. Mouseff, we're talking about two of your top military leaders—Seddiqi and Sharif—being behind a terrorist attack, essentially declaring war on the United States. Your consul in L.A. was also involved. We expect you to arrest General Sharif and Colonel Seddiqi—"

Mouseff interrupted, arrogance in his tone and posture. "That is an internal matter with a great deal of political repercussions. I will have to discuss it with the president and the Joint Chiefs of Staff Committee. Is that all?"

Hutchins jumped to his feet. "Isn't that enough? How deep is the rot in your government, anyway? A lot of good people died—"

Sherwood gripped his shoulders, levering him back into his seat. In his ear Hutchins's boss whispered, "Shut the fuck up." To Mouseff he said, "I apologize for Agent Hutchins's outburst. It won't happen again."

Mouseff aimed his penetrating gaze on Hutchins, who felt like a pot of water about to boil over. "Your report is very interesting. *Very entertaining.* We will, of course, wish to verify it with our *own* internal sources. I assure you I will be discussing this with the president as soon as possible, and I imagine we will be questioning General Sharif and Colonel Seddiqi about this matter."

Hutchins leapt to his feet again. "Is this going to be like how you dealt with A. Q. Khan? The bastard sold nuclear secrets to every shithole dictatorship on the planet. You slap his hand, put him under house arrest, and whine that you can't arrest him because he's a fucking national hero?"

"Sit down, Agent Hutchins. Now." The ambassador's voice was harsh.

Hutchins shook his head. "I'm done here."

Sherwood's voice cut through the babble of voices. "Dale, one more outburst and you'll be looking for a new job. Sit down. We're almost done." His voice was mild; his tone, however, indicated he wasn't bluffing.

Hutchins stared at him. Sherwood nodded. Hutchins slumped into his seat. Firdos caught his eye and shook his head slightly.

Mouseff considered Hutchins for a moment. "As you so vividly point out, Agent Hutchins, sometimes we do things differently in Pakistan. It is, as I am sure you are aware by now, a different country than the United States." He climbed to his feet, nodded to Ambassador Kallendar, and walked out of the room. After an awkward moment, Firdos and his boss got up, made polite goodbyes and left.

When all the Pakistanis had left, Hutchins said, "Is that all we're going to do?"

Ambassador Kallendar raised a hand and said, "Agent Hutchins, I appreciate that you're upset, but this goes beyond standard law enforcement issues. This is politics and diplomacy and—"

The CIA station chief had a soft voice that still managed to under-cut the ambassador's rich tones. "I assure you, Agent Hutchins, that General Sharif and Colonel Seddiqi's crimes will not go unanswered."

Everybody in the room stopped talking for a moment. The State Department people were shooting each other nervous looks.

The ambassador leaned back and said, "Thank you for your good work, gentleman. It's been a long day. We'll be in touch."

On his way out to the car, Hutchins said to Sherwood, "The CIA guy—"

Sherwood said, "It was an interesting word choice."

Hutchins, who by now just wanted to go home to his wife, raised an eyebrow. "What was?"

"*Unanswered.*"

"Meaning?"

Sherwood shrugged. "We've done our jobs, Dale. Good work. Stay tuned."

EPILOGUE

It was January 20 of the new year, a bitter cold day on the Chesapeake Bay, but inside Derek's cabin cruiser, *The Salacious Sally*, it was toasty warm. He moved slowly around in the galley, pulling together a pitcher of margaritas. He had spent six hours in surgery at Cedars-Sinai. The bullet had clipped his scapula, torn through his right lung and lodged only a few centimeters from his spine. During his long convalescence he had been told over and over again about how lucky he was the bullet hadn't severed his spine or a major artery.

He supposed they were right, but it was turning out to be harder— maybe impossible—to get back to his old self physically.

"Need any help?" He glanced over where Sandy O'Reilly lounged on the couch in the salon. Her surgery had been even more extensive, but she seemed to be recuperating better than he was.

At least physically.

Mentally, Derek wasn't so sure. O'Reilly had always seemed confident to the point of arrogance. Since the events in Los Angeles, she seemed much quieter and less sure of herself. It had been a close call, their mission had only been semisuccessful, and she had shot Kalakar to death in order to save her own life. Hell of a couple days in the City of Angels.

As soon as she could travel, she returned to Washington, D.C., to file her reports and turn in her letter of resignation. She had put her condominium up for sale and moved to Dallas. She and Derek kept in touch, primarily through e-mail, and she was hoping to pick up a position at the University of Texas, in either the physics department or international studies. Mostly she wanted to be close to her children.

She had flown back to witness the inauguration. They had been invited by President-Elect Stark to attend the inauguration, as well as several of the balls. They had accepted the invitation to the balls, but passed on the inauguration itself, deciding they'd prefer to just watch it on TV.

Given both of their tendencies to wear out easily, Derek wasn't sure they would make any of the balls either.

He felt a shift in the boat as somebody stepped onboard. *What now?*

"I'll get it," O'Reilly called.

A moment later there was a knock and Derek heard the voice of James Johnston say, "Dr. O'Reilly, I'm surprised to see you here. How are you feeling?"

"As good as can be expected. Come in."

Derek walked over and grinned. "Shouldn't you be back in town?"

"Cleared out my desk and turned the place over to Tom Ross." With a grin, he held up an envelope. "And you know what this is?"

Derek rolled his eyes. "Let me guess. My letter of resignation."

"Yes. I accepted it." Johnston crossed over and rested a hand on Derek's shoulder. "I think you've done enough, don't you?"

Derek sighed. "We'll see, Jim. Ross already contacted me about staying on with Homeland Security."

"Are you going to?"

Derek shrugged. "While you're here, can I get you a drink?"

"Sure."

Derek headed back to the galley. He tuned in while O'Reilly and Johnston talked. She wanted to know what was happening with General Sharif and Colonel Seddiqi. Derek thought Johnston was strangely quiet. After a moment he said, almost casually, "Oh, you didn't hear?"

"No. What?"

Johnston said, "They were in a car accident. They both died."

The salon filled with silence except for the background babble of the TV set. Derek walked in with two margaritas and delivered them. He looked at Johnston and said, "What about John Seddiqi?"

"He'll go to trial, but he's been very cooperative with providing as much information as possible, and given the complicated nature of his involvement, it's hard to say what they'll even charge him with. Conspiracy, perhaps. We'll see how it shakes out in the long run."

They were silent, thinking about the daughter and the wife, who had mostly recovered. And about a father who was in prison facing trial. Derek imagined O'Reilly was thinking about her children.

Finally Johnston said, "So, you think you're going to take Ross up on his proposal?"

Derek shrugged. "Mandalevo asked me to come on board with him, too."

Robert Mandalevo, formerly the director of National Intelligence, had been slotted by President-Elect Stark to be secretary of state. Johnston's eyes widened. "Diplomatic?"

Derek shook his head. "Not exactly."

"Going to take it?"

He shrugged. "I've got some feelers out with some think tanks, too. I really don't know what I'm going to do."

"But it will involve counterterrorism in some way?"

Derek shrugged. "I'm probably too young to just retire."

O'Reilly said, "You told me it was your religion."

"Yeah. It's hard to give up."

Johnston raised his margarita in a toast. "It's been a pleasure working with you, Derek."

They clinked glasses and Derek took a sip. "I don't know if it's been a pleasure, but it's never been boring."

ACKNOWLEDGMENTS

I would like to acknowledge and thank the following people for their assistance with this book: Leanne Terry, Ian Terry, Sean Terry. Irene Kraas, my agent. Everyone at Oceanview Publishing: Pat Gussin, Robert Gussin, Kylie Fritz, Frank Troncale, Mary Adele Bogdon, Maryglenn Mc-Combs, Susan Hayes, and Susan Greger. All the various people at the Department of Homeland Security, Office of the Director of National Intelligence, Federal Bureau of Investigation, and Federal Aviation Administration who supplied information directly or indirectly to me. To my brother, Pete Terry and his wife, Lucia Unrau, for once taking me on a trip to the observatory on Mt. Wilson in California, which stayed embedded in my mind and memory until I needed it.

DATE			